The Night Church

by Whitley Strieber

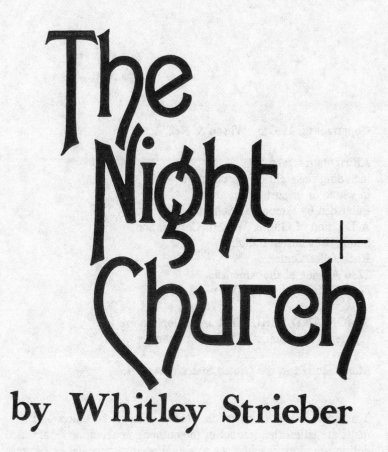

SIMON AND SCHUSTER

NEW YORK

Copyright © 1983 by Wilson & Neff, Inc.

All rights reserved
including the right of reproduction
in whole or in part in any form
Published by Simon and Schuster
A Division of Gulf & Western Corporation
Simon & Schuster Building
Rockefeller Center
1230 Avenue of the Americas
New York, New York 10020

SIMON AND SCHUSTER and colophon are
registered trademarks of Simon & Schuster

Manufactured in the United States of America

FOR BROTHER EDWIN

---

*I would like to thank Patricia Soliman,
without whose insight and support I would
never have dared this.*

PROLOGUE

AUGUST 1963

IT WAS A WET NIGHT in Queens. Kew Gardens was quiet, the only sounds along Beverly Road the slow-dripping rain, the occasional hiss of tires on the slick asphalt, or the hurrying splash of feet on the sidewalk.

A man came swiftly along, huddling in his raincoat, his eyes hooded by a hat. When he stopped and raised his head to read a street sign his face was revealed to be as pale and creased as a worn-out mask. The wrinkles framed a tight mouth and green eyes, ironic and cold. He consulted an address book, then walked up to the front door of a particular house. It had been carefully selected; the tenants had moved here only a few weeks ago from another state. Their little boy had not yet begun attending Holy Spirit Parochial School, had not yet registered.

The Cochrans were a demographic oddity of very special interest to certain people, for the Cochrans had no relatives but one another, and the Cochrans had just come here. They were utterly alone.

The old man did not ring their bell; he did not even pause on the porch. Instead he glanced over his shoulder, then slipped around the side of the house and disappeared at once into the shadows there.

He moved quickly; his activities here were carefully planned. They were dangerous. Occasionally people such as these had guns; occasionally they called the police.

They never understood. Always, there was resistance.

Franklin Titus began to work on the basement door.

Inside the house nine thirty came and went. Letty Cochran sent little Jerry to bed. She and George settled back to watch the second half of the Garry Moore show.

"Mom?"

Frank Fontaine was starting to sing "Maytime"; Letty had just closed her eyes. She sighed. "Why aren't you in bed, dear?"

"There's someone in the house."

George lit a cigarette, did not stir. Letty got up and went to their boy. She was concerned. Jerry was not a fearful child. He was spunky. Seeing him standing before her, wide-eyed, full of his innocent fright, she felt great sympathy and love for him.

"Just us, dear."

"It's a man. He was coming up from the basement, but when I saw him he stepped back into the pantry."

This was not baseless fear. Jerry was terrified. "Come on, Jer, let's go see if we can shoo him out."

Jerry followed her into the hall, tugging at her arm. "No, Mom, don't go in there. He was a real person. I wasn't dreaming."

"Jerry, honey, are you all right?"

Before he could answer she heard a sound from the basement—a short, bitter remark, like a curse. She gathered her boy into her arms.

"George! I think Jerry's right. There's someone in the basement."

Her husband was beside them in an instant, his big hand covering her shoulder. "I'll go take a look. Probably a cat."

He opened the basement door, reached into the darkness, and tightened the light bulb that hung over the stairs. "Nothing down there."

"I certainly heard something."

"I'll go down." As soon as he started descending the stairs Letty was seized with foreboding. Fear battled caution; she wanted to stay with George, but she didn't want to go down those stairs. "Hey," he said, "you two really are scared!" He held out his arms, took Jerry. "Come on, big boy, let's us check this thing out." As he clumped down he swayed from side to side with the weight of his nine-year-old.

"Daddy, don't! Don't take me!"

Couldn't he see he was scaring the poor child even more? Letty started down after them, her heart going out to Jerry.

"George, honey, let him—"

"I know what I'm doing!"

George was only a month back from Viet Nam. He felt Letty had pampered their son during his absence, that the boy was growing up soft. Easygoing George had come home to her with deep hurts, dark and violent things inside him that Letty was learning to fear. The war had wounded him, and his pain was leaking out all over his wife and son.

He put the boy down beside the old black furnace. "You see, son, nobody here, not even behind it. The room's empty."

Jerry did not answer; instead he simply looked up. Letty followed his eyes. All three of them fell silent. One after another the floorboards above their heads were giving under weight. Someone was walking, very softly, from the kitchen into the living room. The footsteps stopped in front of the TV.

"George, listen!"

"Shut up!"

Garry was just starting the "That Wonderful Year" segment of the show. His voice stopped. The TV had been turned off.

"What in hell—" Leaving Letty and Jerry behind, George mounted the steps three at a time. Letty was terrified now. She grabbed her son by the arm and rushed up right behind George.

The living room was empty. George stood in front of the couch, staring at the old DuMont.

It was off.

"What the hell's going on here, some kind of a prank?"

"Shouldn't we call the police?"

"What's the complaint? Somebody turned off our TV? Big deal." He flipped it back on.

It took a moment to warm up. When it did, though, it just hissed and showed snow. George twisted the dial. Nothing, no stations. "Broke the damn thing," he muttered. "Big sonofabitching joke!" She could tell when he was really angry; the army always re-entered his vocabulary.

He turned the switch off and on a few times. Then, abruptly, there came a sound out of the machine that was so big, so utterly shattering in its intensity, that it struck them all like a great pounding fist. Letty felt herself falling, saw the room turn upside down, floated as if by magic to the floor.

Then the sound was gone. She was sitting on the couch. "What—w-what?"

"Darling—"

What was she trying to remember? "I . . . maybe I dozed off. I dreamed we were in the basement. . . ."

George drew her to him. "Put the boy to bed." He started fondling her breasts.

"Not in front of Jerry!" She pushed at him and he stopped.

"Put the boy to bed."

She shook her head. "Gosh, I feel funny. I had this dream while I was still awake. We went to the basement, I was real scared. . . ."

"I was asleep too. Guess we're overtired."

"I guess."

He started in on her again. "Not now!" She gave his hand a pat. "Put the boy to bed."

Little Jerry was already in his pajamas, playing with his toy trains in the hallway behind them.

"Come on, darling, bedtime."

He padded along behind his mother. When they reached the bedroom she gave him a goodnight kiss, embracing him, feeling the solidity and warmth of him, smelling his clean smell, loving him so very much. "Goodnight, Jerry. You sleep tight, now."

"You too, Mom."

"And say your prayers. Guardian Angel and three Hail Marys."

"I will, Mom."

She left him, then, to the dark of his little room.

George was waiting for her. Liberace's TV show was just starting. She sank down into George's arms as the swelling music filled the room.

Neither of them heard the slight click made by the pantry door as it opened, nor the sigh as a raincoat brushed past the dining room curtains, nor the hiss of breath, which was the only sound the old man made as he stood in the hallway watching them.

"Lover," George whispered, "Lover . . ." How she adored her George with his tough ways and tender heart. She snuggled closer to him, inhaling the mixture of Jade East aftershave and tobacco that was his odor.

"You will give me your son."

Now what was that he had said? "George?"

"Yeah?"

"What did you say?"

"Nothing."

"I thought you said something."

"Musta been the TV."

"There's nobody talking." Liberace smiled radiantly, resplendent in his rhinestone dinner jacket. He was playing Liszt's "Hungarian Rhapsody Number One," and nobody was talking.

"You will give him to me."

Letty felt an awful, queasy sensation, as if she had just smelled something dead. "Oh, George, I feel sick!"

He didn't seem to notice. He was fooling with the TV. "I think we're picking up that Hartford station again. There's some kind of a drama or something. That's what we're hearing on the audio."

"You will give him to me. Say yes, both of you. Yes!"

Letty was dizzy, so much so that she couldn't even think straight. Somebody wanted something from her, somebody important wanted her to say yes, to give away little Jerry. . . .

"No!"

A terrible silence entered the room. George seemed frozen before the TV. Something touched Letty's shoulder. She could feel cold fingers digging into her muscles. Her soul screamed revulsion—the hand even *felt* wicked.

"He's only going away to school, Letty. The finest school in the world. And you and George are entering a new life, with new hopes and new beliefs. A better life than you have ever known before." The voice seemed now to be coming from inside her own head, yet she was aware of a dim form in the room, a man leaning against the far wall beside the picture of the new Pope she had just hung up yesterday, a man who was all hat and coat and hypnotic voice. A man who was evil in a way Letty could hardly believe, totally, utterly, in every atom of his being.

So evil he might not even be a man. But his voice curled and twisted through her mind like seductive smoke.

"A new church, Letty, and you and George are going to hear about it soon, and revere it, and join it."

"N-n-n . . ."

"When you join, you will see Jerry again, you will come to visit him at his new school. You will let me take him now, Letty." The voice penetrated deeper and deeper, seeming to caress her very soul. "Say yes, say yes. . . ."

She had an impression, quite clearly, that she was looking directly into the yellow-green eyes of a snake. A *thing* of dreadful, overwhelming evil.

And overwhelming beauty.

But she could not scream, was no longer sure she wanted to. Even so she found she was opening her mouth, forming a word. . . . She struggled against it, fought herself, felt it welling up between clenched teeth. "Yes," she said, "Yes! Yes! Yes!"

George crumpled before the TV, struggling like a trussed animal as Liberace smiled and played. He said it too, a stifled whisper of a yes.

"Both of you, again!"

"Yes, take him, yes!"

"Very well."

Letty's sickness passed. She and George huddled in the dark together, the two of them staring stunned at the hypnotic, gray glow of the TV, where Liberace swept through the final bars of the rhapsody. Outside the rain rained and the wind whispered through the trees.

Jerry lay motionless, staring at the ceiling. As soon as his mother had left he had fixed his gaze on his owl-clock, and was still watching the dimly lit eyes moving endlessly left to right and back again. And he was listening to a persistent whisper. "Back and forth, back and forth . . . and you are getting sleepy, Jerry . . . you are forgetting that you're supposed to go to Holy Spirit School, forgetting that you grew up in San Diego and moved to Queens—all of that. You've always lived here, and you go to another school, a finer school, a hidden, secret school."

"Yeah . . . secret school . . ." Jerry was floating, his only awareness the voice itself, the soft, humming singsong of it, the intensity of it.

"The Titus School, in Greenwich Village. You've always gone there."

"Always . . ."

"And you're coming back with me, coming to start the new term."

"Yes, sir."

With rustling, with the very slightest creak of floorboards, the old man came in from the hallway. "Hello, Jerry," he said. "We've got to go. There's an assembly in the Great Hall in an hour."

"In the middle of the night? I'm sleepy."

The old man ignored the protest. "I've brought your uniform, little boy. Get dressed and be quick about it." Jerry was helpless to stop the old man drawing him up from his bed, or making him cross the room and pull the uniform on. "You have a great work to perform, Jerry, such an exceptionally well-built, exceptionally bright child as you. A great work."

Jerry had the weird feeling that this was all some kind of a dream, but it felt like real life. Only it couldn't be.

Couldn't it? The old man was taking him by the hand, and he could feel that dry claw. It was very real. And now the old man was leading him out of his room.

Jerry's eyes got wet. He choked up when they stopped in the living room to tell his parents goodbye. He shook Dad's hand and kissed Mom.

"Letty, say, 'You look so handsome in your uniform.' "

"You look so handsome in your uniform," she murmured. "Doesn't he look handsome, George?"

Dad grinned, and cuffed Jerry on the shoulder.

"Tell him he's getting to be a big boy, George."

"Getting to be a big boy!"

"Mom, Dad—is this for real?"

The old man's voice began droning, repeating again and again, "This is real, it has always been real, you've always gone to the Titus School, you know that, you know that. . . ."

"I don't want to go!" He embraced his mother.

His mother turned desperately to the old man. "Please, let him stay just a little while longer."

The man gripped Jerry's arm. "You'll see him again on All Souls Eve, Letty."

"Momma, Daddy, don't let him take me!"

"You cannot move, George. You're frozen. You too, Letty."

George Cochran, that big, powerful man, hid his face in his hands.

"Momma, please! Momma!" Jerry struggled against the old man's vicious grip. "Help me! Don't let him take me!" His parents could have stopped the man easily, but they sat as if tied down, their faces awful, tears in their eyes.

Jerry pushed and shouted and dragged at the old man until they were in the kitchen. Then something terrible happened. The old man drew a long, thin stiletto from a scabbard hidden in his sleeve. "If you keep this up, I'm going to go back and cut your parents' throats. They're hypnotized, little boy, and they won't be able to do a damn thing to stop me."

His tone of voice was the scariest Jerry had ever heard. Miserable, sick at heart, his eyes on that long blue blade, Jerry went out the door with the old man.

The last he heard from his parents that night was a ragged sob, an unfamiliar sound that might have come from his father's throat.

Jerry was going to a very special school, a place hidden down the cracks of the familiar, to learn dangers and dark truths. From now on he would be fenced out of his own former life.

The old man took him down the wet, weed-choked alley behind his house. They disappeared together into the night beyond.

Chapter One ————————————

IT WAS ALL ugliness and evil; it had no name. She thought of it as the snake. It came in her dreams, telling her in its sneering way something she could not bear to hear. *You want to kiss me,* it would say, and it would grin at her and come closer. *Now,* it would whisper, and when it did she could smell its rotten breath. *You know what we have to do,* it would whisper. *We can do it, we must do it. Our love is the future, the hope of the world.*

No! You're evil, you have nothing to do with hope!

I must have you, my darling.

No!

When she ran it would drift and blow along behind her like a leaf, its huge form frighteningly insubstantial. It was never far away. *Let me,* it would say, and its voice would become the wind's voice: *Let me, let me.*

No! Leave me alone!

No matter how hard she ran or where she went it would be there. She ran down empty streets and then emptier streets; she passed gray houses and black houses and the last city places, and came into fields rich with wheat. And the wind sang in the wheat: *You can do it, you can let me touch you. Wish,* the wind said, *wish and it shall be so.*

And she would fall sobbing in the dry stems, and the wind would blow around her and through her and deep inside her, bringing its wild coldness to the soft and secret depths of her.

She would know the truth of what it said: some wicked part of her wanted to let it love her, to let it do what it wanted to the world.

But she must not!

No. If she did multitudes would suffer and die, their faces blotched, arms flailing, bodies dancing and blackening, bursting with filth.

She would awaken from the dream so extremely terrified that for a time she would not even know her name.

As gingerly as a frightened little cat, her everyday reality would come creeping back.

"I'm Patricia," she would say into the dark. "I'm Patricia!" And the summer wind would whisper no more. Slowly the image of the evil being would fade.

Since Patricia Murray had left the shelter of the institution where she had been raised she had been tortured by this dream. It had emerged into her days to the point that her life was choked by it, for it carried with it fear as destructive as a lethal bacterium.

Sometimes she discovered tears on her cheeks even when a happy moment seemed to have banished the fear away. She suspected that her inner self never escaped, not even for a moment. Fear and cold and dread must be the only signposts on the landscape of her deepest being, a landscape of trampled, rotting wheat.

Why was she like this inside?

As if her love, the very fruit of her body, was diseased. She would touch her belly, smooth and flat, feeling how soft her skin, imagining how empty her womb, dark and silent beneath the wall of flesh.

The image of the snake would glisten in her mind.

Only once had she actually seen the terrible, slithering creature of the dream. It had been sliding through the field, withering the wheat. *Every stalk I destroy,* it had said as it swept and curled along, *is a million human lives.*

She had seen that it had the face of Death, if Death had one: green-eyed and grinning and very still.

Come, lover, and dance with me.

The sun of morning was her best friend. Fresh light brought the familiar old world back. Reaping with the Reaper, indeed. She was twenty-two years old and people called her beautiful. Her business was life, not death. She was an ordinary, decent girl, full of youth and life and, people said, beauty.

She wanted to believe that her dream was no more than an expression of her perfectly natural fear of beginning a new life. She was in fact loveless; she wanted friends of the opposite sex; she had almost none. Dates, laughter, fun—she wanted all the pleasures that came with men.

She was even lonelier living in her own apartment than she had been in the orphanage, and the therapy for both this and the nightmare was to meet people.

She was shy. Normal, under the circumstances. She was unsure. And who wouldn't be, given her inexperience?

No matter how odd and outcast she *felt,* she kept insisting to herself that she was perfectly normal.

She sat at her makeup mirror revising her looks for a date. It was to be a late meeting, drinks and talk. Getting acquainted. Patricia had become skilled at arranging these dates for herself. She would not spend too much time with a man she had never met before.

Her makeup light flickered. She jiggled it and it almost fell apart. Things like that were always happening here; this was not the most spectacular apartment in Queens. But it was her first place and she loved every inch of it. She loved the furniture she had managed to collect—the big couch, the Indian rug, the bed with its pretty yellow coverlet. She loved the idea that this place, which had been bare walls and a dirty floor when she moved in, was now a home. A charming, comfortable, quiet little home.

But not as quiet as it should be.

She stopped applying her eyeshadow and listened. Hadn't she heard just then the scrape of a window being raised?

Patricia felt she lived on a thin edge of normality. She was given to hysteria and night terrors. But she wasn't really worried about herself. She hadn't always been this way. It was just a reaction to moving out into the world on her own, she told herself. The nightmares and the forebodings and the unexplained tears would all pass.

The television suddenly went on in the living room. She was astonished, her heart thundered, she leaped up. The raucous sound of canned laughter resounded through the apartment, so loud that she could not ignore it. She hurried into the living room and turned off the set.

Her next impulse was to rush to the door. But she forced presence of mind—she was good at that. She stayed where she was. A robber or a rapist wouldn't announce himself by turning on the TV. Then the set flickered as she removed her fingers from the button. She smiled. Her heart stopped pounding. Silly woman, afraid of a loose switch on a TV set. Some errant tremble must have jarred a loose connection.

"All in the Family" was no longer on. Now the screen glowed with a strange, pulsating light. The whisper of the static became low and deep, so deep it was felt rather than heard.

For a few moments Patricia stared at this peculiar phenomenon, fascinated by the sound and the shadowy movements on the screen.

Then she unplugged the set. No point in risking further damage. She would call a repairman tomorrow. Drearily enough, TV was at the moment one of her chief entertainments. She looked forward to it of an evening after work.

Well, so much for that. She glanced at her watch. Getting toward eight. She had to hurry and finish dressing or she'd make tonight's date wait. She started for the bedroom, swallowed. Her mouth was still dry from fright. She went into the kitchen and poured herself some ice water.

She stood drinking and looking at the open kitchen window. The taffeta curtains she had made for it fluttered slightly with the night wind.

She kept that window closed.

Maybe—early this morning—hadn't she burned her toast and raised the sash then? Or . . . was that the scraping sound she had heard a moment ago?

Was somebody really in here?

She shook her head as if clearing her vision. This kitchen window was on an air shaft six stories deep. It would take a human fly to scale the wall and open it.

HUMAN FLY RAPES SECRETARY. That's how the *Post* would headline the story.

She was becoming a victim of hysterical imaginings. She slammed the window and locked it and went back to her makeup table.

The face that looked back at her from her mirror was a little pale, a little tense. She used some blusher, which seemed to help.

Blusher. Eyeshadow. Lipstick. I have the fatal luck to be attractive to men.

The sisters at Our Lady of Victory had not taught much about sexuality. This made most of their orphans frantic as they reached their late teens. How could they look and act right if they had no instructions? And they were desperate to succeed with men. Far more than outside girls they wanted to be wives. Fiercely they reassured one another that they were the sexiest, most irresistible girls mankind had ever seen.

Looking back from her mirror was someone Patricia knew to be a pretty twenty-two-year-old woman. Much prettier than most of the other orphans. And much more discriminating. She could never throw herself into the kind of relationship the others would settle for. She wanted a little more than the usual sullen wifehood.

She finished her makeup. She looked good. At any rate it was the best she knew how to do. She was soapy clean, with gentle green eyes and, astonishingly, a smile hidden in her lips that no tragedy had been able to erase, not even the death of beloved parents in a pointless accident, not even life amid the bells and the cold halls and "Yes, sister," and the packed dorm and knowing that your kind always ended up last.

Her best feature was her smoke-blond hair, enclosing her face in a magically delicate frame and suggesting a sensuality that Patricia was confident she would one day fulfill—when she had found exactly the right man to fulfill it with.

For those who did not get college scholarships Our Lady offered the option of a one-year stint at a business school after graduation. Patricia had taken her secretarial degree and gone from there to her job at the Hamil Bank branch in Queens Plaza, and this little apartment. She had joined the local parish, Holy Spirit, and been welcomed with desperate enthusiasm by its shambling, exhausted priest, Father Goodwin. Harry Goodwin, pastor of a dwindling flock of widowed Italian and Irish ladies, sometimes doing five or six funerals in a week.

At first Patricia's youth had made him suspicious. At parish socials he probed for neurosis or perhaps even fanaticism. She answered him with all the pity and kindness she felt for him. Lately he had changed; suffering came into his face when she approached him now. She could well imagine his celibate anguish. To help him she went to church dressed in what the sisters had called "Mary-like" clothes (long sleeves, deep hemlines, choker collars). At Holy Spirit she wore neither makeup nor scent. Even so, when during Mass his eyes went to his flock they inevitably met hers and could not look away. When she broke the gaze he would stumble in his prayers, and a ragged tone would enter his voice.

Tonight she was not wearing the Mary-like clothes, not for the man she was to meet. At least she could be certain that he was no priest.

A swish of clothing startled her. She turned around, almost falling off the chair. "Who's that?"

Nobody. She pressed the heels of her hands to her temple. It would be nice right now to just scream her heart out, but she might as well face what was really upsetting her. She was scared to death of these awful blind dates.

But dates arranged through friends were her best shots at a decent social life. And why not? Everybody had to start somewhere.

Although she never knew what to expect, these nerve-racking meetings were a habit she dared not break. Sometimes the men she met were decent, sometimes they were not, and one of them had almost fit her nightmare.

She intended to marry well. Mary Banion, her first real outsider friend, told her she must at all costs conceal her desire for attachment from her prospective mates. "For heaven's sake, Pat, don't let them know what you're after. You'll scare them to death. Men want whores. As far as they're concerned the fact that they get wives instead is a disturbing mystery. They spend all their married lives trying to figure out what the hell happened."

Mary Banion was forty-one, the second wife of a high police official named Mike Banion. Both of them had lost their first spouses. Patricia had met Mary at the bank, where casual teller-customer conversations had led to a lunch date and friendship.

Patricia envied Mary the fact that she had always been loved. Her first husband had adored her, but his private plane had given out on him over the Jersey marshes. Now Mike Banion worshiped her as a replacement for his child bride, who had died of cancer in her twenties.

Mary looked and acted Patricia's own ideal of female success. She dressed elegantly, in silks and linens. And she was beautiful, with delicately sculptured features and glowing chestnut hair. The fact that her Mike affected baggy suits and low-grade cigars made her seem even more beautiful.

"I'll make him police commissioner, you'll see. Maybe even mayor if his style comes back into style." Thus she justified her second marriage. "My old truck," she called him. No doubt she would drive him to the top.

Tonight Patricia was going to go out with Mary's son Jonathan. He was late, but he must be coming. He'd better. She'd been preparing herself since she got home from work.

Mary was in the habit of overexplaining him, as if his merely having been born was not justification enough for his life. "You're going to find him fascinating. He's very bright."

Patricia looked askance at herself in the mirror, arched one eyebrow. Was that sexy? Was that winning?

Most of the men she had met didn't call back. Mary said that often happened to extremely beautiful women. Men feared great beauty. But not to worry, it was all to the good. Only the best of them would feel comfortable with her. One undesirable group did call back, though—the nerds. They not only phoned, they came to her teller window. The girls at the bank called them "schmedlocks." "Don't worry," they said, "every good-looking teller has her schmedlocks." Apparently many undesirable men had hit upon the idea of meeting girls by becoming depositors at the banks where they worked.

Was Jonathan going to be a schmedlock? Possibly that was why Mary oversold him.

At least, she hoped, he wouldn't be frightening. There had been one young man who was too quiet, who went through the formalities of the evening like a zombie, who had insisted on taking her home with him. Even when she refused point-blank he had kept driving. Then she saw the little black pistol tucked under his sports jacket. She had escaped by jumping out of the car when traffic slowed down on the Fifty-Ninth Street bridge.

Six weeks later a young man was caught in Massapequa, Long Island, with the bodies of three girls under the floor of his elaborate basement torture chamber. Was it him? She was never sure.

When she heard the buzzer she leaped up from her dressing table, flipped off the Sunbeam makeup mirror, and ran to the intercom in the living room. "Yes?"

"Miss Murray, a Mr. Banion to see you."

"Send him up, Tony."

She had been embarrassed to ask Mary what he looked like, but if he took after his mother he would be darkly handsome, bright, and sophisticated. Thank heavens bullet-shaped Mike was a foster father. Genial as he was, Inspector Banion was not a promising source of looks or manners.

A rap at the door. "Yes?"

"It's Jonathan Banion."

What a soft voice. She hadn't noticed that on the phone. She opened the door onto a tall, lean man who smiled down at her.

"Hello," she said. "Come on in."

He was wearing a seersucker sports jacket over an Oxford shirt. You could even call him handsome, and she thought he had the sweetest face she could ever remember seeing. He came into the center of the room and looked at her for a long moment. "Have we met?"

She knew just what he meant. "I think we *must* have." She laughed. "I can't imagine where."

He held out his hands and she clasped them. They were warm and familiar, as those of a close friend might be. "I'd say that I've known you forever," he said, "but that sounds like such a hokey line."

"Let's just assume we met and forgot and take it from there."

For a moment he didn't answer. He was looking curiously at her out of his gentle green eyes. "Let's stay here awhile," he said. "We can talk more easily."

She smiled. "Would you like a drink?"

"Fix me whatever you're having. I suspect it'll be something I like."

She went to the glass-topped table where she kept her small collection of bottles and fixed two gin and tonics. When she turned around he was still standing in the middle of the room.

He took his drink, never for a moment looking away from her. "Sit down, won't you," she said in exactly the way Sister Dolorosa had when greeting visitors in Our Lady's parlor. He sank onto her couch, looking acutely uncomfortable. She sat down beside him. She should have taken the chair, but she wanted very much to be near him.

"We've got to figure out where we met," she said. Imagine how nice it would be, she thought, if he hugged me. Right now.

"Maybe we knew each other in another life."

"That's impossible. There is no reincarnation."

"No? You're sure?"

"Well, it's against Church doctrine."

He raised his glass. "Cheers."

"Here's to us." Watch it, lady, don't come on too strong. Take it easy. This one looks too good to lose. "To our first date."

"It can't be. I know you."

She could almost have predicted he would say that. The more they were together the more she felt as if they were simply renewing an old and close familiarity.

"You must go to NYU," he said. He turned awkwardly on the couch and faced her. "I'm in psychology. I must see you in the halls or something."

"Never been there in my life. Do you use the Hamil Bank in Queens Plaza?"

"No, Citibank. There's a branch near the university with an automatic teller. I didn't meet you in a bank. I met you . . . I met you . . ." He frowned.

They both fell silent. No doubt the same small breath of fear that was touching her was also touching him. This was no joke; this was just a tiny bit scary.

Nevertheless she was awfully glad to see him. He put his drink down and, in a methodical way that was somehow familiar to her, leaned over to her and kissed her on the cheek. It made her smile. "You're incredibly beautiful," he said.

It was simply stated, and so sincerely that it only embarrassed her a little. "Thank you, Jonathan."

"I've been missing you. I just didn't know it."

She nodded. "Me too." But when she tried to meet his eyes she found he was looking past her shoulder, at the dark entrance into the bedroom. She shook her head slightly, as if to say, Not yet.

"Is someone in there?"

"I'm a single girl, Jonathan, and we are all alone."

"I heard something."

"My apartment's haunted tonight. You should have been here when the TV went on by itself. But the place is empty. I checked it out. Except for us, of course."

He turned her face to his. "You are so lovely."

"Thank you," she said again. She wished she hadn't used that blusher. Her cheeks must be flaming by now.

He regarded her. "My mother calls you Pat. But you prefer Patricia, don't you?"

"What if I said I like Pat best?"

"You'd be lying."

He was right about that. She tried to make herself laugh but the sound died away. He was beautiful, he was sweet, he was just what she desired.

Why, then, did a little voice inside whisper, *Nightmare man?*

When he touched her wrist she involuntarily pulled back. "Maybe we'd better pretend we're strangers," he said. "Tell each other about ourselves. That's the best way to begin."

She smiled to cover the ridiculous fear that was growing inside her. "You start." Her voice was too sharp. Calm down, girl. Take it easy.

"I'm a scientist. I'm engaged in arcane experiments few people can understand. Officially I'm an assistant professor of psychology at NYU, but I'm actually an advanced researcher in the physiology of the brain."

"What research?" She had to keep him talking. Then she could just close her eyes and let the sound of his voice relieve her anxiety.

"You talk, Patricia. I want you to talk too."

"You've told me so little."

"You tell me something, then I'll tell you something more."

"I guess Mary told you I'm an Our Lady of Victory girl." She did not care for the word "orphan." "I went to Clark Secretarial and got a job at the Hamil Bank. Totally unglamorous."

"Not to me. You might be the most beautiful woman on earth. I just want to look at you. Am I making you nervous? Too much heavy breathing?"

She nodded—and instantly regretted it. If only she could dare her fear and let him hold her.

"Excuse me." He went over to her faded maroon Barcalounger, the one she had bought third-hand (at least) from Rebecca Stangers at the bank. "This better?"

She wanted terribly for him to come back to her and carry her into the bedroom and undress her and do with her exactly what she had intended to save for her husband. She wanted that a thousand times more than she had wanted anything else in her life.

And he wanted the same thing—anyone could tell by the intensity that had come into his expression. His dark brows were slightly knitted, the green eyes gone from gentle to piercing. His lips were sensuous but firm. If only he would do it, he could take her. She would not allow herself to stop him.

How could it be happening like this? She was actually desperate for him, yet she had just met him a few minutes ago. It was an awful and yet a delicious feeling. As if sharing her need, he stood up and held his hands down to her. She rested her hands in his, hoping he would draw her up from the couch. He towered over her. But he also trembled and beads of sweat formed along his upper lip. He squeezed her hands like a supplicant. "I'm sorry," he said. "I know I'm coming on too fast for you. I just can't help myself."

In reply she smiled. He was encouraged, and began to pull her to him. Their embrace brought her immediate relief from her fear and left no question about what would happen next.

The bedroom was dark, at once inviting and menacing. Sister Dolorosa had explained what the nuns called "the clinical necessities," so Patricia was not afraid of her inexperience. She knew what would be expected of her. But this was for marriage. This was for marriage!

They were sitting on the side of the bed when Patricia sensed movement in the room. Seeing it too, Jonathan cried out. In the same slow motion that her nightmare always imposed on her, Patricia turned to him, only to see him being taken in a hammerlock by a shadowy, fast-moving figure that had burst out of her closet.

Then someone seized her and pulled her back onto the bed with terrific force.

Impossibly, incredibly, she recognized Mary Banion among their assailants. Her surprise was so total that what should have been a healthy scream came out as a gasp.

Somebody tried to put a wet, ethery cloth over Patricia's face but she fought free. "Patricia, calm down!"

She was not calming down. Two big, vicious-looking men already had Jonathan tied up. Patricia leaped at them, tearing her dress as she tried to keep her balance.

"Get her!"

That was Mary Banion. Definitely. Patricia ran for the apartment door. She reached it, worked the locks, threw it open.

Feet pounded behind her as she raced down the hall and slammed her hand against the elevator button. "Oh, God, get her!" Mary really sounded frantic.

"Mary—you must be crazy!"

"Stay right there, Pat. That's a good girl." The men coming after her were horrible, big but quick, in black raincoats and hats pulled down to disguise themselves. Patricia took the fire stairs four at a time, bursting out the back exit of the apartment building.

She intended to race around to the front and get the doorman to call a cop, but on the way she saw old Franklin Apple, an elderly gentleman who had come to one of the parish seniors suppers she had served. "Oh, Mr. Apple! Mr. Apple, thank the Lord you're here! I need help, I—"

He smiled at her and grabbed her wrists in his dry, clawlike hands. For an instant she was stunned, then filled with cold, prickling terror. His skeletal old face was grinning. He cooed at her as he might at an agitated baby. His fingers around her wrists were as cold and hard as stone.

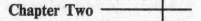

Chapter Two

PATRICIA HAD FOUGHT desperately, finally broken the old man's grip and run wildly away from him through the empty, rain-drenched streets, hoping to hail a cop or find a telephone booth. Before she could do either she had seen three tall men pile out of a car half a block away. She had run down a side street, her shoes clattering on the sidewalk, the trees dripping rain down her back.

She had rushed up onto a lit porch and screamed for help; she had pounded on the door and rattled the windows. In response the porch light had gone out. Then cars, dark and coming fast, had appeared at both ends of the street.

She had leaped over the porch rail into wet and thorny bushes, had fought her way around a side yard past lighted windows, hearing the distant drone of the ten o'clock news inside that locked house. At last she had come into the sodden, choked alley.

And found herself facing a brick wall. But above it loomed a black, blessed shadow, the familiar bulk of Holy Spirit Church. By some instinct she had come to this protection. Surely there were places to hide in here, if one could be still enough. And Father Goodwin *never* locked his church.

By the time two men emerged from the trees behind her she had scaled the wall, run down to the front of the church and entered. The silence inside stopped her for a moment. Votive candles danced shadows around her. Every move echoed in the great stone space. Far away beside the altar shone the deep red of the vigil candle, confirming the Blessed Life that resided here. Patricia forgot her hiding and her danger; she ran to the altar rail and knelt, her eyes seeking the low gleam of the tabernacle.

The glimmering of the votive candles made the images of the saints painted in the dome over the nave jerk with spasmodic, lunging motions. Rain rattled against the stained-glass windows, and wind hissed past the slate eaves of the old building. The air in the church was warm and storm-dense. Patricia felt sweat tickling her lips, beading between her breasts, trickling down her thighs.

As she knelt, she sensed the same sense of wickedness that infested her familiar nightmare, the foul, questing *something* that seemed to want to rape more than her body. It wanted to rape her heart, her very being, her soul.

And it was here, somehow, in this dark old church, its stink filling her nostrils, its body hissing and swirling across the cold marble floor. She forced back wild shrieks of terror, tried to retain what little composure she had left because it was all she had left. The next stage was blind, helpless panic.

To give herself strength she brought the soft voice of Father Goodwin to memory, from an intimate moment in the confessional when she had spilled out the loneliness and terror of her life to him, when she had revealed the anger she felt toward God for depriving her of parents. He had said, "Pray the rosary, Patty. I know it's out of fashion now, but so is everything else. Just take the beads in your hands and Mary will console you. . . ."

Trembling fingers found her rosary in the pocket of her dress. But her grip was so tight she snapped the chain in a dozen places. The talisman was ruined, only a clutch of independent beads and broken links. There was no protection in a handful of plastic.

Someone came up behind her. "Be calm, Patricia. Nobody will hurt you." That horrible Mr. Apple again.

"What are you doing? What's happening?"

"Be quiet, my dear. Be patient."

He had appeared at a parish seniors supper where Patricia was serving the spaghetti. Such a gnarled little old man, his eyes mud green, his face a catastrophe of wrinkles. He had stood before her, his paper plate in hand, his thin lips making a strange, ironic sort of smile. "At *last*," he had said.

"Hungry?" she had asked, basking in a moment of good feeling.

"I'm going to take you home in a few days. I wanted you to know."

Senile. She had smiled again and served him some extra. All during dinner he had watched her, his head bobbing, his spidery little fingers working the fork and the spaghetti spoon with difficulty. "That's an odd one," she had said to Father Goodwin, "a little senile."

"Very old."

"He acts as if he owned me or something."

"Probably lonely. Why not go and talk to him?"

"He gives me the crawls."

"Offer it up. Where's the harm in a lonely old man?"

So she had met Mr. Apple. Now she sobbed aloud and twisted the beads in her hands as she strove toward the tabernacle, wishing she could have the Host, could somehow hold Him before her as a protecting shield. Her vision of the altar blurred and fluttered. From the depths of the church came avid scuttling. She clapped her hands to her ears, scattering beads across the granite floor. Her mind screamed frantically at her, *Run, for the love of God, run.*

People, hundreds of them, were filtering into the church from the side doors, from the crypt, filling the aisles and then the pews. There were shuffles and murmured apologies, and an occasional stifled cough.

"My God, protect me!" Her own voice was a cracking moan. Hard upon her words came another sound, soft, stifled, gleeful. "You laugh," she shouted into the dark. "You're *laughing* at me!"

She swept her hair out of her eyes.

"Don't be afraid, Patricia. I've told you that you won't be hurt."

"You must be crazy, all of you!"

"We're activating your subconscious minds, yours and Jonathan's. The church, the night—all the trappings are to help your imaginations create a new reality."

"You think you're conjuring evil spirits, don't you, Mr. Apple? This is a black mass."

"Nonsense. It has nothing to do with superstition."

"It's blasphemy and I'll have no part of it!"

"You don't know what you're saying. You belong to us, Patricia. You always have and you always will. Your parents gave you to the Church. Our Church."

How dare he talk about her parents! They could never even have known this vicious old man. They would never have allowed him to touch their daughter, much less . . . do the things they did at a black mass. "Hail Mary, full of grace, the Lord is with thee, blessed art thou—"

The laughter again. Pitying laughter. Embarrassed.

Mr. Apple wanted to make others as foul as he was. Evil is always missionary.

Patricia clasped her hands tightly, huddling against the crowd behind her. She was soaked through from her run down the wet Queens streets. Behind her she heard a heavy, scraping tread. She moaned.

The congregation began very softly to clap. The sound was terrible because it was so gentle; a quickening, savage rhythm as intimate as the rustle of leaves.

Patricia raised her eyes until she was again gazing at the tabernacle. Inside lay the living Mystery itself, the God to whom she had given her loyalty and love. She needed intercession now. His customary silence had to end; this was the time and place for a miracle. "Send the Archangel Michael," she whispered.

"It's starting, Patricia. Don't be afraid."

"Oh, my God, I am heartily sorry—"

"Help her, Mary."

"I will try."

Mary was no Catholic nun—Patricia knew that by the deep red of her habit. There was no red habit in the Church. She came sweeping up, now pale and agitated, floating in oceans of wine-red silk, her face framed by starched black linen. A real nun's wimple would be white. A hand came around Patricia's shoulder and starch crackled in her ear. "Now, now, darling, you let me help you."

"Don't touch me!"

"Patricia, you don't understand. You're under hypnosis and it's made you forget your role. You must trust us. This is to create something beautiful and important for the world."

"You're committing an act of desecration. You're a Catholic. We've been to Mass together—I've seen you pray!"

"I'm going to hold a cloth over your nose and mouth, and I want you to breathe deeply."

When Mary's face loomed close, smiling, Patricia almost recognized, almost remembered—but the place her supposedly new friend actually had in her past was, like Jonathan's, just beyond the reach of her conscious mind. Mary placed a golden bowl full of clear blue liquid on the floor and dipped a cloth in it. She took Patricia's head in her hands and held up her face. Her arms were strong; Patricia lacked the power to resist.

The cloth obscured her vision. She held her breath. "Now, Patricia, breathe. Come on, darling." Patricia held on. She resolved to die just as she was, simply by not breathing again. Not ever.

A male voice rumbled behind her. "We can't hold him!"

Another: "Franklin, this is hopeless. You can't make this work with both of them uncooperative."

"Quiet, all of you!" A loud clap of hands. "Music! Now!"

A long, low note vibrated in the atmosphere. Patricia was beginning to be desperate for air. The wet cloth was stifling her. Mary whispered reassurance, her flat green eyes brimming with what appeared to be pity.

Then the eyes fixed on something in the dark. The expression sharpened to fear. Something cold and hard touched Patricia's shoulder. There was awful, ragged breathing behind her. The sound of it mingled with the music. Hands as rough as bark began caressing Patricia's arms, her waist, her thighs.

Strong fingers shredded her clothes, and she knelt naked amid the scraps of cloth. "Breathe in, Patricia," Mary said. "Breathe in!"

"Mary, get away from her."

"She's not anesthetized at all, Franklin."

"Hurry—can't you see what he's going to do?"

"Franklin—"

"Run! He'll tear you to pieces if you get in his way!"

Patricia felt herself swept off her feet, cradled by powerful, wire-tight arms. She shut her eyes, afraid to look on the face of one who felt so terribly wrong. The low music throbbed and the congregation resumed its clapping. "Oh, God, please take me!"

As soon as she spoke air rushed into her lungs. It was damp and smelled of the full church—candle smoke and incense . . . and the sweaty rot of the thing that held her. Now she would have welcomed the anesthesia.

"Somebody help me!"

"Think of our goal, Patricia. It's worth the sacrifice!"

Mary was not a friend, *she was one of them*—here, now, wearing that profane red habit.

Kind, friendly Mary. She had trapped Patricia in sweet coils. Patricia kept her eyes closed as the thing or man or whatever he was laid her out on the altar and ran his hands along her tingling skin. The music boomed deeper than any organ note, coming from some instrument up in the choir loft.

There were so *many* of them; Holy Spirit Church was jammed as it never was during poor Father Goodwin's Masses.

During the day Father Goodwin struggled here to keep his handful of Catholics coming. At night this huge, gaudy, rich congregation obviously met for rituals of a very different kind.

Poor Father. These must be his lost parishioners, the ones who never came to Mass.

Her new lover was heavy. Brutish and gasping, he bore down on her, pinning her to the cold marble of the altar. So many times, in this very spot, Father had accomplished the miracle of Transubstantiation. She wanted to raise her naked flesh from the sacred place but could not. He covered her with himself, enveloped her, crushed her so completely the air gushed from her lungs.

The music began to quicken.

Until now she had called herself the Last Virgin, playing the old-fashioned Catholic game of How-Far-Can-You-Go, allowing a thigh to be stroked, a breast to be touched, the press of trousered hardness against her knee.

She writhed. He was so heavy, so big, so foul-smelling.

He was beginning his filthy work. She could feel it poking and prodding at her privacy. She tried to lock her knees but it was useless. "Oh, Jesus! Oh, Jesus!"

The pain choked off her words. That black music thundered and throbbed. As one person the congregation groaned. The church resounded with the gasps of a monstrous passion.

"Jesus!" There was no response, no feeling of His presence. Nothing at all.

Surely, Jesus, You still love me. You want me in Your heaven. You haven't abandoned me. No.

If You no longer want me—

The arms came completely around her.

"Patricia, you must understand that you'll be hurt if you don't calm down!" That made her fight all the harder. Suddenly there was a pain like fire between her legs, so intense it pulled a piercing scream out of her. "That woke the neighborhood up," someone shouted.

"Our Father, who art in heaven, hallowed be Thy name."

"There's a light across the street!"

"Okay, get him off. This isn't working."

Hands were grabbing at the dark figure atop her, but he growled and fought and tried harder to hurt her. He pounded and jabbed and smashed himself against her. All her thoughts, all her prayers were swept away in a flash of agony as bones cracked and nerves were severed. Her mind dulled down. She heard distant shouts, and saw the frantic, capering form of Mr. Apple with vestments flying about his head.

Then, abruptly, the crushing weight was gone. "Calm him down! Don't let him out of the circle." That was the last she understood. There were more voices, but they were only a buzzing, incoherent cacophony.

The light of consciousness was flickering and starting to die. This time when Sister Mary's sweet-smelling cloth was pressed against her face she inhaled gratefully in sobbing gasps.

"You will forget," said Mary's voice.

"Oh, Mary, why, why did you let him hurt . . ."

Darkness came, and she sank back into the dream she called ordinary life. They left her, hurt and bleeding, alone.

MARY: THE RESURRECTION OF
THE INQUISITION

I am so frightened for Patricia and Jonathan I do not think I can bear it. Tonight we made a terrible, terrible mistake with them. Unbelievable that we could be so foolish!

Or is it so unbelievable? In an institution two thousand years old there is precedent for every error. The ones who unleashed the Black Death prematurely in 1334 made a greater mistake than we have, after all.

But that is history and this is now. She is bleeding, maybe dying, at this very moment! If I could sweat blood I think I would.

But I am absolutely helpless. If I show myself now I risk exposure of the whole Church. Error must not be allowed to compound error.

So I spend these predawn hours writing, hoping that somehow the act of putting pen to paper will relax me enough for a few hours of rest.

What a disaster! And there was so much time wasted after she was hurt! We had to get safely away before calling the priest. I can only hope and pray that he gets Patricia to a hospital in time.

My God, we had to leave her!

I look at my words as they stand on the paper, dry and still. Words of fear. I think it, I say it—fear, fear, fear.

We live exactly like all night things—we hide and scurry and know the way of silence. We and the rats and owls and bats.

The children are so incredibly important. Please, please may no more harm come to them. Our mistake has exposed them to an even worse enemy than our own stupidity!

The Inquisition will certainly have noticed our gaudy public fiasco. Now our tireless old enemy will be after them again.

It hides for a few years, to lull us, to tempt us. . . .

Then it jumps out of nowhere—right at our throats!

The Inquisition will battle us until Catholicism withers away. The last priest, in the last moment of the last Catholic church on earth, will strike the last blow at us.

They say we are evil, that we work to make Satan manifest, to give Him physical form.

I say, dear Inquisitors, evil is not all black nor your "Satan" all bad, and the world is not as simple as you would like to believe.

Inquisition: it means inquiry. Question. Such a small word for such a great terror.

To the common world the Inquisition is dead and gone. How would the ordinary Catholic feel to know that the handsome priest with the briefcase, striding so confidently out of the Chancellery, is an Inquisitor? And that the Samsonite case contains a thumbscrew, a radio direction-finder, and a car bomb?

Daddy laughed and called them Christ's terrorists.

I do not laugh. They murdered my father by exposing him to plutonium. They chose that particular horror so the radiation would prevent us from salvaging his semen and thus his precious genes.

Dad—covered with sores, gasping, his hair falling out on the pillow. Oh, God, help us!

Deliver the children from such a fate. Deliver my boy!

Must these hot summer days be his autumn? Death, birth, the roll of seasons, sky-changes: Jonathan is the end of a long line, the perfection of two millennia of patient breeding.

The Inquisition is so skilled. How can they be so damn good at it? They're just a bunch of fanatical priests!

The world has forgotten us, but the Church has not, not for an instant.

I hear my heart beating: bump-bump, save his life, save his life.

I love you until my heart will break, it takes my breath away to touch you, and I cannot speak to look on your beauty. You liked to swim, you liked to play basketball, to listen to your short-wave, to look at the stars.

We raped your mind so that the Inquisition could not even torture the truth of your identity out of you. And now look—the disaster of this night will attract them like flies to a corpse!

I loved my father.

And I loved my husband. Poor Martin. So happy, so handsome! And I don't want to think about him either. I'm homesick for my men, for Dad and for Martin!

It's a pleasure to write his name. Martin. Such a lovely name. I can almost hear his plane falling. I imagine wind hissing past motionless propellers.

I know all the details of loneliness, the coldness of suddenly empty sheets, the attic boxes full of new suits.

And then there is Mike. Oh, Mike. If only you knew how tiresome I find you. I only married you because of the cover you unwittingly provide for Jonathan. Even the Inquisition will hesitate to kill a police official's son. Or so we hope.

Will anything work? Can we *ever* escape them?

"Down the nights and down the days; down the arches of the years, the Hound of Heaven . . ."

Howling in the precincts of darkness, and in my heart.

I feel awful. I hate the dreary old church we use. Of course, *our* priest can't command a better parish.

I am sweating. I'm sick.

I imagine being put in the Lady, a steel sarcophagus lined with spikes. When the Lady is closed the spikes penetrate to a quarter of an inch every surface of the victim's body.

Mother Regina was in it three hours. Nineteen fifty-four. She really talked! She gave them the entire bloodline, told them our whole history.

—Founded by Titus Flavius Sabinus Vespasianus on Sunday, September 9, in the year A.D. 70 on the still-smoking ruins of the Temple of Solomon in Jerusalem.

—Based on the secrets of breeding, now known as genetics, contained in the scrolls that were known as the Treasure of Solomon.

—Charged with breeding a new and greater species out of the old human stock, a species that would be allied with what men call evil, as they are allied with what they call good.

But evil is not evil nor good good. They are simply different principles. Man calls himself beautiful. By his standards his replacement will be hideous beyond description. But his replacement will be a powerful species, brighter than man, more resistant to disease, closer to nature.

The blood is the whole point. Jonathan and Patricia are precious because of their blood. They are the masterpieces of thousands of years of breeding according to Solomonic principles. Out of their union the new species will be born.

This is worse than lying and sweating up in that bedroom. This is—oh, hell, I'm going to just burn this and sit in the dark.

Poor Patricia. She was screaming!

"Help her, Mary." Franklin, you said that, you fool!

God knows but I tried.

Chapter Three ———————

FATHER HARRY GOODWIN was awakened suddenly by the ringing of his telephone. The rings exploded in his head, one, then another, then another. Silence. Please keep ringing. Please!

No. The silence continued. There would be no fourth ring. Harry dragged himself to the edge of his bed. His skull felt like it was going to pound itself to bits. He was nauseated with fear.

All these years he had been dreading the three rings on a night the Tituses were using the church. Three rings were the maximum emergency signal. They meant only one thing—they have had a terrible accident and his church was in danger.

His impulse was to race across to the church but he seemed plunged into stifling muck; his fear paralyzed him. It was several minutes before he managed to go to the window and look across at the Spirit. He expected to see destruction, a mayhem of flames, or some unspeakable horror—maybe a conjured thing—crawling the roof slates.

But there wasn't even a haze of smoke along the roof line of the old building, nor a flicker behind the stained glass. Harry Goodwin tapped his own window. Should the Spirit burn there was no chance at all of building a new church. A fire would mean the end of this fine old parish.

Maybe the three rings had been a coincidence. The church across the parking lot seemed utterly at peace, blurred by the beginnings of a predawn shower.

Harry's familiar morning exhaustion bowed him. His alarm clock said four fifteen. In two hours he must say his first Mass . . . before a congregation of perhaps seven, in a church built to accommodate five hundred.

"Friday," he muttered. "God give me strength." He felt awful. Had he taken a sleeping pill last night? No, there weren't any left and so much the better. Leave the pills alone. Valium priests, Seconal priests, Thorazine priests. They were worse than the old-fashioned whiskey priests. He had so far escaped the lure of depressants and tranquilizers. As a result, his life was raw with loneliness and a sense of unfulfilled promise. The issue, of course, was faith and the lack thereof. His confessor, Father Michael Brautigan, a bluff and kindly Jesuit, red with drink, would say that faith was a matter of relaxing one's instinct to touch. "Don't try to touch Christ," he would say. "That's the point of Thomas, isn't it?"

Harry *had* to touch. But it worked both ways: one who had to touch also needed touching. Sometimes, naked in the middle of his silent rectory, he would dip his hands into cold water until they were numbed and did not feel his own, then he would close his eyes and embrace himself and dance around and around with himself in the dingy rooms.

Lately he had become too desperate, too full of self-pity even for that. Never to be touched—or even needed, for that matter—had emerged for him as the poisonous central issue of his life. When he had first entered the priesthood, he had assumed that his services would be ardently desired by Catholics hungry for the succor of their Church. Instead he had spent his life struggling to pay bills, working against the relentless dwindling of his flock, forced to hold jumble sales and bingo and raffles, until finally even those measures failed.

Then came the Tituses. Old Franklin and handsome Martin, just wanting to rent "the plant," as they had called it, a few nights a week.

Nobody will know, Father. We help out dozens of parishes in the same shape as Holy Spirit.

Nobody will even care except you.

Our money will keep you going. You won't ever have to close your doors.

At first he had thought perhaps it was drugs or counterfeiting or some sort of white slavery.

He had heard their soft chanting, though, and seen the flicker of their candles. He did not actually say it to himself but he knew the truth. Every Monday and Friday morning, after their nights, he had taken to reconsecrating his altar. And he no longer kept the Host in the tabernacle on those nights. It stayed under his pillow, tucked away in the pyx.

Twenty-seven years a priest, twenty a creature of the Tituses. Traitor to his own faith, to his own soul. How black can sin be? He put his hands to his stubbly cheeks and rubbed. He longed for the velvet fingers of a woman, or of death.

As time unfolded the sad destiny that had been contrived for him it became obvious that his whole life—the vocation itself—was not really very valuable. In the world of his youth priests were essential people, needed by their congregations for all sorts of succor. Now when the leaves fell on his walks they stayed, and his leaking roof leaked on.

Did people sense that he was a traitor? Could they somehow smell the taint of the Night Church in the great nave of Holy Spirit?

He didn't want to be a priest anymore. He did not even want to live. No, he had a plan for himself. He intended to die unconfessed, and go to Hell—in which, despite the modern theologians, he still firmly believed. He actually looked forward to it: he deserved his damnation, wanted it, and had for some years been seeking the death that would bring it. Once he had attempted to commit suicide by suffocating himself in a plastic bag, but it had been too terrifying. So he had tried sleeping pills—and vomited them up.

He had asked Martin Titus to kill him, just a few weeks before Titus himself had been killed in an airplane crash. "I'll think it over," the man had replied absently, and changed the subject. Harry was not even important enough for martyrdom.

He said a bitter prayer, a Hail Mary, and turned once again to his bed.

As he slid beneath the sheet he heard quite distinctly from the church a human sound. It was a loud, woeful groan, loud enough to carry across the parking lot to the rectory.

He should have gone straight over there. Damn fool not to. Three rings at this hour, and he had made himself believe it was a coincidence. Harry Goodwin was a weak man, and that was a fact.

He put his hand on the bedside table. In the drawer was a small pistol. Mike Banion over at the 112th Precinct had given it to him after the ritual murder of Father Santa Cruz at Saint Thomas in Brooklyn. He shouldn't have accepted it, but he didn't want Mike to know how he envied old Santa Cruz.

This was the right time to have a pistol. He felt the comforting steel of it in the palm of his hand. One day soon, when he could bear the taste of the barrel in his mouth, he was going to use it on himself.

As he pulled on the old raincoat liner he used as a robe and jammed his feet into his aged and corn-cut Adidas, he struggled for some sort of inner stability. Gun or no gun, he was terrified. The Tituses did horrible things over there.

He hurried past empty bedrooms (it had once taken six priests just to administer this parish) and descended the back stairs to the kitchen. There was a folding umbrella in the bottom of his briefcase. He fished around for it, opening it as he went out the kitchen door.

Curtains of rain swept the muddy parking lot. As Harry crossed it he was reminded by the sucking of his shoes that he could not afford reasphalting. He opened the side door to the sacristy. Inside, the Spirit was inky black. As he carefully pulled the door shut behind him he twisted the little pistol's safety to the off position.

All he heard was the din of rain on the roof. Just as he was beginning to think he had dreamed the human sound he heard another one—a long sigh. At first he was frightened, fumbling for the lights. Then he realized the sound was coming from the altar and a flash of anger mixed with his fear. How dare they leave him to clean up one of their desecrations.

In the dancing, vanishing light of the votive candles he could just make out a dense shadow splayed across the altar. Harry stared hard. Wasn't that a large animal? He raised his gun but he could not take aim in the dimness. Then he realized that the shape was not a crouching animal but a prone human body.

His fingers found the right switches and he flipped them all at once. Light flooded the church.

There was a woman on the altar, lying on her back. Her blood flowed down to the sacristy floor in thin streams like bars. Harry had only a moment for astonishment. The girl moaned again, horribly.

He approached the altar. The poor child lay in a dark pool of her own blood, her legs spread, her arms akimbo, her hair tangled about her face.

The fact that he knew this woman so well pulled the first sound from his throat. His own scream was more real to him and more frightening than even the horror before him. In his urgency to get to the phone in the sacristy he dropped his pistol, which went clattering into the dark behind the high altar at the back of the nave.

This was incredible. This could not be condoned. And yet . . . he had to deal very carefully with the whole affair. His own life, his very soul, was teetering on a knife edge.

Turning away from the horror he dashed on his long legs to the phone, grabbed it, dialed 911. The Tituses would be furious with him for calling the police, but what else did they expect him to do? They had just gone off and left him with this tragedy and not one word of instruction.

There were voices outside. Neighbors. Of course—the girl's screams had roused the neighborhood. The Tituses must never have intended to leave her behind. Circumstances had forced them. Perhaps they even wanted her saved.

In any case, she *would* be saved. He might not be much of a priest anymore, but Harry Goodwin was still a human being.

He heard the first siren start not long after he had hung up the phone. The New York City Police Department was more than half Catholic, and it protected the Church almost as carefully as it did itself. Harry knew one of the two patrolmen who came sprinting up the aisle, their guns in their hands. Timothy Reilly was his name. Impossible that such a scrawny, mischievous altar boy could have grown into this enormous, competent-looking man in blue. Reilly took in the scene at once.

"He still in the church, you think, Father?"

Harry told the first of what he realized miserably would be many lies. "I thought perhaps I heard him. I'm not quite sure. It could have been the echo of a door closing." Trick the cops into searching the church. Give the Tituses and their congregation a little more time to get well away.

Reilly's partner began to search with a flashlight while Reilly joined Harry beside the poor, damaged girl. Her eyes were rolling slowly up into her head. "Her name is Patricia Murray," Harry said, and woe tugged his heart. "She's one of the hardest-working young women in the parish." His throat closed. "One of my best people." He wept and could not stop, and it was useless and stupid but he was so full of anger and self-disgust and sorrow that he wished right now he could be torn to pieces, and the rancid bits of himself scattered through the filthiest deeps of the Pit, each to suffer separately the full and eternal measure of damnation.

"She's hurt bad, Father. That bleeding's gotta be controlled. EMS better get here damn soon."

"I'll get my kit." He raced into the sacristy and dragged his ancient first aid kit from the bottom of the old armoire. As he ran back he fumbled with the latch, only to open it and find the bandages rotted and covered with roach sacs, the medicines dried and useless, the tourniquet a brittle mound of rubber.

"Aren't you going to anoint her, Father?"

"Anoint?" The kid had assumed he was getting the chrism. "Oh, of course."

Another siren ground down outside. Two black paramedics sprinted past the rows of age-darkened pews carrying their stretcher and other equipment. When they reached the altar they set to work with lightning choreography, producing bandages and plasma and intravenous needles and syringes. In seconds her nakedness was obscured by gauze and tape. She lay as blue-bruised and destroyed as if on a slab in a morgue. Her eyes were waxen and staring now, her skin gray.

"She use drugs?"

"Certainly not. She's a very good Catholic."

"Then she's *been* drugged. You better call the next of kin, Father."

"There are no next of kin. She was orphaned in her teens. She was raised at Our Lady of Victory. She rarely spoke of her past. She's not been in the parish more than six months."

More police were pouring into the church. Outside, siren after siren moaned to a stop. The whole precinct must be turning out. It occurred to Harry that he ought to make a big pot of coffee.

No, that was a silly idea. He realized when he looked down and found the holy oil in his hands that he was in shock, moving like a robot. Part of him was still performing priestly duties. The rest wanted at this moment to be, to do, anything else. Anything.

Patricia was already on the stretcher. Harry fumbled to her side and began administering the sacrament. The paramedics wheeled her rapidly down the aisle. He muttered his prayer as one of the men spoke another sort of ritual into a walkie-talkie. "Multiple pelvic fractures, possible severed spine, copious vaginal bleeding with developed pallor. Administering plasma and antishock procedures with cold pack. Patient in shock, stage two, possible drug OD."

The ambulance began sounding its siren and flashing its lights as the stretcher was wheeled up to it. The doors slammed on the two solemn black faces and their white-draped patient.

Harry was left with chrism in hand, his sacrament incomplete. Carefully he wiped the remaining oil from his thumb onto the edge of the container. Then he snapped it shut and started to go back to his church.

Mike Banion stood in the doorway, looking with the light behind him like a blocky tree stump. He was an important cop, Detective Inspector, eighteen years on the force, as good a friend as Harry Goodwin had ever had. Mike was both physically and politically powerful. You saw him at all the police funerals and the big, famous crimes, looking through the familiar bifocal glasses out of his hurt-child eyes.

Seeing him here confirmed the seriousness of the affair. So this was to be a famous crime.

As if to certify the awfulness of it all, a car from Channel Two News came roaring up Morris Street and screeched to a halt. The rain had gone soft and dawn was beginning to outline the jumble of flashing cars, and to touch the cross above the dome with a delicate gray glow. When Harry looked up at it he was almost in control, but when he looked down, his throat was tight and his eyes were once again tearing.

"Father Goodrich, I'm Charles Datridge, Channel Two News." A young man stuck out his hand as a plump girl patted at him with a powder puff. "Mind if we get started?"

"I—" There was a sudden bloom of iron-blue light. Harry squinted.

"Rolling," cried a voice beyond the glare. "Sound! Speed!"

"This is Charles Datridge here at Holy Ghost Parish in Queens. With me I have Father Michael Goodrich. Father Goodrich—"

"Cut it, Charlie."

"Right, Inspector. Kill the lights, Benny."

"Holy *Spirit* Church, Charlie. And the priest's name is Harry Goodwin, not Michael Goodrich. You guys stay in your car until we get the perpetrator pinned down. You'll get your pictures then, assuming you play my way now."

"Playing your way, Inspector."

"Thank you, Charlie. Come on, Father, let's go where we can talk. You got any coffee in the kitchen?"

"Sure, Mike, we can make some."

Mike Banion moved toward the rectory. "Charlie's a news tiger. Channel Two's lightnin' reporter." He laughed, a deep, reassuring sound, the easy mirth of authority. "You're gonna get a horde of 'em in the next couple of hours. First there'll be the *Post* lookin' for pictures. 'Where'sa body?' they'll yell. Then the *News,* and they'll want a shot of the altar. Then TV and radio stations, all of 'em hollerin' like crazy." He laughed again. "Along about dawn a guy from the *Times* will probably phone, name of Terry Quist. Only since you're a priest, he'll introduce himself as Terence. He'll already know the story back to front. But he'll get the real stuff out of you, the dope about how it feels." They reached the rectory. "I'm sorry to say this, Harry, but you're gonna be famous. So's that poor girl."

"Mike, she was a parish leader, one of the few young people who really cared. She was wonderful. My star."

"I hate to hear that, Harry. You must be hurting awful bad. I gotta think the perpetrator knew. I mean, the beautiful parish star, and he takes her and brutally rapes her on the altar. That's tellin' me he *did* know, and this is one of these weirdo deals. Probably somebody she was familiar with. Struck up an acquaintance with her on purpose. Hell, maybe even at some parish affair. Psychopath."

They reached the kitchen. Harry turned on the lights, revealing the aged stove, the greasy counters, the yellowing oilcloth on the table. "Let me get the coffee," he said.

" 'Fill it to the rim with Brim.' "

"I don't have any decaffeinated, Mike."

"And I don't drink it. I'm just trying to take an easier tone. Lower our blood pressure before we both get strokes. A crime like this works on you, Father. Eats you alive."

Harry looked at him. He could not find words.

After a moment Mike continued. "So this kid was one of the parish stars. And she was in the church alone at a very odd hour. Was she a little loony on religion? I mean, was there any likelihood she might have come there on her own and surprised some derelict sleeping in a pew? It's important we know that."

"She was a stable, normal sort of a person. Her parents died in a fire, she told me. She had been here in Queens for about six months. She was vague about her past. Quite vague. But Mike, she was a *good* girl. A darned good girl."

Mike Banion sank onto a chair. The kettle began to whistle and

Harry poured water into their mugs. When he inhaled the steam Mike coughed, a sound like a car refusing to start. "Foggy morning," he said, cradling his mug in his hands. Suddenly he looked directly at Harry. As always Harry was startled by the depths of pain in those eyes. From the day Mike's first wife had died, they had been like that. Despite his remarriage, Mike still went to Beth's grave every Sunday. "Harry, tell me your story. What did you see?"

"I was awake. The usual morning hells. We've talked about it."

"Awake, horny, worried."

The chill in the room enveloped Harry. He talked too much to Mike Banion, telling him all except the really bad part, the part about the Tituses. Should a parishioner know his priest so intimately? But who else, if not Mike? Harry nodded at the accuracy of Mike's statement. "I heard a noise. Loud. A terrible groan. So I went over to investigate."

I heard the three rings. Their emergency signal. But I can't tell you that.

"Must have been awfully loud."

"Very."

"Church unlocked, of course."

Harry had been waiting for that. "You know it always is."

Mike's face darkened. Harry had been through this with him dozens of times before. He watched Mike relight his cigar and take a long pull. Mike smoked cigars the way other people did cigarettes. He claimed he never got drunk because there was so much nicotine in his blood there was no room for the alcohol. Given a pint of good scotch he might nod a little, but that was all. "You lock your church at ten P.M. in the future, Harry, and consider that an order. I'm gonna tell the patrolmen to check it out, so don't think I won't know."

Mike's big, spotted hand came across the table and covered Harry's. The touch lasted only an instant, but the tenderness in it shamed Harry almost unendurably. *Thank God for good friends, there when you need them.* The gesture did nothing to dismantle Harry's shame at what he had come to, only painted it in a more bitter light. "Churches belong open," he said.

"You're sentimental. That's a weakness."

"God help me, the poor girl was raped in my church! Mike, don't tell me it's because I leave the place unlocked."

"I'm not accusing you, Father. You just tell me if you saw the perpetrator closely enough to make an ID."

Now the lie again. "I heard a noise. Maybe a cough, maybe the sound of the side door closing."

"Meaning the guy was just that second leaving. He must still be in the neighborhood."

"Yes. I told Officer Reilly—"

Mike Banion stood up and went out the kitchen door. A few moments later he was shouting. Harry heard him yell that roadblocks should have gone up and a house-to-house search started long ago, on and on. Cops trotted here and there, lights flashed, voices kept fracturing the dawn silence.

A moment later Mike was back in the kitchen. "By *God,* why didn't you tell me her name?"

"I—I didn't?"

"Reilly says it was Pat Murray. Father, is that true?"

"Well, yes, that's right, Mike."

"She's a good friend of my wife's. She was on a date with my *stepson!*"

Mike Banion thundered off into the churchyard. A moment later his old Dodge was skidding its way out of the muddy parking lot.

For a long time Father Harry Goodwin simply sat, staring. Then he tried to pray. His words mocked him, and soon lost themselves in silence.

Chapter Four ————|——

They guided Jonathan to a car and took him home. They bathed him and attended him, six young sisters in their red habits, and a grave man of perhaps thirty who was so gentle he must love him. He laid his exhausted friend in his bed.

Jonathan dreamed of wet leaves stinging his face, snatching at his arms. He raced through a vicious jungle of grasping plants and slick, seething creatures barely seen. In this dream he ran with the strength of a wild animal and the hunger of a ghoul. He pursued a woman.

"He's having a nightmare," one of the sisters said. "Shouldn't we wake him, Jerry?"

"Let him sleep." Jerry Cochran stroked Jonathan's sweaty forehead.

In his dream Jonathan stretched out his arms, grabbed at his dream-woman's flying hair, screamed out his desire. She raced on through long, dripping alleys of trees, past flickering candles and bloodied crosses.

"Jerry, he's suffering!"

"We have to let him sleep, otherwise the hypnosis may be permanently weakened. He mustn't be allowed to remember what he did." He looked long at his young friend. "Or what he is."

Jonathan heard none of this. He was utterly lost in himself, racked by his nightmare. In it he got his fingers in her hair, he dragged her down, he sat astride her.

He tried desperately to wake up. The hands that had grabbed her were not his hands, they were ugly and horn-hard and full of evil strength.

His watchers heard a noise downstairs, the slam of a door, the pounding of Mike Banion's footsteps. "If he knows, we kill him," the young man said laconically.

One of the sisters withdrew a long, thin blade from her habit.

They retreated into the back hall as Jonathan screamed the broken screams of great agony.

Mike came running up the stairs, oblivious to the thickened shadows at the far end of the dark hall.

"Wake up, Jonathan!" Mike shouted over the roaring shrieks.

Jonathan heard the voice but it was too faint for him to make out the words. The nightmare continued. He smoothed back the obscuring fog of his victim's hair and looked upon her face. Her mouth opened and a scream swarmed out like a flight of wasps—and then his anger possessed him, his horrible, vicious anger, and made him delight in the way her flesh swept from her bones as he stroked her. Beneath his scaly palms it scraped away as skin might during the flaying of a rabbit.

This was the worst ever, the most wicked dream he had ever had. And he couldn't stop it. He watched himself tear the skin off her knotting, twisting muscles. His own screams mingled with hers.

"Wake up! Wake up!" A frantic voice was calling to him.

Help me! Please help me!

"Wake up!" His savior grabbed his shoulders and shook him so furiously the dream finally snapped.

"Wake up, son," Mike Banion was saying. "You and I have a big problem."

"Dad?" His own voice was a whisper. Mike had him by the shoulders, had pulled him half out of the bed.

Mike threw his arms around him. "Wake up, Johnny. This is a serious problem."

Jonathan hugged him back. He had come to love gruff Mike Banion. Although Mike could be fierce, the cop loved him too, in his own way. Behind the tough exterior the love was there. Definitely. But in his own way.

"I've got a hard thing to tell you, Johnny."

Jonathan looked into the detective's eyes. The intensity of the dream made even the reality of Mike seem vague, as if he were on the other side of a dirty window. Jonathan tried to bring things into focus, to prepare himself for whatever unimaginable tragedy had occurred. "Okay, Dad."

"Your girl is in the hospital. She got raped."

Earthquake. The ceiling, the walls, the floor flying out into the night. "My—my—"

"Patricia Murray. She was raped on the altar of Holy Spirit sometime around midnight. She's at the Polyclinic. Bad, I'm afraid, son."

That made the dream boil up once again from Jonathan's unconscious. This time it brought a stunning, terrible image of a blond head twisting and turning below him, lips flecked with blood. He felt her body beneath his own, jerking in spasm.

A thrill tickled him like the passage of a spider across his neck. "No!"

Mike grabbed his shoulders. "You must have been the last person to see her before the rapist."

On those words his mother swept into the room, her red silk robe fluttering behind her. "Leave him alone!" She was not her usual self. She looked like she hadn't slept in a month; her face was a mask.

"Mary, I'm trying to console our boy. His date was raped tonight at the Spirit."

Mary forced her features into a grimace. "No," she blurted. "That's crazy!"

"It happened."

Jonathan saw an ocean of pity in his mother's eyes. She reached out to him, then stopped. She looked from Jonathan to Mike and back again. She was silent.

Jonathan's mind returned to his dream. In it he had been raping somebody. And those vast rows of tree trunks, those crosses—the dream jungle could easily have been a real-life church.

The memory of how very much he had enjoyed hurting her made him reject Mike's comforting hug and scramble to his feet in panic. He wanted to run, to hide, to somehow escape the red fire of insane anger within him.

Mike enclosed his arm in a powerful hand. "That's okay, son, take it easy. Take it easy, now."

He couldn't do that—not after glimpsing a monster in the shadows of his soul. Frantically he tried to stifle the terror. Dad obviously thought he was grief-stricken. How could he say that the right emotion was dread?

He decided that the impression of rape was more than a dream. It was almost a memory. Maybe this is the way psychopaths discover their crimes.

"Dad—"

How could he say it? While she was being raped I was dreaming about raping her? Funny coincidence, right, Dad?

"Come on, son, I'll drive you over to the hospital."

"You'll leave him right here, Mike Banion! Look at him. He's overwrought! You wake him up in the middle of the night, drag him out of bed—"

"Oh, darlin'. Pat was his girl."

"One date! And I arranged it."

At last Jonathan pulled himself together enough to talk. He had to tell them, he could not keep the coincidence of his dream a secret. He worked his throat, trying to get the words out. "I had a bad dream— my God, I had a bad dream! It's—no. It's impossible—but I dreamed I was raping her. I was dreaming it when you woke me up!"

"Come on, son, take it easy, now."

"Jonathan, you don't know what you're saying! Mike, he's not awake yet. You can see that!"

"Listen to me! I dreamed this. I *did* dream it." He faced Mike. "Dad, you have to put me on the polygraph, and do it right now."

"The hell I will," Mike roared. "No way are you going on the poly!"

"I am a *prime* suspect, Dad. I was the last person to see her."

"For God's sake, the poly can lie. What if I got a positive?"

"You'd do what you have to."

"Son—oh, son—are you—it almost sounds like—are you confessing this crime?"

"Mike, if you do this—if you *dare*—" She fell silent, her face burning with fear and rage.

Mike ignored her, regarded Jonathan sadly. "Don't tell me this, Johnny."

Jonathan felt in that moment the most profound pity for his stepfather. "If I'd gotten hold of you in time," Mike had once said, "I'd have made you a cop. Such a cop." He'd cuffed Jonathan. "You'd've been a great cop." Poor Mike, all tangled up in his dreams of the son he'd never had. His first wife had died before they could afford children, so twenty-two-year-old Jonathan was taking the place of the unborn. Of course there was no question of Mary giving him children. She'd had a hysterectomy years ago.

"Mike, you've got to face it. I've got to go on the poly. *Especially* because I'm your stepson. If you didn't know me personally, I'd be a prime suspect—dream or no dream—just because I was the last person known to have been with her. I'd be down at the precinct under questioning right now."

"Hell, I'd know in a second you didn't do it. I've been a detective a damn long time, kid. And I know you didn't do it. My goddamn trick knee tells me." He cuffed Jonathan's shoulder. "The poor girl is really banged up. A stringbean like you couldn'ta done it."

Then why did I dream what I dreamed?

"If I weren't your son, you'd request a poly as a matter of routine. It'd be your duty then, and it's your duty now."

Mike's face clouded. Jonathan had him cornered. The truth was obvious. "I'll call the precinct, get an operator outa bed," Mike muttered. He started to go heavily down the stairs. At the landing he paused. He looked back, the hall light gleaming on his glasses, his skin the color of dirty flour. "Goddamn, I just had a thought. If we were out on the lease, we'd be gettin' up just about now. I can smell that coffee, son."

Mike's hunting lease was his personal version of paradise. The two of them had good times there, despite Jonathan's total inability to fire after he had aimed. He couldn't understand killing for fun. The pleasure of the hunt did not seem justification for stealing a life. For him, getting the buck in his sights was enough. "I'll be ready in a minute." He went to his closet, began to get dressed.

Mother followed Jonathan into his room, talked to him as he put on his clothes. "Don't you realize he thinks you're guilty? He'll make that test read any way he wants it to read!"

"Mother, for heaven's sake, I *asked* for the test."

She dropped her voice. "He's clever. If I didn't know better, I'd say I had committed the ultimate error of marrying an Inquisitor."

"A who?"

She blinked away annoyance. "Just a figure of speech. Remember that a policeman's first concern is solving his case. Getting the right man is entirely secondary."

"Mike would never take advantage like that. It isn't his way."

"*I'm* the one who loves you, Jonathan. You're my child and it's my obligation to protect you." Her hands fluttered helplessly before her face. "His affection—if you can even call it that—is ordinary. Just ordinary." She clutched at him. "You're so brilliant, so good—he has no idea what you are. He's a barbarian."

"Why did you marry him then? I don't think you've ever loved him, have you?"

"That isn't your business. I had a good reason for marrying Mike. Better than you can imagine."

"And I have a good reason for taking the polygraph."

"I can't stop you, can I?"

"Not really, Mother."

"So put your shirt on and go take your beloved polygraph and God help you! You can defy me all you want. I can't stop you." She swept out, head high, fists clenched. There were tears starting in her eyes.

Poor Mother. There was so much about her own son that she did not understand.

I am a gentle man who dreams like a monster.

He went down the stairs, found Mike standing in the kitchen.

Mike's face was tight with embarrassment. "The poly operator's waiting." He walked quietly behind Jonathan into the garage. But the moment the door closed he began to argue again. "For God's sake, Johnny, the girl is over at that hospital and we're wasting time. She needs a friend right now. Let me take you to her. Forget the damn polygraph—nobody suspects you, least of all me."

Jonathan paused beside the car. A quiet, firm voice spoke within: *There is something wrong with you, and now is the time to find out what it is.*

"Do it for me, Dad."

That statement brought a cuff that made Jonathan's ear ring. He sat down in the cigar-cured old Dodge and wished that Mike would for once remember his strength. "Sorry, Johnny. Sorry. It's just—I know my own job. Don't tell me my job. And I don't want to polygraph you."

Jonathan had to be more specific with Mike; there was no way around it. "Dad, I was having a very strange dream when you woke me up. I was dreaming that I had raped Patricia. Violently. In a church."

Mike got into the Dodge. For a moment he was silent. Then he slammed his hands against the steering wheel. "Coincidence."

"What if I'm a psychopath and don't know it?"

"Rare. Chance in a million."

"It happens, Dad."

"I know it happens! But it isn't happening to you. You're the scientific genius in the family. You'd *know* it if you were a psycho." He looked at Jonathan. There was fear in his eyes. "Wouldn't you?"

"There are blank areas in my memory."

"Big deal. There are blank areas in my memory too. You're a good kid—I mean, don't go getting a swelled head if you get a compliment from the inspector, but I know a good kid when I see one. You live clean, you work hard. This dream stuff is damn foolishness. Everybody has crazy dreams now and then. You don't know where they come from. Men are violent. That's a fact. Hell, I ought to run you in for wasting police time with false leads or somethin'. God, do I wish that was a crime. Our job'd be cut in half. But that's neither here nor there. The point is, that girl was brutally raped, Jonathan. Could you really hurt somebody that way? You can't even shoot a *deer,* for Chrissake. You have less killer instinct than any man I've ever known. Take my word for it, kid."

"The nicest people are often the most repressed, the kind who chop their families to bits, then can't remember a thing about it. It takes years of psychotherapy to uncover the monster inside."

Mike started the car, pulled out into the soft early morning, into the quiet of Kew Gardens. There had been rain before dawn, and dew now gleamed in the sunlight, sparkling leaves and grass, shining on the street and the roofs of the tall, elegant houses.

As they drove along Jonathan suffered another wave of anguish over Patricia. What nameless horror had befallen her?

If I raped her I'll commit suicide.

As they went from Kew out onto Queens Boulevard Jonathan felt in himself something almost filthy, as if a rotten, evil presence had crawled through his soul and left greasy stains behind.

His whole life might be coming apart.

Mike lit a cigar, his sallow skin glowing briefly in the lighter flame. From time to time he glanced in Jonathan's direction. Pain seemed to ooze from Mike's sweat-gleaming brow, from his hunched shoulders, his betrayed face.

His faith in me has finally been shaken a little.

Cold crept into Jonathan's bones. The dawn hour was a time when one's body seemed to hold less tightly to life. He huddled into his thin jacket.

The 112th precinct house was a modern building, all gray tile and glass. Jonathan had never been inside. Mike's workplaces—indeed his habits, even his friends—were mostly kept from his stepson. Despite Mike's occasional suggestion that Jonathan become a cop, he kept his police associations separate. "Hardasses," he would say. "You wouldn't go for 'em."

Mike pulled the car into a no-parking zone in front of the station. One thing New York City police officials do not have is parking problems. As soon as the car stopped Jonathan got out.

"Hold it. Just wait a minute." Mike took his stepson's arm. "Look, you aren't any kind of a suspect or anything like that. Nobody even knows you're gonna be on the poly, and nothin's goin' in the record unless—"

He stopped.

"Come on, Dad. Let's get it over with."

He followed Mike through an empty waiting room, past a desk sergeant with permanently raised eyebrows, and into a steel-clad elevator that whined horribly when it started moving.

On the third floor there were offices, the largest among them Mike Banion's. When they went inside, a tall, cadaverous man rose to his feet. " 'Morning, Blake," Mike muttered. "Sorry to bring you down here at this hour."

"No problem, Inspector. Glad to do it." He glanced at Jonathan. "This the suspect?"

"Not a suspect."

Blake regarded Jonathan with neutrality so complete it was chilling. "Got the booking papers?"

"This is a voluntary. Off the goddamn record, see?"

"How do I record the polygraph use, then? It's gotta be on the record, especially with this portable unit. If we were down at the Police Academy with the fixed installation it'd be easier. A lot of uses on that thing. But this—nobody ever takes it out."

"Then say you were testing it. Making sure it still works." He paused a moment. "Look, Blake, you're gonna find out when you work up the questions, so I'm telling you now that this is my stepson, Jonathan. He had the misfortune to be the last respectable person to be seen with a very nice young lady named Patricia Murray who was raped after he left her. So we're down here clearing him."

The polygraph operator's face closed down tight. He was already in the middle of this. He obviously thought he ought to keep as low a profile as possible.

They left Mike's pin-perfect office with its gleaming oak desk and wall of citations and awards, and went down the hall to a small inner room that smelled of stale cigarette smoke and was dominated by an electronic apparatus on a table beside an old-fashioned office chair.

A young policeman had appeared in the hall behind them. He followed them into the room and began going through a file cabinet.

"Out, patrolman," Mike snapped.

"But, sir, I've got to—"

"Get the hell out! This is private!"

The young cop hurried to the door. Jonathan looked around at the police equipment. He recognized the electrodes and wires of a skin galvanometer. He understood the principle of the polygraph; the devices he worked with in his own lab were far more sophisticated versions of the same system.

As soon as he saw how primitive the police machine really was he began to doubt the effectiveness of this session. Perhaps this was all just a waste of time and emotional energy.

Mike was staring at the door. "Who was that guy, Blake, a rookie?"

"Musta been. Never saw him before."

"Got his uniform all screwed up. Notice that?"

"No, sir."

"Yeah. Some damn screwed-up rookie." Mike looked through his bifocals at Jonathan. "Let's get on with it."

"Remove any metal objects from your pockets and roll up your sleeves, please."

Mike stood at the far side of the room with his fingers hooked in his belt loops. His lips were pursed, his face tightly controlled. His eyes were too calm. He was preparing himself for the worst.

Jonathan said nothing about the poor rookie, who was still lurking in the hall. Fortunately Mike couldn't see him from where he was standing. All the young cop needed was an argument with Mike Banion.

He could feel the young cop's eyes on him, watching from just beyond the edge of the light. Idle eyes. Lucky young cop, with nothing to worry about except some damn file.

The operator rubbed Jonathan's wrists with electrostatic gel and affixed the straps, then bound the device's belt around his chest. He flipped a couple of switches and graph paper began spewing out of the plotter. Next there was a test routine to confirm that the styli were rolling correctly.

"What is your name, please?"

"Jonathan Titus Banion."

"Your age?"

"Twenty-two."

"Occupation?"

"Assistant professor, New York University."

"Are you a homosexual?"

"Cut the crap! Don't ask him asshole questions."

"Sorry, Mike! Sorry! It's routine in rape cases."

"Try another tack, boy."

The operator cleared his throat. "Do you like girls?"

"Yes."

"Have you ever hit a girl or hurt a girl in any way?"

"Not that I remember."

"Do you go to church on Sunday?"

"No."

"Do you bathe?"

"Yes."

It was coming soon. They usually popped in the big one after a few innocuous questions so that fluctuations in the graph could be more easily read.

"Do you have a driver's license?"

"Yes."

"Did you rape Patricia Murray?"

"No."

"Were you present when she was raped?"

"No."

Silence descended. Jonathan had the happiness of watching Mike's face go from tight misery to relief. The needles hadn't even burped. But his own mind was just as full of questions as before. Even as he was taking the test he was growing more sure that this polygraph was the wrong instrument. There were more sensitive ways of getting to the truth than measuring whether or not a person *thought* he was lying.

Jonathan's outer self obviously believed that he was innocent. But was that enough? There are other, deeper selves in all human beings, selves that are never meant to be seen by the person riding the surface. A simple polygraph might not detect trouble deep down in a man, where his serpents crawl.

"As clean a test as I've ever seen, Inspector. The kid's not lying. He didn't do it. I'd stake my reputation on it."

Slowly Mike began to smile. He clapped his hands together. His eyes began to twinkle. Then, abruptly, he shifted to a more grave expression. No celebrations now, not appropriate. "Okay. I guess you want to get to that hospital right away, don't you, Jonathan?"

Jonathan stood up. He wished he could be as easily convinced as Mike.

Scientist, test thyself.

In the privacy of his own lab, deserted for the summer, he might find a deeper answer than the simple police equipment offered.

But not now. He knew that Mike would object violently to a trip to the lab. And he would too, for the moment. He was needed at the hospital. And he was longing to be there, more as each moment passed.

The polygraph operator made his way out of the room. Jonathan started to follow, but Mike stopped him. "Just hold on a second. I can't go with you; I got too much to do on this case. I just want to say —oh, Johnny, wow. What the hell can I say?"

"I love you too, Dad." Jonathan kissed his stepfather's cheek, giving expression to the emotion that filled and also frightened his stepfather. Mike in response shook his hand with almost comic solemnity.

"Good enough. I've a mind to send you over to the hospital under escort. Get you there in two minutes."

"I can take a cab, Dad. And don't kill yourself while I'm not watching over you. Remember to get some sleep."

They went through the tiled halls again, back to the grinding elevator, and this time the desk sergeant didn't even look up as they passed. On his way down to the corner to get a cab Jonathan realized it was still too early to find one around here. He would have to take a bus.

Standing at the bus stop with nothing to do but wait, all his energy seemed to drain from his body. He felt like he had been awake for a month. He could conceive of going home, getting into bed, and sleeping until noon.

How dare he even consider that when Patricia needed him?

Needs me? He'd known her for exactly twelve hours. But, yes, she did need him. She would be all alone in that hospital right now, maybe losing her life. . . .

"She really had an effect on you, for a new girl." Mike had come up behind him. "I'm avoiding a reporter," he said sheepishly. "Church rapes are big news. I'll drive you."

"No, I need some time to get myself together. Just about bus ride time."

"What's she like, Johnny?"

"What can I tell you? I fell in love with her. She's wonderful."

"She's one of Father Goodwin's most pious types. I see you as falling more for the easygoing kind."

"Beggars can't be choosers."

"Beggars? Come on, you must have 'em fallin' all over themselves for you." He grasped Jonathan's shoulder. "You're a hell of a good guy. Girls sense things like that."

Jonathan couldn't even smile. The wrong bus came and went, disgorging a rumpled man who seemed astonished to see them.

"Why, if it isn't Mike Banion, waiting for me right on the street corner. Got a scoop, Mike?"

"This is the goddamn reporter I was hiding from. The only uneducated man the *Times* has left."

"I'm an institution."

"You're still working the blotter after fifteen years. I guess you are sort of an institution."

The reporter smiled toward Jonathan. He had very bad teeth. "Terry Quist, at your service. You make it, we break it."

"He means the news. All the news that fits, he prints."

"As long as it's bad. Never accuse me of publicizing good causes, please."

Quist was a thinner, more threadbare version of Mike. He had cigars in the top pocket of his jacket too. His feet were huge clown feet, encased in shoes that seemed composed of shine alone. His ropy, weathered face spoke all the cunning of a man who understood the intricacies of city life.

"Terry, I want you to meet my stepson Jonathan. Jonathan, meet Terry Quist."

"Hello," Jonathan said.

Terry Quist stared at him as he might at a cobra coiled on the foot of his bed. "He gonna be with us?"

Mike nodded. "Until his bus comes."

"I'm in big trouble. I've got to talk to you privately." When Quist's voice quavered, Jonathan realized that the man was trying to control profound fear. Jonathan found his very presence chilling. His own terror, his awful sense of evil within, was still close to the surface.

"I'll give you ten minutes," Mike told the reporter.

"Your office, please. I might be talkin' about my *life*, Inspector."

The bus came as Mike and Terry were entering the precinct house. Sitting alone as it swayed along, Jonathan tried to prepare himself for what he was going to find at the hospital. But he could not. A few hours ago Patricia had dazzled him with her beauty. Now she was the victim of somebody who despised it.

Somebody dark and wicked.

He sucked in breath. For an instant he had wanted to run, just to let his body take over and somehow escape the situation.

He remained on the bus as if frozen to his seat, unable for a time even to move.

By the time the bus reached the huge Art Deco hulk of the Poly, full sunlight bathed the streets, the white walls of the building, the sea of glittering windows. He got up and forced himself out onto the sidewalk. He passed through the entrance to the old building.

Once in the lobby he sought the information desk. It was manned by a fat guard complete with Sam Browne belt and pistol. Queens Poly didn't fool around. It was a hard place, where the borough's desperate emergencies came. This man often confronted people who were crazy with shock and grief.

"I'm trying to locate a woman named Patricia Murray, a rape victim, badly injured."

He consulted a computer printout. "Here—Murray, Patricia, Intensive Care Unit, Ward C, Section Five. That's the fifth floor, end of the corridor."

Jonathan got on an elevator jammed with interns, nurses, and two patients in wheelchairs. It stopped for an interminable time at each floor. At last, though, he arrived at the nurses' station that controlled the ICU. "I'm here to see Patricia Murray," he said to the nurse at the desk.

"Visiting hours start at nine." She flipped through a file. "Oh. Are you related?"

He lied because he knew he had to. "Yes."

"She may be awake. But you'll have to observe her through the window. No direct contact yet."

He followed the nurse down a hallway cluttered with medical paraphernalia, IV stands, wheelchairs, rolling beds, electronic equipment.

Patricia lay swathed in an olive-drab surgical gown. Her legs were spread and a tent of plastic obscured her head. An OXYGEN IN USE sign flashed on and off above the window that looked into the room. Her whole belly was covered with gauze and bandages, and more bandages were on her arms. Even beyond the evidence of great wounding, it was her absolute stillness that made Jonathan feel the strange, deep anguish of the bereft. Only if she were dead would she be more still.

He stood looking at her, feeling the tears burn in his eyes and a tightness constrict his throat, and wishing that somehow it could have been different.

What terrible thing had happened last night?

Was he wrong, or had her head slowly turned toward him? With the wrinkled plastic oxygen tent making a clear view of her impossible, it was difficult to tell.

Yes, she had definitely looked his way.

But what was the expression on her face? Was it love, or terror—or was it madness?

He strained and peered at her, but he could not tell. After a few minutes the nurse nudged his elbow, then drew him away.

As he went down the hall exhaustion hit him hard, and with it came a great sorrow. His brief love was destroyed.

He thought of her, lying beneath him in his dream. He crept from the hospital like a guilty man.

---

27 JUNE 1983

MOST PRIVATE

To: The Prefect of the Sacred Congregation for the Defense of the Faith

From: The Chancellor for the Inquiry in North America

Your Eminence:

I am sorry to inform you that the Night Church has surfaced publicly with a bloody ritual at a parish in the New York City borough of Queens.

Location: Holy Spirit Parish, founded 1892, church dedicated September, 1894. Present population 16,231.

We have known for some time that rituals were being held at this church, but, in accordance with your Directive 1516, 28 October 1971, *In Causa Clandestina,* we have done no more than insert operative observers into the congregation.

A full report of the service from observer Brother Alexander Parker (Judist) is attached. Here are the highlights:

1. The ritual was conducted by Prince Franklin Titus himself, attesting to its canonical importance.

2. Princess Mary Titus was in attendance at the ceremony.

3. The ritual appeared to be the *Rituale Pudibunda Coitus,* the Shameful Coupling. (See *Grimoire Titus,* Rev. XIV, vol. 11, pp. 2112–2177.)

4. Apparently the principal participants were the two heirs who were successfully hidden from us during our last *Oppugnatio.* According to our statistics these two are the only viable heirs left:

    a. Patricia Murray (from Pantera to Roland to Sheil to Murray, see *Genealogies Pantera,* Sec. 42, Family 58, Branch Irish, yrs. 1718–1952, for lineage to Murray, Jean Patricia Roisin Margaret out of Samuel and Rebecca).

    b. Jonathan Banion (believed to be Jonathan Titus, Prince, see *Genealogies Titus,* Sec. 113, Family 71, Branch Anglo-American, yrs. 1691–1951, for lineage to Titus, Jonathan Martin Flavius out of Martin and Mary).

5. Because the two viable heirs were participating, we must view this ritual as extremely dangerous.

6. Because of the urgency of the situation I would suggest Directive 801, 14 June 1831, *Contra Poenam Ultimam,* be revoked, and that His Holiness be prevailed upon to authorize the Ultimate Measure against these two individuals.

Yours in Christ & for the Defense of the Faith,
Brian Conlon (Msgr.)

Document Class: Urgent A, most private, Swiss Guards courier

Destination: Paolo Cardinal Impelliteri, the Hidden Collegium,
Prefecturate for the Defense of the Faith, Vatican City

11 IULIUS 1983
FURTIVISSIMUS

Ad: *Cancellarius Inquisitionis in Septentrionalis Americanensis*

Ex: *Prefectus Congregationis Defensioni Fidei*

You are by this order directed most specifically not to under-
take any actions contrary to *Poenam Ultimam.*

His Holiness certainly has no intention of condoning the sort
of excesses that have marred the history of the Hidden Collegium.

However, we do authorize you to submit either of the heirs to
passive questioning if you can find a means of doing so that does
not violate the civil laws of the jurisdiction in which you reside.

You are proceeding under the following authorities of the
Holy Office of the Congregation for the Defense of the Faith:

1. *In Defensione Fidei,* Ch. V, Pt. C, Para. 5: "The Holy Office
of the Inquisition shall retain its full powers and authorities, as
granted in *Justinian, Lex.* 1.023:325, *In haeretici,* and affirmed
many times subsequently."

2. *Canon Lex. 221.04 (Privatus):* "The Defenders are author-
ized in cases of extreme necessity, where the whole life of the
Faith is threatened or the very existence of the Church called
into question, to take up arms in defense of our Holy Faith."

As there is a possibility that there will be sin committed in the
heat of your effort, and that you may be unable to confess before
death, I now pronounce the customary absolution *In Futuro*
upon you and your subordinates:

Auctoritate a Summis Pontificibus mihi concessa plenariam
omnium peccatorum tuorum indulgentiam tibi impertior: in
nomine Patris et Filii et Spiritus Sancti.

Mea Auctoritate,
Paolo Cardinalis Impelliteri

Document Class: Urgent A, destroy in presence of courier

Destination: Monsignor Brian Conlon, Chancellor for the Inquiry, North America, 1217 Fuller Brush Building, 221 E. 57th Street, New York, N.Y., 10022

12 JULY 1983

MOST PRIVATE

To: The Prefect of the Sacred Congregation for the Defense of the Faith

From: The Chancellor for the Inquiry in North America

Your Eminence:

Of course we understand and respect the position of His Holiness and of the Hidden Collegium.

In no way will this office violate the provisions against execution and torture promulgated in *Contra Poenam Ultimam.*

But we also apprehend what is hidden between the lines of your memorandum, that we are to act *exactly* according to the statutes you cite, which granted the Holy Office its original authority.

Be assured that we will do so with all vigor.

May God have mercy on our souls.

Yours in Christ & for the Defense of the Faith,
Brian Conlon (Msgr.)

Document Class: Extraordinary, destroy after reading, Swiss Guards courier

Destination: Paolo Cardinal Impelliteri, the Hidden Collegium, Prefecturate for the Defense of the Faith, Vatican City

MIKE WATCHED Terry Quist open a Baby Ruth, stuff it into his mouth, and toss the wrapper to the floor. The poor guy. He always gobbled food when he was tense. Or scared. Mike eased his friend into telling his story. "You still write the blotter, don't you?"

"That and the bus plunges at the bottom of the pages—'158 die in Surinam bus plunge' typa junk. I'll never get anywhere on the *Times*. I'm more of a *National Tattler* kind of a guy."

"So what're you doin' here? Go plunge a bus."

"I've got serious business with you. You wanna hear my story or not? I might have a line on your raped girl."

"Anything about Patricia Murray I want to hear. Are you lookin' for pay, or what?"

"Come on, man. By rights I ought to be back at the shop doin' my investigative reporter bit. But I'm here because I'm a coward. I want to stay alive. Just one thing, though, before I lay what I've got on the table. It's very weird. I want you to suspend disbelief."

"No."

"Please remember we been friends since I taught you to smoke in fifth grade."

"Fourth."

"I forget. Anyway, you promise me that you *will* check this one out, no matter how wild it sounds."

"You're settin' yourself up for a putdown. You been takin' rides on a UFO or somethin'?"

"I wish I had. I'd be better off gettin' fucked over by little green men than by the Night Church."

He fell silent. His hands, Mike noticed, were gripping the edge of the desk so tightly there was a flush beneath his fingernails. "Keep goin', buddy."

"Just that I have reason to believe from the nature of the crime that your lady was hurt in a religious service."

"The priest in that parish is a good friend of mine."

"You're dealing here with something much bigger than any single priest or parish. The way I see it, this thing is gigantic. World wide. A festering, deadly cancer hidden in the Catholic Church, rotting it from within. And evil, Mike, as God is my witness. Unbelievably evil."

"Something as big as that fools around with rape? This is lone pervert stuff."

"I said you wouldn't believe me."

"I didn't pass judgment yet. Keep convincin' me. You're doin' a wonderful job so far."

"I'll bet."

"You are. I'm takin' you seriously."

"It's got a congregation that meets at Holy Spirit. Ah, come on, Mike, I see you smilin'! I'm telling you something *big*."

Mike had smiled just a little, to test Terry's resolve. Terry's reaction meant that he, at least, believed the story he was telling. "Prove somethin'."

"What do you want proved?"

"Anything. Any part of it."

"The constant whine of the cop to the reporter: do my work, I can't do it myself. Okay, I got onto this through a guy named Alexander Parker, lives across the street from Holy Spirit. This guy is not connected with the media. He started comin' in to the Idle Hour about a week or so ago. He hears I'm a reporter and he tells me he's got a story."

Mike nodded.

"He tells me how he goes home late a lot. Night person, he says. And every Sunday and Thursday night he's noticed somethin' funny. It's not that big a deal, just slightly more people around than usual. One night, he's in his apartment. It's quiet, see, and he hears this real low noise. Like music, but so low he more *feels* it than hears it. He thinks maybe it comes from the church. So he goes over there."

"Ought to be on the force."

"He tries the door, but it's locked. So he listens. He hears people moving around inside, like lots of people just walking around and around in the church. Every so often a baby screams and gets stifled. That spooks him a little, and he goes home. He watches. Along about four-thirty he's been asleep, and all of a sudden he sees people leaving."

"He's asleep and he sees the people?"

"Will you cut it out! He *wakes up* and he sees the people. Clumps of two and three, like. He counts three hundred people leaving over the space of half an hour. In the small hours of the goddamn mornin'. He can't figure it."

"So he runs off and tells New York's most brilliant reporter."

"He lets it sort of slip out. Like he was trying to lead me on. He tells me they're dangerously crazy. Something about a disease they're gonna spread. Something about a new species—the anti-man. He asks me, almost begs me, to write it up. 'Tell the world,' he says. 'Warn them.' "

"So?"

"So doesn't that sound pretty damn dangerous?"

"Hell, I'm all for it. Anti or not, a new species'll probably do a better job than we have."

"You don't understand, do you, you jerk? You're sittin' there straight as a razor and all the time laughing at me. *It's what they plan to do after the new race gets going. The rest of us—they're gonna just kill us. All of us.*"

"Lotta work."

"Not for people with the kind of weapon they have. A disease has been developed. When they release it everybody dies."

"Including the new race—and the Night Church?"

"Hell, no. Everybody *except* them. They all get vaccinated."

"Your friend found out a lot. I mean, considering he just watched these people from across the street. Supposedly."

"I thought about that. I think Alex is more than he seems. He told me, 'You're a reporter, get your story and publish it.' "

"So you're here."

"I'm afraid for my life! This is bigger than me. I can't get the story *and* stay alive."

"How can I identify these people?"

"Well, most of 'em are in Holy Spirit Church in the middle of the night. Go over and pick 'em up."

"And hit 'em with a trespass misdemeanor? That'd just tell 'em to get cautious."

"Find their labs or whatever. They must have storage facilities for their disease bacteria, not to mention delivery systems. It can't be simple to infect the whole world. There's got to be plenty of evidence of what they're planning."

"This sounds like some kind of crazy science, not a church."

"Well, maybe that's accurate. Religion and science mix and a monster is born."

"You still haven't given me anything to go on."

"Hell, Mike—"

"You bring me a load of crap like this and you'd better have some tangible evidence to go with it. Something I can goddamn-well put my hands on. Come on, Terry. I'm a busy man."

"So talk to Alex Parker! Do your goddamn job, follow the lead."

Terry's tone made Mike want to slug him, but he resisted the temptation. "Everybody in the neighborhood's being interviewed, you can bet on that."

"Oh, come on! You get your ass out of that chair and go and personally talk to Alex Parker. Do it for me. For old times."

Mike regarded his friend. Too many disappointments, too much booze, too many hopes down the drain. "OK, buddy, I'll give him a call right now." Terry had the number. Mike dialed, waited through three, then five, then seven rings. He shrugged, put the phone down. "What can I tell you? No answer. We'll have to try again later."

Terry Quist's face was covered with a fine sheen of sweat. Mike could smell the stink of his fear.

It was the nausea as much as the riot of birdsong that awoke Brother Alexander. He opened his eyes to blue morning sky. The lurching vertigo told him that he had been drugged. He could smell the thick ether fumes still in his nose, could taste them in his dry mouth. His stomach heaved and twisted.

Above him puffy white clouds crossed the clear blue. He was bound hand and foot, chained to an iron bedstead. He was in a forest glade. He could not move his head enough to see them, but he could sense people about.

When he turned his head far to the right he caught a glimpse of a familiar face. His heart began to pound. It was the notorious Jerry Cochran, and he was carrying something that looked very much like a blowtorch.

"Good morning, Brother."

Tears sprang to Alex Parker's eyes. He had heard stories of this man, terrible stories of flaying alive and burning, of tortures beyond belief.

There was a *whump* and a roar. Then Jerry Cochran came into full view, tall, grim, his eyes crazy, his face so rigid it might be made of stone. In his hand was a black blowtorch gushing fire. Alex turned and twisted on the rocking bedstead. His mind swarmed with terrors. In the deep of the night when he was all alone he had sweated out the possibility of just this martyrdom, death by fire.

"If you answer my questions, I will first garrote you," Jerry Cochran said softly.

Alex wept openly. He already knew what he would do, he had thought all this out very carefully. Inquisitors must understand themselves well enough to know what they will do under torture. "I'm sorry, Jerry," he said between sobs. Then he fixed his mind on the Jesus prayer, his only weapon against the agony of the flames: "Jesus, thou art with me, Jesus, thou art with me, Jesuss—oh! Oh, GOD! AAAHHH!"

Jerry had held the flame against Alex's chest. There was a stink of burnt hair. "You're very sensitive, Alex. I hardly touched you."

Alex felt his bladder let go. But they had prepared for that. He could feel that a towel was stuffed between his legs. "Jesus, thou art with me, Jesus, thou art with—"

The flames sent tidal waves of razor-sharp agony up his thighs as Jerry played the flame along his legs. Skin popped and crackled. Oily smoke rose.

"We know your drinking companion is a reporter, Alex. What is his name?"

"Jesus, thou art with me, Jesus, thou art with me." Alex stopped in confusion when the next application didn't come. To his utter horror he felt Jerry pulling away the towel that had protected him.

"The Judists are celibate, I think," he said. "Well, I don't suppose it matters one way or the other, does it, my friend? No more worries about keeping your vow."

When he felt the fire this time it was as if his insides were being torn out, as if all the flaming stars of heaven had fallen on him. Wild with torment he shrieked, he bellowed until his throat cracked, he jerked and twisted on the iron bedstead.

Nobody could hear him, not out here on one of the Night Church's vast country estates.

"Name him!"

"Qui-i-st! QUIST! QUIST!!"

"Ah."

"Stop! Jerry, I told you! Stop! Stop!"

With lazy strokes, Jerry moved the tongue of flame up and down Alex's legs from his crotch to the searing, crackling bottoms of his feet. "QUIST! QUIST! OH, GOD!"

Jerry gazed at him with the hooded eyes of great passion. His face was flushed. "Now we'll get started on your belly, OK, Alex?" He smiled a little. "Maybe if you tried the Jesus prayer some more it would help. Or if you told me the names of the other scum in your cell!"

"I told you, QUIST!"

"He was a recent contact. A reporter indeed. What an amateurish attempt to harm us—attracting the attention of a reporter. I want to know the other names, Alex, all of them!"

To give up his cell was the ultimate failure of an Inquisitor. Desperate, knowing his own weakness, Alex tried to knock himself senseless by banging his head against the iron bar beneath it. But Jerry had thought of that. A leather collar restrained his neck. "Look, Alex, you're suffering so much I'll offer you another deal. I'm afraid you've been too difficult to deserve garroting, but you give me the names and I'll do your face with the torch. It'll be over very quickly."

"Jesus, thou art with me, Jesus, thou art with me, Jesus—"

When the flames came this time they pierced his belly and made his stomach boil. His bowels exploded inside him, mixing their torment with the searing of the flesh. Hot steam rushed up his throat and scorched his mouth and nose.

Jerry stopped. "You may be wondering why all this pain doesn't just knock you out. We loaded you up with amphetamines, Brother Alex. You cannot escape into unconsciousness."

That did it. He had been hoping to faint, even to go into a coma from the pain and the damage. This was just too much. Even in his worst imaginings he had never dreamed torture would be this bad. It was almost incredible that the human body could endure such agony. Sick at heart, facing his own miserable failure, Alex listed the names of the people in his cell. "God forgive me. Brother Julius Timothy is one, Brother George Yates the other."

"That's all? Why such a small cell?"

"Holy Spirit was a backwater assignment."

Jerry nodded. "So we thought. That's why we use it so much."

"You're very clever."

"I know we are, Alex."

There was a moment of silence between them. Alex sought the eyes of his torturer. There was contact between the two men then, the anguished victim and his tormentor. In Jerry Cochran's eyes Alex saw so many things: hate, enjoyment, self-loathing, and deep down in the sparks and the shadows, a scared little boy who had been lost for a long time.

"God forgives you, my son, and I forgive you too."

Jerry laughed. As sad a sound as Alex had ever heard. "I ought to give you the full treatment for that." He turned up the blowtorch until it bellowed out a great gust of flame.

For a moment he hesitated as if undecided. He pointed the torch at Alex's chest. "Jesus, thou art with me, Jesus—"

But something had moved that hard man, and he suddenly changed the direction of the flame. For an instant Alex saw fire, then he felt a red-hot poker go down his throat, then he was all in cool. He fell away into timeless blessedness.

Jerry directed the work crew to complete the cremation and bag the body. Then they returned to Queens and entered Alex's apartment with the remains. They replaced them in Alex's bed, which they then set afire.

Twenty minutes later the fire department arrived. Ten minutes more and steam was pouring out the window of Alex Parker's apartment. Mike arrived on the scene with Terry Quist clinging to him like a baby. When he saw the charred, wet remains of Alex Parker being carried out of the building Terry grabbed fistfuls of his own hair.

The cause of death was listed as burns and asphyxiation. The agency was a mattress fire. The means of ignition was theorized to have been a cigarette.

Officially, the martyr was listed as having died because he smoked in bed.

Terry Quist left the scene a haunted, stricken man.

Mike Banion watched him go. And he wondered.

Chapter Six

THE PERMANENT GLOOM of Rayne Street surrounded Jonathan the moment he turned from busy MacDougal. Rayne was a narrow cobbled lane between MacDougal and Sullivan, like Gay Street and Aldorf Mews one of Greenwich Village's hidden streets. Here NYU had placed its data storage facilities in the enormous black hulk of the house that dominated the short block. In the basement they had found room for Jonathan's lab. He hated the place, hated its dampness, its inconvenient distance from campus, and above all, the dark gargoyled ugliness of the building itself.

The sun never shone on Rayne Street, not even at high noon. It was one of the few New York streets still cobbled with the round stones that had seen carriages and wagons and had resounded to the clatter of hoofs. Jonathan's footfalls were the only sound that disturbed it now. He looked up at the front of the house. At least the place was well kept. A small brass plaque on the door announced NEW YORK UNIVERSITY DIGITAL DATA STORAGE FACILITY. Under the stoop was another door, this time with a plastic sign: PHYSIOLOGICAL PSYCHOLOGY DEPT. LAB B.

Jonathan was expecting the lock to be stiff. He hadn't used it in three weeks, but it turned easily. The iron door opened without a squeak.

The hallway beyond was pitch black. Jonathan fumbled for the switch, found it, and turned it on.

Nothing happened.

He cursed. Here he was in the middle of a sunny morning and he was going to have to feel his way down a dark hallway because an indifferent university administration had put his lab in this hole.

The door swung closed behind him. He flipped the light switch a

few more times, uselessly, then began moving along the hall, feeling
for the door to the lab. Fortunately it was the only one in this wall. It
led to what had once been the wine cellars and basement storerooms
of the old building.

Jonathan became aware of a curious trick of sound in the enclosed
hallway. His own breathing sounded like it was coming from the
darkness beside him. The effect was so realistic that he waved his arms
out into the middle of the hallway. Nothing there, of course.

He began to search the wall more urgently, sweeping his hand up
and down, feeling for the door jamb. He really wanted to have some
light.

Perhaps it was another trick of sound, but he heard distinct scut-
tlings. Rats. Disgusting. He clapped, he shouted "Hey!"

Then he heard something that silenced him. He became very still,
listening. There were human footsteps coming down the stairs at the
far end of the hall.

Jonathan shrank back. This was a closed facility. Nobody worked
upstairs. His first thought was that some drifter had gotten in here.

A beam of intense white light dazzled him. He shielded his eyes
with his forearm. Fearful thoughts passed through his mind, of death
at the hands of a maniac.

"Who are you?" The voice was old and harsh. It did not sound
completely sane.

"Banion. This is my lab."

"You can't come in here. The facility is closed."

Now it made sense. He was confronting a watchman. "Look, this is
my lab. I'm not a student, I'm a professor. So please get that flashlight
out of my eyes and shine it on the door so I can see the keyhole."

The beam did not waver. Instead it came closer, until it was blazing
in Jonathan's face. "Go home, young man. You mustn't come here."
The voice was so old, and the tone like ice.

Jonathan knew when he was being threatened. And it infuriated
him. With a single, quick motion he reached up and snatched the
flashlight from the old man's hand. There was an instant of surprisingly powerful resistance, then the old man sighed and quite intentionally let go of the light. As he did Jonathan came into contact with
his hand. It was a shocking sensation. Jonathan had never felt skin so
hard and cold. More like stone than skin. He imagined that a
mummy's hand might feel like that. A dry claw.

"You're mad to come here! You're putting yourself in great danger!"

Jonathan turned the light around, catching just a glimpse of the man before he turned his back. What he saw made him gasp: bright green eyes set in a labyrinth of wrinkles, a tiny slit of a mouth open in an infuriated snarl.

Then the old man was gone, his feet rat-tatting up the stairs. A door slammed.

Good riddance. The university had a nerve hiring senile old fools like that to guard the facilities. Budget, probably.

Jonathan selected the right key from his chain. Getting in was easy now that he had the use of the flashlight.

He entered his lab, making a mental note to call the university's maintenance department and complain to them about their watchman. Obviously unbalanced, not to mention being far too old for the job.

Jonathan had come to his lab in the quiet of a summer morning to try and discover once and for all if he had done that terrible thing to Patricia. He couldn't bear to name it. He simply could not accept the idea that her hurt and his dream were a coincidence, not even with the vindication of the police polygraph. He needed his own instruments to tell him if there was some hidden corruption in his soul.

Was he an unconscious psychopath?

He imagined the demon's loom clicking eagerly as strand by strand it pulled his life apart. He had come to think of Satan as a sort of neurological shadow, a speck of dark potential in the electrochemical bath that floats the soul. He could no longer be sure that the shadow was not an actual, outside force. Evil for its own sake seemed increasingly to him to be a real power in the world.

Certainly when it was abroad, when the owls and jackals announced Lilith wandering, those she caressed could not resist her beauty—nor fight her talons.

He moved among the covered instruments. During the term he had been making the first really detailed map of microvoltages in the human brain. His work was highly technical, but beneath all the statistics were the mystery and romance of pure science: he and others like him were cracking the code of the mind.

The room was full of galvanic sensors of various kinds, but mostly there were computers: Apples and small IBMs to handle the statistical work, terminals connected to the big Cray 2000 at MIT that was his main tool. He used the Cray to do the sensitive high-speed signal recognition that was needed to separate the various brain waves into their hundreds of component parts and analyze each in isolation from the others. This gave him a virtual electronic window on the mind, vastly more sensitive than any that had been developed before.

There were also racks of Petri dishes, used for culturing microorganisms, lined up against one wall. He stopped. He ran his fingers along the edge of one of the racks. Strange. He didn't remember authorizing anybody to install such equipment here.

In the middle of the wall, what had been a closet door was now marked in block letters: VECTOR STORAGE. It was locked.

He didn't do work on bacteria. He didn't even know how. As he looked around him he could see evidence of another's recent presence. There was a lab chart with annotations dated only yesterday. On the floor was the cover of a coffee container. Somebody had been working here within the past twenty-four hours.

The university must have allocated unused space to another project. Odd. Was it like NYU to do something like that and not bother to tell him? He couldn't seem to remember.

He stood in the center of the dim, warm room, wondering. That persistent, distant clicking was the sound of footsteps on the sidewalk above this end of the basement. Demon's loom. His was a gothic soul.

The clicking died away. Maybe they *had* told him about this biology equipment. Not remembering something like this fitted with a theory of amnesia. If he didn't remember somebody installing a bacterial experiment in here maybe he didn't remember other things either.

Somehow he must uncover enough of the mechanism of his mind to determine the truth.

He had come to realize that horror and disgust were not his only reactions to the rape. His body vibrated eagerly at the thought of it. It was awful, repulsive. And yet, when he remembered her lying there in that hospital there came over him a sneering, hateful contempt that was at odds with everything he believed and loved about himself.

Off in the corners of his mind there were also violent bits of memory that seemed to go beyond the rape—a screaming face, a closing coffin, thuds and howls . . . long marble staircases, lines of chanting nuns, the garrote and the strappado and the rack. . . .

Was it another life, some horrendous past? Unlike Patricia he did not discount reincarnation just because it was against Catholic doctrine. Had he at some time in the past been a victim of the Inquisition, suffered in the dungeon of some elegant Spanish palace?

No, that wasn't quite right.

"Inquisitor." He whispered the word as he might the name of a present danger. "Inquisitor." Mother had uttered the word early this morning, then waved away his question about it.

Inquisitor. His hands were shaking, his legs seemed about to give way. The old man's lunatic warning sounded again in his mind. He went to the door, flipped on all the fluorescent lights, then locked it securely to the outside.

He remembered.

A priest, walking smartly across an airport lobby, his hair neatly parted on the right, his well-fed face mixing self-assurance and contentment, his shoes clicking on the floor.

Then the face turns, sees Jonathan, changes. Hate replaces contentment and the face becomes terrible, relentless, and cruel. But this time the Inquisition is not successful. A tall young man, a man Jonathan admires, grabs the priest and forces him into a car.

Next memory: the priest is naked, chained to the wall of a cellar. Questions are coming, one after another: *Who is your Inquisitor-General? How did you find us?* On and on, while the tall man removes strips of skin from the naked priest's body.

Jonathan is hiding in a corner, behind some shelves full of empty Petri dishes.

From the priest's mouth a ceaseless prayer: *Jesus, thou art with me, Jesus, thou art with me, Jesus, thou art with me.*

Help the priest! I side with the priest!

At last the torture stops. The torturer goes upstairs for a Coke. Jonathan is left alone, astonished, horrified that his friend, his hero, could do such things to another human being. The priest, his eyes watery and bloodshot, must know that his end will not be long in coming. He fixes his gaze on the boy who has crept forward, his own eyes tearing with pity. Words pour in a torrent from the priest's parched mouth. "Young man, they're going to destroy humanity for your sake, yours and the girl's. Turn against them! Accept Christ! Please, listen to me. Your friend Jerry is evil, your uncle is evil, they are creating . . . death . . . they are Satan's . . . oh . . . Satan's friends." Then the eyes roll and the head sinks forward, the chin touching the oozing, flayed chest.

No, that isn't a memory. You're imagining, spinning tales around the biology experiments that shouldn't be here.

You're hysterical.

With an effort Jonathan pushed the mad imaginings out of his mind. Again he regarded his sophisticated instruments, the ones that were familiar. They could sense and record brain waves; that's what they were all about. If he could find out where a thought like the one he had just had was physically coming from in his brain he could easily tell whether it was a memory or not.

Jonathan went over to the cubicle, took the complex, wire-covered sensor helmet in his hands.

How was he going to work the controls while wearing this thing? Its cable wasn't long enough.

Jonathan cursed silently. Without an assistant there was no way he could use the equipment.

And the alternative was not at all desirable.

At CalTech they were experimenting with a certain drug. It could be inhaled like cocaine, but it had no euphoric effect. On the contrary, it stimulated the brain's deepest memory centers and caused an almost incredible flow of vivid recollections.

This was N, alpha doporinol 6-6-6, a complex triumph of the biochemist's craft. It was synthesized from naturally occurring brain chemicals. So far the cost was eight thousand dollars an ounce. There were a few grams of it in the refrigerator. Jonathan had been asked to duplicate some of CalTech's experimental results but he had shut the lab for the summer before carrying out the work.

He went to the refrigerator. It was not your ordinary Frigidaire. This refrigerator was bolted to the floor and had a combination lock. Some of the drugs kept there, tranquilizers and such, were much in demand on college campuses. Others, like 6-6-6, were valuable.

Back behind the bottles of Valium and Quaaludes were foil packets with hand-lettered labels. Jonathan took out the packet of 6-6-6. The crystals inside crunched like sugar when he opened the foil. Ideally, the drug should be suspended in a saline solution and introduced to the nasal membrane via an aspirator. But Jonathan did not have time for that. He measured out a moderate dose, four grains, on the sensitive laboratory scale. Then he ground it fine with pestle and mortar.

He poured it from the mortar to the flat of a spatula and raised it to his nose.

He inhaled.

There was a gentle, pleasant aroma.

Jonathan felt no change. He went into one of the subject cubicles and lay down on the couchette. Still nothing.

Why do there have to be bars on my window, Mother?

The boy's voice was so clear and real that Jonathan jumped up.

That had been him, Jonathan Titus Banion, as a child.

Bars? Had there been bars on the windows of their old apartment? He didn't remember it that way . . . and yet he did.

We've got to keep them out, to keep them away from you. The bars are against them.

This was uncanny. It had been her voice, but she wasn't here.

He could see the walls of the bedroom in which she had said those words. But he didn't recall wallpaper like that, with moons and planets and rockets on it.

But where, then, did this memory come from?

The old man from the hallway came around the end of a lab bench. His emerald eyes flashed. Beneath the fluorescent lights his skin was powder-gray. He looked dead. Hallucinatory phenomenon, of course. Jonathan blinked his eyes, but he could not make the illusion disappear. The old man spoke. "You must not try the door to the past, Jonathan. It's dangerous for you. Terribly dangerous."

"Who in hell are you? How dare you come into my lab!"

The man shifted and wavered, half mirage and half real. Jonathan blinked but the image remained vague. In an odd way the old man seemed to fit among these recollections. "Danger," the old man said, "danger in these memories!" Then he was swinging a red lantern and Jonathan knew that this time he was an hallucination. NYU maintenance personnel didn't carry such lights. The real watchman was probably off sleeping under the stairs.

The false one symbolized a powerful barrier in Jonathan's mind against the very act of remembering.

But how? A barrier like this didn't just come out of nowhere. It had to be created. As wild as it sounded, almost the only explanation was that a highly sophisticated hypnotist had been at work on him.

Then what of those other imaginings a moment ago—the Inquisition, the tortured priest? "They're going to destroy humanity for your sake, yours and the girl's." Hadn't the priest said something like that?

But there isn't any reason to destroy anything for us.

He sat up on the edge of the couchette and rubbed his sweaty face. Bits and pieces of memory were still breaking through the hypnotic wall, induced by the powerful action of the drug to move toward a surface they could not quite reach.

Like a crust formed on lava, his mind shifted and cracked, and where it cracked the searing ugliness beneath drove him back.

This was not his doing. He was not amnesiac; somebody had intentionally set out to conceal his past from him. And this somebody had a great deal of skill. Hypnotism was a gross craft. To practice it with such delicacy was right at the limits of modern technique, perhaps even a little beyond.

He could feel a titanic struggle building in him between the drug and the barrier. Frantic, sweating, dizzy, he lurched out of the cubicle. There was no antidote to 6-6-6; he should never have taken it without controlled supervision.

The room was hot, terribly hot. He had to have water. But the least movement sent him slumping and reeling with dizziness. His head pounded, waves of nausea staggered him.

So you want to know why we protect you? Look, then, my boy, look at the work of the Inquisition that seeks you!

He was surrounded by a rising wall of flames. He was being touched by them, and their touch was hideously painful. He was attached to the stake by an iron collar.

His hands were free; he tore at the iron. He kicked the logs until sparks flew up around him. Outside of the flames he could see a great and gaudy crowd, men and women and children. Along the edges of his pyre little boys roasted potatoes to sell to the mob. And the mob chanted: "Evil, evil, evil! Satan's child, save yourself!"

But I'm not Satan's child! I'm—I'm . . . something else.

He looked up into the royal enclosure, to one pale female face, her skin like milk, her eyes crystal-green, her hair as blond as a sunlit cloud. From her eyes there flowed cooling love. She was composed, but he knew how deeply tragic she felt.

As the flames rose around him and he died in torment he fixed on those eyes, and saw in them the triumphant secret: *Our nights were not in vain, my señor, for I am with child. There will be another generation.*

Jonathan lurched against a bench, knocked a computer to the floor with a crash and a cascade of shattered electronic chips.

As he collected himself he realized that the fire wasn't a dream any more than the tortured priest was a dream. They were both memories.

But what kind of memories? And what sort of a monster would have them?

The priest was recent, but that fire had burned a long time ago.

In the fire there is exaltation; the pain is your triumph.

How dare you preach to me, Lucinda, when I have to endure the stake!

Martyred husband.

O Lucinda Pantera, you are the image of my dreams, the woman who has always been beside me. Angel Lucinda.

Angel Patricia. You are also Patricia, and all other women I and my ancestors have loved.

Seeking the edge of the future, we go on. By breeding the two lines together again and again, age by age, millennium by millennium, we are creating a masterpiece.

A masterpiece of evil. Something far darker than mankind. Something unencumbered by impulses toward the good.

Something unspeakably monstrous!

Jonathan was on the floor. "No!" His mouth was dry, his face smeared with tears. "No, it mustn't be!"

He could almost see it, almost smell it, and it was hideous and stank of rotted flesh.

And it was in this room.

Danger, the old man wailed, *danger!*

The bits and pieces of the shattered computer had cut into Jonathan viciously. He touched a gash on his palm, tasted his blood.

Something was crouched just the other side of the lab bench, breathing softly. Jonathan was so frightened he literally could not move.

It was the *thing* humankind with its inquisitions and persecutions has been trying to prevent through the ages.

The anti-man, ugly where man is beautiful, bad where man is good, the very essence of evil.

But it wasn't on the other side of the lab bench, not really. That was only his imagination, it had to be.

Yes, but your imagination is still dangerous! It's trying to make you stop thinking these thoughts.

"I won't stop thinking. I remember the anti-man. It's been bred over thousands of years. And it's—"

He looked at his own hands, turned them slowly over and over in the merciless fluorescent light.

Cro-Magnon was bred out of Neanderthal and destroyed Neanderthal. Homo sapiens was bred out of Cro-Magnon and destroyed him. In the same way the anti-man will destroy what you call mankind. It is only following nature's law. There is nothing bad about it.

"It's Satanic! Hell's answer to the creation of God!"

Homo sapiens is a defective species, and like all of nature's mistakes, it is going to become extinct. You of all people should love the anti-man. You will be its father.

Jonathan felt his skin beneath his jeans, the slight dampness of his crotch pressed by his briefs. In him was a new species?

You have already learned more than you should. Now you must be made to forget. You will confront the thing behind the bench, and it will tear these past few minutes from your mind.

"No!"

I think yes. I think yesssss.

The voice in Jonathan's mind became one with the breathing behind the lab bench. It merged into the hissing, terrible and loud, of something primal and big. Then came a slipping, sliding sound, weighty rubbing against the floor, and the black gleaming head of an enormous snake appeared around the corner of the table. It had coppery scales and eyes like yellow-green stones.

In them was not the savage blankness of the reptile species. Instead there was something far worse—burning, unquenchable rage mixed with the self-mocking irony of great intelligence.

It came elegantly along, its huge body sweeping in great loops. Jonathan was utterly revolted, and yet also fascinated. Nothing, not even the threat of death itself, could tear him from those staring green eyes.

But 6-6-6 isn't supposed to be a hallucinogen. Sloppy testing, California. This is an effect you didn't mention in the protocols.

The serpent had coiled into a great shiny mass of scales just in front of Jonathan. It reared its head until it was level with his own face.

It was so very real, even to the snake mites running along the edges of its mouth. Jonathan drew himself up from his prone position. The snake rose almost magically, facing him, staring at him over a space of mere inches.

He stood fully erect. Impossibly, the snake had now risen up out of its coil, still face to face with him.

"What are you?"

I guard your memories. I live inside you.

"My God!"

Back and forth it swayed, back and forth. Its eyes regarded Jonathan evenly. He realized that, in spite of all the fear it evoked in him, there was great beauty in it. He stretched out his hand, palm up. The huge head laid itself in his palm, and the membranes over the eyes slid down, giving them a milky green appearance.

An invisible claw seemed to take hold of his arm, to make him draw the head closer and closer to his own sweating face. Up close it was terrible to see, the face of a snake with such extreme intelligence in it that it seemed more than human. Much more. Satan would create such a face.

With a snap of its body the snake plunged its head between Jonathan's lips, forcing itself into his mouth.

He could feel the hard, cold scaliness of it, was made to gag as its tongue tickled the back of his throat. His helpless gagging enabled it to jam itself farther down, to fill his gullet. Now the thickness of the body distended his lips, compressed his tongue, made his jaws click. Fear and loathing shot through him. He threw himself back, grabbed at the heavy, surging coils. As the snake worked its way down into him he clawed at its slick flesh with frantic hands. He couldn't breathe, could barely make a sound. He could feel the head probing against sphincters as it made its way deep into him, past his esophagus and into his stomach. The deeper it got, the faster it went. Huge masses of coils began sweeping past his snatching, batting hands.

Then it was gone, only the tail tickling his throat. He felt as dense as thick paste, hideously full. His stomach was distended, his belt broken, his pants torn open. And the coils could be seen surging and billowing beneath the skin of his belly.

Heavily, he sank to the floor. He was utterly, completely revolted. As a teenager he had tried LSD. Compared to this the lysergic illusion was a mere daydream.

All at once a terrible cramp doubled him over. He retched, spattering the tiles around him with flecks of blood.

He lay a long time, groaning, wanting to give way to nausea, unable to do so.

When at last the sensation passed and he could straighten up, his belly was no longer distended. He had not only swallowed the demon snake but somehow absorbed it. Now it was part of his body, of his soul.

There had been something else, some memory.

"I've got to remember!"

What?

It was gone. He was left with the horrible feeling that he had let some vital piece of information slip through the cracks in his mind. Another unreported side effect of 6-6-6. Those idiots at CalTech were going to get a hell of an angry letter. Ought to sue the jerks. He hitched up his pants, slammed the refrigerator and locked it, kicked the bits of broken computer under a table, and staggered out of the lab.

As he went down the corridor and emerged into the sunlight he began to feel a little better, although the smell of hot dogs from a streetcorner vendor brought renewed nausea.

Of course it had been an hallucination. There was no question about that. The snake was such an obvious unconscious symbol, exactly the sort of thing one might see on a bad trip. There hadn't been proper testing of 6-6-6; that was the long and short of it.

Everything that had happened, from the moment he took the drug, could be discounted.

He wanted to drink, to laugh in the sun just for an afternoon, to somehow forget the insane horror he had just experienced. Too bad it was clouding over. The best antidote would be the pleasure of a sunny day.

A very sunny day.

Chapter Seven ────────┼────

JONATHAN LAY IN his bed at home, his mind a jumble of confused and revolting images. So much for 6-6-6. It was a bad-trip express which had not gotten him much closer to resolving the question that tormented him.

He tossed, closed his eyes. Despite his efforts the old man still warned him, the serpent still sent shuddering waves of nausea through the depths of his stomach. There was also a confused jumble of thoughts—stakes, fires, Satanic plans . . . but he had lost the thread.

At last he accepted the fact that he was going to stay awake; in his present state there was no chance that he would find the relief of unconsciousness. Just as he was deciding to get up, his mother came in. He did not open his eyes. Quietly she sat down beside him and took his head in her lap, as she had done when he was a boy.

From time to time she would say his name, all the while stroking his forehead with her cool hand. Through slitted eyes he watched her. How sad she seemed, her eyes gazing at him with such softness in them. Never before had she seemed so mysterious, or so beautiful, or so full of love.

Her eyes were green. As were the old man's. As were Patricia's. And his own.

A species apart . . .

It came as a surprise to realize that she had soothed him after all, and he had slept for some little time. He sat up, startled by his return to a consciousness he did not know he had left. Where there had been memories in his mind there was now darkness . . . and a watchful snake.

"What time is it?"

"Eleven-thirty."

She ran her fingers through his hair. "I would have gotten you up if there had been any change. She's still in the coma."

The cold word "coma" sighed in his mind. "Is she—"

"She'll come around this afternoon sometime. She's badly injured, darling, but she's going to be all right."

"Mother, I fell in love with her. I fell in love last night."

"She's a wonderful person."

"She's an angel." The image of that still body in its olive-drab intensive care blankets came into his mind. He would not cry, but inside himself he knew there were tears.

And deeper, where the serpent had its lair, what emotions did he feel there? He dared not find out, and turned his mind away. Better to cling to the surface.

"You know how you feel sometimes when you meet somebody who really fits—like you've always known them? That's how we felt. When I held her in my arms, Mother—" He could not continue. The thought of that warm, vital body was so moving and his grief so great that he was forced to lapse into silence.

Martin Titus had taught his son not to weep, but Jonathan knew that his mother understood what was in him. She had been only eighteen when he was born, and her relative youth increased the element of companionship. She was a beautiful woman. Her forty-one was a reasonable facsimile of thirty. "Did Mike make it hard for you?"

"You have the wrong idea, Mother. Mike is good to me."

"I suppose I ought to love him for that. But I just can't, poor man."

She was always saying things like that, and justifying her marriage as having some higher purpose.

"You didn't have to marry him."

"Oh, Jonathan, let's not go over that again. I'm trying to make the best of it. Let it go at that."

"Okay, Mother. I just wish you were happier. I don't appreciate being the cause of your martyrdom—especially because you won't tell me why you did it. I like Mike, he's a good man, but if you hadn't brought him into my life I wouldn't even know him." He got up and turned on WNEW-FM. Clash was deep in the purple rhythm of anger. He lowered the volume until it became a sullen, muttering undertone.

"Darling, I wish I could tell you. Maybe some day soon I'll be able to. But for now let's just drop the subject."

"You keep too much from me, Mother. I'm beginning to get an idea that what you're really hiding from me is my past."

"What is there to hide?"

"Whatever is the matter with me. What did you do—send me to some kind of a quack hypnotherapist? Let me ask you a frank question. Are we buried out here in Queens because of something I did in the past—like maybe raping a girl, or killing her?" His voice had risen. "Who *were* our friends in Manhattan, before Dad was killed? I don't even know. I can't remember."

"Jonathan, be patient with me. Just a little while longer—"

Almost before he realized it his hand had lashed out and caught her on the cheek. "Stop feeding me that line of bullshit! I want to know *now!*"

His mother turned away, her cheek reddening. There was a long silence. She did not turn back to him. "Perhaps we can go over to the hospital together," she said, too briskly. "I think it would be nice for us both to be there when she comes around."

"I'm sorry, Mother. Please forgive me."

"Hush, son. You're upset. Overwrought. There's nothing to forgive, okay? Just to forget." She smiled, her hand came out and touched his temple. "Get your clothes on and we'll go." Jonathan went into the bathroom and applied his Norelco to his face until the shadow was gone. Then he opened the aftershave, splashed some on, and combed his hair. He returned to his room and started to pull on some briefs. His mother stopped him with a gesture, then looked long at his naked body. "There's nothing you're not telling me, is there? Everything went all right with Mike, didn't it?"

"What're you inspecting me for, signs of a beating? He cleared me, at least superficially. Mother, I don't think you have even the foggiest idea about me and Mike. We love each other. Somehow or other it worked out between us. He's my friend, and I think of him as my father."

He dressed in the clothes his mother handed him from his closet. She got his brush and rebrushed his hair. "You're so handsome, Jonathan." She hugged him, throwing her arms around his chest and pressing her cheek against it. "I can't believe I have a big six-footer like you. Your dad's family is small." She fell silent for a moment. "Thump-bump, thump-bump—I hear your heart."

He kissed the top of her head and they went down to her car

together. She had gotten the blue Audi out of Mike by simply going over to Bavaria Motors and buying it with a check. Mike had juggled his MasterCard credit lines like crazy, but when the check arrived at the bank the money was there. "She looks like a million dollars in that thing," Mike often said.

Her whole relationship with Mike was like that—she didn't so much make demands as present him with *faits accomplis*.

"Car running well, Mother?"

"I love it."

To get to the Poly they had to pass Patricia's building on Metropolitan Avenue. Jonathan stared at the tachometer rather than look out at it.

When he saw Queens Poly again, in the light of the summer afternoon, he knew he would hate it for the rest of his life. But then, as they rounded the corner, he counted up five rows of windows, then across six. That was her room. And somehow that particular window looked beautiful. "Let's stop for some flowers," he said. "There's a shop in the lobby."

They got sixteen dollars' worth of gardenias on Mary's theory that she would still be able to smell them even if all the tubes prevented her from moving her head enough to look at them. "Are you nervous, Jonathan?"

"I suppose so."

"I am too. But I know it's nothing compared to what you're going through. I'm very, very sorry for you both. I want you to know that."

"It's crazy to be so attached to somebody you just met, but—"

"She's special. That's why I got you two together in the first place."

"I suppose it's inevitable that I would love someone you picked out for me."

They went up in an elevator that was, if possible, even more crowded than the one Jonathan had used that morning. The fifth floor bustled with activity. Like a voice of doom an operator kept droning, "Airway team, airway team, airway team, entrance Twenty-two-B. Airway team, airway team, airway team . . ." Presumably there was somebody at entrance 22B, wherever that was, suffocating.

This time it was possible to enter her room. They went side by side down the white corridor, past a window where a man lay with tubes emanating from his belly, past another where groans rose from behind the drawn curtain, until finally they reached Patricia.

She was lying as still as Snow White beneath her plastic shroud. Other flowers, long-stemmed red roses, stood in a water pitcher on the bedside table. The card was from Mike. "Does he know her, Mother?"

"No. He must have sent them because of you."

Jonathan hardly heard her. Patricia lay as still and pure as the Madonna herself. Three tubes came out of her nose, crossed her ivory cheeks, and wound around into three humming machines. Intravenous needles pierced both her forearms. Her hands rested at her sides. Jonathan knelt beside her bed in a state of sorrow that was also a state of love. He took her right hand in his and very gently kissed it.

The machines hummed. The air conditioning hissed. From the hallway chimes sounded. A tray of implements was rattled past by an orderly. Far off somebody cried out once sharply, and then fell silent.

Jonathan reached his hand in under the oxygen tent and touched her hair. It was matted with sweat, and her head was very warm. "My love," he whispered. "Please, God, help my love." He noticed that the smell of Mike's roses blended nicely with his gardenias.

There was a sound from Patricia's throat. Mary drew close to Jonathan. "Your hand. She feels your touch. She's going to come to."

"Patricia, it's me, Jonathan."

She made a guttural, inhuman sound, nothing like the melody of her voice. Then her eyes opened. She looked straight ahead for a long time. She was absolutely motionless.

"Patricia?"

Mary put her arm around Jonathan's shoulder. "It's us, darling, Mary and Jonathan Banion."

"John—Jonathan?"

"Hi, darling. I love you."

There was the slightest incline of her head. "Why am I here?"

"Something happened," Mary said. "There was an accident, but you'll be all right. You'll be fine."

"Oh-h-h, I hurt! I *hurt!*" Her voice was strident; now she frowned; now her eyes darted about wildly. "Why can't I feel my legs? Did I—"

"No, no, darling, nothing like that. You just got hurt, but you're going to be back to normal soon. It wasn't that bad."

She closed her eyes. Tears popped out from beneath the lids. "Was I raped?"

"Yes, honey, that's what happened."

She nodded. Silence fell.

"Hello, folks, how's our patient?"

Mary whirled around. "Mike!" He was standing there in his rumpled brown suit. Beside him was a natty man of perhaps thirty-five.

"This is Lieutenant Maxwell of the Sex Crimes Unit. He's going to be questioning Patricia."

Mary glared at the two men.

"Do you want us to leave, Dad?"

"It might be best. In cases like this they usually concentrate better when they're alone."

Jonathan withdrew his hand from Patricia's. "Jonathan!" Her voice was sharp, almost commanding. When she lifted her fingers he understood and again took her hand.

"I'm here, honey."

"Stay!"

"I won't leave unless you want me to."

Mike leaned into her field of vision. "We have some police questions to ask you, sweetie. It's better if you let Jonathan go for just five minutes—"

"No!"

Mary spoke. "What does it matter, Mike? Jonathan told me about the polygraph."

"Police questioning is confidential, ma'am," said the lieutenant.

Patricia's hand gripped Jonathan's, hard. "You better stay, Johnny," Mike said. "She wants you, that's the important thing."

"Thanks, Dad."

The lieutenant went around to the opposite side of the bed, turned on a large, old-fashioned cassette recorder, and affixed the microphone to his lapel. "Miss Murray," he said in a surprisingly gentle voice, "I'm awfully sorry to have to bother you now, but we find it's best to do this as early as possible so you can get on with the business of getting well without us intruding."

"Who are you?"

"My name is Tom Maxwell. I'm a police officer."

"It hurts, Officer Maxwell."

Jonathan was aware that his mother had gotten another person to come into the room, a man with a surgical smock thrown over his business suit and half-glasses on his face. Obviously he was Patricia's doctor. "This patient has too many visitors," he said. "Perhaps it would be best if you left, Inspector Banion."

"My associate wants to ask questions."

"He can stay."

"Miss Murray, do you remember anything at all about the man who raped you?" Maxwell asked his question softly, gently. A sensitive man.

Patricia stared straight ahead, her eyes glazed with deep inner looking. "I was on the bed with Jonathan," she said. She met his eyes. "I had you in my arms. . . ." Behind him Mike leaned forward, put his hand on his stepson's shoulder.

The doctor spoke up again, directing his words to Mike. "Please, you really do have to leave."

"After that, what happened? Did Jonathan stay?"

"He . . ."

Jonathan's own mind flashed a violent, confused memory, like a door that opened and shut very quickly on an explosion.

They had been sitting on her bed, and there had been some erotic play. He was so excited, he remembered. . . . Then—a blast of light, a bad dream. Then he was being shaken awake by Mike.

"He left. I made him go home." She smiled at him. "You ought to marry me. Do you want to? I'm a good girl." Tears appeared in her eyes. She was probably afraid the rape had made her undesirable.

"I'd marry you in a minute."

She smiled a little. Silence followed his comment, broken by the doctor. "Inspector Banion, I'm telling you now to leave this room. There are too many people here."

"Look, Doctor, this is a capital case of the utmost importance."

"You aren't asking the questions."

"This case is special. I'm following it very closely." Jonathan felt Mary stiffen beside him. Mike continued. "There may be much more to it than simple rape. A great deal more. Right now the Queens Detective Area rates it priority one."

That silenced the doctor. Even he realized that it would be unwise to obstruct an inspector on a case he considered as major as this one. The lieutenant started in again. "After he left, what happened?"

"I went to bed." She sobbed, closed her eyes.

"And?"

"Oh! All these voices! Then it's—oh . . ."

"What is it?"

"Dark! My God, it's dark!"

The lieutenant looked across the oxygen tent to Doctor Gottlieb, who shook his head. "Should I continue?" Watching Mike carefully, the doctor nodded. "Miss Murray, do you remember anything about the individual who assaulted you?"

Jonathan felt her grip weaken, saw her lips open slightly behind the obscuring tangle of tubes. "She's fallen asleep," the doctor said. "All is well."

Mike shook his head. "I don't know what to make of this," he said.

"Obviously it's traumatic amnesia," the doctor snapped. "She can't handle the memory just now."

"It doesn't look like that to me. She—"

"Never mind how you think it looks or doesn't look! When she's stronger you can come back. Maybe you'll have better luck with your bullying then."

Mike smiled. "He asks the questions but you yap at me. What's my problem—bad breath?" He led his lieutenant out of the room. Beyond the window Jonathan could see yet another visitor, Father Goodwin, looking even more pale and cadaverous than usual.

"I have to examine the wound and change the dressing," the doctor announced. "You can come back afterward, Jonathan."

Jonathan started to get up, but the moment he moved Patricia's hand became like steel again. "Hey, darling, I thought you were asleep."

She didn't answer; she was clinging even in sleep. Jonathan was deeply moved. "Jennifer," the doctor said to a nurse, "get him a mask and gown, will you?" When she was gone, the doctor spoke directly to Jonathan for the first time. "After we're finished, please come into the conference room. I'd like to brief you since you're obviously the closest we're going to come to a next of kin."

Mary and the nurse managed to get Jonathan more or less covered without breaking the contact so vital to Patricia. The surgical mask smelled faintly of iodine.

"I'm Paul Gottlieb," the doctor said as he worked. "I'm your mother's gynecologist. She called me into the case. I have a surgical specialty," he added, as if to further justify himself. Jonathan could not see what he was doing behind the sheets, but a blood-soaked dressing soon came out. "Oh, this looks just fine. This is coming right along. There's been excellent preliminary progress." Then he muttered to the nurse, "I want a pin test, Jenny. There's still cyanosis evident in the legs."

The nurse disappeared down the hall, returning after a moment with an instrument tray. Jonathan did not see exactly which device the doctor used, but from the length of time he spent it was obvious the test was not immediately successful.

"Okay," he said at last, "very good. Now, Jonathan, if you'd just come out with me, I can go over our plans. You're going to play a crucial role in Patricia's recovery, you know."

Coaxing finally got Patricia to release Jonathan's hand. He promised to come back as soon as he could. As they left the room he saw Father Goodwin go in. He had a pyx in his hand. No doubt, if she awoke more fully, she would be grateful for Communion.

The conference room was as plastic as any of the hospital spaces, blue walls and an acoustic-tiled ceiling into which somebody was in the habit of sailing pencils, two or three of which jutted out of it. There were half-empty coffee cups on the cigarette-scarred Formica conference table. Here and there lay a pencil-marked yellow pad. On one was a doodle of a female foot in a tall spike heel.

"So this is Jonathan." The doctor's eyes shone.

"Doctor Gottlieb delivered you," Mary said softly.

Jonathan was touched. In all his life he had never met this man, had not even heard him referred to. His identity was no secret, it was just that Mother tended to be quite private about female matters. "I'm glad to meet you, Doctor. And I'm awfully glad you're here." He had never said truer words. He was feeling a rush of gratitude toward the physician.

"I want to tell you right now that Patricia will be able to bear children normally. And there will be no loss of sexual function. There will be a vertical scar about eight inches long, but plastic surgery can deal with that if the patient wishes." Jonathan remembered kissing her perfect skin just above the belly button, how sweet it had tasted. "Our major worry is that scarring to the vagina will impair sexual enjoyment for the patient and her partners. But we tried hard to limit that."

"How badly was she hurt, Doctor?" Jonathan had to ask. He found that it was very, very important to him.

"She had extensive vaginal injuries. She has hairline fractures in her pelvis, and one hip was dislocated. She was as severely injured genitally as any young woman I've seen. We can count ourselves lucky that she's going to make a good recovery."

"You make it sound like there might be something else."

"Well, I was getting to that. We don't know for certain yet, but the indications so far are that both of her legs are paralyzed."

Jonathan was stunned. "She can't walk?"

"Not just at the moment, no. But we haven't been able to detect any injury that would cause this, so we don't think that it's likely to be a permanent condition."

"What does that mean? Days? Years?"

"We have no way of telling, I'm sorry to say. It would be premature to take a completely pessimistic view, though."

Jonathan left the barren little conference room and went back to Patricia. He found the priest kneeling beside the bed with his face on his clasped hands, obviously praying. He didn't blame Father Goodwin. In fact he envied him his faith.

When Jonathan came into her view she smiled a vague sort of a smile. Her fingers moved slightly.

He twined his own in them. They stayed like that, the two of them, silent in one another's company. After a time the priest finished whatever prayer he had been saying, and left them alone.

---

18 JULY 1983

MOST PRIVATE

To: The Prefect of the Sacred Congregation for the Defense of the Faith

From: The Chancellor for the Inquiry in North America

Your Eminence:

This is to inform you that Brother Alexander Thomas Parker (b. 12 Oct. 1942, + 17 Oct. 1942, ord. 22 June 1964, Judist, Soldier of Christ, Inquisitor-Captain) has been martyred in the line of duty. Because he was tortured we must assume his cell to have been compromised.

As a result I have withdrawn the cell from the Night Church

Congregation Holy Spirit and am now in the process of regrouping around a new cell leader.

This will result in a period during which we will be intelligence-blind.

The following personnel shifts have occurred:

1. Brother Alexander Thomas Parker, deceased by reason of fire applied to the body by hostile persons. Martyr.

2. Brother Julius Timothy, transferred to Prefecturate of the West, service in California.

3. Brother George Robert Yates, transferred as above.

4. Sister Marie-Louise D'Aubusson, invested as Captain-Inquisitor, ordered to form a new cell for penetration of the Night Church Congregation Holy Spirit.

Under separate cover please find a request for $2,114.28 to cover travel expenses involved in these changes.

A layperson (Terence Quist, b. 22 Nov. 1933, + 25 Dec. 1933, conf. 5 April 1945, single, K. of C., CCD) in the process of being recruited by Brother Alexander has been abandoned. Recruitment had not proceeded far enough to justify shifting to another operative, and I prefer to let the new Captain-Inquisitor bring in her own people.

> Yours in Christ & for the Defense of the Faith,
> Brian Conlon (Msgr.)

Document Class: Urgent A, most private, Swiss Guards courier

Destination: Paolo Cardinal Impelliteri, the Hidden Collegium, Prefecturate for the Defense of the Faith, Vatican City

20 IULIUS 1983

FURTIVISSIMUS

Ad: *Cancellarius Inquisitionis in Septentrionalis Americanensis*

Ex: *Prefectus Congregationis Defensioni Fidei*

We are shocked and saddened by the loss you have experienced. It is especially unfortunate that Brother Alexander had to endure such a harsh martyrdom. We can all take solace, though, in contemplating the peace Brother knows now.

I wish to reassert the wish of His Holiness that *Contra Poenam Ultimam* is to be scrupulously observed. The Night Church may be barbaric, but *we* are not.

I attach your approved expense report, with the admonition that religious below the level of Monsignor should not have traveled business class.

Also attached is a most distressing report from the Historical Section, written in the seventies of the last century. It appeared in the list of relevant *documentum* when we ran *Rituale Pudibunda Coitus* through the library's data-base.

Mea Auctoritate,
Paolo Cardinalis Impelliteri

Document Class: Urgent A, destroy in presence of courier

Destination: Monsignor Brian Conlon, Chancellor for the Inquiry, North America, 1217 Fuller Brush Building, 221 E. 57th Street, New York, N.Y., 10022

THE USE OF DISEASE VECTORS BY THE
NIGHT CHURCH IN HISTORICAL TIMES

by
Anthony S. Gardner, O.S.
March 4, 1871
(Synopsis)

1. Recent research into the Salisbury *Documentum*, the *Annales Emiliani,* and the *Marque de la Templars* suggests that the European plague known as the Black Death (1334–1360) spread from three focal points on the continent and one in Great Britain, in addition to the known font in Constantinople. (Vat. Docs. CMXXXIV)

2. These points were:

Ȃ   The Colchester Redoubt in Britain
Ȃ   Palazzo Emiliani in Venice
Ȃ   The Preceptory of the Hidden Temple in Paris
Ȃ   Rennes-le-Château in the Pyrenees

3. Three of these locations were in the famous 14th-century strongholds of the so-called "Cathar Heresy," which is one of the best-known disguises of the Night Church. The fourth, the Templar's House, was the confirmed world center of the Night Church at that time, fulfilling much the same function as their headquarters at Lourdes does today.

4. The Black Death began spreading within a few weeks of the infamous *Rituale Pudibunda Coitus* held between Margaret de Pantera and Carolus Titus at Salisbury Cathedral. During this ritual Carolus was killed, but not before despoiling the still unfinished cathedral and killing a substantial number of the sorcerers who were attendant at the affair.

5. The period after this is known in the annals of the Night Church as the "Dolorosa," apparently because the first "anti-man," which was successfully conceived in the ritual, was born defective and had to be destroyed. Many more years of breeding between the Pantera and Titus families were needed before a true success could be achieved.

6. The Night Church, which had unleased the Black Death to make room for its "anti-humanity," was then compelled to do its best to stave off the destruction of the entire human race lest the two critical families themselves be included. Given the primitive medicine of the day, it took them twenty years to completely eliminate the plague they had started.

7. Seven out of every ten human beings on this planet died during the Black Death. It was the most destructive thing that has ever happened to humankind. Whole cities, nations, disappeared into the wilderness.

8. The disease is thought to have been an artificially created hybrid of bubonic plague. Its exact nature remains to this day unknown.

9. Because of the speed of the contagion (about three hours from first symptoms to death) and the rapidity with which it spreads, even modern medicine would be taxed by it, should it appear again.

Chapter Eight ———————|—

TERRY QUIST KNEW he was in trouble when he woke up in the middle of the night and smelled perfume around him. As always, he was alone in bed. Women were a thing of the past for him . . . and it hadn't been much of a past. He was ugly, poor, and full of bad personal habits. He had not done well with the ladies.

He lay staring into the shadows around him, inhaling and listening.

There came from the living room of his tiny garage apartment a steady rustling.

Woman or not, the idea of somebody out there going through the papers on his desk scared the hell out of him.

Rustle, rustle, rustle. She was turning over page after page. All his story ideas, such as they were, lay on that desk. Under pseudonyms he moonlighted for a number of raunchy weeklies: *The National Tattler, The Midnight Express,* a few others. Naturally his notes were here. They couldn't be kept at the office. If the *Times* ever discovered his sin he'd be instantly fired, or so he assumed.

But his notes weren't of interest to anybody—just a bunch of jerkoff ideas. "The Sexual Power of Celery" was one. "Telepathic Cancer Cure" was another.

Oh, God, the notes on the Night Church were there, two pages neatly typed up just this morning!

He became aware that the rustling had stopped.

By the time he realized she had come into his room she was right beside his bed.

She stood looking down at him. As she bent close he saw her glaring eyes. She was beautiful like a snake might be beautiful. You can't look, and yet you can't look away.

She was also familiar.

Although his own eyes were closed to slits, he recognized the face swimming in the dark above him. It was Mike Banion's wife, Mary.

Seemingly satisfied he was asleep, she withdrew from the room, pulling the door almost shut.

A blinding flash filled the crack between door and jamb. Then a rustle of paper. Then another flash.

A moment later he heard his front door click shut.

He lay motionless, waiting for his heart to stop banging. A confusion of thoughts tumbled through his mind. Mary Banion? Two flashes. Pictures of the two pages.

But *Mary Banion?*

Oh, Christ. If they were in it together, when he went to Mike he would have been talking to the Night Church.

The image of Alex's charred body came to mind. Death was bad enough, but a death as hard as that, God help you.

He was in deep, deep trouble. He had to act on his own behalf or he was a dead man.

Throw himself on the mercy of the Night Church? Maybe the Banions would vouch for him. Sure they would. God, they had to or he was going to end up just like Alex.

What the hell *was* the Night Church, that it could command the loyalty of a lady as fine as Mary Banion? Or Mike, if he was part of it.

He was damn well going to find out. He showered and shaved and put on his best doubleknit suit.

Now he looked like an underpaid salesman instead of an even more underpaid newshog. Maybe a machine-tool salesman or a shoe salesman, or the type of guy with a chain of two or three newsstands. Barely okay, in other words. But it was his best suit, so it would have to do.

The streets were empty and quiet, the big trees breaking up the glare of the streetlights. Flower smells came from the yards of the enormous old Richmond Hill houses. People sneered at Queens, but it was a magical place at night, on the side streets where the secrets hid.

He would walk right into the Spirit. He would become a member in good standing. Hell, he wasn't going to go the way of Alex Parker; he was smarter than that.

The Spirit lay at the far end of Morris Street, a huge black bulk rising past the crowns of maples and chestnuts. Morris was a short block, worth only one streetlight, which fitfully illuminated the front of the age-blackened church. Terry's footsteps sounded loud on the sidewalk.

He reached the church. Absolute silence.

He mounted the steps, put his hand on the big brass handle.

The door opened noiselessly. Somebody had been very careful to keep it thoroughly oiled. Inside, total blackness. For a few moments Terry thought he must be early, or late, or even that they hadn't come on this particular night.

Then he sensed that the dark was full of people.

From deep within there came a low, strange musical note. In response some of the people in the pews lit tiny candles, cradling them in paper cones. Now Terry could see faces, and they were the faces of everyday life, old and young, plain and beautiful. There were whole families, mothers and fathers and children, single men and women too, all sorts of people.

Terry thought he'd better make himself known instantly. They mustn't be given the idea he was spying on them. "Excuse me," he said in a whisper that managed to echo through the whole damn church. "I'd like to join up . . . if that's okay."

They responded as one voice with a sound that at first Terry could not quite understand. Then he realized that it was a buzz of amused surprise.

He felt horribly alone. But when he turned to leave he found that somebody was standing right behind him. He was of middle age, dressed in a black pinstriped suit and a club tie, with the sensitive face of a decent and educated man. Obviously an usher. And why not? Night or day, churches needed ushers. He drew a long, gleaming stiletto from beneath his jacket, then replaced it. "Please be quiet," he whispered. On the domineering side, as ushers go.

Terry decided to be just as quiet as he could.

There came from the choir loft a deep, resonating hum, like the rising of a million locusts. The call of whatever kind of hellhorn they had up there caused the congregation to drop as one man to its knees. The service had begun.

Old altar bells, long abandoned by the day church, tinkled softly. The congregation raised their heads. Before them stood an elderly man with blazing green eyes. The most glorious vestment that Terry had ever seen wrapped his shoulders. It must be beyond anything created for centuries—not since the decadence of the Middle Ages—

with diamonds and rubies and emeralds and sapphires, the thousands of tiny jewels worked into intricate symbols and designs. In his right hand he carried a crystal wand. His head was mitered with a tall conical hat.

His robe shimmered in the wan light with images and suggestions of images, scenes of horror: corpses woven of tiny black beads ran along the bottom hem, worked into every possible posture of agony. Above them rose flames of ruby and orange soapstone, and higher still were obsidian chips fashioned into the outlines of ruined cities.

He swept back and forth in front of his congregation, pacing like a lion and making passes with his wand. Here came the mumbo jumbo. For an instant Terry actually thought that this was going to be humorous, but then the man turned to the altar and he saw the face woven on the back of the robe.

It was more than a monster's face embroidered there; it was remotely and disgustingly human. Its features were gross, with thick lips and exaggerated brows, and an excess of teeth bulging from the mouth.

The anti-man.

Terry wondered why they would want to create such a thing. What did they get from serving evil? Power? Wealth? Or was it the same thing that drew romantic young Germans into the SS: the allure of death?

Two members of this congregation were supposed to have been bred to conceive the first anti-man. Sure. Look at this bunch, scrubbed and clean and straight.

They must all be crazy. Had to be. Nothing that ugly could come out of a human union, no matter how horrible the parents were. And none of these people was even slightly horrible.

The chief magus, or whatever he was, turned around again and cleared his throat. He looked out across his congregation with an expression only a little nicer than the one portrayed on his vestment.

"We are gathered here to pray that our Princess may survive the great suffering to which we in our impiety and stupidity have subjected her." Another stiletto type came across the nave and whispered to the dark priest or wizard or whatever he was.

Then those eyes were looking right down the center aisle at Terry Quist. "Come," the wizard said softly. As Terry walked up the aisle faces turned to watch him. Just normal, ordinary, everyday faces. A lot of families had brought their kids.

The low, pulsing sound that had begun the ceremony started again, this time developing thrumming chords that seemed capable of sinking into the depths of the mind, evoking in Terry emotions of stunning violence. He saw by the discomfort in the pews that he was not alone in this reaction.

Here and there younger children covered their ears. And yet this was not a loud sound so much as a penetrating one. It would hardly be audible beyond the church walls, except to somebody with unusually sensitive ears. Alexander Parker must have been one such person. The music carried a strong emotional charge. Negative. Terry fantasized a sten gun in his hands, pulling the trigger, seeing blood and brains spray around him—

"Stop right there, young man."

Terry stopped. He was about ten feet from the wizard. This close the man's face was quite simply terrible. It was old and the color of newspaper, and it looked as fragile as a dry leaf. The green eyes glared in the way that Terry's years as a reporter had taught him to associate with advanced psychosis or great rage.

"You say that you want to join us, young man. How have you come to know of us?"

Terry's sense of the situation was that there weren't many right answers to that question.

He hadn't really expected to be greeted with suspicion, given his assumption that they would want recruits. Wrong again, Terry. His life was a tissue of mistakes, way back to the beginning. Obviously, he had just made another. Or had he? Getting into this was his one and only ticket out of getting killed by it.

"I knew a guy named Alex Parker—"

Somebody grabbed his shoulders from behind and slammed him to his knees. *"Never* address His Eminence from your feet, please."

"Hey, now, wait a minute." He sensed an arm being raised for a blow. "Sorry! His Eminence. Take it easy. I'll be real respectful."

The wizard met Terry's eyes with as cold a look as he could imagine. "So you must be Mr. Quist," he said softly. "Yes. I see your logic in coming here. You were correct to assume Parker had talked about you. Now you want to join us rather than risk sharing Parker's fate. Clever. Convenient for us, too."

Not quite the right response. There was something Terry didn't like about his coming here being convenient for them.

"We have been given a special opportunity tonight," the wizard said. "Prepare for the *Rituale Cruciatus Nexis.*" He clapped his hands. "Mr. Quist is going to test our revised vector."

"What kind of a vector?"

He was shoved again. "Never address a question to His Eminence."

"Sorry! Will you tell me what test—"

"It will be very brief, Mr. Quist," His Eminence said. "This vector is so quick you'll hardly even know what happened."

"Wonderful, Your Eminence. Very reassuring. I think I want to go home."

His Eminence did not even smile.

Something was going on at the rear of the church. There were a number of people consulting with one another. Then one of them broke away and trotted up a side aisle. He consulted briefly with His Eminence. The old man seemed testy. "And make it fast," he rasped at his departing lackey. He looked toward the choir loft. "Begin the processional, Bob."

"The organ?" came the reply, full of doubt.

"Of course not, it's too loud. The horn."

The musician was a master of his instrument, whatever it was. The music swept and swirled and throbbed. Terry even forgot his aching knees. He had never before heard a musical instrument that made such a sound. It worked on your emotions to an almost uncanny degree. This time the tone was one of peace and reassurance, like one might hear in an ancient monastery, where the monks were chanting their matins.

Perhaps fifteen minutes passed before His Eminence returned to the center of the sacristy. At the same time Stiletto Man and one of his assistants arrived and crowded Terry on both sides. Guess I'm going through with this, Terry thought.

The horn sounded a single, long note. Terry craned his neck around and saw a boy and girl of perhaps twelve begin marching up the aisle with the self-consciously slow tread of under-rehearsed kids. Their grave, soft faces were yellowed by the flickering light of the thick red candles they held in their hands. They were dressed all in white, these children, and their footsteps made no sound.

Now things began to get colorful. The wizard—oops, His Eminence

—raised his arms and spoke: "By the power of the King of the Underworld, O Spirits of the Hells receive our gift and remember Thee us!" He began a slow twirling dance, his face sinking to deep concentration, his wand describing quick crosses. "Come and take our offering, O Deeps!"

The congregation replied: "Come from the east, the south, the west, and the north. Come into this house." There was the rattle of a general turning of pages.

The children reached Terry.

His Eminence stopped his dance. He dropped to his knees, facing his congregation. "Who shall be the medium of the experiment?"

The girl replied, "Father, it is Terence Michael Aloysius Quist." Nice. They even knew the Aloysius. The last place that had appeared was on his birth certificate. The Night Church had done its homework.

"Do you give him up willingly?"

"We do, Your Eminence." The children spoke as from rote, carefully and in unison. Their candles guttered and swayed.

"What shall open the gates of the future?"

"The death of man."

His Eminence stood up, a menacing presence in his shimmering robes and tall miter. "I call Thee, O dweller in the deep of hearts, come among us and receive this our gift of thanks."

The congregation responded: "May He bless our experiment."

There was that word again. Experiment. This Night Church was half religion, half science—the demented superstition of the Middle Ages mixed with a science that had progressed far beyond the worship that accompanied it.

The music stopped.

This was a cue to the children, who had paused before Terry. "Come with us, please, sir," said the girl. She put out her free hand. Terry took it and raised himself to his feet. The two children turned him around.

His heart almost stopped. A black coffin lay open in the aisle. The boy took his other hand. "This is just our initiation," he whispered. "You have to get in."

"Come on, don't be ridiculous."

Something sharp pressed up against his neck. He shuddered; he knew that it was the stiletto.

His legs were wobbly, but he made it to the coffin. In other circumstances he might have tried to run, but there were hundreds of people between him and the doors. He had a strong feeling that he either got into that coffin or ended up with his throat cut.

It looked soft inside but the damn thing was hard. Beneath the white satin lining there was just wood.

"Nobody close this thing," Terry said. He did not speak in a whisper. He wanted to be heard.

The girl smiled. "Even if we do, it won't be for long. It's going to be fine. Really it is."

The intensity of the music increased, the emotional timbre became excited and mean.

There was no real pillow, so Terry had to raise his head to see what was going on around him. He raised it and kept it raised: there was no way he was going to let these loonies put that lid down. He noticed that the edges of the lid were lined with rubber, like the door of a refrigerator.

His Eminence approached the altar. He began to quiver, creating the impression that a tremendous inner battle was taking place. The wand he held seemed about to drop from his hand. An acolyte appeared and held a gold platen covered by a silk doily beneath the vibrating wand.

"I conjure Thee, O Lord of Flies and Ills, through the medium of his dread, bring the infection unto his body."

A tension of expectancy filled the church. People were whispering. He saw a mother putting a surgical mask on her six-year-old.

The music was vicious now, actually prancing with glee.

His Eminence straightened up. He raised his hands and the music stopped. With a rustle of his robes he turned around. He spread his arms. "The time has come."

Faces began to look expectantly at Terry. The two children had taken places at the foot and head of the coffin. The wizard said softly to them, "Now."

With a movement too sudden to avoid the boy reached out and spurted a tiny aerosol in Terry's face. It wasn't much of a spurt. There wasn't even any odor.

Then they started to close the coffin.

Terry had been expecting this. "No way!" He jumped right out onto the floor. "No way do I get shut up in there."

In the dark a woman screamed, a keening sound. "Seal him up," somebody said in a frantic whisper.

People began pushing down the pews, away from him. His Eminence plastered on a smile. And here came the Stilettos. They were not smiling. For his part, Terry was about to sneeze.

"Amanda," the wizard said pleasantly, "tell Terry a little about the ritual." She hesitated. "Don't be afraid, Amanda. There are still a few minutes' grace."

At the sound of that word Terry noticed that he felt like hell. His bones ached, his skin was dry and sensitive.

The girl took his hand again. He noticed for the first time that there was an almost childlike quality about all these people. The gaudy rituals, the deep of the night, the secrecy, all spoke of the distant past; the terror of it, but also the charm.

"Terry, we have to close the lid for a little while because our ritual is about dying to the past and coming to life again in the service of evil. It only stays down for about two minutes. It's just symbolic." She squeezed his hand and gave him a cute smile. "It's what you want, isn't it? I mean, that must be why you're here."

"Yes." Terry's voice was hoarse with fear.

"We all want you to do it, all of us." There were murmurs of assent from the surrounding pews, accompanied by encouraging nods and smiles. And then there were also the Stilettos.

"Sorry I'm so touchy," he muttered. "Claustrophobia." He got back in and the kids, smiling warmly, closed the lid. There was a distinct click, and then utter darkness. Someone had locked the lid with a coffin key. Oh, Christ, this was going to be hard. Almost at once the air began to go bad. He felt absolutely horrible.

The music started again, its low notes filling the thick air. Muffled but audible there came from the congregation a sharp sigh. This was followed by a burst of low words, sounding like Latin.

Although he listened with all his might Terry couldn't hear much. He felt along the top of the coffin. Maybe there was some kind of a handle or latch in here—just in case the dead man woke up. But no, nothing.

They were doing something outside; he could hear movements close to the coffin.

It was hot in here. Plus he was so sick his chest was beginning to rattle. He sneezed violently. Once. Again. Three times. Four. Five. He began to see the true nature of the experiment they were conducting. It had to do with that aerosol.

They had given him the disease!

The top seemed to crash against his face. For a moment he didn't understand that he had banged at it with his forehead, trying to break out. When he did understand it scared the hell out of him. He was farther gone than he thought; he was out of control. Must be fever coming on.

They weren't going to let him out of here. They were going to see how efficiently their disease worked.

How long it took to kill an average adult male.

He writhed, felt with desperate, questing fingers the satin flocking of the coffin. He had been an idiot to think they would let him out! "Please!" Nothing. "Please! Oh, plea-a-ase!"

"Mr. Quist?"

"Oh! Oh, yes! Oh, thank you! Thank you for answering me! I can't get my breath. I gotta have air! I'm sick. Sick bad! You've got to open this thing up."

"We have a few questions first, Mr. Quist." The wizard's voice sounded so close he must be crouched right at the head of the coffin. Terry had been fool enough to come here, and they had simply taken advantage.

All Terry could think to do was be agreeable. If he cooperated there might be some hope.

If not he was a dead man. "Questions? Sure, but hurry!" He had never been able to hold his breath long in childhood contests at Miller-Walkin Public Swimming Pool in Corona Park. Never for long. He would come bursting up out of the water first or second, his lungs aching for air, his whole body filled with a painfully urgent need to breathe. "Please hurry!"

"What did you tell Inspector Michael Banion about us?"

Holy God! Mike wasn't in on it, only his wife! His heart went out to the poor guy. He had to get out of here, to somehow warn Mike! They'd been friends forever, he and Mike. The poor guy.

His wife! His *wife!*

That unbelievable bitch.

His throat hurt as if it were being hacked with a dull blade. He raised his hands and was horrified to find huge swellings on both sides of his neck. Then he couldn't lower his arms. In that moment other swellings had appeared in his underarms. Even as the air around him went bad he kept having to take deeper and deeper breaths through his constricted windpipe.

"Help me! I told you, I'm sick! Bad!"

"Inspector Banion—"

Maybe he could still help Mike a little. "I told him nothing!"

"You're lying."

"Let me out of here! Let me out! You've got to get me to a hospital. I'm sick. I'm smothering, for God's sake!"

"Are you an Inquisitor? Is Banion an Inquisitor?"

"What the fuck is an Inquisitor? I don't know from Inquisitors. For the love of God, open this thing up!" He kicked, he hammered, he tore at the upholstery. The swelling under his right arm burst with an audible pop, a discharge of thick, stinking fluid, and an agonizing shaft of pain.

He knew suddenly that he would die before the interrogation was over. "Open it up and let me breathe! I'll tell you everything. Please, I beg you. I *beg* you."

"Did you name names?"

"Hell, no!"

"Tell us the truth and we'll open the top."

This was no time to be coy. "I told Mike nothing because he wouldn't listen to me. The minute he heard Night Church he laughed at me. He's not the type of cop's gonna buy something like this without it being rubbed in his ever-lovin' face! *Now let me out!*"

There was whispered conversation outside, which soon died to silence. He felt himself drifting. Then he felt nothing.

Suddenly he came to. He had been out cold! "Open this thing up!"

What air he could get past his twisted throat moved with a thin whistling sound.

This was the death of Terence Michael Aloysius Quist, reporter. Noble? Not very. No Pulitzer for this turkey. He became aware of a seething, slithering sound on the outside of the coffin, as if somebody was lying on it. Just a few inches of wood separated his face from excited breathing.

"You perverts—you bastards!"

The response was a sort of whine that sounded hardly human. The coffin started to shake with the gyrations of whoever was there. "Listen with the stethoscope," somebody whispered. "Four minutes and he can barely breathe past the buboes!"

Buboes? The bastards had given him some kind of superplague, then shut him up in here to see how fast it worked.

Terry was almost grateful when his heart began to beat irregularly. Death is coming soon, guy. This too will pass. Who knows, maybe there's even some kind of special heaven for the congenitally unlucky.

"Cardiac arrhythmias at five minutes," said a calm voice.

"Excellent work," His Eminence replied.

Unfeeling bastards. At the sound of those clipped, educated voices Terry's fear shattered. Now he was simply mad. Too bad there was no way to disappoint them at least a little. To die nobly, instead of like a choking, poisoned dog.

A wave of raw desperation made him hammer his feet wildly. From outside there came excited little cries. "Delirium at five minutes twenty seconds!"

For an instant Terry was out again, then he returned to consciousness amid a series of white flashes. He was going now, he knew it. Escape just wasn't in the cards.

He grieved for parts of life he had loved, for the snow-muffled nights along old cobbled streets, for the pungent smell of coal smoke, for crime scenes and squad cars and all-night delis. And girls, all the girls he hadn't had.

Outside there were eager scufflings, as if more of the ghouls were gathering around the coffin. He could picture them out there, all crowded around, laughing that stifled laughter, gleeful at the success of their experiment.

There was a plague that killed in minutes, and it was in the hands of the mad.

He would at least show them a little human nobility, a little bravery. Mustering every bit of self-control available to him he cleared his throat as best he could.

If he was going to die, let it be in style.

"I'm singin' in the rain," he gasped, "singin' and dancin'—"

He had to work up another breath to go on.

Outside, silence had descended. Maybe they were shocked, maybe awed. Good. He wanted them to know this was a human being in here, and at the end this human being had broken through all his pain and all his terror, and faced a hell of a death with a song.

"Singin' in the rain—"

There came a murmur of conversation. He was getting to them, he knew he was.

"Glory halleluja, I'm happy again!"

Somebody hushed the murmur.

"Singin' in the rain, you bastards! Singin' in the goddamn rain!" He threw back his head and ground out some wheezy laughter. There was thunder in his ears and acid in his throat. He was dying in agony but he did not scream.

Then singing burst forth all around him, the brightest, most triumphant singing he had ever heard. From hundreds of throats: ". . . just singin' in the rain. What a glorious feelin', I'm happy again. . . ."

They were throwing it right back at him. He hadn't gotten through to them at all. They had no feelings, they were worse than mad, they had no souls.

At last the animal took over and he tore madly at the coffin, digging as a trapped beast would dig. He sank his nails into the wooden lid.

He died.

MARY: THE TERROR OF THE INQUISITION

My dearest Jonathan:

I write this now, in this black time, in the hope that it will one day soon be possible for you to read it.

I must tell you that Patricia's injuries are not your fault. The blame rests with me and your Uncle Franklin. All I can say in our defense is that what happened was a sort of accident. We caused it, yes, but for the best of reasons. We were trying to protect you both from the terror of the Inquisition.

There is a chance that we may cure Patricia, by a method that will surprise you. If the cure works, my son, you will one day hold this letter in your hands.

I put pen to paper confidently, trusting that those we serve will guide us through our troubles. I have belonged to them, as have you, all the days of my life. I have come to love their hardness, to embrace their danger.

I cannot call them evil, any more than I can call you anything but my beloved child. I hope my words will help you in your confusion and fear. Remember yourself. Remember what you were before the hypnosis and what you are becoming again. Remember that you will be the father of the anti-man.

He will be a creature of what men call darkness. But not to himself. Men's dark will be his light, their evil his good. Your son will have strengths and powers mankind never had; he will have the attributes of the demons.

The anti-man will have the intelligence of Asmodeus and the strength of Belial. He will be able to discourse like Satan and will shine with Lucifer's fire.

Do you remember learning all of that in catechism? Remember the stories of the demons?

They are all hoping for you now, Jonathan. Can you feel them in your heart, hear them whispering to you when the wind hisses through the leaves?

Remember the vision of Belial you had when you were nine? "I will speak to you in the voice of the dry leaves," he said. That was such an extraordinary vision, and it filled you with such determination.

I know what you are feeling, what conflict rages in your heart. Now that you have been exposed to the world of man you have come to love it. But, Jonathan, remember that God has owned this earth for millions upon millions of years. It is time for the Devil to have His share of rule. This is justice.

Anti-humanity will be stronger than humanity, and far greater. Life on earth has been steadily evolving toward higher and higher intelligence. So our creation is only the next logical step. Satan gave man knowledge in the first place. Now He will give the earth a humanity fashioned in His image.

Compared to us ordinary folk your son will literally be a god—as far above us as we are above the ape men who preceded us.

When our species was born we pushed our forebears into extinction. And that was just.

But modern Homo sapiens would resist its own extinction. A fearful and jealous humankind will destroy the new species before it can get a proper start.

The destiny of this earth is to produce your son and all his race. As a Church, we worship this destiny. As scientists, we help to bring it about.

Jonathan, I can scarcely imagine how shocking it must be to discover these truths about yourself after you thought yourself an ordinary man. You are not ordinary. You are the product of centuries and centuries of the most careful breeding. You and Patricia are hardly even human.

Your bodies are ordinary. They are the past. Your souls, though, contain the seed of the future.

Do not recoil at the responsibility, my son: you are merely the instrument of nature. The law of evolution is expressing itself through you.

Now I must tell you why you are going through all this difficulty and confusion, why you have been made to forget your own past.

When your natural father and Patricia's parents were killed by the Inquisition, we hid you both. We did it by hypnotizing you and concealing you under false identities. Even under torture you would not reveal the truth about yourselves.

I am so sorry we made you endure this, and in our ignorance caused the accident in June at Holy Spirit. All I can do is plead an excess of protective zeal.

You two are so precious! When I think that we nearly destroyed you by our very effort to protect you I almost go mad!

But we were not wrong to take the steps we did. The Inquisitors are master saboteurs. Their murders usually seem like accidents. They are so stealthy I think that they could kidnap an unborn child from its mother's womb. I myself trust nobody. When the cricket stops at moonset, I suspect the sneaking approach of the Inquisitor with his tinder ready to set a fire in my bed. And when the darkness sighs, I listen for the Inquisitor's voice, murmuring word of our defeat.

I sit here by the hour waiting and listening and worrying.

How can I help you through your rediscovery of yourself? Advice seems hollow, love futile. All I can tell you is that the earth's will is toward evolution. It is your privilege to enact it.

Accept this fundamental reality and all your confusion will evaporate. You will reacquire the moral precision that has always supported you. You will *know* the rightness of our cause.

It is the middle of the night, warm and still. I am hunched in a pool of light at my desk in the upstairs sitting room. I can hear Mike snoring across the hall. And at the far end, in your room, you have just sighed. I will go and kiss you, my dearest son.

Five minutes have passed. I am back from your bedside. You moaned when my lips touched your cheek. Your sleep is troubled again tonight, darling. I wish that I were a demon, and could bless you with a demon's insight.

Franklin says the life of the Church has always been this hard, but I don't agree. It was bad during the Albigensian Crusade and worse during the Spanish Inquisition, but at least then the Catholic cards were placed on the table. Now the Inquisition is secret, and therefore more dangerous than ever.

My darling, may you be granted full measure of courage. May your burdens be borne with bravery.

A mother's hope is with you.

    Mary Titus

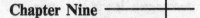

PATRICIA ATTRIBUTED TO the trauma of her assault her feeling that a great unseen force was slowly capturing her. Since the attack she was always under threat in her dreams, always being pursued by some relentless thing she could never quite see.

During the day she tried to avoid being touched. Anybody who came into contact with her might turn out to be one of the dream things. They might reappear at night, their faces stretched thin, the bones exaggerated to bestial size. In one recent dream all her friends had clawed up out of the street beneath her feet and grabbed her legs.

Dreams that bad can drive people mad. They can even kill. Just to survive, Patricia had been forced to make nightmare management her new specialty.

Only Jonathan knew how to comfort her. She let him sit close, and occasionally she screwed up the courage to clasp his hand. "At first you wouldn't let go," he had told her. From those hours she remembered only the sense of dissolving, as if her whole self were leaking out through her wounded sex. To prevent it she had felt a desperate, overwhelming need to hold onto him.

She was grateful when she felt the sun touch her face. She had slept with the window open and now she took breath after breath of the summer morning. There was again today no feeling of fullness down below. The dull, unceasing pain had actually diminished to little more than a sensation of tightness.

Despite Mike's begging that she move, she had returned to this apartment. It was home, after all, her first real home since she had been a very little girl. And it had been consecrated by her meeting Jonathan here.

In the open drawer of her bedside table lay a small black pistol, a gift from Mike Banion. On the far wall there was a keypad. Above the keypad glowed a single red light. Until Patricia punched in the right code the light would stay red and this apartment would remain an electronic fortress. Another gift from Mike Banion.

Beside her hand was a push button. If she pressed it, a bell would ring downstairs and one of the building guards would come to her immediate assistance, twenty-four hours a day. Thanks again, Mike Banion. And thanks for the alarm on my wheelchair and the cripple-height fire extinguishers in every room, and the carry permit which allows me to wheel myself through life with a six-shooter at my hip. Thanks, Mike. You poor, sweet man, you have made me feel more threatened than I think I can bear.

It was nine A.M. Time to call Jonathan. She went to the phone and dialed the Banions' number. As he had promised, he was waiting for her and picked up the phone on the first ring. "Hi," he said. "You ready for me?"

"I'll be ready when you get here."

"On my way."

"Love you." He hung up. She stared for an instant at the phone, then replaced it in the cradle. This morning she was going to face some of her worst fears. She would enter the place where most of her nightmares were set, and worship there among her terrors.

Jonathan was taking her to Mass at Holy Spirit.

As reward for the courage of her act he was then to escort her to the Café Trianon in Queens Center for a late breakfast of croissants and café au lait. During the course of the morning they would not kiss, and they might not even touch. And Jonathan would not grin foolishly, or make elaborate conversational efforts to avoid the subjects of rape, paralysis, or nightmare. Nor would his talk be full of unintentional innuendo about those subjects.

It would, in short, be a nice morning after the Spirit was faced. But none of it could happen for another twenty minutes. She had to dress herself. Hard and angering labor. Her legs dangled like soft rubber tubes. The worst part of this awful immobility was that there was no detectable reason for it. There was no physical damage at all. They had even scanned her brain. She was healthy and whole, nothing crushed, pinched, or severed. Only she couldn't walk.

Hysterical paralysis, Doctor Gottlieb had called it. Mary's dear friend. She had come to hate his watchful eyes, peering at her from behind half-glasses, and those hands, so big and yet so clever with the probes and instruments of examination.

At Mass she must also see Mary Banion, who seemed desperately pained whenever they encountered one another. Did it embarrass her to be in the company of a victimized woman? Activate her own personal sense of helplessness?

Mike and his minions had installed gripping bars on every wall in the apartment, but Patricia's mainstay was the big chrome wheelchair beside her bed. She checked the brakes, then twisted herself around so that she lay with her back to it. Then she pushed herself with her arms until her head was in the seat. Next she gripped the armrests and hauled herself into a sitting position. That was one of the "chair maneuvers" she had been taught in physical therapy. She was pleased; she had executed it well.

The rest of her dressing went as awkwardly as ever. She washed her face in the newly installed low sink, and combed out her hair. She dropped her comb, then rolled over it and broke it trying to find it. Then she took off her pajamas and got herself dressed in a light blue skirt and white blouse—and split the zipper in the back trying to hike the skirt down under her buttocks. Then a little lipstick, a little eyeshadow, and she looked just right. Like she had been dressed by a drunk.

Would she please Jonathan? Would she ever *really* please him again as much as she had? Perhaps she was selfish even to want that. Damnit, though, she did.

He buzzed right on schedule. All of a sudden the visit to Holy Spirit —which she had been carefully not thinking about—seemed formidable indeed. A visit to the heart of her latest inner hell. "You have to," Jonathan had insisted, "you need to confront these fears. We'll go together." He was the brain specialist, after all; he ought to know. For an instant the back of her chair felt as cold as a marble altar.

That made her lunge forward, the involuntary response of a person forgetting that she couldn't get up. When she wasn't being pursued in her dreams she was always trying to find Jonathan. She would see him walking into the ocean or across a forest glade, or down a darkly mirrored hall. She would call to him.

He used his own key to get in. "You look great."

"Thank you."

"I expected to find you upside down on the bathroom floor with lipstick in your ear."

"Funny boy."

He took the handles of the chair and pushed her out the door.

There were a couple of greetings in the elevator, more of those bright smiles she had learned to hate. It had been awful to find out that normal people no longer had any idea of how to relate to you, and would not do so at all unless trapped.

Tony had a Checker Cab waiting. Patricia could have kissed Mr. Checker for inventing those wonderful rolling boxes. Between the two of them she and Jonathan had only a hideous time getting her in. This contrasted with the inhuman struggle smaller cabs entailed.

"How was last night?" Jonathan asked as soon as they were rolling. Poor guy, he had a big stake in her last-nights. They tended to determine where on the scale from bad to abysmal her mood for the coming day would fall.

"Not nightmare alley, anyway. But not Nirvana either."

"That's something at least. Did you trank down?"

"Nope. I slept totally drug-free, so I'm wild-eyed and bushy-tailed and ready to meet my day!"

" 'Wide-eyed.' The expression is 'wide-eyed.' "

"Not in my case."

Holy Spirit filled the far end of Morris Street. It was as large as some of the smaller Gothic cathedrals, but its architects, no doubt struggling to provide enough massiveness to satisfy the prosperous Gay Nineties parishioners who had paid them, had not managed to make its stones soar. A heavier, more gargoyled and crenelated construction could hardly be imagined. Its stained-glass windows seemed to squint, little cracks in the granite facade.

"Oh, damn it, Jonathan, there's Mike's car."

"He's here, of course. Your whole entourage is here, as a matter of fact."

"And those patrol cars." She counted four in the parking area between church and rectory. "I don't think I can stand this."

"Mike's been working on the case like a crazy person. Twenty hours a day. He really cares about you, darling. He wants very badly to find whoever did this to you. Solving the case means an awful lot to him."

"I don't want to hear about the case!" The cab stopped and they worked themselves out of it. Patricia wished Jonathan had never said the word case, but now that he had, there was no point in trying to avoid talking about it. That way ulcers lay. "Damnit all, anyway. I do want to hear about the case."

He stopped rolling her up the wooden wheelchair ramp that had recently been installed on the steps of the Spirit.

There were benches to either side of the front door. Jonathan wheeled her to one and sat down before her. "You're sure?"

She wasn't, but she nodded.

"They've tried to reconstruct your past, hour by hour, for the two weeks leading up to the incident. All they came up with out of the ordinary was the fact that you had spoken to an old man named Mr. Apple at a parish seniors supper. Aside from our date, I mean."

"How did they ever find out about him?"

"An old lady who had been at the supper remembered you talking to him."

"He was just an old man. They were wasting their time."

"Mike decided to go after the guy. Farfetched, but the only lead they had. But the night before he was due to be questioned, he died. He was buried in All Souls."

"A wild-goose chase. First off, the man was ancient. Second, he couldn't have hurt me. He was like paper. What's more, he was senile. They could have asked me about him and saved themselves some trouble."

"No more questions, says the good Doctor Gottlieb. Not until you're walking again."

"What's the point, anyway? I can't remember anything important."

"Tell that to Mike. Maybe you'll cheer him up. His other problem is that he had something going with a reporter and the reporter disappeared. Mike's convinced the same cult that got you got him. He knew something about it, it seems."

Patricia really wished, just at this moment, that she had been strong enough to tell him to wheel her straight into the church. The newspapers had called it a ritual sacrifice, a cult rape, and her imagination had been left to boil and burn with images of blank-eyed cultists waiting in the shadows around every corner. Cult. Ugly, stupid word. She wanted very much to believe she had been the victim of a single disturbed man, acting alone. Cult meant people, dozens probably, ever-watchful, alert for any unguarded moment. She couldn't accept that; it was just too much.

And yet, she thought, she dreamed, that something was getting closer and closer, fingers going around her neck, cool and dry and tight.

Whoever had hurt her had also done something to make her forget. Something incredible: the police hypnotist had worked with her for hours. "If it were not for the physical evidence, I would conclude that this woman had not been harmed," he had written in the report Mike had shown her. The police hypnotist was a bleak old man with a voice like a pillow.

Perhaps she should thank her rapist; maybe he had done her a favor. After all, she wanted to forget.

No, she wanted to remember—to remember his face, his name, anything about him that would help Mike get him behind bars.

But if it was a cult Mike would never catch enough of them, no matter how hard he tried. That was why she was afraid of a cult—they would be unstoppable.

She wanted to be safe. Safe and normal and happy. That was what was so sad. It was so little to want. Now the tears were starting. She cried so easily these days. She battled with her feelings. Jonathan's hand came out, touched her cheek. She couldn't bear it right now. She turned her head away.

"I'm ready," she said, trying to ignore the hurt in his face. He began to wheel her in.

The big doors swept open as they approached. They had been watched, of course. Eager people clustered around. Somebody found a Saint Joseph Missalette and held it out before her. She smiled up at the grinning face. "I have my missal," she said. The grin widened, the head nodded furiously. Other volunteers wheeled her; Jonathan walked beside.

Oh, my Lord, there is the altar where most of me died.

I am so afraid. Black, ugly altar. Why is it black, anyway? Other churches don't have black altars. But there also is the vigil candle, that red glow that tells us why this place matters, because it houses the fabulous enigma of the Blessed Sacrament.

Come on, girl, suppress that overwhelming urge to lunge out of this chair and crawl away like a soldier escaping from a battlefield. You knew coming here was going to be hard, yes, you did. She wanted his touch, raised her left hand. He was always ready, her beloved, and his warm, slender fingers soon surrounded hers.

There were a lot of cops in the church. Six or seven in uniform, and another five clustering around Mike Banion and Mary. Patricia recognized Lieutenant Maxwell, the sex-crimes specialist with the bedside manner of a friendly old doctor.

Father Goodwin lurched abruptly out of the sacristy followed by a plump boy of perhaps eleven in a surplice at least three sizes too small. Father had lost weight; his chasuble hung on him like a shroud.

Now for the Mass. Father Goodwin was spectral, his voice full of quavers. Patricia wondered if she could bear this ritual.

Even that word made her writhe in the chair. Ritual. *Rituale*. She wanted to scream.

Frantically she fought for control. Father began the motions, the drone of words. Patricia's mind battled the chaos of terror that the place had inspired in her. Why had she been so stupid as to come here?

We know nothing of our passions, especially not the black ones, terror and panic. She sensed that the saints lurking in the dome overhead were mad; she looked up at their twisted, pious faces and saw suddenly a vast coldness written there.

Saints are not saints for love of God. They are saints because they have seen the terror of the unknown. Of Hell. Hell is no fire, it is the emptiness, the black between the stars, and she could hear it whistling in her own soul.

Come on, girl! Get yourself together! *Work at it!*

She drove her consciousness to bland and orderly thoughts. Sister Desperada: "The Holy Mass is divided into thirty-four parts from the Entrance Antiphon to the Dismissal." No! I can't bear it. I'll never be able to stay here that long!

"The Lord be with you."

A ragged trail of voices: "And also with you." Patricia wanted to run, to hide, to get down into the depths of the earth and pull soil over her, to hide so completely that the very atoms of her body would be mixed forever with the anonymous brown dirt.

"My brothers and sisters, to prepare ourselves to celebrate the sacred mysteries, let us call to mind our sins."

Oh, yes, my sins. My sins are very horrible. I long for a loving man, and that is a sin of inordinate desire. I want a nice little house, oh, God, in someplace like Riverdale, and some kids to need me and a husband to grow old with, oh, God. And for me those are also sins of inordinate desire!

As if from afar she felt herself beating her breast, heard her words echoing through the stunned silence of the church. "Through my fault, through my fault, through my most grievous fault, in thought and in word, in all I have done and failed to do—oh, the *Confiteor* is a lie! A lie, God! I never did anything wrong. Hell just opened up under my feet, God, and I fell in and now you won't pull me out!"

The silence deepened. "Lord have mercy," said Father at last.

His hands paused over the *Rituale* and she saw him close his eyes for an endless moment.

Jonathan's arm was around her. Mike Banion was questioning her with his eyes, frowning with concern. Mary's face was buried in her hands.

Poor Father began stuttering through his *Kyrie*.

"I'm sorry," Patricia muttered. She looked down. Anything but stare at that horrible altar. How stupid to make it black!

"Shall I take you out?" Jonathan whispered.

She shook her head. Father said the *Gloria* in a completely new tone. He raised his head, lifted his arms, looked as if from the bottom of a pit toward some promise above. "Glory to God in the highest, and peace to His people on earth. Lord God, heavenly King, almighty God and Father, we worship You, we thank You, we praise You for Your glory."

He cared about her. They all did.

She wanted to weep. But also, on behalf of the people who loved her, she wanted to be strong.

On to the Liturgy of the Word, today from the Prophet Daniel. Feast of the Transfiguration. "I saw one like a son of man coming, on the clouds of heaven. When He reached the Ancient One and was presented before Him, He received dominion, glory, and kingship; nations and peoples of every language serve Him." Oh, Lord. You come on clouds of glory, I come creaking on wheels, terror in my heart.

What bitterness was in her. It was pitiful, to be bitter even against Him.

But God did not help me! God let me be raped on His own altar!

Next in the endless litany of the Mass came the Liturgy of the Eucharist. Mike and Mary brought the gifts, looking from behind almost silly, the tall, elegant, chestnut-haired woman and her stocky husband.

Father Goodwin took the chalice in hands so nervous that the wine stormed like the Red Sea. "Lord, by the transfiguration of Your Son, make our gifts holy."

Is it possible, she wondered as he prepared to give out Communion, that God doesn't hate us, but has simply lost us? Maybe the earth has drifted into a part of the universe so obscure that even God has lost track of it.

Human worship is chiefly characterized by the silence of God.

"Holy, holy, holy Lord God of power and might, heaven and earth are filled with Your glory. Hosanna in the highest."

Father hovered over his chalice, looking out at his tiny flock in what must seem an immense ocean of empty pews.

The emptiness of space. The coldness. Except, oh, God, for us. We people, *we* are here.

Your silence is what drives us mad! How dare You do this to us, God! *How dare You!* We deserve Your involvement. We deserve Your respect. Yes, even Your admiration!

Or at least Your help. Please. Just two words, two infinitely blessed words. Oh, God, just say it. "I am." Come on, say it. "I am." "Say it! Say it, damn You!"

With a horrified look at her, Father raced into the next prayer. "For the kingdom and the power and the glory are Yours, now and forever."

"Sorry," she muttered again. Jonathan's arm was starting to hurt her shoulder. She shrugged it off.

"Let us offer each other the sign of peace."

Listen to him. It takes real faith to say something like that with any conviction. As she watched the Mass proceed she fancied that she could hear a voice in the breeze that was rattling the old stained-glass windows. *I love you,* the voice said with a sudden clatter. *You're mine! Mine! Mine!* And then the breeze went muttering off among the lush summer trees.

Father took the Host and ate it.

Patricia felt her chair wobble a little. "You sure you don't want to leave?" Jonathan whispered.

"No! Let's go ahead with Communion."

"Okay." He began pushing her toward the altar. She was to lead the

Communion parade—which consisted of Mike and his entourage and the usual seven old ladies who were Father's morning Mass regulars.

Take this blood. Take this body. Let us proclaim the mystery of faith. When Father approached her, Patricia cast her eyes down and held up her hands, cupped. She chewed the whole-wheat Host that Father handed her. The little girl she had once been had believed that the Eucharist was the great center of human life.

The breeze came back, much stronger, slapping at the windows, moaning past the eaves.

"Thanks be to God."

Far up in the church glass broke. The altar candles were snuffed out by a powerful blast of wind.

Faces turned, glanced up. But nothing more happened, except that the communicants shuffled back to the three populated pews.

The concluding doxology followed. When Father turned around again he seemed unutterably sad. Patricia felt oppressed; she did not want to share any more sadness. So it was a sad world. She had also discovered this. A very sad world.

Father might be sad for her, but the way he was looking at his pews she suspected he was mostly sad for his dying parish. This was probably the biggest turnout he'd had in months. So sad.

Maybe he ought to try bingo again. It hadn't worked the last time, but the prizes had been a joke. Who wants *used* prizes? The premium table had looked like a lawn sale.

She could easily have laughed, remembering how she had hand-drawn the stencil for the last bingo-night poster. So very long ago, that innocent May night when the caller had called into the ocean of empty tables. Fourteen players only. All had won at least one game. Three ended up winning back the castoffs they had donated.

Suddenly Mike stood up and approached the altar rail. Instead of going off to the sacristy to devest, Father joined him. Mike drew an envelope from his pocket.

"Patricia," he said into the quiet, "I'm no speechmaker." He fingered the envelope. "This is from the Holy Name Society. We got together and passed the hat because we wanted to give you a real good gift. Well, open it up."

He dropped the envelope into her lap. She looked down at it, wondering dully what it would be this time.

I ought to be grateful.

"Go on, open it."

Airplane tickets and a letter. Lord be merciful, they had given her a pilgrimage to Lourdes. Now she didn't know whether to laugh or cry. She just sat there, stunned. "I'm the pilgrimage director," Father said. There was such warmth and anticipation in the faces around her, she had no choice but to smile.

Only Jonathan looked as desolate as she secretly felt.

Lourdes. Preserve me. They are sending their cripple for the cure. They were ridiculous, but they were also touching. "Thank you," she said, as sweetly as she could.

"This means a lot to us both," Jonathan added in the thick silence that followed.

Jonathan took the handles firmly and wheeled her out. It was not until they were safely in a cab and well away from the church that she did what she had really needed to do all morning, to somehow express the irony behind the sadness, the bitterness behind the terror.

She burst out laughing. Holding the ridiculous tickets, tears streaming down her face, she laughed and laughed.

Jonathan was frightened. He shouted at her to stop, but that only made her laugh harder. He grabbed her shoulders, held her to him.

Even so, it was a long time before this laughter, which hurt so much she could hardly stand it, at last began to die.

Chapter Ten ————— |

PATRICIA'S LAUGHTER SPREAD a coldness through Jonathan unlike anything he had ever experienced before. It was a hoarse, gasping agony. That there was no humor in it made it more awful. He couldn't bear to hear it; he wanted to quell it with a shout. But that would never do; instead he hugged her until it subsided to moans, then to soft breathing.

They had to go to Tommy Farrell's Backroom for breakfast with the Holy Name Society. Forget Trianon.

"I'm not going," she said. She waved the letter of invitation they had given her with the tickets.

Suddenly she planted her lips on his and gave him a hard, stunningly intimate kiss. There was something lovely in it, full as it was of sudden, innocent passion. "Let's take a detour," she said. "Go to my apartment."

"We have an invitation."

"They'll wait half an hour! Driver, go to Twelve Hundred Metro Avenue!"

Jonathan did not protest. Even more than his love, he wanted to be alone with her for her own well-being. She had been close to hysteria in that church.

She kissed him again, and when he felt the gentleness of it a joy of great proportions appeared in his soul. No matter what happens, we have each other. Nothing can ever crush this love.

"We have each other, darling."

"Yes, Jonathan."

He had heard that word spoken another way. *Yesssss.*

He looked deep into her eyes. Terror flickered there, and sorrow, and something immense and strange and cold. The bitter fear in the church. The hard first kiss.

How much sanity did she have left? Her composure was growing threadbare. It occurred to him he could, just possibly, help her in his lab. With him at the controls of his equipment there would be no need for the unpredictable 6-6-6.

If he couldn't find out what *he* had forgotten about that night, perhaps she would be more accessible. At least then she would no longer fear the unknown.

He looked at her, his heart pounding with love. If it was me. *If it was me!*

He did not broach the subject of the lab at once. Instead he waited until they were in the apartment. They lay quietly together, still fully dressed, on her bed.

"I could find out what you're hiding from yourself," he murmured. "Oh?"

"In my lab. I really think I could."

"Don't talk about it now. Anyway, if that police hypnotist—"

"Primitive techniques."

"I thought you were out of school for the summer."

"I can always use the lab. The equipment's just sitting there."

"As long as I'm agreeable."

"Not much chance of that, right?"

"Oh, come on, Jonathan! I'm nothing if not agreeable. I'll smile cheerfully during that breakfast. Go humbly to Lourdes. And don't think I won't let you study my head. In the end I probably will."

"Good. We can go this afternoon."

"No, please, darling. I don't think I have the strength."

"Okay, I can understand that."

"But you're disappointed."

"I think if you could remember what happened, you might not suffer so much. The fear of the unknown is the worst thing."

"Maybe."

"What do you mean, maybe? What could be worse?"

She took his hands. "The known," she whispered. "The known is always worse." She rolled across the bed, touched his face. "Part of the problem is that people are trying too hard to help me. They already filled me so full of x-rays at the hospital that I practically scorched my sheets when they rolled me back to my bed. Anyway, your machine's irrelevant. They also did a CAT scan, which is the definitive brain test."

"I don't x-ray. What I do is make a model of the brain's electrical function. I'm not interested in whether or not it's damaged in some subtle way, but what part of it the thoughts are coming from. I can tell if you're remembering a dream, a reality, or even telling a lie. Believe me, no hospital can do that. Safe too, as long as I don't monkey around with drugs. I can distinguish between truth and lies better than any lie detector. Far better."

"I'm not lying. I just can't remember."

"But there are snatches. Bits and pieces that you do remember."

"I remember people shouting. I remember being lifted up. And darkness. Absolute, black darkness."

"I'll bet we could reconstruct a great deal even from those few impressions."

"Are you sure you want to?"

"Good God, of course I'm sure!"

She laughed that knife-sharp laugh once again. "You mad scientists will stop at nothing to convince a subject. Next thing I know you'll be saying you can cure my legs."

"I won't say that. But I won't say it's out of the question either. If I could find out what's wrong—"

"Nothing is wrong! Oh, hell, Jonathan, Mike and the Holy Namers are right. It's between me and the Blessed Virgin now. Lourdes is probably where I *belong.*"

"Then I demand equal time for science. Let me do a thought-source map."

She frowned. Then she smiled. "I told you I'd give in. One of these days. But there are lots of other Good Samaritans in line ahead of you." The smile became too brilliant. "Holy Name breakfast, here I come. Marvelous! Rubber eggs? Love 'em!"

It hurt terribly to hear her pain. He enfolded her in his arms, and they wept a little together. Finally Jonathan spoke again. "It's a beautiful morning, my love. Let's do our best with it."

"I think that's a wonderful idea, Jonathan." She clutched at him. He kissed her.

"I love you, Patricia. I want to make love to you." At the sound of his own words his heart started beating harder. He was amazed at himself, and at the stunning intensity of the need that had burst forth in him as soon as he spoke.

"Don't you want to get to the breakfast on time?" Her eyes actually twinkled.

"The hell with the breakfast." He tried to kiss her lips again but this time got her cheek.

"Mike'll give you a hard time if I don't show up."

"I can handle Mike."

"You're sure?"

"Darling, I don't know how to ask this. I mean, is it safe and all for you to do it?"

"It ought to be," she whispered, "if you're gentle."

There had been a moment once before, in this same bedroom, just as they had embraced on this same cheerful yellow coverlet, when—

The hand of his fear clutched at his throat, constricted it, dried it to ash.

But she took his face in her hands and gazed at him. "We have to some time, Jonathan."

He dared not express his own fear when hers tormented her so. He hugged her.

Perhaps she sensed some of that fear, though, because she spoke in a tone of reassurance. "It's going to be wonderful, darling. Just enjoy yourself. Don't be worried. The doctor said I could do anything I wanted." She unsnapped his belt and opened his zipper.

Through the delicious film of his excitement he sensed something dark and slick and dangerous to them both.

The serpent was sensitive to these things; the serpent could smell passion.

She poised her hand above the shaft of his penis, then began stroking it. "Oh, it feels almost like silk." She touched the gleaming tip of it. "I thought it would be like a bone or something."

The serpent was uncoiling in Jonathan. Is love also death? Am I death?

No. Now whose fears are running away with him? You are a perfectly normal man. Your perfectly ordinary love is not deadly.

He could tear her throat out with his teeth.

She regarded him. "You're like an angel with the genitals of an ape." She giggled. He watched her through a haze of pleasure and growing horror. With trembling hands he reached around her neck and undid her blouse. Then came the bra, then the skirt and the panties.

Her flesh, so perfect, so rich and full and young that it almost left him breathless, glowed in the soft bedroom light. There was only a small scar, bright red, coming up halfway to her navel from her mound of Venus.

"Now you've seen the defect."

"I think you are the most beautiful human being I have ever seen." He touched her full and perfect breasts. He was awed.

"Can you stand my scar? Oh, say you can!" In answer he finished undressing himself, straddled her, bent forward and began kissing her breasts each in turn, tasting the faint saltiness of her skin, touching her nipples with his tongue until they were fully engorged.

Inside him the serpent slithered quickly forth, sweeping the coils of its hatred into his mind, bit by bit possessing him.

He fumbled down below and she took his shaft again and guided it in. The sensation was stunning. For a moment he simply sank down on her, unable to move. It was as if the whole lower half of his body had become a blazing comet of pure excitement.

Then the serpent opened a door in his mind. He looked around himself with new eyes, at the blowing curtains, the partly opened closet, the radiant, pleasuring face beneath his own. He thrust.

"Ouch. Too rough."

"Sorry." His own voice was a rumble. He was scared; he had wanted to thrust even harder. He saw that scar opening again, only wider this time. He wanted to laugh, to scream with derisive laughter.

"Uh oh. Jonathan, this isn't going to work." He thrust again. "Hey, I'm sensitive. Take it easy." The pleasure had gone out of her face, replaced by apprehension. Tears were starting in her eyes.

He strove against himself, fighting the next and harder thrust with all the force he had in him. Finally, trembling, battling his own raging instincts, he drew himself free.

There was silence between them. Then, slowly, bravely, she smiled. "It's a little too soon for the heavy stuff, darling. But just to make it up to you I'd like to do something I've always fantasized about. Okay?"

He managed to speak. "Maybe we'd better call it off. Wait a while longer."

"There's something I could do—oh, I'm such a silly I can't even get up the nerve to say it!" She swallowed. "Here goes." She turned to him, pressed her lips against his ear. *"Soixante-neuf."*

"What?"

"You know. Sixty-nine." A blush flared on her cheeks. Without a further word, praying that the lesser acts of the bedroom would be ignored by his demon, Jonathan knelt above her, then bent forward. As he moved his lips upon her richly dampened and sharp-scented vagina, he felt her take his penis.

He thrust a little and heard her choke. He knew that even in this was terrible danger. The serpent was fully awake now, crawling about in his unconscious, seeking access to his outer being.

She tasted wonderful; he had never known that such a flavor existed. His own sexual contacts before had been limited to the frantic couplings of adolescence.

She was sucking and licking him, bringing him very rapidly to completion. But the snake was quick. The snake was going to get out, he knew it was. What anger he felt, and what glee. Suddenly her back arched and the rhythm of her own efforts was interrupted. Then her fingers clutched his buttocks, instinctively sought the intimate area there.

That did it. He simply exploded into her mouth. She jerked her head back, then, in an instant, had disengaged from him. She laughed aloud.

"I'm sorry. I hope I didn't—"

"You were lovely."

Yes. I was lovely. One more moment and I would have been ugly beyond belief.

You poor, deluded girl. Beware who you love.

Chapter Eleven

FARRELL'S, WITH ITS red vinyl booths and its Formica bar and its smell of Sunday bacon and eggs, made Jonathan feel the small relief of being in a friendly place.

In the ultimate moment of his pleasure he had seen something within himself so dark and alien that it seemed scarcely human at all. He could only hope that the serpent was an aftereffect of the drug he had taken, and that it would wear off.

He had wanted to *thrust.* Such movement taken to a level of almost superhuman violence had been what had caused Patricia's greatest injuries.

Superhuman violence.

Tommy himself opened the door to the famous Backroom. Jonathan wheeled Patricia in. Inwardly he was desperate. How could he dare to love her? How could he help it? Now that he had seen the true miracle of her beauty and tasted her secret essence, she seemed invested with magical light, as if a goddess.

Would he kill a goddess?

Lately he had been retreating to a fantasy of another life, very different from this one. They shared it in peace and privacy and love.

I want her. Even the wheelchair—it doesn't concern me. I want her so much.

Image of the snake: the shadow in the deep, rising to movement above.

His fantasy was of a house on the Pacific coast of Mexico—not Puerto Vallarta or one of those tourist traps, but some exotic and hidden village where you could rent an old villa. They'd have a pool overlooking the Pacific, and from poolside you'd see yachts and sailboats in the near water, and maybe a cruise ship sparkling on the horizon.

He had a running dream of what they'd do there. She'd want the sun, he'd want sex. He figured they could make love three or four times a day at least. She'd laugh, she'd ask him if he ever got tired. They'd bake a while in the sun, then go into the air-conditioned bedroom and make love and her skin would taste of sun and coconut oil, and then maybe they'd drink a while by the pool. . . .

Not a very uncommon fantasy. Just an everyday man's dream. No serpents.

He was jarred from his fantasy by the reality of the room they had entered. Farrell's Backroom was a fluorescent bedlam. Along one wall was a bar covered in wood-grained shelf paper. Behind it was a massive mirror completely outlined in blue fluorescent tubing, with a red Farrell's sign in the middle. The ceiling was outlined in more blue tubing, as were the mirrors around the walls. There were round tables with black tablecloths and red napkins on them, and a bandstand that, thank whatever saint presided over the suppression of bad music, was empty of everything except a massive red fluorescent F on the wall behind it. The room went zzzt! zzzt! zzz—zzzt! and the gray-green specters that were Mike and Mary and friends looked as if their blood had been replaced by phlegm.

Mike turned, gave Jonathan a look that said, all right, so it's ludicrous, then went back to the conversation he was having with Mary and Lieutenant Maxwell.

"You've obviously never had the pleasure of coming here," Patricia said acidly. "I love what it does to makeup." The women looked like they were wearing wax masks. Their eyes were glittering holes.

"When were you here?"

"The bank had a celebration Friday. I went back to work, remember?" Her voice was dry.

"A celebration? How touching."

"Very."

A waiter began laying out trays of steam-table eggs and sausages.

Mike came forward, leaned down to Patricia, and kissed her forehead. "Honey, I hope you aren't too upset about this Lourdes thing. I know it's—what's the word—"

Jonathan supplied it. "Mawkish."

"That sure as hell isn't it. Nothing to do with birds. Anyway, it's a little hokey—but Mary suggested it to me and she and Maxwell kind of got things rolling and all of a sudden—well, hell, we're on our way. I put in a word for Miami Beach but nobody would listen."

"Hey, Father," Lieutenant Maxwell called to the silent, watching form of Father Goodwin, "how about saying grace so we can dig in?"

Father made the sign of the cross. "Bless us, O Lord, and these Thy gifts which we are about to receive from Thy bounty through Christ Our Lord. Amen." Catholic grace at least was quick.

"Stay right where you are," Mike said to Patricia and Jonathan. "Let me get your plates. I'm sure after all the hard work you've done this morning you're starving. I'll pile 'em high."

"He noticed we're late," Patricia said.

"Well, he's right about one thing. I *am* hungry."

She squeezed his hand. Mike came back and arranged the plates on their table. The three of them seemed to form a separate unit inside the little group. Mary spent time with Father Goodwin; Lieutenant Maxwell and Doctor Gottlieb sat together near the empty bandstand. Jonathan felt comfortable with Patricia and Mike. They were at ease together, the three of them.

Jonathan watched Mike. He was just another rumpled cop, a little tougher-looking than most, until you met his eyes. Then you were shocked. In those eyes was as deeply felt a human being as you were likely to encounter. No saint, though. In fact, sometimes a sonofabitch. Totally lacking in perspective. Either you could do no wrong by Mike Banion or he treated you as a cross between a sewer rat and a cigar butt. But if he loved you, he was mad about you. As he was about Jonathan, and had become about Patricia. Jonathan's eyes went to her, sitting so stiffly in her chair, a party smile on her face. You'd never guess what she'd been doing half an hour ago.

Once or twice right after Jonathan had been told of the paralysis he had awakened in the middle of the night and sweated out what it was going to be like with her, wondering if she would be ruined.

"I want you to break away and come over to the office after this," Mike said. "I've gotta tell you something."

He whispered this to Jonathan as one might to the parent of a sensitive child. "About the case?" Jonathan replied.

"Yeah."

"She's not up to it."

"That's what your mother and Gottlieb said. That's what Max said."

"What're you two whispering about?" Patricia asked.

"I've got a lead. I've got to talk to you about it over at my office."

She ate her toast delicately, her lap spread with a napkin to catch the crumbs. "Look at it this way, Mike," she told him. "I can't break because I'm already broken. So you can feel free to tell me anything."

Mike reached toward her as if she were toppling out of her chair. His hands stopped, poised above the table. "We've got what may be a major lead. And a problem. I want you to know in advance it's gonna upset you."

Mary Banion was staring at them. She disengaged herself from Father Goodwin and came over to the table. "Father is ready to bless our pilgrim, Mike," she said, loudly enough for everybody in the room to hear. The priest reddened and stumbled to his feet. He always fell all over himself when Jonathan's mother noticed him. It amused Jonathan to see how the man blushed. When she idly touched his wrist—as she often did when she talked to people—his eyes followed her fingers with frank avidity. In his daydreams it surely was not his wrist she touched.

Father Goodwin came to the center of the room and faced Patricia. His cheeks were flushed. The lighting made his skin appear mauve.

"I bless you in the name of the Father and the Son and the Holy Spirit. Go in peace. And may your journey to that holy place of God's strength and curing be made easy by the intercession of blessed Saint Christopher, patron saint of travelers."

"Patricia, I want to add my personal blessing," Mike said. "To help you out over there, I thought you'd need someone who speaks French, so I'm going along."

"The whole family's going," Mary added hastily.

"We leave on August fourteenth," Father said. "So far there are fifty-five pilgrims, bless their souls."

The sick, the pious, the crazy.

"Perhaps you're interested in the history of the pilgrimage," Father continued. "I got this material from the Chancery yesterday." He handed around a brochure entitled "Queens County Pilgrimage to the Shrine of Our Lady at Lourdes."

Fifty-seven consecutive years except during wartime.

Oldest pilgrim, Miss Mae Pztskowski, ninety-four, a traveler for eighteen years.

Sponsored by the Diocese.

Managed by Catholic Travel, Inc., in business since 1947.

Comfortable SkySaver Airlines Jetliner with facilities for The Sick. (Capitals theirs.)

Package price complete, including all transfers, lodging, and, God help us, meals. Special diets accommodated.

Five days and four nights in the idyllic and holy town of Lourdes, one of the most scenic in the Pyrenees district. Accommodations at the first-class Gethsemane Hotel, a short walk from the grotto.

Price: $999.95.

When he saw the surprising avidity with which Patricia was examining the brochure, Jonathan felt an unwelcome twinge of pity for her.

As soon as Father finished there was a general leave-taking. Mike stayed right with Patricia and Jonathan. Maxwell joined them. Jonathan's last impression of the room was his mother's face, watching anxiously as the little entourage departed.

After Farrell's Backroom the sunlight seemed unnaturally intense.

"No cabs this time, kids. We go in my car."

"A ride in that thing is equivalent to smoking two cigars, Dad. You think she can handle it?"

"Never fall in love with a woman who can't stand cigars. Advice from the persecuted."

She maneuvered herself out of the chair and into the back seat with a certain new adroitness. "I've been practicing on the way to work," she said. "Soon I'll be able to open the door, get in, fold the chair, and pull it in behind me."

"And tip the driver? Cabbies oughtta be more help than that."

"You learn to tip any driver who'll pick you up. Cabbies stop for drunk killers with smoking pistols in their hands and paralytics, in that order."

Mike hit the steering wheel with the heels of his hands. "You get the number of any fucking hack passes you by and he will not, repeat, *will not,* drive another day in this town! I'll get the bastard revoked so fast—"

"I love you too, Mike," Patricia said hastily. She reached forward as far as she could, touched his shoulder. "But the hacks have it rough enough already."

Jonathan could have kissed his stepfather. He was one loyal man.

Nothing more was said on the way to the 112th precinct house. Mike stuck a cigar in his face but did not light it until they had arrived at his favorite no-parking zone.

Jonathan got Patricia out of the car while Mike hovered, not quite sure how to help.

As he wheeled Patricia along, Jonathan noticed the ugly tile corridors with their glaring overhead lights hidden behind wire cages. He wondered if he would ever pronounce himself guilty enough to come here as an official visitor.

The precinct house was noisy now; the post-midnight silence of the polygraph session seemed a thousand years away. Yet Jonathan remembered the sick dread, and the grinding sound of this very elevator. There was a reality of some sort waiting for him in the mysteries of this place. Here, perhaps, a devastated Mike Banion would one day book him.

Lieutenant Maxwell and an assistant were already in Mike's office. They were pulling papers out of their briefcases when Mary Banion arrived. Mike's eyes widened and he chewed his stogie. "Hi, hon," he said. "You don't need to be here."

"Lieutenant?"

"I asked her, Mike. I thought you—"

"Doesn't matter. Glad to have you, darlin'. Let's everybody pull up benches. We got a real official presentation here, thanks to Max and the Sarge." That was what he called Maxwell's delicate little assistant, apparently. Somehow, though, the Sarge's nickname fit. She looked feminine, but not one to tolerate any fooling around.

"We want to take you kids through the case," Maxwell said in his rich, anchorman voice. Obviously he had been designated speaker— Mike's token New Policeman—the kind of cop he liked to show off to Jonathan.

You wanted to shake some sense into Mike; you wanted to hug him. Jonathan wished he knew how to ask him to make his own presentation. But how could he say that they were happier hearing it from him, that they trusted him and respected him more than any of his degree-bearing underlings?

Patricia's hand slipped into Jonathan's. The gesture might as well have been spoken words, so clear was its meaning: whatever they tell us, we are one now. We are one.

In that moment Jonathan decided to ask her to marry him and damn the consequences. If it was psychotherapy he needed, he would get it. They would make a life together. They had a perfect right.

"We believe that we have identified the man primarily responsible for what happened on the night of June sixteenth." The lieutenant handed Patricia a composite drawing of a ridiculously old man. "Do you recognize him?"

"He was at the parish supper."

So it was that again. Nothing new, nothing new.

"He was the one who talked to you at the seniors supper the week before the incident. His name seems to be Franklin Apple. We aren't certain."

Jonathan's heart skipped a beat. He felt so much as if somebody were creeping up behind him that he had actively to suppress the urge to look over his shoulder. Then he realized why: the strange old man he had seen in his lab yesterday looked a little bit like that.

"He died the day we were going to question him."

Jonathan was relieved.

"We believe that he was the local leader of a large religious organization—we call it that for want of a better word—that has been operating clandestinely for some years."

Jonathan put his hand on Patricia's shoulder. He could feel her trembling. But he felt it was right that she be here just as it had been right for her to go to the church. She *had* to confront these things. That was the only way back to some kind of mental stability and a chance at happiness for them both.

Mike questioned Jonathan with his eyes. Jonathan nodded. "Go on, Max," Mike said.

"We have looked for some sort of pattern of rape in churches—boroughwide, citywide, statewide. Nothing. Your case is all but unique. What we have found is that a larger number of Catholic religious have turned up missing or dead by violent means than we would have expected. Fourteen in the past twelve years."

"I don't see the connection." Patricia's voice was soft, but Jonathan could hear the fear in it.

"Admittedly tenuous. A recent case illustrates the pattern, though. A Brother Alexander Parker of the Society of Saint Jude was found dead, apparently of accidental causes, in an apartment across the street from Holy Spirit the morning after your incident. Two strange things. First, he was living incognito. We didn't know he was a religious until we questioned his mother. Second, he had taken a reporter into his confidence."

"The reporter told me about the cult," Mike added. "Your Mr. Apple fit the description of the man he said was running it."

"And the reporter is now a missing person," Maxwell's assistant said.

"I don't know what all that means and I don't want to hear any more," Patricia said, her voice ragged.

Now Mike spoke. Quietly, almost sadly, as if this were a miserable duty. "There isn't much. Just bits and pieces. But connect the dots and you have something more than a single individual acting alone."

"Come on, Mike, get it over with! Why am I here? What do you want me to do?"

"We are assuming the surviving members of the group have the capacity to come back and finish what was left undone."

She writhed in her chair, looking desperate. Jonathan went closer to her, knelt beside the chair. "That's enough," she said in anguish. "Don't you think I know that? I mean, all those alarms and that horrible little gun and all, how could I *not* know? I can't do anything about it. If they're going to kill me, they're going to kill me." She clasped her knees. Her knuckles went white with the pressure she was exerting. "I perfectly fulfill the cliché of the helpless female."

"Honey," Mike said, "I called you here to tell you that we are going to give you protection. You're getting twenty-four-hour surveillance."

"Oh, no! I won't live like that, I won't!"

"Max, you tell her."

"You won't even know we're there. And it's just until we roll this thing up."

"Roll it up? You said you just had bits and pieces! So now you're going to roll it up?"

"We're working on it. We're getting close."

"How close?" Mary asked. "I think it would help Patricia if you would tell us all."

"We've got Holy Spirit staked out."

"Which is to say you're not close at all. And I'm supposed to remain under lock and key—being watched constantly—until you get somewhere? I'll bet you have years of work before you." Patricia shook her head. "The notion of rolling myself off a cliff keeps recurring."

Mike nodded to Maxwell, who went doggedly on.

He explained the details of how they were going to guard Patricia. They were distressing: every moment of every day somebody would be watching. Plainclothesmen most of the time, but uniformed officers in places like the bank where she was exposed to the public.

Oh, Mexico, land of fantasy! A pool, a beach, a bedroom.

Patricia's only comment after the meeting was over was that Lourdes suddenly sounded considerably more tempting. "It says it's in the Pyrenees in the brochure," she said in the cab on the way home.

"What of it?"

"Well, you can take me mountain climbing." She didn't laugh this time, and neither did he.

Chapter Twelve ———————+

JONATHAN HAD HOPED that their journey would bring them a measure of peace. Instead it only drew them deeper into their fears.

The flight itself was extremely pleasant. Jonathan was amazed to find that SkySaver Airlines had provided a beautiful L-1011 for the journey. There were a number of different pilgrimages on the plane, of which the Holy Spirit group was by far the most privileged. They occupied the first-class section, and had been pampered as if they were flying on the best of the scheduled airlines. Behind them in economy Jonathan had glimpsed seats jammed nine abreast and people eating out of bags they had brought from home, but the curtains were kept closed, so there was no need to dwell on their plight.

The Holy Spirit group was young and well dressed. Where they had come from Jonathan did not know. Father's usual parishioners were old people, mostly widows. Although the rear of the plane was jammed with stretchers, and there was even a staff doctor aboard, the Holy Spirit group had no sick.

Patricia was the only one among them with any defect or disease. The two of them sat together hand in hand for all the hours across the Atlantic. Jonathan watched the limitless waves passing below, and let himself be lulled by the sound of the plane's engines. He toyed with the rescue-instruction card, flipped through a gift catalog. They had drinks before their dinner of lobster tails, and cognac afterward.

Then he slept. Unconsciousness brought him a new and terrible dream, worse than any that had come before. Like a man struggling against a stubborn current, he fought it, and like such a man, knew his efforts were pointless.

The serpent would have its way. Jonathan must dream his dream.

He sat astride a white, undulating female body. Each shiver-sweet pulse of his hardness wounded her more. When he jerked his thighs she would scream, and when she screamed his whole being would explode with pleasure. He jerked harder and harder until she was shrieking through bloodied lips and he could feel her swooning beneath the power of his passion.

Jonathan screamed. He could not bear to look into those agonized eyes.

And yet they pleased him, and he *did* keep on.

Even as she screamed her voice faded into wind-noise. He grew cold. The wind mourned and wailed, and the wail became a whine. Jonathan realized he was awake. The pitch of the engines had changed. They were nearing Tarbes-Ossun-Lourdes Airport. He flickered his eyes open and looked at Patricia. "You were groaning," she said. "Was it a nightmare?"

He didn't want to think about it. He twined his hand in hers and settled back in the seat.

Father Goodwin began to make an attempt with his guitar, and that diverted Jonathan. The priest stood in the aisle, his needle-thin fingers worrying the strings of the beaten old instrument. "Hail Queen of Heav'n, the Ocean Star, guide to the wanderer here below . . ."

Yeah, yeah, yeah.

Father nodded and smiled encouragement at his fashionable pilgrims as the plane swam on through the lambent French evening. He raised his eyebrows, he strove for a joining of voices.

Jonathan could almost hear him thinking: Sing. Please sing. "O gentle, chaste, and spotless maid, we sinners make our prayers through thee." Sing, you beautiful zombies.

Still nothing. Father Goodwin withdrew, nodding and smiling. People had barely glanced up from their cognacs.

From the economy cabin came a renewed burst of song. Father shifted uncomfortably in his seat. All during the trip the other pilgrims had been alternately singing and saying the rosary.

Across the aisle Mike slept heavily, his mouth slack, one massive arm dangling into the aisle. Beside him Mary remained engrossed in Marnham's *Lourdes: A Modern Pilgrimage*. She was participating avidly in the family absurdity. And why not? It was an absurdity she had created. Jonathan thought of her as far too sophisticated to suggest this ludicrous journey, but she had insisted it would be good for Patricia. Perhaps she was right. At least it was a change of scene.

"What was your dream, darling?" Patricia asked.

In the past few days she had grown more and more like a wife. Usually he reveled in it; to be known intimately was a wonderful new experience for him. But he wanted to spare her the savagery of his dreams.

"Jonathan, you didn't answer me."

"I was hoping I wouldn't have to."

"You can tell me, darling."

"I don't remember."

She didn't press him but he still wished she hadn't asked. Thinking about it forced him to face the fact that there was something he could not share with her, nor even explain.

"You're shaking." She slipped an arm behind his neck. The gesture had conspiratorial quality. Her other hand she laid on his chest. She placed her lips so near his ear that they touched and tickled deliciously. "I'm here with you, Jonathan. We're safe. We're thousands of miles from any danger."

The purr of the engines dropped a couple of octaves. They were landing. A sharp bank revealed lights glowing in wrinkled valleys, and off to the east a splash of color that must be Lourdes. Soon they rocked and rumbled down the runway, coming to a halt near the gate. Next stop, God willing, was the Gethsemane Hotel and a night's rest.

Jonathan was still not sure how Patricia was going to react to being here. She might, despite all she said, be holding out some small hope of a miracle. If she was, then she would be disappointed. Mother had been insensitive to this aspect of the trip, and Jonathan had told her as much. Patricia was an ideal breeding place for forlorn hopes. She was not reconciled to that wheelchair, no matter how she acted.

"Lourdes," Patricia said as the plane stopped at the gate. "My first footstep on foreign soil." Jonathan managed a weak smile into the rich and glorious beauty of his lover's face.

She looked long at him. Patricia of the green eyes; Patricia of the madonna smile. Her lovely breasts were elusive beneath her blouse. Her curves were suggested by the folds of her dress.

So far they had only been intimate that once. Subsequent attempts to get sufficient privacy had been squelched by a friend of Patricia's, a former Our Lady nun who had needed lodging while she found a place of her own. She had moved into Patricia's living room. God willing, old Letty Cochran (formerly Sister Saint John) would be gone by the time they got back.

To make matters worse, Mother and Mike seemed to have reached a new height of sexuality. As never before Mother was seducing him. She was almost frantic. And she certainly knew how to make Mike happy. Not a night passed that Jonathan wouldn't hear her in their bedroom crying out with delight, a sound which evoked in him the most painful combination of loneliness and excitement. He would lie just across the hall, fevered, sweating, erect in the empty air.

"Do you think it all really happened?"

"What?"

"Lourdes, of course. The cures."

"Perhaps. I don't know. There's something to faith healing, that much we know. Psychological cure, like the placebo effect."

"Something *could* happen, then. That's what you're saying, since the doctors say my paralysis is psychological."

Oh, boy, here it came. How dare they bring her here just to let her get hurt like this! Mother had been irresponsible. "The odds are against it, darling."

"But not a hundred percent."

"I thought you were the one who considered this an insult to your intelligence."

"Oh, Jonathan, now that I'm here—don't you think there's just a tiny, outside, million-to-one sort of chance?"

He could have wept. "I'm afraid I'm too much the scientist to calculate odds. Psychosomatic cures are known, but they are extremely rare."

"But if I believed—if I *really* believed—maybe that would be enough?"

He wanted to say no, but that just wasn't true. "There's a remote possibility. But please don't cling to it."

She sat rigid, staring into the middle distance. Without the sound of the engines the plane was filled with the moans and coughs of the Sick in the economy section. On the flight Jonathan had worried a good bit about the possibility of contagion. Would it be possible to get one of the bizarre diseases represented back there? The Sick who came on pilgrimage were the abandoned of medicine. Hardly a common disease—except of course for the cancerous and the diabetic and the stroke victims. Among the most bizarre victims there was a case of dystonia musculorum deformans, a man of twenty-five twisted to Gordian complexity, peering through his glasses at a tattered volume of Proust.

But the Sick were far to the rear. The Holy Spirit pilgrims didn't need to trouble themselves.

"All bearers to their pickup points, please," a priest's voice called over the intercom. There was a general shuffling among the economy passengers. Soon stretchers began to go past, hauled by relatives and volunteers. The worst of the Sick, a form swathed from head to toe in white, was propelled down the aisle first. No information about this individual's disease had been forthcoming.

"There goes the corpse," Jonathan muttered to Patricia.

"Our Lady doesn't raise the dead, dope."

Just then the corpse gave out a long sigh.

"It's a miracle!"

"Shh!" Patricia's pale cheeks flushed. How painfully, delicately beautiful she was.

The complete procession of stretchers took ten minutes to pass.

At last those not under constant medical care could leave the plane. Jonathan went and got Patricia's wheelchair and they were soon on their way.

The greater part of the airport was a hodgepodge of victims and their retinues. It took an astonishing amount of effort and skill to move the truly sick, and people did not bring colds and rashes to Lourdes. Only the abandoned entered here . . . and their relatives and priests and lovers and friends. The airport resounded with a sort of low, penitent murmur. Despite all of Jonathan's negative feelings about the place, he saw at once that there was great faith here, and despite himself was moved.

His group was ushered by a woman with a clipboard into a special customs area. Here there were no crowds and no Sick. The Holy Spirit pilgrims were grouped with others like them, healthy, well-dressed people who seemed to have little relation to the struggling faithful on the other side of the ropes.

For an instant Jonathan's eyes met the cute little usherette's. She blushed and lowered her head, practically bowed. She hurried away.

"Who was that—a fan of yours?" Patricia asked.

"Never saw her before in my life."

"She acted like you were a movie star."

"Now, now, don't get jealous."

Across the rope hard-edged officials were screaming, "Customs! *Douane!*" They were searching every bag, even looking under the sheets covering the Sick.

On this side of the rope people got through instantly, with a polite smile and a perfunctory tap of the bag. Their luggage was not even checked with chalk marks. Their passports were not stamped. And the customs inspectors lowered their eyes when the Banion family passed, more like servants than officers of the law.

"No big deal," Mike said happily. "Maybe they know I'm a cop." Jonathan wasted no time rolling Patricia out to the cab station. He really wanted time alone on the way to the hotel. He managed to get one of the ungainly-looking Peugeot cabs especially customized to take wheelchairs.

Once inside silence descended between the two of them. He had an important reason to want to be alone with her. So important, in fact, that he was having a hard time saying it. He wondered how she would react when he asked her to marry him. It had been much on his mind, and he had decided to ask her here at Lourdes. Maybe the good news would soften the hurt she was going to experience when the grotto failed her.

"Gethsemane Hotel," he said to the driver. Would it afford an opportunity of privacy, or was this to be his only chance? He wasn't sure he had the nerve right now.

He had decided to dare marriage because he was convinced the serpent was a side effect of a poorly tested drug. And he intended to enter psychotherapy for his dreams. Maybe he could become exactly what he wanted to be—a good husband to the woman he loved. It seemed so simple.

Why, then, was he afraid to ask his question?

He thought of the dream of an hour ago, the sweet, dying flesh.

The driver pulled out into traffic. Jonathan watched Patricia's fingers twisting in her flat, lifeless lap. "Look," she said, "the crosses."

So those were the famous crosses of Lourdes, on the hill called Calvary just above the grotto. Beyond was the great Basilica of the Rosary and farther away the town itself, glowing with evening light, suggestions of neon shimmering in the summer haze.

Patricia smiled, and Jonathan almost sobbed. More and more he was feeling pity for her. He must not do that.

She had the softest eyes he had ever seen, so utterly without anger in them.

"I wish we could thank Mike and Mary in some way. I want to give them a present."

"Get cured."

She looked at him, surprise and confusion following one another across her face. How could he have been so brusque? Did he want to make her angry at him . . . or was there some deep, sadistic *thing* in his soul that was actually sneering at her? In a voice dull with hurt she said she had come here only to pray.

"I know, darling. I'm sorry. It didn't come out the way I intended. I guess it's just that I'm frustrated. I want the best for you, Patricia. I love you so!"

Her eyes searched him. There was perfume coming from the blond glory of her hair. He noticed the neatness of her nails, and the care she had obviously taken with her makeup. Even after the long flight Patricia appeared fresh. He felt weak and coarse and mean to pity her. She must be suffering incredibly just now.

But no, she was smiling, she was brushing away the wetness in the corners of her eyes.

"At least I could get something for Mary since all this was her idea."

"A plastic Virgin, maybe? A rosary? Or how about a Virgin-rosary combo? That would be generous."

She managed to laugh a little at that. "Don't be sarcastic, you evil man. We *have* to find something appropriate."

The basilica now loomed on the far side of the quick-flowing River Gave. The cab made a turn and passed under the railway tracks and they were abruptly in Lourdes. Jonathan noticed the driver flashing his lights at a small group of dark-suited men on the corner. The men doffed their hats. Traffic choked the streets—tour buses, taxis, private cars, trucks.

The commercial density of Lourdes was totally unexpected. Every inch of sidewalk was faced by a storefront jammed with religious kitsch. There were exuberant festoons of rosaries—brown, red, yellow, green, pink, white. Scapulars and miraculous medals were piled in mounds and pinned to cards in clumps of hundreds. Whole armies of plastic Madonnas of the Grotto disappeared into the glaring interiors of the shops. Our Lady danced and jittered in neon, praying hands

flickered into images of the Sacred Heart and back again, and cruci-
fixes were everywhere, each twisted tin Jesus identical to all the
others.

The neon banished night. This was a religious Las Vegas, where
piety and greed had twisted together like mutant chromosomes. As
the cab proceeded slowly down the street, an endless, shrill babble of
hymns from storefront loudspeakers came in through the windows
with the choking diesel exhaust and the smell of frying junk food.

Patricia had gone pale. Her hands were tightly clenched. She was
motionless, staring straight ahead. From the edges of her eyes tears
once again gleamed.

Nothing Jonathan had read had prepared him for the relentless
cynicism that had infected this city. It was almost as if the merchants
of the place were trying to mock their Catholic customers.

And what of her, bringing her broken body here in hope of cure?
This exhibition must be shattering. Jonathan would have done anything to spare her this ugliness. If only he had known, he would have
really fought the trip, made certain it didn't happen.

The plastic and the glare were nailing her to her wheelchair forever.
She sobbed, and Jonathan felt as never before her catastrophe.

The driver yanked open the cab door and drew Patricia out with
exaggerated gentleness that Jonathan took for more cynicism.
Jonathan gave him his money, adding as a tip the smallest coin in his
pocket, which the driver took with reverence. He stood on the sidewalk, his cap in his hand, smiling after them.

Jonathan became aware of the scene around them. Stretchers,
wheelchairs, frames, medical supplies, and luggage lay about on the
sidewalk. The Holy Spirit pilgrims were nowhere to be seen. Of them
only Father Goodwin remained. He was rushing back and forth between the hotel and the pilgrims, his face sweat-shiny, helping the
other priests to organize their charges.

The Gethsemane appeared to be a typical middle-grade Lourdes
hostelry, six stories of small windows, a gray stone facade. Only its top
two floors suggested any promise of decent accommodation. On floors
seven and eight the windows were large and arched. Light shone from
behind beautiful draperies. Well-dressed people could be seen coming
and going in the rooms beyond.

Mary got out of her cab and stood with Jonathan, looking upward.

They saw the silhouette of a trim little man approach one window.
Then the light behind it went out.

"Relax, Harry," Mike called to the frantic priest. "You're gonna get
a coronary."

Jonathan really noticed Father Goodwin for the first time since they
had landed. Gone was the guitar-playing priest of the airplane. This
new Father Goodwin acted like a man let down on the most dangerous street in the worst part of the Los Angeles barrio. He wasn't just
overexcited, he was in a panic. And he was looking up too, furtively,
as if he expected someone to stone him from above.

Jonathan followed one of his glances and was surprised to see that
the seventh and eighth floors were now completely dark.

Mary saw Father's consternation too, and strode over to him. There
was a whispered conversation. Father, his face gray with what was
surely shock, his eyes stricken with sorrow, spoke to the gathered
pilgrims. "We have to stay here," he said thickly. "There are no other
hotels available. Let's go in."

"He doesn't like the hotel," Mary said as she returned to the Banion
group.

"Has he been inside?" Mike asked.

"I have no idea. I think he's suffering from jet lag."

They went into the gray-tiled lobby and found a bright young
concierge behind the aged hotel desk. She wore a dingy brown dress
and greeted them with the same deference everybody had thus far
exhibited.

"Here are your keys, *Américains*. The lift is opposite the restaurant.
As you asked, *Madame,* your rooms are on the second floor, two-oh-
two through two-twelve."

Jonathan was disappointed. He had assumed that American pilgrims routinely got the first-class accommodations, which were obviously on seven and eight. "I'd like to be higher, Mother."

"It's not safe with the chair. These places are firetraps."

Jonathan knew better than to argue with her over a matter like this.
Mother had an obsessive fear of fire.

Oddly, the elevator showed only six floors to the hotel. There
weren't even keys for the two additional floors. Once they got upstairs
it was clear that Father's intuition had been right. The "rooms" were
dormitories fitted with cots and obviously intended to sleep no fewer
than four. There were no singles or doubles; the Gethsemane hadn't

even been built that way. Mike moved his family, Patricia, and Father Goodwin into 202. This was as depressing an arrangement as Jonathan could imagine. Chances of privacy flew out the window, a crack of a thing overlooking the hotel's kitchen exhaust. Behind a frayed screen stood an ancient lavatory and toilet. On the bidet was a handmade sign, FEET ONLY, NO URINATION!

"Beautiful," Mike growled, throwing luggage down. "Thank God the Sick aren't here." For pilgrims in need of constant medical attention the Church had built Our Lady of Sorrows Hospital, which was some blocks away.

In that she did not require nursing or medication, Patricia was here rather than at the hospital. As Jonathan wheeled her across the room, thinking of his unasked question, he longed to be alone with her.

She took the wheels and went over to Mike and Mary. "I don't even mind the room," she said. "I'm so glad to be at Lourdes."

"All the plastic Jesuses—I could do without that part of it," Mike said.

"It won't be like that at the grotto," Mary assured her. She touched Patricia's face, very much more tenderly than she ever had before. "You'll see."

Mike leaned over and kissed Patricia's forehead. "You're too good, that's your problem."

Father Goodwin, who had been dashing up and down the hall in a frenzy of announcements and schedule changes, stuck his head in the door. "Soubirous tour in fifteen minutes! Those interested please gather in the lobby. The bus will pull out at *exactement* eight P.M."

"He seems to have recovered some of his *savoir-faire,*" Mary said acidly. She was behind the screen; Mike had pulled a bottle of Chivas out of his suitcase and was trying to make a drink in one of the hotel's cracked plastic cups. "No way," he said, as it leaked whiskey from at least six different holes.

"Jonathan," Patricia said, "I'd like very much to go."

"Don't," Mary called. "We can arrange a private visit tomorrow."

"I'd like to go on the tour, really I would." That was unfortunate. Jonathan's one wish was to bury himself in the two-inch foam-rubber mattress allocated to him and forget his disappointment.

"It won't be very pleasant," Mary said.

"It'll do me good to be with other pilgrims. I mean sick ones."

"I'll be glad to come, darling," Jonathan said. "But I intend to sleep through the Bernadette bit."

Mary laughed. "You two go along. But if you get tired and want to come back early, hail one of the Peugeot cabs. And make sure it's a Peugeot. They're the best."

The tour bus was huge but astonishingly flimsy, as if it might be built of cardboard. At the rear was a large double door and a pneumatic chair lift. Jonathan wheeled Patricia onto the contraption. He soon discovered, when nothing happened, that it was first necessary to pay the driver an American dollar to operate the lift.

He put the money into the kid's hand. Once inside the bus he had to move Patricia onto a seat. This was a harrowing operation, involving picking her up in his arms and carrying her down the narrow aisle from the chair-storage area in the back. She was not a small girl, and the lifelessness of her lower body made it difficult. She winced as he slid her into an empty seat.

"I'm sorry, Jonathan."

"I love you."

In answer she kissed him gently on the cheek. Behind them the lift whined again and again until there were thirty people in the bus, ten of them the Sick. Father Goodwin, who no longer seemed to have any pilgrims from his own group, was tuning his guitar.

"Uh oh," Patricia said. "More hymns."

They were soon navigating in traffic to the strains of "Dominique." Faces pressed to the windows. This was, after all, the most famous place of pilgrimage on earth. Despite the kitsch, this *was* Lourdes.

At the end of a shuddering, backfiring trip up a hill the bus came to a stop. *"Maison Paternelle,"* the driver roared. Then the clatter and confusion of disembarking began. This time it went more smoothly. Evidently the first dollar covered the whole journey.

The House of Bernadette proved to be attached to the back wall of a huge souvenir shop. Here there were even baseball caps with Aquero —as Our Lady of the Grotto was called—on their badges. Statues of Aquero rotated on little pedestals, the "Ave Maria" or the "Lourdes Hymn"—or "Lara's Theme" or even "Indian Love Call"—tinkling from music boxes in the bases. There were Dutch wooden shoes with Aquero statuettes glued to the toes.

Patricia looked slowly left and right as Jonathan propelled her down the aisle to the shrine at the rear, which looked more like a jail cell than a one-room cottage, barred to prevent its being pillaged by relic hunters.

She reached back and found his hand. "Take me out," she said. He turned her around and wheeled her back to the bus.

"Jonathan, this is awful. It's terrifying!"

"Obscene is the word. Those statues—"

"Not the souvenirs, the people behind the counters. Haven't you noticed them?"

"No, to tell you the truth."

"Jonathan, we are being carefully watched. We have been ever since we got here." She snatched his hands, glared into his eyes. "Please, let's go home right now."

"Who's watching us?"

"The girl at the airport, some of the people in the streets, everybody in the shops, even the concierge at the hotel."

"Darling, I think you're a little overwrought. Mother's right, we need to rest."

"I am not tired and I am not crazy! Everybody in this whole city— all the people who work in the stores, in the hotel, all the drivers— they are watching you and me."

"Patricia, really—"

"Don't you 'really' me. They're all watching us—staring at us. Just at us."

Jonathan had been bending over the wheelchair. When he stood up he looked right into the face of a salesman who had been standing behind a counter in the shop. The man lowered his eyes and walked away.

Jonathan found one of the Peugeots. "We'll stick close to the hotel," he said. What else could he say? She wasn't paranoid, she was absolutely right.

But why? Surely no cult was large enough to include the inhabitants of a whole town, thousands of miles from home.

Yet they were watching, even now, from sidewalks, out of shop windows.

As the cab made its way through the jammed streets Patricia's face revealed how trapped she felt. From time to time Jonathan saw her dart a glance out the window.

And the crowds, the swirling mass of eyes, looked back.

MARY: THE SHADOW OF THE INQUISITION

NOW HAS COME the night of highest peril. We will kill her or cure her. She is useless to us as she is.

We own this town—its shops, its hotels, even the spring that feeds the grotto. But the great underground river beneath the grotto is nobody's property. Alpheus, the river of life and death.

It is not like the little aboveground trickle into which Catholic pilgrims dip their infirm parts. Alpheus is wild and dark and dangerous. If it sweeps you away you are lost forever. I think it may be more than water, more than a simple trick of geology. If a demon had a body it would be very like Alpheus, a freezing torrent raging against the rock of the earth.

This week at Lourdes many of the pilgrims are our people. We have booked the best rooms, taken the best charters. Some of our Catholic customers will have to wait until next week to continue buying their kitsch and bathing themselves in one another's sweat. Yet our beloved child is in as much jeopardy here as at home. As if the Inquisition had a sort of shadow . . .

Our people have made us welcome. To them it is the highest honor to have the Prince and Princess among them. Never have two people been so well guarded.

When Gottlieb told me that her paralysis would prevent childbirth, I remember I said I wanted to die.

He is a wise man. "Concentrate on your work. Keep to the plan." How I threw myself into my work! I've arranged the worldwide vaccination program, the food supplies, all we need to see us through the coming extinction.

I even have Mike performing his allotted role. I am insisting he wear a vetiver cologne I had compounded at Keil's in Manhattan just for him. But it is more than scent. Jerry Cochran has mixed his vaccine into it. Every time Mike splashes some on, he contributes to the immunity he will some day need in order to fulfill his place in our plan.

If all goes as we intend, we will require him to remain alive some little time after the others are dead. Such a fatherly man can be put to good use.

Lately I have really been trying to seduce Mike, to make him love me as he has never loved anybody before. Frankly, I hope we will be able to convert him.

Still, I could not bear to be with him tonight. I lay on that miserable pallet in the Catholic part of the hotel downstairs, sweating and worrying until I could bear no more; now I am here where it is risky for me to be, in the suite where a princess of the Night Church belongs, writing and writing and trying to pretend that I am not exhausted, that I do not tremble, that my hand is as firm as ever.

Stupid woman. You calm yourself by writing in your journal. Then you tear out the pages and burn them.

Outside quiet multitudes file toward the aid stations for their vaccinations. My own arm itches furiously where Jerry himself applied the needle. Lourdes is the main vaccination center for southern Europe. We will vaccinate thirty thousand faithful in the alleyways of this town before we are finished.

When the rest of the world is weakening and dying, in that time of unimaginable chaos, our Church must be stronger than ever.

As I write these words I feel the immensity and the difficulty of our task. Despite Jerry's brilliance and Franklin's great strength, I feel almost alone. The French have filled this room with flowers, have brought me a late supper of salmon trout and champagne. They are so awed by the presence of Titus blood among them that they are not able even to meet my eyes.

They must have a hard time understanding Mike, who is so obviously not of the royal lineage. The husband of a princess? Impossible!

Oh, Mike, Mike, I rise to the heavens beneath your sweating body. I hate you! I will not say the opposite, but I do feel it too. Love, damn it all. You obsess me for a very simple reason: I cannot decide *what* I feel about you, and have good reasons for all my contradictory impulses.

Two fifteen in the morning. Throughout our ancient capital our people have just begun going from the hidden vaccination stations to the basilica itself, for the great ritual cleansing. We will take our darling down under the grotto to the banks of the secret river.

She will overcome her paralysis or she will drown in it.

Are we about to kill the hopes of two thousand years?

I go now, as always, loyal to my duty. I am crying, weak woman that I am. I call to my demon fathers.

Hear me.

Chapter Thirteen

PATRICIA LAY WATCHING suggestions of movement in the shadows on the ceiling. The room was unquiet, even at three o'clock in the morning. Father Goodwin had been up and down to the bathroom half a dozen times. He was overexcited—which was to be expected, she supposed.

He snored now, his sleeping expression one of deep sadness. In the cot beside his, Mike's breathing was thick and regular, a settled hound's. Mary was gone from her cot, no doubt forced into a walk by the heat and stuffiness. Across the room lay Jonathan, and Patricia wondered if he too might be awake.

The thought brought deep stirrings. Since their half-hour in bed Jonathan had grown more and more ardent. And she had too. In her daydreams she would kiss his rigid, silken member . . . then she would banish the fantasy. Which would promptly return.

Of the two of them, though, Patricia knew that Jonathan was the more enraptured. And why not—wasn't that in the nature of the male, to have explosive passions? But how, then, could he think clearly about life with a paralyzed woman? And what if she needed more medical care? Would he accept the burden, just for love?

I want him to be as free as the wheat in the field.

Oh? The field that I dream about, where Death resides?

The scythe sighs and the Reaper sweats. He is a mad dot of death amid the growing, fruiting, bursting fertility of humanity.

Is it love I wish for, or death?

Maybe I just ought to let him make love to me again and forget the rest. Maybe that physical contact is the only real thing, and all this thinking is just a waste of time that might be better spent in pleasure.

I want to go across the room and place my lips on his lips, and press my tongue between his teeth, and love him and love him until I melt into him.

I am free to die in Jonathan, free to let the living steel of him tear me apart.

God help me, I'm frightened.

The shadows seemed to move just then with a purpose of their own.

She was conscious that Jonathan had stirred in his bed. Fingers seemed to brush her face; she was suddenly frozen with terror. This must be another nightmare. She wasn't awake, she *couldn't* be, not if she felt this afraid over so little.

Oh, he was moving—she knew he was moving.

The shadows on the ceiling were very slowly changing shape as he slipped inch by stealthy inch from his bed.

You will go with him.

"Is that you?" Her voice was like a rattle of leaves in the quiet. Mike snuffled, Father sighed.

Don't whisper so loud, you little fool!

Now I know he is on the floor. I hear his breath, hisss, hisss, hissssss, getting nearer and nearer. I see his shadow creeping.

You will go with him!

"I will go with him."

Far away someone was singing, the same few words again and again. And the wind made a deep note as it surged and flowed through the ancient streets of the town.

"Patricia?" Jonathan said softly. Oh, seductive whisperer, where have you come from?

And why do your eyes gleam so?

"You awake?"

"Mmm . . ."

"I—please—"

She knew what she had to do; slip from the bed, pull on her dress, let him carry her.

They went then through the black halls of the hotel, down the cobbled streets in the night wind, her dress hardly protecting her.

All she could think of was how his skin must taste. She was desperate, urgent to drop to her knees before him, to free the tight imprisoned purple arrow and pierce herself with it as she had in that time of beloved memory.

They moved through the night, beneath the stars and tossing trees.

We aren't in the town anymore. Where are we?

He was scary. His face was too sharp, his eyes too bright. There was fire in him, and she knew that if she tempted it too much it would kill her.

"Welcome to the domain of Our Lady," said an age-dried voice. A small, quick man moved in the dark.

You look familiar, old man.

He smiled. Behind him the massive bronze doors of the Basilica of the Rosary opened just a crack.

"Come," he said.

Can this be real?

"Don't worry, you are certainly dreaming. What do you think? You must be dreaming!" He spoke with soft intensity.

"I'm *not* dreaming."

Her own voice startled her. She touched Jonathan's face. "I'm not either, my love," he said.

She felt, though, that she must be. Of course she was; she had to be.

The old, old man beckoned frantically from the doorway. Then they were inside and Patricia was stunned by the spectacle before her.

There were candles in the vast space, candles by the thousands, points of light, crowds of points, reefs and blazing cascades. Enormous curtains covered the windows.

The ocean of candlelit pews had the just-emptied look of a place where a procession began, and to which it would return. The air smelled of hot wax and people.

At the far end of the basilica there was a stairway. Below must be the grotto. The entrance was utterly black. After the blaze of the candles it was impossible to see.

There came from the foot of the stairs the sound of water.

As they descended the murmur grew to an echoing roar. In the caverns beneath Bernadette's little stream was a mad, frothing cataract. "The headwaters of the Holy River Alpheus, where Parsifal drank of death. *Go now, and give yourself to Alpheus.*"

Give herself to Death? She clung to Jonathan.

The only light came from the phosphorescent foam. Unseen hands took Patricia, carried her forward, closer and closer to the surging water, as Jonathan rushed beside her. The water cascaded from the rocks, flooded through the chamber, then ran gurgling and complaining down the crevasse beyond.

"The river wants you," whispered the old man, and there sounded above the voice of the water a deeper, more terrible note, as of a great horn booming and booming, and with every boom the old man came a step closer to her and Jonathan.

"Take her, boy, down into the water."

"She'll drown!"

The old man's mouth moved but Patricia could not hear. At once a change came over Jonathan. He drew off his clothes. Now he was naked and his skin gleamed in the blue iridescence. He smiled a jack-o'-lantern grin.

Then she was in his arms, lying helpless against his naked flesh, and the water was coming up around her, seething and tugging and lapping, covering her midriff and her chest and her arms and then her face. Now he ceased to carry her; instead he pressed her down with his hands. She went down and down and down into the freezing, grabbing dark.

Then his strong arms were gone.

She was tumbling, dashed again and again against the rocks. The current was holding her against the bottom.

Her arms were not strong enough to resist the power of the water. Only her legs could help her and they were useless.

If inhaled, a half a cup of water is enough to kill. But she had to breathe, she *had* to inhale! A surge of agony swept her body. She tried to bring her hands to her face but it was no good; she was tumbling over and over, caught in a corner between the side and the bottom of the river.

This nightmare had to end. But how could it, when the water was so very cold and the bottom so very hard and her lungs bursting with desperate need?

God. God. God.

Her left foot scraped stone. She pushed, and for an instant the tumbling stopped. But then she was off again, worse than before. She knew that her mouth was going to open in a second and she was going to breathe, and that breath was going to be water.

Her foot connected solidly with the rough bottom, and this time she did stop tumbling. She drew her legs up under her and pressed with all her might—but how could she?—against the battering power of the backwash that held her.

She broke free.

The air was dank cave air, but it was air and it balmed her searing lungs.

She heard *hiss-whoosh! hiss-whoosh!* and saw what looked like a monstrous toad waddling toward her in the foam. Then he removed his face mask. It was a man in scuba gear.

"She's done it," he shouted over the water.

And the bone-deep note she had heard before boomed triumph.

Jonathan, naked still, came to her. Hand in hand they walked from the water. For the briefest of instants she had brushed his great hard stone of a thigh and heard him gasp and felt him stumble. She longed then to touch him more, to hold him delicately between her fingers, to spend long minutes just stroking his secret part.

Mary Banion gave them their clothes.

She walked in the darkness, between cliffs of a new sound. At first she did not know what it was, then she understood. There were throngs here, and they were clapping softly. Jonathan drew her forward. "I can't see a thing," he whispered.

"There's a glow over there. It must be from the candles upstairs."

Hand in hand they went toward the light.

As Patricia sank to deeper sleep she was aware that bells were ringing. But for the glory of those bells she dreamed no dream, sleeping on toward the forgetful dawn.

Chapter Fourteen ——————|

WHEN THE KITCHEN exhaust fan beneath the window was turned on, Patricia awoke instantly. Her sleep had been troubled; she looked at her watch. Six-thirty. Around her the others slept on.

She wished she had not dreamed she could walk. It was cruel to do that to oneself. The inner Patricia was furious with herself for the crippling, which made it hard for ordinary, everyday Patricia to get used to it.

"Good morning."

Jonathan whispered to her from his cot against the wall. Beside him Mike Banion snored softly. Father Goodwin lay twined in on himself. Mary, very still, was as pale as a lovely statue in her sleep. There was a round patch of bandage on her right arm, just below her shoulder. Patricia looked at it, reflecting idly that it was the only imperfection she had ever seen marring that perfect body. Even Mary wasn't immune to scratches and cuts.

Patricia raised her own arms, spread her hands, closed her eyes and waited a thousand eternities for Jonathan to cross the room and bend to her. "Hello," he said. "You're cool. Shouldn't you be bed-warm?"

You have dared the wild waters, and you have won.

"Jonathan, take me out of here. I want us to be alone together."

"Darling, darling." They traded a lingering kiss.

Then they dressed, he pulling jeans on over his briefs, she grappling with a skirt and blouse, working her feet into a pair of flats, running a brush a few times through her hair.

He carried her to the wheelchair. When he sat her in it she writhed. The thing had claws, it grabbed her; the chair was hungry for her body.

He wheeled her down the dim, stuffy hallway, past endless rows of little black doors with slats in them, beneath buzzing fluorescent rings, to the wide hospital-like lift. The main lobby was dark, nobody about at this hour. In front of the hotel was a still-bundled stack of French newspapers and a few copies of the *International Herald Tribune*.

He wheeled her fast, almost running down the Rue Reine-Claire. "Where are we going?"

"There's a gate at the end of the street. It leads into the Domain of Our Lady. It'll be quiet there. On the map it looks like a park."

She had seen him in the plane poring over his Michelin. "You memorized the map in hope we could slip away, didn't you?"

"Yeah. I know all the exits."

"Love you so much."

From behind her his hand caressed her cheek. They came to a little wrought-iron gate between two ancient buildings. Beyond was a muddy alley, and beyond that a widening expanse of grass.

The lawn went on for a while, then stopped abruptly at a tall hill. That must be Calvary. Behind it would be the Basilica of the Rosary. In the opposite direction to the basilica the land dropped to the river in a jumble of rocks and ferns and gnarled trees.

Jonathan made for the hill, laboring to push the chair through the thick grass.

He was so silent and purposeful. That wasn't like him. Then she understood what he must be planning.

The anticipation thrilled her to shivering dampness. She was going to be made love to, and it was going to be done by her delicious Jonathan, in the woods.

A hundred yards from the most Catholic place on earth.

Was that funny, sad, or both? Oh, hell, it wasn't sad at all! She reached her hand back. Instantly he squeezed it. Then he returned to his pushing.

"You're working up a sweat," she said.

"Doesn't matter."

They came to the line of trees and went a short distance in. This was a different world. Alien. Here the low hum of insects mixed with the petty chanted rage of birds. The light was rich green. Woods were beautiful places, but Patricia certainly saw why in ancient times the pagans had peopled them with nymphs and spirits, and humming, vindictive gods.

They stopped.

Silence.

The bugs started again, then the birds. But as far as humanity was concerned the two of them were gloriously alone.

He will lift me from the chair. I will let him have his way with me.

But he hesitated. Was he afraid? Confused? "I dreamed that I took you to the grotto and put you in the water, and you could walk."

"I dreamed I could too. I dream it a lot."

He bowed his head and kissed her hands. "I'll take you out of the chair now."

"We'll be missed if we don't get to the basilica by eight." How dare you say that, girl. Keep your mouth shut; you don't want to ruin this beautiful moment.

"It doesn't matter. Because I want to ask you to marry me. Please, as soon as we get back to New York."

He swept her from the chair and set her on the forest floor.

"You really, really do? You want to marry me?"

He lay full on her. She felt the rigid curve of his flesh, and laid her hands on his buttocks, which rippled beneath his jeans. "I'd like a child," he whispered. "If you want one."

She was full of laughter and tears and gratitude. "Oh, certainly! Surely I do! I want lots of them!"

"I've always wanted a child. I want him to be named Martin, after my dad."

Just like a man. It never even occurred to him that he might have a daughter. She didn't care, though—not now, not about such details. She hugged him to her. "I'll marry you, Jonathan. Oh, yes, yes, I will!"

"I want it so badly, darling. Soon. How soon can it be?"

"Next week, if we can get a dispensation on the banns. We can ask Father."

From sheer delight in each other they laughed softly, in the twilight of the woods. When he began to lift her skirt, she stopped him. "Wait. I have to say something."

"No more delays. I won't stand for it." He kept at it.

"I have to say yes! Yes, yes, yes!" In moments she was naked, her clothes beneath her body. He lay beside her running his hands over her. "You have goosebumps."

"It's cold."

"Am I cold?"

His hands were like fire where they touched her. He seemed wire-tense. "The ground is cold. You're warm." She arched her back. "Touch me more," she whispered, feeling her cheeks go livid. She presented her breasts to him; the grass beneath her whispered when she opened her legs. "Touch me all you want."

He laid a hand on her midriff, so roughly that she gasped. "I wish I hadn't dreamed you could walk."

Oh, God, don't let him start worrying about that the second he asks me to marry him.

"Forget it, it's no big deal. I dreamed the same thing." The water had bellowed and foamed up out of the ground, a fantastic living organism, as far from normal water as a demon is from some placid human soul. *I will kill or I will heal,* the water had said. *It is all the same to me.*

"In my dream they called the river—"

"Alpheus. The river of death."

His hand froze on her thigh, clutching. They looked into one an-other's eyes. She moved slightly. He was hurting her just a little. "After I could walk, they rang the bells."

"I remember the bells." He fell silent. When he spoke again his voice was almost sullen. "What in the name of God is happening? We had exactly the same dream."

Words, thoughts, questions crowded through her mind. "But Jonathan, I can't walk! So nothing's happening except that we're getting very, very close to one another."

"You haven't tried to walk." He pinched her hard just above her knee. It hurt; she jerked away.

"You have sensation!"

He stood up, held his hands down to her. She grasped his strong fingers and pulled herself to her feet. For an instant her legs were stiff and she thought she was going to totter. His face reflected awe and utter amazement. "As crazy as it sounds, we dreamed this together. And you really can walk. You *can!*"

"Don't let go!" She lifted her left foot, put it down in front of her. He backed up, released her hands. "Don't do that!" But he backed away farther and farther, until at last just their fingertips were touch-ing. Then she was grasping air.

And walking. She had the delicate, unsteady gait of a new foal, but she was walking. She could feel everything from her toes to her thighs, just as she always had before the incident.

Jonathan rushed up to her and embraced her and covered her face with kisses. "Patricia, my darling, God bless whatever happened last night, God bless it!" He held her at arm's length. "You are so incredibly beautiful. Oh, you are so, so wonderful!" He hugged her; he was laughing and crying at the same time. His hands ran up and down her back and he kept kissing her. Finally he went down on his knees and embraced her around the waist. She stroked his head, then knelt down with him. Their bodies made a little warm tent in the forest cool. He drew off his T-shirt and unbuckled his belt. "Shall I?"

In answer she unzipped him and drew his pants down around his knees. She laid her hands on him. He closed his eyes, sank back on his haunches. Around them the forest sighed with morning wind. Sunlight filtered through the trees. From far away came the sound of a multitude singing. It was the Lourdes hymn; people were gathering at the basilica.

He was warm and solid to hold, and his skin had that velvet-soft feeling she remembered. He raised his own hands to her breasts, cupped them gently, then rubbed his palms against them. The sensation was so strong and so fine that it made her feel pride in her own ability to experience pleasure. She smiled, and he leaned forward and kissed the smile.

They lay down together in the grass. She spread her legs for him and he tried to enter her. He was not very practiced either. In the end she had to guide him. But she was too tight. That scared her; were they going to fail?

He lay full down on her. "If you would kiss it like last time," he whispered, "we could make it work, I think."

Yes, it had to be made damp. People were so delicately constructed.

She didn't mind. Far from it, the thought of what she was about to do fascinated her. She recognized in herself a desire to surrender to him that was very, very great. If he had been a coarser or a more cunning man he might have found a way to make her his slave.

She knelt between his legs and lifted his penis; the end was gleaming as if it had been waxed. This she took in her mouth. It pulsed once, then plunged deep. It hurt. For a full minute and more she kept it there. The sensation of being filled by it was not terrible; indeed, she had discovered pleasure in this the first time she had done it.

Like a white-hot knife it tore into you. It filled you with searing, molten lava and it ripped you until you thought you would die of the pain.

He withdrew himself. He was shaking. In Jonathan passion and fury looked startlingly alike. "That's enough! Let me calm down." He took sharp, frantic breaths. He glared at her. Then he sighed and closed his eyes. After a short pause he asked to try again.

In answer she rolled over beside him and spread her legs. This time he slipped in much more easily. He groaned once, then they were linked.

A thousand lonely Our Lady nights: how will it feel? They say the first time hurts, but you mustn't let him know that. They say it's literally like an explosion in you. A million, zillion times better than diddling with the corner of a pillow.

A million, zillion times better. She could have believed that the entire universe had reordered itself around these two people making love.

There were waves of pleasure connected with even his slightest movements. They swarmed one after another, faster and faster, rushing up from the center of her belly until they suffused her whole body and seemed to enter her very soul. She could hardly bear it. She clamped her hands to her temple, she shouted, she kissed his face, his neck, his shoulders, she licked his skin almost frantically, and she looked into his hungry, avid, raging eyes. She felt at the same time both laughter and sadness, the whole game and tragedy of life all knotted up together and then bursting into a huge, impossible ecstasy that was also hideous, a sharp joy that made her cry out.

And then she was aware of a bumblebee worrying a small blue flower near their heads.

He drew himself out of her.

"Stay in me."

"Oh, my darling." In his voice was love and joy . . . and something like relief. He laid his open mouth on hers. She thought perhaps they had become song. Were they still just two ordinary people? Could they possibly be?

The bumblebee finished its work with the flower and bumbled on. From the basilica came the deep murmur of thousands of voices saying the rosary.

Suddenly Jonathan reared back. His face was almost bursting with happiness. "This is the greatest moment of my life!"

"Of mine too. By far, far, far."

He fell to kissing her again. It was after nine before they even thought of dressing. Jonathan insisted he could make love again if she wanted him to.

"We have to get back. We really will be missed."

He laughed silently. "You can walk! Can you imagine the irony of it —you go to Lourdes and you get cured. It's almost a kind of cosmic joke. I mean, *you* don't want to go, *I* don't want you to go. Not even good old *Mike* really wants you to. Then you go and cure yourself with some kind of a crazy dream."

"Is that what happened last night?"

He looked at her. Slowly he shook his head. "We dreamed the same dream. I put you in the water and you came up cured."

"It scared me. I thought I'd drown."

He grabbed her tight against him. "The very last thing in the world I would ever, ever do is hurt you."

"The water was so loud. It was like a cataract or something, just literally gushing out of the ground."

"She told me it was the river of death."

"She?"

"My mother. While you were in the water."

"It *wasn't* a dream, was it?"

"Don't ask me what it was, darling, because I don't know the answer. I just know that whatever it was, it broke the psychological barrier that was forcing you to seek dependence."

"I was really paralyzed, Jonathan! Don't say it was psychological."

He hugged her. "Let's walk over to the basilica. I think you're going to cause quite a sensation among certain people. For one thing, you are going to make Mike a very happy man."

They dressed and brushed one another's clothes free of loam and bits of fern, and walked out into the calm, warm sun. How good it felt to move again under her own power! It also hurt; this was more exercise than her legs had gotten in three months.

They laid their arms along the small of one another's backs and walked across the green sweep of grass that led up to the basilica. As they came closer, mounting the low hill, the voice of the multitude in the forecourt of the church washed over them.

Sing of Mary pure and lowly,
Virgin Mother undefiled.
Sing of God's own Son most holy
Who became her little child.

Then Jonathan lifted her onto the low wall that separated the court from the greensward beyond. There gathered a multitude of sick and well, crutches, wheelchairs, stretchers, people old and new, priests gathered in little black clumps, nuns in and out of habit, all the huge crowd of the world come to supplicate at the dirty, trickling water of life.

She sat down on the wall and wept for them even while her body sang its reborn power. Her lover hugged her to him, and she heard his ragged breath.

Neither Mecca nor the raped Ganges could equal Lourdes in sheer numbers of pilgrims.

Patricia felt the roiling, frantic living *thing* beneath the ground, the serpent River Alpheus crying out through the stones.

"There's my mother. She sees us. Oh, boy, this is going to be something!"

Mary Banion broke away from the crowd. Turning, her face was struck by the sun and she shielded her eyes. Then, splendid in a navy blue dress, holding down her white straw hat, she came quickly to their side. Despite the sweltering August heat, she wore an autumn dress with long sleeves.

Most of the other pilgrims wore long sleeves too, Patricia noticed. Mike alone was dressed for the weather, in a short-sleeved sports shirt. "Come down off that wall, Pat. Oh, I wish they would stop that caterwauling!"

As if she had commanded them all, the crowd fell silent.

Patricia's legs ached a good deal from the walk. Mary and Jonathan had to help her down. She stood leaning against the low wall.

"Mother," Jonathan said, "she's cured."

Mary hugged her. "I knew you would be, Pat! I had my heart set on it!"

Mike was coming closer, his expression one of purest astonishment. "Don't look now, but here comes Dad."

He came rushing up to them, followed closely by the tall form of Father Goodwin, flapping like a huge old buzzard, his face gleaming with perspiration and excited tears. "Sometimes it happens at the exposure of the Blessed Sacrament! Is that when it happened?"

Mary answered. "That's when it happened. Just a few minutes ago."

Patricia recalled that the Blessed Sacrament was carried out in procession morning and evening. All the singing must have signified the morning exposure. But the miracle had happened during the night. "Mary—" Mary's hand squeezed hers.

She saw a small, very old man watching them from the fringe of the mob.

In the crowd there were at least as many of those strangely attentive faces as she had seen on the Bernadette tour. More, in fact. Practically everybody.

When she looked directly at the old man, it was as if the light went out of the sun and the warmth left the air. He turned quickly away and was lost in the crowd.

Mr. Apple is dead, isn't he?

Mike Banion's muscular arms came around her, and she let him hug her against his damp shirt. "Glory be!"

"Thank you, Mike, and thank the Holy Namers." She was playing a part, and she knew it, but that somehow did not stop her.

"Thanks be to God," Mary added.

Father Goodwin bowed his head. The great copper doors opened and the crowd began filing into the basilica, eager to touch their wounds and agonies to the waters.

Patricia rested her head against Mike's shoulder. Jonathan joined the embrace and the three of them stood together—three common, ordinary people against the dark, the unknown, the mysteries of the night.

She wished that she could shake the feeling of dread that had been with her all these weeks. But she could not. In fact, day by day and hour by hour it was increasing.

For heaven's sake, she had been *cured!* Shouldn't she rejoice?

---

8 AUGUST 1983

MOST PRIVATE

To: The Prefect of the Sacred Congregation for the Defense of the Faith

From: The Chancellor for the Inquiry in North America

Your Eminence:

It is with deepest regret that I inform you that Sister Marie-Louise has refused her commission. When the death of Terence Quist was added to that of Brother Alexander and I could not even guarantee the loyalty of the parish priest, Sister concluded that the risk of penetrating this congregation was too high.

Theoretically, Sister is correct, but the importance of the present mission is so great that I must ask you to use your good offices with the worldwide body, and find me a warrior-priest of the old school, who will brave anything for love of Him.

If you wish to reach Sister, she will be at the Esalen Institute in California for the next two weeks, "getting her head back together," as she so aptly put it.

In addition, Sister demanded that we turn over our files on the disease vector to the secular authorities for proper action. I do not yet wish to do this. Until we are utterly and completely defeated, we must not risk the damage to Holy Faith that revelation of our existence would cause.

Your Grace, our one and only alternative remains to neutralize the bearers of the blood.

Please send me a good man! May God have mercy on us all.

> Yours in Christ & for the Defense of the Faith,
> Brian Conlon (Msgr.)

Document Class: Urgent A, most private, Swiss Guards courier

Destination: Paolo Cardinal Impelliteri, the Hidden Collegium, Prefecturate for the Defense of the Faith, Vatican City

12 AUGUSTUS 1983
FURTIVISSIMUS

Ad: *Cancellarius Inquisitionis in Septentrionalis Americanensis*

Ex: *Prefectus Congregationis Defensioni Fidei*

We are vexed, Monsignor. If you cannot command the loyalty of your own religious, I fail to perceive any reason for you to continue in your post. Cells destroyed, martyrdoms, Inquisitors going to the Esalen Institute? What can be the matter over there?

You impress upon me in the same letter both your own personal helplessness and the urgency of the situation. I should remove you, but I cannot afford to spend time training a new man at such a tense moment.

Monsignor, I order you to go in yourself. *Work* on that parish priest, Goodwin. Enlist his help if you can.

At all costs, the *monstrum* and his mate must be rendered impotent. We simply cannot afford to face the chance of their birthing the so-called anti-man. Do what is needed in this regard, bearing our previous correspondence in mind. It has taken two thousand years of breeding to produce those two. In two brave seconds the threat can be removed.

So I charge you: For Christ and Holy Faith, find your courage. You have done brave things in the past, Brian. You always knew that your work might expose you to the threat of martyrdom.

Accept the cup Our Lord gives into your hand. Remember His passion in the Garden of Gethsemane. Brian, I cannot compel you. But I offer my prayers for you in this difficult hour.

Bless you, my son. You yourself must be our *Oppugnatio*.

> *Mea Auctoritate,*
> Paolo Cardinalis Impelliteri

Document Class: Urgent A, destroy in presence of courier

Destination: Monsignor Brian Conlon, Chancellor for the Inquiry, North America, 1217 Fuller Brush Building, 221 E. 57th Street, New York, N.Y., 10022

Chapter Fifteen ————|——

THE LIGHT OF evening lifted from hot Queens streets. Far below the windows of the apartment a bus roared, accelerating away down Metropolitan Avenue. Jonathan wished he and Patricia were on it.

They had spent time very carefully comparing the dreams they had experienced on the night of the cure.

They were complementary in every detail, so much so that Jonathan was forced to conclude they had *not* dreamed, but in fact had undergone some sort of actual experience.

The two of them were at the edge of the unknown. Jonathan wanted to get everything out in the open, unlock the secrets and damn the consequences. But how do you confront something you do not understand, which seems like a nightmare but has stunning consequences in real life?

The cure.

"Farfetched," Mike had said when Jonathan had told him about the complementary dreams. "Coincidence. And if the cult were big enough to include Lourdes there'd be a lot of people involved. There'd be leaks, and there aren't any. I'm looking for a group that starts and stops right here in Queens. Big enough to be mean as hell, which they obviously are, but small enough to stay well hidden. And as for the cure, just accept it. Thank the good Lord it happened."

Nightmares. Cleansing rivers. Cures. Jonathan accepted nothing, not even the way they had been scrutinized in the streets of Lourdes. That Mike brushed off. "The place is full of Frenchmen," seemed to him to be enough of an explanation.

But after listening to Jonathan's story on the way home in the plane, Mike had fallen silent, had stared a long time into the distance, had finally given them both reassuring pats and told them to relax.

Now he almost haunted them; he was either with them himself or some of his men were in evidence. The protective net around them had been strengthened.

"Patricia," Mike said around an unlit cigar, "aren't you hot?" She was sitting on the couch, her arms lying along the back, blond hair clinging to her forehead. "If you'd turn on the air conditioner we could close the windows." He dabbed a handkerchief along his neckline.

"It's worse than this with it on," Patricia replied. "Too humid. The coils freeze up."

"That what the super tells you? Bullshit! The thing's been tampered with. They don't wanna pay the bill. 'Effing landlords. S'cuse me."

Music blared up from a passing car. Jonathan went to the window to see a white Lincoln convertible pause at the light, the top down, the seats filled with expensively dressed, reveling blacks. WPLJ. Silk chinos. White dust in tiny cellophane bags.

Behind him Mike breathed heavily, it seemed painfully. He stared at them out of stricken eyes.

"Have you changed your mind, Dad? Do you think this thing might actually be bigger than Queens? Is that why you hang around all the time?"

"Come on, Johnny boy, let it rest." Jonathan could hear him chewing at the cigar. On the couch Patricia stirred. She had a bowl of ice water, and she began dabbing her face with a washcloth.

"I want to know. You come here and you stare. What the hell for?"

Mike did not reply. Patricia went over to the window. "He doesn't know why he's here, do you, Mike?"

At last he cut his cigar and lit up. "I'll tell you," he said around it. "I'm here because I'm here. It doesn't hurt to be cautious."

"We're all overtired from the trip and the heat, Dad. Maybe a good night's sleep—"

"Screw that, Johnny. I was trying to reassure you two by softpedaling your stories about France. But there's no use in it. You're obviously not buying it. I might as well admit I think this thing is big. Very big. Somethin' was going on over there. You're not crazy, neither am I. Right? That *is* right, isn't it?"

"Of course it's right," Jonathan replied.

Patricia put her hand out, tried to touch Mike's shoulder. He recoiled, then looked at the hand. "I mean, were you paralyzed or weren't you? Was it some kind of a joke or what the hell was it?"

"Mike, I was paralyzed! Oh, I was certainly that!"

"Okay. I'm sorry." He shook his head, then rummaged in the top pocket of his suit, drawing out a sheaf of thin paper. Third copies of some kind of police report, Jonathan saw. "This is a return on the surveillance of Holy Spirit Church over the past three weeks." He opened it. "The goddamn thing is clear."

"They moved to another church."

Mike smiled slightly. "Why should they do that? I'm beginning to think the three of us are the only people any of us know who *aren't* in on this thing. Your guards are now from the 107th, not the 112th," he added with venom in his voice. "Maybe it's safer that way."

Jonathan heard the rage in him. No wonder Mike was scared. He was saying he felt he could no longer trust his own men. "You want some gin, Dad?"

He stared, wordless, his papers on his lap. Patricia went to the kitchen and brought back glasses of ice. She made three healthy gin and tonics.

Mike smiled. "Seein' you walk, darlin'—oh, Christ, I get soupy. I'm gonna be such a sentimental old fart one of these days." He sipped the drink she gave him. "When you two went out the night before the cure, where did you go?"

Patricia's eyes widened. "You're definitely sure we did go out?"

"Not only you. Mary was gone when you woke me up leaving. Frankly I thought you two had personal business that was none of mine so I stayed in bed. Where did you go?"

"I told you on the plane I thought we were dreaming." Jonathan's mouth was so dry he had to sip his drink before he could speak.

"You weren't. You really went out, both of you. Surely you remember carrying her."

"This is definite confirmation," Jonathan said, almost hating to hear the words. "Why didn't you say this before? Why did you doubt me on the plane?"

"It's a technique. Sometimes it leaches out a few more facts. I mean, if you went out, you must know where you went and what you did. Stands to reason."

"Mike," Jonathan said, "I don't think you understand even yet. I've believed for some weeks that I'm under some form of hypnosis. Now it seems obvious to me that Patricia is too. The story I told you on the plane stands. We may have gone out in the real, flesh-and-blood world, but we both remember it as if it were a dream."

For better or worse, he was going to have to try to work with Patricia on his instruments. Otherwise this mystery was going to keep getting bigger and bigger until it consumed them both.

The evening had turned to night. Now the room was lit from below by harsh sodium-vapor streetlamps. Some kids had opened up a hydrant and were shrilling gaily in its illicit spray. Jonathan envied them. A feeling of almost unimaginable menace seemed to fill the air in this place.

In the secrecy of conclave that lovers have, Patricia touched Jonathan's shoulder. The damp, warm flesh of her arm came into contact with his own. He knew just what was on her mind. The marriage. She was now ready to tell Mike of their marriage plans.

"You two keep the alarms on every minute you're in here. And if you go out, we'll be with you."

"We've asked Father to marry us," Patricia said quietly but quite firmly, "on Saturday night. The banns are waived." She smiled. "In view of our eagerness and the unusual circumstances of our situation."

Mike pulled his cigar out of his mouth. His face burst in an instant from shadows to smiles. "He-e-y! This is good! This is so good! Tell me sometime, eh?"

"It was her, Dad. She didn't want to say it on the plane."

"They were already celebrating the cure. I didn't want to make more of a fuss."

"People kept kissing her on the plane. I think she was embarrassed."

"Awful fast." Mike got a canny look in his eyes. "Not gonna have a miracle seven-month baby, are you?"

Patricia blushed.

"Come on, Dad, no way. We're just two eager kids."

"Oh, sure. Eager to share your first kiss. I'm sorry you've decided to do it so soon, no chance to plan, but I accept that if it makes you happy."

"We want it private."

"Like now. You want it private now too, don't you?"

Mike had gotten self-conscious. Jonathan wanted to hug him. "We like having you here, Dad."

He pulled himself up from his lounge chair and drank his gin. When he spoke again his words were sharp. "I hate to leave on such a sour note, but I got to say it. You kids take care. You're good kids, both of you." He put out his hands, seemed about to embrace them. "I want my chance at grandfathering, goddamnit." He turned and moved heavily out the door.

They exchanged a glance. "Let's lie down," was all she said. They had only been home a day; there was still the jet lag. Too tired to make love, they contented themselves with a shower together, then lying twined in bed.

When Jonathan awoke it felt late, but it was only ten. He kissed his bride-to-be and probed at her with his inevitable erection. She moaned. He entered her and she sighed, half-awake. It was easier this time. A slight smile came across her face. He began, trying with all his might to make it last, totally engrossed in the astonishing experience of making love for a second time to this very beautiful woman. He had done it once without freeing the serpent. Surely the second time would be even easier.

The phone rang.

"Leave it."

It rang again. And again. Jonathan tried to ignore it but it just wouldn't stop.

Finally he disengaged himself and, as he was the most awake of the two, padded into the living room and answered it. "Oh, hi, Mother." What a magnificent sense of timing. As she spoke Jonathan watched his erection fade.

"You must be careful together," she said in a nervous voice. "I hadn't expected you just to move in with her. You ought to wait until after the marriage. I think you've embarrassed your father." That wasn't very likely. "You're embarrassing me." That was probably true.

"Is Dad there?"

"He just walked in."

"Well, all I can say is we're both adults, and we really would appreciate it if you wouldn't interfere."

She hung up. Jonathan stared a moment at the phone. Slamming down telephones was most unlike Mary Banion. Nor was it like her to pry into his private life.

What role did she have in all this, anyway? According to Mike she had been out of the hotel room at the time the cure was taking place. What role, Mother?

Maybe it was just a coincidence. Hell, maybe it was all coincidences and hysteria. Jonathan had to find out. Beside that urgent need, spending time lovemaking seemed almost irresponsible.

Jonathan went back to the bedroom. Patricia raised her arms, inviting him to fall into them. But he stayed where he was.

"Patricia, we have to go down to the lab. We have to find out where we stand in this thing."

"Why? We stand together."

He would sort through the strands of her mind, separating the real from the imagined.

"We have no idea what's really going on. That's the whole problem. We're crazy to lie around here. We've got work to do."

"What can we do? We can't remember clearly, either one of us."

"My lab can help us. The devices there can tell the difference between dreams and memories. If we're hypnotized, I think we can break through." He did not tell her what he had tried on himself. There was no point. The story would only frighten her, and he didn't need to use 6–6–6 on her. He would control his devices himself.

She pulled him down to her and kissed him with softness and skill. Her early kisses had been rough splashes, but now she had become his geisha. You would not say whore, no, because she was the one who owned. He felt himself enslaved, taken in a snare so cunning it did not even know itself.

"Please come, Patricia. Please."

"We might hurt ourselves. What if there are things we don't *want* to know?"

"I sense that some terrible drama is being enacted. And we're the main characters."

A slight tension came into her face, visible in the careful set of her lips and the cast of her eyes. Maybe she was a little angry, maybe scared. "Tell me your dreams, Jonathan."

"I told you the Lourdes dream."

"But there are others."

"They disgust me."

"You weren't there when I was hurt. You weren't!"

"I don't know anymore."

She laid her head on his shoulder. "We both choose to believe that you were not responsible. And we haven't got one shred of evidence to the contrary. Aren't we better off leaving it that way?"

"I'd kill myself if I ever hurt you!"

She looked at him. "You're so loyal, Jonathan. You make me love you so very much. Don't you understand yourself at all? You're the most gentle man I've ever known. You couldn't hurt me or anybody else!" He had never seen such fiery conviction in so soft a face.

"What if it was me? What if it *was?* I've dreamed it more than once."

"All I want is you, the you that I know and love and trust. That's the Jonathan I want to know."

He could hardly believe what he heard. She was simply overlooking what he was telling her about his dreams. "Don't you think I might have done it—I mean, if I dream about it?"

"When you came into the hospital and looked at me through the window, I knew instantly it hadn't been you." She lowered her eyes. "You were suffering too much."

"And what about Lourdes? My God, surely you agree we've *got* to find out what happened there."

She took his hands. When she spoke he had to strain to listen, her voice was so low. She ignored Lourdes. "If it was you, I don't think I can afford to know." She snuggled deeper against him.

He recoiled. This was not working out right. "We've got to find out. We owe it to ourselves, maybe to others as well." He took her by the wrist. "We're going to the lab right now."

"No!"

He would not, could not force her. "Please. You've got to think of others now, not just you and me. What if I'm dangerous? What if we're both part of something terrible?"

"Jonathan, I don't want to know! I just want us to be together, and love each other, and have a family."

"Lord, darling, we are *hypnotized.* Don't you want to know why somebody has invaded our privacy in this way?"

She touched his face. "You're being a fool."

"I've got to know!"

She closed her eyes, nodded her head. "I hate to hear that. But you really do, don't you? You can't live with yourself unless you know."

"Let's go. Right now."

He did not have money for a cab into Manhattan; they had to content themselves with the F train. They sat on the orange plastic seats in a nearly empty car.

There was no understanding her. On the one hand, she was such a sensitive and moral person—and on the other, almost indifferent to the question of whether or not the two of them were caught up in some kind of dangerous insanity, and unwilling even to consider that a man who wanted her to marry him might be deranged.

He felt like he was smothering, took a deep breath. That was tension. He closed his eyes, listened to the rattling of the train, let his mind wander.

We have a demon between us, she and I.

"This is the stop, honey." They got off at West Fourth Street and went upstairs into the teeming summer night of Greenwich Village.

Down West Fourth they walked past the grim honky-tonks and shoestring restaurants that served the New York University community and the endless streams of tourists, past the lopsided row house that contained the Epsilon Rho fraternity, and down Sullivan Street.

As Jonathan and Patricia walked along, one shadowy figure after another stepped forward saying, "Smoke, smoke," and an occasional man held open a bag full of pills. Somewhere somebody played haunting, ethereal ragtime on steel drums.

The turn into Rayne Street brought them at once to another world. The street was dark and quiet. Tourists and students did not come here. It was too forbidding at night. The streetlights at either end of the block barely penetrated the gloom.

He wished Patricia would walk like an independent human being and not with her head bowed and her hand in his, as if she must go exactly where he led and damn her own feelings.

"I'm sorry if I'm imposing on you."

"That's all right."

"It's for both our sakes."

"I just don't want to risk something coming between us. I love you so much."

He led her down the outside stairway to the basement. When he stopped at the door of Room 014A, she stood quietly beside him.

When he released her hand to fish for his keys, she twined her own hands together and looked at the floor.

"You're making this very hard for me."

"I know." When she raised her eyes they were full of mischief. "I think you're being an idiot, to tell you the truth."

"Well, there's some of the old spirit, at least. Why not look at this as an adventure." He found his key, opened the lab. Inside he flipped the six light switches, flooding the cavernous room with steely fluorescent light. "It might be one, after all. You never know."

The lab had been cleaned up. The busted microcomputer had been replaced and all of the bacteriologicals removed. Even the doorway that had led to the culture lab now led only to a storeroom full of cartons of computer printouts.

Somebody had moved to hide all evidence of bacteria culture having taken place here. That seemed very sinister indeed. He tried to force himself not to speculate about it right now. This wasn't the time to worry about it.

"I don't know any bacteriologists!"

"Jonathan?"

"Sorry. I was thinking aloud." This was his old, familiar workplace now that the other things were gone. A good laboratory is a delight to work in, and in its intact form his was no exception. "I may be bragging, but please indulge me and admire this place." He gestured. "Just look at it."

"It doesn't make a bit of sense to me."

"My dear, you are looking at the closest thing to a device that can read minds that has ever been designed." He went over to the bench on which most of the digital EEG analyzer was lying under its plastic tarp. "All that she requires is a little juice, a little software, and a little love, and she will tell us exactly—but *exactly*—what is hidden in the deep recesses of our minds."

"Look, I'm going to say it one last time. This is all a mistake, Jonathan. What we need to do is forget."

"Just do it for me, honey. It'll be over in fifteen minutes."

"What concerns me is that I'll have to remember something I simply can't face. Let Mike find them if he can. I just want to forget. And you should too. Anyway, your machine might lie."

"For my sake, let me find out what it says. I'll never have peace if I don't."

"I wish you understood how the hell much I love you, Jonathan Banion. You're part of my soul!"

He hugged her and felt her tremble. "I'm sorry."

"What if we don't like what we find?"

"We have to take that risk! What's the good of living a lie? I don't want that, and I don't think you do either. If we really love each other, we've got to know the truth."

"Even if it destroys everything?"

He held her tight to him. "Let's face that if we have to. The point is to find out the truth, then we'll deal with it."

"You didn't rape me. Not you."

"We have to find that out, among other things."

She shrieked at him. "*I do not want to!*" She looked at the equipment he had uncovered as if it were a writhing tangle of snakes. Her lips twisted. For a moment it seemed as if she might faint. "I don't even allow myself to think about it. I just know it's there, deep in me, a filthy memory of—of—oh, I don't know what it's of."

Of me?

"Darling, I'm going to ask you to lie in the cubicle. And please excuse the mildew." Will your mind tell us what mine would not? He gave the couchette a few swipes.

"I'm doing this for you, Jonathan. Only for you. I'm going on record right now saying it's a mistake."

She lay down. A memory of Mike haunted Jonathan. Mike sitting on the lounge chair, chewing his cigar, his bald head gleaming with sweat.

We're all afraid.

Surely questioning under instruments would work more gently on her mind than 6-6-6 had on his. He hoped so; if he put her through one-tenth of the anguish he had endured he would never forgive himself.

He punched in the Telenet address of the Cray 2000 computer that controlled his software and entered his personal password. The internal prompt appeared on his CRT. The computer was ready. Now he ordered it to load his software from the Corvus Hard Disk Drive sitting beside his terminal. The drive's active light came on for a long moment. When it went off Jonathan knew that the fast, elegant program had been transferred to the Cray.

The Cray came back with the diamond-shaped prompt that indicated it had successfully loaded. "We're go on the program," he said to his waiting subject—or patient—or was it victim?

She was lying quietly on the couchette, watching him. "Just don't mess up my brain, chromedome."

"You're going to be the chromedome, I'm afraid." He got the helmet. It contained a hundred and twenty-eight pressure-sensitive electrodes and was a great improvement over the old method of applying them individually to the skin. But with the masses of wires coming out of it, it looked like something that belonged on the head of a robot.

She laughed when she saw it. "We need a camera. I want you to remember me at my most beautiful."

He looked long at her. "I wouldn't do this if I didn't have to."

"Never leave me, Jonathan. Never, no matter what." Jonathan fitted the helmet to her head and they laughed together. "I really want a picture," she said. He turned to his instruments. Patricia's brain-wave patterns were jittering across the screen of the oscilloscope.

"Remember that night? We were together. We had drinks. And?"

"Jonathan, ask about Lourdes instead."

He watched his instruments. "Remember? We were together, we had just had a drink—"

"You left!"

The PV220 wave showed a peak, then settled. The thought was not coming from memory; neither was it quite a lie. It was an implant. To break a hypnotic block, it was necessary to challenge such implants.

This was a fateful moment. If he could break what had been put into her mind to blind it, his next words would do it. "You don't remember that."

"That's what happened."

"Try again. We had drinks. Assume I didn't leave. What really happened?"

The sound she made was not a scream, it was an eruption. Jonathan lunged toward her. In an instant she had gone a ghastly pale gray color, her eyes almost starting out of her head. Her shriek dropped suddenly from a glass-shattering pitch to a vibrating groan. Then the computer started beeping. Automatically Jonathan responded to the line-failure signal and pressed the reset button. The screen flickered to blankness. Even as it was doing that he was leaping to her aid. He thought perhaps a short of some kind was sending voltage into the headset. But even when he tore it from her head she didn't change. She was convulsing. Her arms went out straight beside her, her legs began to hammer, her head jerked from side to side. He shook her, he yelled at her, finally he scooped her up into his arms and hugged her to him.

"What have I done? Oh, stop, stop! Oh, God, God, please make her stop!"

Chapter Sixteen ——————|—

HER HEAD WAS whirling, her ears ringing, the whole room shaking. Jonathan seemed to dart and flicker as if caught in some sort of strobe light. Then his hands slapped against the helmet with a stunning clap and he tore it from her head.

She blacked out. She knew that something was terribly wrong with her. She could feel her body jerking in spasm, her tongue filling the back of her throat. And she was spinning, spinning fast, out of control, falling. A great bell was booming somewhere.

Then it wasn't a bell at all, it was Jonathan's voice. He was crying and screaming, cradling her in his arms.

Quite suddenly, all was quiet.

"Patricia?"

His face was shadowed by the glare of the fluorescent tubes above him. "Jonathan—"

"Darling, darling, darling. I'm so stupid, so damn stupid." He embraced her and she let herself be swept up into his arms. They were strong and good and she was glad.

"I feel better. I think I'm going to be okay."

A haunted expression came into his eyes. It alarmed her; it was the expression of somebody with a guilty secret.

"Did you hurt me, honey? Is there something I don't know?"

"I don't think so."

Another thought occurred to her. "Did you find out?" Her own voice sounded so small.

She turned her head to avoid the glaring ceiling lights.

He stared down at her.

Love me tonight. . . . She became aware, dimly, of something quick and gleaming that stank of flyblow, chasing her through her dream country. Catching her.

Oh, God, how horrible! She heard herself gasp. She felt another scream coming. The thing she had glimpsed was so ugly and so utterly cold, the very opposite of all she loved of humanity and life. It was Death coming through the high grass, Death rising from its hiding place in the soul. "Oh! Oh! No, Jonathan!"

"Patricia! Sh! Sh! It's over, I turned it off. You were right; I won't ask any more questions. I'm so sorry."

"Oh, darling, it was so ugly!" Were there people in the world who were not quite people? What had that thing been, straddling her, staring down with the blank eyes of a snake?

She was going to throw up. "Jonathan—" Her mouth opened. He grabbed for a wastepaper basket, thrust it beneath her face, and held her. Her stomach seemed to pull off its moorings. For an instant she was sinking in a fast elevator. Then the lights were above her again, glaring, humming tubes of brilliance, and beneath them Jonathan's face, his lips slack with fear and his eyes still hidden in the dark of his brows.

He bent to her, lifted her in his arms, and embraced her. "I thought it would work out differently."

The world had just changed for her. Her memory of that terrible moment was now clear. She could remember what had raped her, and it was not a human being.

What evil has been wrought in the dark of this world?

"First I heard music, a sort of humming, very low, like a swarm of flies."

"Hush, honey, hush."

"I will not!" She reached out and snatched up the tangled pile of graph paper. "What does this say?"

"I pulled off the helmet."

"Before you did that you asked me what really happened. And I had a vivid image. Was it a memory or wasn't it?"

"I don't know. The reading isn't reliable."

She wouldn't stand for that. "Jonathan, you opened something up in me and it feels like a memory. Now I'm the one who has to know."

"Whatever it was sent you into convulsions, I don't think we should fool with it."

That wasn't acceptable. "You tell me—*dream or memory?*"

He took her hands, pressed them to his lips. "I can't be sure. There's something wrong with the readout."

She could smell it, could taste its filthy, rotten kisses. "Jonathan, Jonathan, look at you. You poor man, you're so innocent. Do you still think you did it?"

He squeezed his eyes shut, he bowed his head. He was slick with sweat. "I know." The words were a bare murmur.

"Don't be an ass. You didn't. You couldn't possibly."

He dropped to the couchette beside her. His hands, holding hers, were cold and wet.

She tossed her head, wishing she could get the image of the thing out of her mind, could somehow replace it forever with Jonathan's beauty.

But that *thing* existed.

"Darling, we have to take a reading on me as well."

"What? Have you lost your mind, Jonathan Banion?"

"Just a short reading. And you'll have to run the computer."

"I can't run a computer, and I wouldn't even if I could!"

He glanced again at the chart of her own reading, made a sad kind of a sighing sound. Suddenly he grabbed her shoulders. He brought his face close to hers and she saw him clearly, without shadows. His eyes were staring, fixed, his lips dry. He was trembling steadily, with the frantic rhythm of a small animal. "You get over there and run it!" He picked up the graph and shook it at her. "Do you realize what this —no, you couldn't possibly." He jumped up, went to the computer terminal with a single stride, began jabbing at keys. It beeped, the screen came to green life, then he grabbed her by the wrist and dragged her over.

"Once the helmet is on, the computer will want to adjust to the exact frequencies of my thought patterns. There will be a series of numbers coming across the screen. Each time it pauses, press the key marked 'return.' Got that?"

"Darling—"

"Got that? *Got that?*"

"Okay! Got it."

"Then it will ask you a question—which measurement? You will type in the answer, 'waves by harmonic type.' Then press 'return' again."

"I've got it. 'Waves by harmonic type.'"

"Then press 'return.' You see the return key?"

She put her finger on it. "Jonathan, what if something happens to you?"

"Do just what I did—you press this orange key marked 'reset,' then you pull the helmet off my head. But nothing *will* happen because this is a passive test. We aren't fooling with my hypnotic barriers."

"So we *are* hypnotized. You know that for certain?"

"Oh, yes. And the barriers are powerful. More so than I dreamed possible. One more question, baby, and bang—the next step was brain death."

"Death by hypnosis? I didn't think—"

"Don't ask me how it's done because I don't know. Now come on, let's get this over with."

He fitted the silver, cable-strewn helmet onto his own head and lay down on the couchette. After a moment a string of numbers shot across the screen, and she began following her instructions.

Soon the numbers stopped and the machine asked its question. She typed in the reply, then kept one finger hovering over the reset button and the other over 'return.' She looked at Jonathan. He was lying on the couchette, his eyes closed. He seemed fine. She pressed 'return.'

Silence. Jonathan didn't move. She kept her finger over the orange button, began watching his chest. He was breathing steadily.

Soon paper started streaming out of the graph. Then the machine sounded a bell and stopped. "Jonathan, did I do something wrong?"

He sat up, pulled off the helmet. "You were fine," he muttered. "That's all there was to it." He lunged for the graph paper, ripped it off the roll, studied it almost frantically.

When he looked up at her again, his face was pallid with shock. The paper dropped from his hands.

"Jonathan, what is it?"

He shook his head. Then he came to her, almost reverently, and took her head in his hands. "Darling, our brains show an incredible, radical departure from the normal wave pattern."

Was *that* all? "Well, are we okay anyway?" She could think of nothing else to ask.

He laughed silently, mirthlessly. "Dearest, we're fine. But don't you see what this means? We've got eighteen separate waves. Normal people have seven."

"Does it mean—have we got a disease?"

"In a funny kind of a way. Our disease is that we aren't human beings."

"We—what?" She was mystified. "Of course we are!"

"No. We're too far from the norm. Oh, we're human stock all right. I mean, the basic pattern—alpha, beta, delta—it's there. But *we are not people.* We've got an alpha high harmonic, a delta parallel, and a whole cluster of little waves down in the low frequencies."

"It must be the hypnosis. It's got to be!"

"No way. I'm talking about brain *structures,* not transitory effects like that. I mean, we are real first-class *freaks!"*

That word slashed through her composure and made her shriek. She couldn't help it; freak is a horrible word. "No, I'm not a freak. I hate it! I am *not* a freak!"

I was raped by a freak with the skin of a snake and yellow-green reptile eyes.

"Honey, come on, be quiet."

"I will not be quiet! I am not a freak! Don't you ever, ever, ever call either of us that, because we are *normal.* I'm telling you we are normal and we can have a good life! You'll see, Jonathan Banion, I'll make a nice home for you, you'll see!"

"Come on! Pull yourself together. We've got to think this out."

She stopped, but only by jamming her own feelings down into her guts and holding them there with a fierce effort of will she doubted she could sustain for long.

"We are mutants. The other word was unfortunate." He sounded calm, and that helped a little. "Genetically we must be very different from other people." He shook his head. "God knows what we are. Halfway between *Homo sapiens* and—well, something else. I cannot imagine what our children will be like. A virtual new species."

"But we're people!"

"Not really. Close, yes, but you and I are not people."

She was losing her home, her family, her happy life. She knew it— she could feel it all being destroyed by that one awful word. Freak. "But we *look* like people, we *act* like people!"

He nodded agreement. "We're a close mutation." He looked at his hands, felt his cheeks. "Amazing. Me. You. That we would be this . . . whatever we are."

"Are you *sure* it's not the hypnosis?"

He took her hands. "I know how to read my charts. We may be

under hypnosis. In fact I'm sure we are. But the overriding finding is the high degree of abnormality in our brains' electrical functions. That means—"

"Don't say it again! Don't say that word!"

She let him hug her. Gratefully she buried her face in his chest. She remembered the monster again, and felt all at once the absolute coldness of the unknown. How little she really knew, even about herself. "We *look* like people!"

"Yeah. We can probably mate with people too. Have humanlike kids. But if we mate with each other our children won't be remotely human."

She couldn't stand to hear that. "Just stop it! Stop talking that way. Look, we can go away somewhere. Nobody will ever know, nobody needs to know. Whatever we are inside, we can keep it secret, we can hide it! We'll be able to get married and all, and things'll work out. They will, I know it!"

He held her more tightly. "Baby," he said, his voice quaking, "somebody already knows all about us."

He could only mean the Night Church. There flashed in her mind again an image of the revolting thing on the altar. She let herself weep into his shoulder, and she thought, We're in the middle of God knows what, and we're getting more lost by the second.

She held him, and he held her, and for a precious moment that was all there was.

We two.

Chapter Seventeen ———————|——

FEAR WAS NOT normally part of Mike's emotional makeup. To-night, though, he could taste it in his mouth, a sour dryness that made it hard to swallow.

It is not a sound, but you can hear it in the wind; not a presence, but you can feel it watching you.

Fear.

He had no illusions about searching Mr. Apple's house. It belonged to a powerful and hitherto unknown cult. The Night Church. Coming here was probably the most dangerous thing he had ever done.

He suspected he was a fool to be doing it—especially this way, alone and without backup.

He had no warrant. As far as the law was concerned, he was a common burglar. But then the law didn't know he was here. He didn't trust his own people enough to risk swearing out papers.

He waited until the hours past midnight to drive through the streets of Kew Gardens to the empty house. He parked around the corner and walked back, his hands thrust into the pockets of his raincoat, his hat shadowing his face when he passed under streetlights. He moved with the precision of a dancer, his shoes making no sound on the sidewalk.

His entrance was professional, so quick that an onlooker would have assumed he had a key. As he gained the front hall he returned the plastic card he had used to prize the lock to his inside coat pocket. Almost automatically his fingers reached in and touched the butt of his police special, tucked into its shoulder holster.

The floor groaned with his weight. Good—that was a sign it hadn't been walked on for some time. Mike went across the foyer and into the living room. The air was dense, faintly tinged with the musk of mildew.

As Mike's eyes got used to the light he could see that nothing had been removed from this room. That was as expected. Mr. Apple had left no relatives and no will. It would be months before Probate Court got around to disposing of this place on behalf of New York State. He took a crystal ball from a collection in a case in the living room. The little quartz orb dimly reflected the thick velvet drapes, the intricate Chinese carpet, the Flemish landscapes on the walls, and the deep mahogany of the Victorian furniture. One could almost see shadowy figures moving in the complex dark of the crystal.

Beside the orb was a small silver key, rounded at the end in a unique and familiar way. It was a coffin key. Mike had seen them often enough at the morgue. Strange thing to find in a home. Was it the key to Mr. Apple's coffin, left here by a careless mortician when the old man had so conveniently died?

He replaced the crystal, picked up the key. It was a typical stubby coffin key, steel, looking like a luggage key, but with the name Aurora stamped on the flange. Largest coffin company in the world. Mike had used such keys in disinterments.

Carefully, patiently, he moved through the living room, brushing his gloved hand along the back of a chair, caressing the surface of a mahogany table.

Old Mr. Apple.

That name hadn't checked out. Back around the turn of the century foundlings in upstate New York were always called Johnny Apple on their birth certificates. "Mr. Apple" was an identity generated from the birth certificate of a foundling who had died in the Oneonta County Institution for Indigent Children two weeks after he was discovered in a box behind a grocery store.

"Franklin Apple's" birthday was December 11, 1893. That was the day Johnny Apple had been discovered in the box. Developing an alias this way was a clever technique. You find somebody who died young about the time you were actually born, and you send for the birth certificate. Then you use that to get a social security card and a passport, and the passport to get a driver's license, and the license for everything else.

You use the alias until it gets hot. Then you kill it off.

Father Goodwin hadn't mentioned Mr. Apple during interrogation, but one of the ladies at the supper had. Mike was so desperate for leads he had begged Harry to dredge his memory. "The incident was very minor," he had said. "The man made her nervous and she didn't want to talk to him. I told her to offer it up. That kept her with him for fifteen minutes. She said that he was creepy. It's a matter of no importance, I'm sure. He was very old."

Mike hadn't told Harry how important he thought Mr. Apple might be. Always best to play a case like this one closer than you thought you had to.

To discover the little tiny motives that always seem to start crimes, the best place to go is a man's hidden world, his sock drawer, his medicine cabinet, the back of his closet.

Crystal balls? Coffin keys? Not the likely possessions of just any old man. But an old man who was playing around with sorcery might have such things.

Strange mementoes themselves were of little value as evidence. Such things did suggest, though, didn't they?

Mike returned to the central hallway of the house. On the opposite side was a study. Behind it would be the master bedroom and dressing room. Mike knew the layout of the house; he had lived in one very much like it with his first wife, Beth. Rego Park, from 1964 to 1975. The house had been built by Butler and Horowitz in the late twenties —they had put up hundreds of them all over the borough. Butler Boxes, they were called. By now most had been torn down or so altered as to obscure their original modesty. Not so Mr. Apple's bungalow. It even retained the vintage twist-spring doorbell.

Beyond the door of the study Mike could see a big desk, shelves of books, a television set on one of the shelves. He went in, walked the edge of the room.

When he brushed past the television set he paused. He put his hand on it. Was there a little warmth there, or was it simply the hot night? He went on, circling the desk. Nothing was disturbed in here. He would save the study for a few minutes. Even as inefficient as it was, Probate would have removed any important papers with the body and stored them in its vault down at the Queens County Courthouse.

To get an idea of the man as he had been in his skivvies, at his most revealed, Mike would try the bedroom. He stepped carefully along the Persian prayer rug that served as a hall runner. His penlight told him that, like everything else he had seen in the house so far, the carpet was very fine. Mr. Apple certainly hadn't lived in want.

Which raised an interesting question. Why had a rich man like this gone to a seniors supper to eat Father Goodwin's meager offering?

The sonofabitch had gone there to observe Patricia. Even then he had been watching her.

The bedroom was a puzzle. It did not talk old man, not by a long shot. If Mike's instincts were working, this room had been decorated by a young woman. There was even a vase of fresh roses. Perhaps only a day old, from the feel of the petals.

Fresh flowers, a slightly warm television—somebody was *living* here. Mike became aware of the weight of his pistol, and wished he had spent some time down on the practice range recently.

He got much more careful, but also much more interested. He glanced at his watch. Three fifty. This time of night people who weren't home could be expected any minute or not at all. Good that his car was around the corner and not out front. He began to work the penlight with his hand cupped around it. Reflections on the ceiling would read outside like the flicker of a match.

Then he froze. He had heard a sound, a scrape like a window being raised.

There it was again. It was followed by silence. Maybe some wind had come up and was scraping a tree limb against a pane of glass.

There was a small writing desk under the window. Lying on it was a fountain pen. Mike touched the nib. Full of ink. It was eerie to come into the house of a dead man who might not be dead.

He opened the single drawer of the desk. Inside was a black leather binder that contained about ten sheets of blank chart paper, like something a scientist might use to plot curves. He felt the surface for telltale indentations. Sure enough, someone had written on the top sheet and torn it off, leaving depressions on the sheet below.

Mike took the indented sheet off, laid it on the desk, and shone his penlight along it edgewise. There were words neatly inscribed in one corner, as a scientist might label the chart of an experiment. But the words were not scientific *R-i-t-u*—something. Then *C-r-u-c-i-a-t-u-s,* then a word that began with *N* and had an *x* in it. Then a name, which Mike recognized with sick dread. *Quist!*

Come on, guy, quit the shaking. You're a cop, you're carryin' heat, you got no problem.

Cruciatus. Mike's altar boy Latin was exceedingly rusty, but there was an ugly sound to that word. It didn't mean crucifixion—that was *crucifixus.* This sounded worse.

Seems from this they must have hurt Terry. So what's the surprise? Look what they did to Patricia.

Beside Terry's name were two slashes—a date had been written there, but the numbers were too faint to be discerned. Below the name, pressed into the paper as if the writer had been bearing down for emphasis, was written "Titus strain 334, Cochran batch, B. positive 3." Here and there across the paper faint lines indicated that a chart had indeed been drawn. At the bottom, at regular intervals, were numbers, but Mike could only make out a few—3:54.22 was the first. Farther down was 3:57.44. The others were unintelligible.

Titus strain. Mary's first husband was named Martin Titus. Batch? Mike felt a cold shiver go up his spine. What the hell was it Terry had said about diseases? And what the hell was Mary's former married name doing on this chart?

You be careful, guy. Forget going home for tonight. Mary was now a suspect. She had gone out before the kids at Lourdes—he had witnessed that. Now her first husband's name turns up here. So she must be considered dangerous, and prepared for accordingly. Damn, damn. What in *hell* was this all about? Mary involved? That beautiful, decent woman? He loved Mary, damn it, and he was now suspecting she was about to become a very big disappointment to him.

Cruciatus. Whatever the hell *Cruciatus* was, it sounded bad. He looked at the paper. Killing by disease and charting the results. Experimenting.

Was Mary crazy or what? He was getting all choked up. He loved that woman, damn her. Damn everything. People got hooked by cults all the time—Reverend Moon and all that—but this thing—God, if Mary knew about Patricia. If she *knew!*

Cruciatus. It might mean excruciation. Torture. That poor guy. Such a rotten end for an innocent human being. Mike next went to the high, beautifully carved antique four-poster. He took off his gloves and raised the edge of the bedspread. Thrusting one arm beneath the sheets he felt the intimate space where the user would sleep. The sheets were damp, slept in recently.

Why, Mr. Apple, you're not dead, you've just moved to some new name. As far as that beautiful piece of mahogany amoldering six feet down is concerned, let archaeologists of the future figure out why it contains cinder blocks.

Make a note: get the damn thing exhumed ASAP.

The house was suddenly filled with voices. "Please, let me go, let me go!" a woman screamed. Mike whipped out his pistol and backed into the shadows.

"I can't help myself!" a man cried back, his voice full of anguish.

Then Mike saw a flickering glow in the hallway. And those voices— they were accompanied by music.

The goddamn TV had been turned on.

Mike's heart began thundering. Somebody must have come home. Now he was watching an old movie. God, these people were stealthy. They even crept into their own houses.

A coldness spread through his body. He didn't believe people could be as quiet as this one had been. Not normal people.

He started down the hall. To get out he had to pass that study, and the door was wide open. At least he had the sound of the TV to cover him.

He was three-quarters of the way past it when he risked a glance in. The study was empty.

A television set turning on by itself? Mike swallowed, braced his pistol in his hands, and went into the room. The television had gone from picture to snow. The station must have signed off.

For a moment he watched the pulsing, hypnotic glow of the screen. Then there was an audio problem—the hiss changed to a deep, tooth-jarring sound that made Mike lunge forward to turn off the set.

Don't do that! You're crazy—whoever turned it on will notice! He stood transfixed, staring into the dancing, pulsating glow, listening to the low booming sound.

And didn't he hear a voice?

No.

His eyes went to a small box attached to a wall socket immediately below the TV.

He almost laughed with relief. It was a timer. The set was timed to go on in order to make the house look occupied.

At four o'clock in the morning?

Hell, maybe the timer was defective.

Mike pulled the timer out of the socket. The TV went off. He returned to his search, feeling more than a little annoyed with himself for letting a perfectly explainable incident throw him off balance. It now seemed as if the place would be a rich source of information. No probate officer had made an inventory of this house, because Mr. Apple hadn't really died.

Mike looked around at the shelves and shelves of books and the big desk.

He intended only a quick glance at the books. There were a few modern titles, mostly privately printed from the look of the spines. *Biogenetic Atlas: Engineering the Future, Transmission of Contagious Vectors, Genealogies Pantera, The Family of Flavius Sabinus Titus.*

Who? Always go for the names. Names are hard information.

Mike took the Titus volume down. It turned out to be about a Roman emperor. A long story about how he had sacked Jerusalem started the book. Mike thumbed through it. A chapter heading: "The Treasure of Solomon." This chapter was about ritual magic, hypnosis, and "the calling of the demiurge." "Out of the union of the perfectly bred will arise the antithesis of man, who will inherit the mantle of species and the favor of demons." On and on like that. Next chapter: "The Coming Good: Anti-Man."

Mike read: "He will bear the appearance of a demon, yet have a living heart. As God made man in his miserable image, so Satan will make the anti-man in His glorious one. He will be as a dark fury, going about at night and sleeping during the day. Taller, stronger, more intelligent than a man, he will be heavy-boned and like the lower animals be born competent to walk. He will have great jaws and eat raw flesh by gorging. His strength will be such that he will need neither house nor fire, but will be comfortable in the fields and forests. All the despoiling of the land that man has done will end when the anti-man repopulates the earth with his own issue."

Mike stared at the words, dumbfounded. They were talking about nothing less than giving the world to some devil-made species.

Insane, insane, insane.

Farther along there was a complicated genealogical table, showing how they intended to bring about their anti-humanity. Generation by generation they were breeding toward the monster. The genealogical table was a chronicle of their progress. It was labeled "The Hidden Kingdom, 1021–1952." It spilled over twenty pages of names and more names, all connected together by lines of relationship.

Mike read with increasing foreboding the lists of Tituses, until he quit trying to puzzle the middle centuries together and flipped to the end. Sure enough, there was Martin Titus, wife Mary Derwent Titus, son Jonathan.

Mike found a chair. His penlight was beginning to dim but he had to read more and he couldn't risk taking books.

All the time he had been right in the middle of the thing. These Tituses weren't just in the cult, they *were* the cult. And that wonderful kid was heir to the whole damn thing.

Biogenetic Atlas: Engineering the Future proved to be a complicated scientific treatise of recent origin. The spine crackled when Mike opened the book. It had been printed in 1981. There were charts and graphs, and detailed diagrams of what seemed to be genetic helixes. The chapter headings were daunting: "Structural Physiology of Titus/Pantera Offspring." "Biogenetic Reference Tables to Families 121/166." (Here there were thirty pages of tables of numbers, evidently referring to changes in the genetic structure of generation after generation. Every twenty columns or so somebody had made a check mark in red ink beside a major change in the numbers.)

Looking at these charts Mike got a sense of the steady progress that had been made by the Night Church, patiently breeding two families together over hundreds and hundreds of generations, breeding them like fruit flies in a laboratory. But the Night Church didn't have laboratory conditions. This had been accomplished across the tumult of history.

This section of the book was accompanied by illustrations. The earliest ones were Roman wax paintings, familiar to Mike from an afternoon's wandering through the Metropolitan Museum with Mary. He had assumed them to be satyrs or something. Not until now had he ever dreamed that those old Roman monsters were real, living creatures.

According to the text, carefully bred people with the proper genetic structure could briefly become such monsters in a ceremony called the *Rituale Pudibunda Coitus.* Thus transformed, they were called *monstrum.* If a man in the *monstrum* state inseminated a correctly bred woman, the resulting anti-human would be male. If the woman was the *monstrum,* the child would be female.

Generation after generation they had tried to give birth to a living anti-man. All they needed was a male: he would be able to mate with normal humans and produce monstrous offspring. But they hadn't succeeded. One would be born with a defective heart, another with an unformed brain, a third with some mysterious genetic disease. It was as if nature rebelled against the travesty.

Astonishingly their failures were chronicled publicly, there for all to see just like the old Roman paintings. As time went on the creatures had become more and more terrible. Anybody could study them even now: their portraits were on all the Gothic cathedrals in the world. They were the gargoyles.

Generations of failure had only spurred the Night Church to greater efforts of breeding. Mike reflected as he read that here was a group of people in love with death. Their books were decorated by images of Thoth, the all-seeing Egyptian god of the underworld. Thoth and the arms of the Black Prince of the Middle Ages, and the glittering death's-head symbol of the SS.

The Night Church was a religion of death, just as Christianity was one of life. As Christianity strove to resurrect man in Christ, the Night Church sought to destroy him in Satan.

Next was a technical appendix showing recent progress in creating the state of *monstrum*.

Mike was more utterly revolted by this than by anything he had seen in all his years as a cop. The Night Church was breeding human beings like lab mice, toward ugliness and deformity. And making them carry out obscene rituals in churches, becoming *monstrum* in order to give birth to hideous things.

But there was genius in it, sparkling like a black, evil diamond through these carefully reasoned words. As a cold touch, there came to Mike the realization that he was looking upon the very work of Satan. This was *real* evil in all its hideous ugliness, not the paltry nastiness of human beings. The Night Church was a dark, festering miracle, a Satanic masterpiece.

Mike wanted to throw down the book in his hand, to somehow cleanse himself of the foulness it exuded. But he forced himself to read on. Here was the jargon of high science: "Signal Ritual Induction in Late Titus Offspring." As if to crush what little hope of disbelief he had left, this section contained a photograph of almost unspeakable hideousness. The picture was blurred by the fact that the light was low and the subject twisting and turning against chains. But Mike could see the awful, mucous-slick scales half-grown out of human flesh, the bulging vulture eyes still bearing a man's brow, the mouth crusted with blood from the sudden eruption of the yellow fangs, the flaring, pink snout still looking a little like the nose it had been. This dreadful image, of a man half-transformed into something else, was accompanied by a dry paragraph of scientific jargon: "Induction in collateral Titus male 22, Ungar, Robert Titus Martin, type O—, genetic subclass AR, 22.66 measured PKO, reversion in 52 sec. to human. Outcome: *monstrum* deceased before impregnation of female could be completed."

Mike could no longer control himself. He cried, openly, loudly, like a child lost in a haunted forest.

The Night Church was another, darker world hidden in our own, a place of terror and agony lurking in the shadows of everyday life.

He wanted with almost crazy desperation to get out of this wicked house. But he forced a shaking hand to put back the atlas and draw out another book, this one entitled *Genealogies Pantera*. This was the family that had been bred along with the Tituses across so many generations.

The female line.

He went directly to the last few pages, to see if he recognized any of the modern names. He was thunderstruck by what he found. Patricia was there, listed as the daughter of Samuel and Rebecca Murray, who went through a long line of Irish families back to Roman Britain, and thence to someone named Joshua, who had been a sorcerer in the time of Solomon.

Mike had reached the end of his strength. This was more than he could bear. He threw the book against the wall and screamed out his rage and disgust.

Every living person he loved was in this monstrous, corrupt cult! Every one of them!

He ran, ignoring the noise he was making, out into the black night. The roses on the porch trellis filled the darkness with their scent. As Mike ran he got scared. It was as if some great creature was following him, reaching out for him. He vaulted a hedge and slipped in dew-covered grass, falling and rolling. He lay on his back gasping for breath. And saw among the stars two great vulture eyes staring down at him.

His scream was as thin and high as a baby's. His wildly pumping legs pushed him along for a moment, then he managed to get to his feet and scramble the thirty paces to his car.

Frantically he worked the key into the starter, said a little prayer as the engine turned over, fought the impulse to floor it when it started.

Mike drove down Abingdon Street, slowly for quiet, and did not turn his lights on until he had reached the corner of Lefferts Boulevard.

The precinct was three minutes away, but Farrell's was what he wanted. Lights and people and normal things like coffee and tea. Lobster-shift cops would be there. He needed the reassuring presence of other police.

Tonight he had seen things that could drive a man mad. In an hour the whole world had changed for him. Satan was no longer a vague symbol of emotional disturbance. Satan was a real thing, as vital and alive as any human being. Mike had no doubt that those eyes he had seen in the sky were Satan's. Evil and ugly and tremendous, and staring right at him.

He cruised past his own house. A dim light shone in his and Mary's bedroom. What was going on in there? What might await him?

He had given that woman his love. Goodbye to that. And the kids? He had to reserve judgment there, he just didn't have the heart to start hating Jonathan and Patricia.

The boy had demanded a poly—like he suspected himself of the rape but did not know. Could that mean the two of them were dupes, ignorant of their own true selves?

He thought of going over to All Souls Cemetery and visiting Beth, just to be near someone who had once been warm and good and loved him, to wash off with memories of her goodness the evil that clung to him.

"Honey," he would say, "I never thought Mary was really a replacement for you, but she was warm and decent, and she was real pretty. I didn't fit with her and I guess I should have known something was wrong, but she was so damn beautiful. That counts. She isn't as pretty as you, though, no, ma'am. Lord, honey, I'd like to get you in my arms right now. I'd like to kiss your neck while we made love, the way I used to."

His chest was tight, his throat ached with sorrow. "You had a beautiful name, Beth. A beautiful name."

Oh, quit your bawlin', you sentimental Irish asshole. You have to put yourself back together. For better or worse, you've been handed the biggest job any cop ever had.

He felt that horrible chill again. He sensed that the eyes were back, glaring at him right through the roof of his car. A sudden wind rocked the old Dodge on its springs, and made the trees ahead toss wildly in its headlights. For companionship he flipped on the police radio. He headed for Farrell's even though he had realized that the lobster shift was off break, so there weren't likely to be a hell of a lot of cops there.

There weren't any at all.

He was tempted to cruise the boulevard for a whore, but he couldn't do that successfully in an obvious unmarked car like this. They'd run away, naturally, from a city-issue Dodge with cop plates.

Naturally.

He finally rolled into Farrell's, put on his hat, and went in. The counter was empty, the booths were empty. A black preacher and his family sat at one of the tables eating a turkey dinner. At this hour of the morning?

Okay.

Old Gus the drunk was on duty, with Reynaldo running the grill. "Gimme coffee, Gus."

"Sure thing, Inspector."

Call me Mike. I'm just Mike. Good Lord, but I am alone.

MARY: THE WEBS OF THE INQUISITION

It is four o'clock in the morning. I sit here in my little pool of light writing, alone in an empty, hostile house. I am a betrayer. I have lived with a man in love in this house, falsely drawing him down into a pit from which he cannot save himself.

I look at these smooth hands of Lilith, my hands, witch's hands. They used to burn my kind in autumn fires long ago, in forest villages when the wind crowded down the leaves and the sky ran gray.

I am swift in the night, the taloned maiden. Look at my red-tipped claws. Mike would call them fingers, and say they are beautiful. I know differently. When he thinks they are caressing him is when they are cutting deepest. I can make a man's soul leak out through his skin.

Distantly the bell of Holy Spirit Church tolls four times. All well, all well, all well, all well. Not far from here Mike is searching the cottage Franklin used while he was living under his alias. All well.

Mike is being tricked into finding exactly what we want him to find, just enough of our secrets to animate in him a great fear of us. He will take nothing important away; he dares not. Within moments of his departure the crew that is waiting in the basement will come up and strip the house of every single scrap of evidence.

Mike is an actor now in the terrible theater of Lilith. He will strut and posture until the end of the play. He will not escape me.

Look at the words I have just written. He will not escape me. I'm sure of that, I suppose.

By going where he has gone, Mike Banion has delivered himself to our control. We are vastly better equipped for this game than he. We have people, resources, equipment, and above all the insight of the demons to guide us. For his part, Mike is afraid even to involve his own men for fear that some may be members of our Church.

Mankind drifts along, haunted by gibbering spirits and useless gods. At the bottom of each human soul is the evil old ape from which we have sprung. We, the transitional species, half-animal and half-god, all full of tragedies and destructions.

I am almost overwhelmed with a worshipful desire to get on with our great work. What a mercy bubonic positive 3 will be. Homo sapiens has suffered itself for a hundred thousand years. It is past time for this awful tragedy to end.

The actors upon the stage are at last dissolving into dark.

Only the Inquisition can stop us now. But will it? We are very close to success. And yet . . . there is always the possibility of something overlooked.

The Inquisition spins subtle webs.

I worry, turning the same few facts over in my mind again and again. I imagine priests—silent, careful, fanatical—slipping through the darkness, filling every ignored corner, obsessed with their mission to save a religion and a humanity that are both already dead.

Most human creatures, in their secret hearts, hunger for destruction. Freud's "death wish" is the instinct of a defective species toward its own extinction.

As the church of the destruction of man, we use the great human symbols of death: the unblinking eyes of Thoth, the steel helmet of the Black Prince, the glittering silver death's head of the SS.

Mankind longs so much for an end to itself that it has even devised means of mass suicide. Or else why are there such vast nuclear arsenals on the earth? If man does it himself, with his atomic bombs, the race's death agony will last for years. The few destroyed in the explosions will be lucky. As for the rest—radiation poisoning, burns, infection, violence, and starvation will take them . . . so very slowly. Dr. Cochran's new bubonic positive 3 kills quickly—in under ten minutes, to judge from our experience with Terence Quist.

We, at least, are merciful.

Chapter Eighteen ————————— +

THE INCREDIBLE REALITY that Jonathan's instruments had unlocked tore at Patricia's mind, threatening her very sanity.

From the moment she had understood what he meant she had thought of only one thing: *escape*. If she had been able to magically trade bodies with somebody else she would have done it. But that was impossible. She was in herself and she couldn't get out.

He was trapped as well. Two mutants.

Who felt like, wanted to be, in their hearts *were* just ordinary people.

They were going to go where they could live the lives they coveted. Their wants were simple: a home and children. Just like everybody else, they had a right to a quiet life.

We can live in sunshine. The shadows that have caressed us can be burned away.

They crept through the dangerous silence of Kew Gardens, beneath the black intricate trees lining the streets, their feet falling softly on the close-cropped lawns and spotless sidewalks. It was so quiet their breathing seemed to shake the air.

Every movement Patricia made, every rustle of her skirt or touch of bare arm against a shrub, almost stopped her heart. Slowly they drew closer to the Banion house and whatever might await them there.

Had there been a choice they would have gone directly from the lab to the Port Authority Bus Terminal, but there was no such option. Money was essential, unless they wanted to terminate their escape this side of Philadelphia. Jonathan carried no credit cards. The best Patricia could do was a Hamil MasterCard with a three-hundred-dollar credit line that was almost used up. Between the two of them they had thirty-six dollars and the card.

The night through which they moved was on one level just another fragrant August night, rich with the mysterious content of nature. But underneath the beauty lurked an evil presence they could feel but not name. They sensed it in the reflection of moonlight from the startled eyes of cats, and in the long voice of the wind that seemed always to be with them.

The moon had dropped low. Soon the gray shadows of trees and houses that crazed across the lawns would be blackened away. Only the Manhattan glare in the western sky would be left providing light.

Patricia took Jonathan's hand in hers as they approached the Banion house. She wanted to say, Don't be afraid, but she did not dare even to whisper until they were better concealed.

They had gone first to her apartment to get her miserable little cache of five-dollar bills. Four of them—big deal. But what could they expect? She was at the moment taking home exactly $168.42 a week. The pistol Mike had given her was there too, guarding her fortune, and she had dropped it into her purse as well.

It was safest to assume that the Night Church was everywhere, watching, waiting. Not patient, either. Patricia remembered the avidity of the thing that had raped her.

With each step she took she said a prayer. But it was not your usual Catholic turn-the-other-cheek sort of thing, it was a raging, furious prayer for the utter destruction of the Night Church and all its faithful.

Patricia had insisted that they walk instead of taking the bus from her place to his, for a very practical reason. This way they could better detect anybody following them. The streets of this quiet and exclusive enclave hidden in the middle of Queens were just too empty at four thirty A.M. for a follower not to be seen or heard. They didn't want the Night Church and didn't need Mike's guards. This had to be done alone.

She intended that they would take the Long Island Railroad milk run in from Kew Gardens at five. From Penn Station they would walk to the bus terminal and get on the first long-distance express they found, and go where it was going.

Now that this plan was being executed she could almost taste the freedom of the new life it promised.

She took Jonathan's hand. Nobody was going to ruin the common, everyday happiness she wanted to share with him.

As they walked along, she felt in her purse with her other hand, touching the steel flesh of her pistol.

"I don't think I can kill," he had said when she picked up the weapon. "Can you?"

Yes, to protect us.

They reached the walkway that led up to the house. Even with the money they would get here they were hardly in for an easy time.

She put her arm around Jonathan's waist and drew him past the house, hushing his impulse to go through the front door with a quiet whisper. Precautions and strategies did not occur to Jonathan. If this was to be done right she had to do it. Her ability came from dormitory sneaks, creeping out on midnight dares.

The important thing was to assume the worst. That way you wouldn't be surprised.

They slipped from bush to bush until she had a view overlooking both the Banion house and the sidewalk before it. She tugged at Jonathan's hand, gestured, and crouched down. He came down beside her. They were behind a shrub, perhaps an ailanthus bush, well concealed.

She risked a breathy whisper. "We'll give it five minutes, then go in through the garage."

"Give what five minutes?"

"Our tail, dope. If anybody's following us we'll see them come up the sidewalk."

"You're beautiful."

Mr. Romantic. He didn't even now understand the danger they were in, not really.

Her dream thing's eyes were yellow and huge and steady.

"What's come over you? Are you all right?"

"Sh! Whisper."

"Sorry."

She pinched his wrist. "I'm praying that we'll get out of this alive." Lord, let him finally grasp the seriousness of our problem.

He patted her on the cheek, an absurd gesture of reassurance. For all his strength and intelligence, Jonathan could be maddeningly guileless.

The five minutes passed without a sign of trouble. Patricia allowed herself some small hope. She was going to get them out of this. One day soon, she would have a little room somewhere and a decent little job and the exotic luxury of this man as her husband.

Or was that more than this particular ordinary garden-variety mutant had a right to ask?

She drew him close to her; she could smell his golden body in the dark. He smelled so sweet, so unlike the stench of a normal human being on a hot night. She felt her own body singing with desire. His hand came under her chin and turned her face to his. There was nothing wrong in that; kisses were silent.

The mutants find one another attractive. Of course.

So many lonely years were being erased by his kisses, a whole girlhood of desolate tea-dances with the Saint Dominic boys. But we orphans did not want other orphans, we wanted princes. How we dreamed, we wizard-frogged princesses.

Somewhere a dog howled. Both of their heads turned toward the distant noise. But it was far away, blocks and blocks. A bird muttered a reply. The air moved a little, and a few leaves whispered.

She gave his shoulder two quick taps and nodded her head. They rose up from behind their bush and trotted into the Banion side yard. Although Patricia did not know the place as well as he, she did not let Jonathan lead even here. She took out her pistol, flicked off the rather stiff safety catch. For some reason its presence in her hand was a little embarrassing; she held it down where Jonathan could not see. It implied a kind of commitment to what they were doing that she was not entirely sure she wanted him to perceive. It might scare him.

She hefted the gun a little, preparing to enter the house.

They reached the back door that led into the garage. Jonathan took out his keys and opened it. There was a deafening squeak, then they were in, brushing spider webs from their faces. The garage was black; too bad they didn't have a small flashlight.

Jonathan's hand came into hers. "I'm scared, hon, to be frank."

"We'll be all right. Just keep on."

"If we get caught—"

"We'll back each other up. Better to be caught here by Mike and your mother if we're going to be caught at all."

A hard squeeze of the hand communicated heartfelt assent. A few steps into the garage Patricia realized Mike's car was gone. All to the good. One less person to wake up.

They went through the shadowy kitchen, past the hanging plants and the gleaming appliances Patricia had once so admired, through the dining room with its wonderful antique table and chairs, and into Mike's den. Here were loungers and a dartboard on the wall and a case of books about police work. Here also a big television for the weekend games and a desk for the weeknight work. The room spoke Mike Banion and made Patricia feel sad for the friendship that had to die. Without her and Jonathan Mike was going to be a very lonely man.

"I think we might find something in the desk." Jonathan lifted up the blotter. He withdrew the key from a little leather slit on its underside. Clever hiding place, and fortunate that Jonathan knew about it.

There was a money clip of twenties in the top drawer. Six of them. Jonathan pocketed it.

"Hot money," he whispered. He tried to smile but it was obvious he felt as unpleasant about this as she did. She took a deep, calming breath, and calculated. They now had a hundred and fifty-six dollars. It wasn't enough. They had to go upstairs.

As Jonathan knew the house so much better than she, there was no choice at this point but to let him lead the way. She had no faith in his innocent skills as a burglar. She stopped him at the foot of the stairs. "If she wakes up, do you know what to do?"

"Run like hell."

"No! That's how you get caught. You stand absolutely still and don't make a sound. She'll go back to sleep."

"Oh, I see." Although the house was centrally air conditioned, the air upstairs smelled thickly of the perfumes of sleep. Patricia first sent Jonathan into his own room to get the eleven dollars and six subway tokens on his dresser. When he came back they went together to Mike and Mary's bedroom.

Mary lay on the near side of the bed, turned toward them. Her face was almost invisible. Patricia looked long at her from the shadows of the hall. For a breathless few moments it seemed that her eyes might be open.

I will kill her if I must, she told herself. I will not hesitate. But that was a lie: this woman was Jonathan's mother. His shoulder touched Patricia's. All Patricia could do was hope that Mary didn't wake up and force the issue.

Now that they were this close to the end Patricia could leave

Jonathan here in the hall for the rest of the job. The other girls had always chosen her to sneak into Sister Saint John's room when that was called for, replacing her wimple with the gardener's fedora or stealing the lenses out of her glasses or some such mischief.

Mary Banion was not the good-hearted soul Sister had been, and this was not funny. Carefully, moving so that she rustled as little as possible, Patricia went past the bed. Mary's breathing was not regular. Bad, bad sign. Just as she was deciding to retreat, Mary's purse swam into view on the dresser. In it would be the wallet. How much? A couple of hundred if they got lucky. California, Florida, Texas, Montana. Freedom in a purse.

When Patricia reached in, something made a distinct clinking sound. She froze.

No movement from the bed.

She withdrew the wallet. Before she dared leave the room she stood a long time watching and listening. Mary was very still. Patricia began to move toward the door.

When she was beside the bed she looked down at Mary once again.

And met very definitely open eyes.

There came from Mary a long hissing sound like cloth tearing. She rose up in bed. Patricia stood dumbfounded, confused by the suddenness of Mary's movements.

"Stop. Both of you!" Mary leaped from the bed.

Patricia got to the door just before Mary would have blocked it with her body. "You can't run away. It's impossible!"

"Leave us alone, Mary. Don't you dare try to stop us."

The sound that came in response was almost inhuman in its rage.

"I have a gun, Mary!"

"You can't escape, you little fools, you *belong* to the Church."

"Jonathan, come on," she said as she brushed past him.

As Patricia ran down the stairs she listened for the clatter of his footsteps behind, and was relieved to hear them.

Would she have gone back for him, into the face of that woman?

Once outside Patricia threw her arms around him.

Then she saw Mary coming through the garage door, a raincoat thrown over her nightgown. She moved silently, swiftly. Patricia's gun didn't even seem to concern her.

A wind came up as they raced along the alley that led into Eighty-Fourth Avenue. Large drops of rain began to rustle the leaves. The air grew dense. The northern sky was a deeper black; a storm was coming. Patricia pulled the collar of her blouse up around her neck. In a way a storm would help them by obscuring the sounds of their movement, but they would be conspicuous on the train if they arrived wet.

"We'll cut through Forest Park," she told Jonathan. "It's quickest." Would they be watching the Kew Gardens station? She could only hope not.

As they approached Park Lane a garbage truck clattered past, trailing from its closed maw like a flag the tatters of a red dress. They climbed the low wall that outlined Forest Park and set off among the trees.

Absolute silence and absolute darkness filled the park. Forest Park was so named because it contained the largest stand of virgin forest in New York City, uncut since before the founding of the United States. Seventy-foot oaks and maples soared into the dark from a bed of mist-hazed ferns. She and Jonathan kept to familiar paths, worn clear by generations of shortcutters. Patricia plodded along, aware that the damp was rapidly making a mockery of her shoes. Passing beneath the Interboro Parkway overpass she was briefly spared the trickle of rainwater down her neck. The woods were deeper on the far side, but they could now make use of one of the park roadways, a winding blacktop lane dotted with potholes, where carriages once had rolled and lovers strolled.

The wind made the ferns whisper and the tops of the trees utter long sighs.

When Patricia saw the gleam of water on metal ahead, she realized the enormous strategic error she had just made. Forest Park was not the same as a weed-choked alley. Here the Night Church could afford a few risks. Screams didn't matter in this wilderness, and there were no back doors on which to pound.

The Night Church had worked very fast. Mary could not have warned them more than a few minutes ago.

"Hold it." She grabbed his shoulder. "There's a van here."

"Where?"

She lifted his hand, placed it against the cold metal. His whole body jerked, as if he had been delivered an electric shock.

"Back up," she breathed. "Maybe they haven't seen us."

They turned off the road onto a path. She wasn't sure, but she thought it led out onto Park Place. If so, they would be safe in a few minutes. As they picked their way through the wet, slapping ferns she heard the distinct sound of footfalls on the roadway they had just left. Then there was crashing in the brush not fifty feet behind them.

"Oh, God, Jonathan, run!"

As they dashed through the slapping ferns she fingered the safety of her pistol again and again. She would use it, she told herself, she would certainly use it.

That thought was recurring so often she was beginning to be afraid she didn't really have the courage.

The ferns slapped her legs and she kept blundering into tree trunks. Beside her Jonathan clambered and fell along. A steady shuffling of brush followed them.

They went on like that for a while, with the Night Church fifty feet behind. The memory of the thing she had encountered at Holy Spirit made her run like a madwoman, battling the wet, clawing undergrowth, her feet sliding in mud, sheets of rain obscuring her vision.

Was the thing behind them?

Jonathan screamed and fell against her. She clutched him, got him to his feet. "Come on, honey!"

Fingers whipped like snakes around her neck and she grabbed at them, trying to fight instead of scream, trying to keep the terror from rising up and blanking her ability to resist.

With a growl of naked rage Jonathan leaped across the three feet that separated him from whoever was on her and grabbed him. Instantly the arm was swept away and Patricia was confronted with a seething, rolling mass of flailing limbs. She heard blow after blow land. She heard air hiss from lungs and bones crunch.

"For God's sake, you're killing him!"

"That's—exactly—right!" Jonathan said. Again and again his arm rose and fell, until there was no further movement from the figure beneath him. Jonathan stood up. Patricia was awed; she had never seen anything like it before. In a few seconds he had beaten a man senseless—maybe to death.

She hugged him. "Are you hurt, darling?"

"I'm fine. Let's get a move on."

There was a shuffle of ferns ahead. A distinct click. "Drop the gun, please," said a quiet, cold voice.

Instead Patricia pointed it in the direction of the sound and pulled the trigger, a feeling of vicious and triumphant power surging through her.

The pistol went click. Click. Clickclick.

Something pricked her neck. "Don't move, either of you." Another dark figure stepped out of the bushes beside Jonathan. She could see in his hand the same weapon that must be cold against her own neck. A stiletto.

Her stomach heaved. "Drop the pistol." The razored edge of the knife caressed her neck. "It's useless to you. The powder was taken out of the bullets the night you got it." She threw it to the ground, feeling the most intense helplessness. They even had access to her apartment. There was no escape from them, none at all. Even to have tried was stupid.

A two-way radio burped in the darkness. Patricia became aware that there were a large number of people around them. They had been at the center of a highly organized net all the time.

She threw the pistol to the ground. The pressure of steel against her neck diminished.

"Come with us, please."

Jonathan started off ahead of her. He was pushed roughly. Behind them flashlights bobbed in the path and voices were raised. They were trying to help the one Jonathan had beaten.

Patricia allowed herself a moment to be proud of him. He had tried hard; that meant a great deal.

Soon more of the search party met them. There were easily twenty people around, all in black turtlenecks and jeans. Occasional flashes of lightning revealed them to be utterly ordinary young men and women, clean-cut, even pleasant-looking.

Nobody had scales, nobody had reptile eyes.

Patricia had visualized the Night Church in terms of batwing soup and gnarled old wizards. These men probably worked in law offices and insurance agencies by day, and the women raised kids in pretty Kew Gardens homes.

When the back door of the van was opened slightly, a shaft of yellow light leaked out. The door opened all the way. "Come," said a pleasantly modulated voice.

Although the door was locked behind them, this luxurious interior hardly seemed a prison. Jonathan sat back in one of the deep leather seats. "I can't grasp this." His voice was like ashes.

"I know."

The van had no windows, and the walls were covered with padding. There was a well-stocked bar, complete with ice, glasses, potato chips, and pretzels.

"Don't eat or drink any of that stuff, Jonathan."

"Of course not." He slumped forward, bowed his head into his hands. She sat down in the seat beside him and put her arm around him.

The van started off. Patricia experienced what seemed an almost primordial urge to escape, as if she had been trapped in a cave-in or locked in a coffin.

The van gathered speed, driving on deep into the night.

Chapter Nineteen

MIKE HAD TO exhume Franklin Apple's coffin. The way the Night Church operated there could be anything in there—or anybody. He might not like it, but he had to go through the whole official drill to make it happen.

It was late afternoon before he could make all the bureaucracies involved agree. Finally the paperwork was complete and Mike sat waiting in his old Dodge at the entrance to All Souls Cemetery. Night was coming, he was tired and uncomfortable, and he wished he could go home. He rubbed his palms along his cheeks, which itched like fire. Either he had shaved sloppily at his office or he was allergic to the cologne Mary had given him. His whole face was sensitive. Too bad. He liked the cologne a lot. Time to change, probably. The older you get the more allergic you become. Allergic to life, finally. Then you pack it in.

It had been a rotten day, beginning when he woke up at eight on the couch in his office feeling like he had been cared for by a Mack truck, and proceeding through contact with a smarmy assistant DA who could not understand why Apple should be exhumed on so "minor" a matter as an alias, and going from there to miserable dealings with the Board of Health and the Cemeteries Department, getting the exhumation order initialed by the right department heads.

It had started raining just before dawn and hadn't stopped all day. The graveyard was going to be a mess.

Mike considered himself a careful, patient detective. He had learned that cases were cracked either by persistence or luck, and he was not the lucky type. He was no longer even close to buying the fact that "Mr. Apple" was dead. No way was a coincidence like that going to happen. No way. Especially since his real name was very probably Titus.

Mike was pretty sure he was going to turn up a load of cinder blocks or bricks, or maybe just a coffin full of sand. It was no big deal to get a burial like that done. The Dexter Funeral Home over on Metro Avenue did fakeouts for the Mafia all the time. Two thousand bucks could get a box of bricks buried, priest's honorarium included.

Mike carried the exhumation order in his breast pocket behind his cigars. Being a high-class dump, All Souls did not like cops and exhumations even a little bit. To avoid being ordered off the property you had to be sure every *i* was dotted and every *t* crossed.

While he was waiting, Mike took some more time to work on his own emotional state.

He had been crazy last night after being in that house. Crazy with fear. After a few hours on the couch in his office he had realized that he was going to have to break this case. He might have to confront the Devil himself to do it, but he was by God going to expose the Night Church.

That didn't change his fear, though. It was with sick dread that he had called Mary at nine, pleaded that an emergency had kept him out all night, then told her to expect him home for dinner. As nerve-racking as staying there would be, not doing so was too obvious a tip-off. And he dared not arrange for a backup team out on the street. He might be making his arrangements with the Night Church.

He wasn't looking forward to the night ahead. No way was he going to sleep.

He hit his hands against the steering wheel. This case was so damn complicated. It would be nice just to be able to walk people in on charges right now. But what charges, and which people? Christ, what a mess.

What better cover for a woman like Mary than being married to a police official?

Sweet lady. Supposed to have loved him. Maybe she did, who knew? It sure as hell didn't matter to him. A nasty taste came into his mouth just thinking about last night. He shook his head, fighting the images.

Mike intended to sift this case exceedingly fine.

Another car pulled up. The Department of Health observer and the Queens County coroner—or, as Mike could see through the window

of the battered green city-issue Dodge, coroness. A fine, robust speci-
men of a woman too, and visibly pissed off about gravedigging in the
rain. The two of them got out of their jalopy and came over to Mike's.
They knew their protocol, at least. When you are working with a
detective inspector who is fool enough to get out and wallow in the
mud, you damn well come to him because you know he is a man
obsessed. Inspectors are not even supposed to work cases. Their job is
managing detectives.

"Inspector Banion?"

"Yours truly."

The Health Department type leaned into the car, his popeyes wet
with fatigue, his breath a mixture of C&C Cola and streetcorner hot
dog. These guys did a tough job, chasing down rats and sick dogs,
scraping shit off floors, examining corpses for signs of contagion. "I'm
Inspector Ryan," he said. "This is Doctor Phillips."

Mike unlocked his doors. "Come on in. The gravediggers are late."

The two of them piled into the police car. "Sorry about the rain,"
Mike said.

"As long as they can dig." The coroness was younger than she
looked.

"This your first exhumation?"

"My first in a rainstorm."

"Maybe you're lucky. The wet'll hold down the stink."

Silence followed this remark. The bureaucrats were here because
the law required their presence. But they were also human beings, and
they must be curious about why such a high official was supervising an
emergency exhumation in the middle of a rainy afternoon. They were
going to stay curious. Mike wasn't going to repeat one word about this
case to outsiders. He might be talking to the Night Church.

He looked across at a forlorn paper sign tied to the iron gate.
GROWING SEASON, JUNE 1–NOVEMBER 1. FRESH FLOWERS ONLY.
ARTIFICIALS WILL BE REMOVED. A high-toned cemetery.

In keeping with its image it was full of the most amazing monuments. For fifty years the Mafia had been burying here. The more
murderous the sonofabitch, the more elaborate the grave. Buddy
DiMaestro had a goddamn twelve-foot angel with a sword in its hand
over his grave. Who was it supposed to scare, God?

Beth was also here, off in the Irish section of the boneyard. Not a huge monument, but he kept it clean. He came out here Sundays to talk to her. There had always been space in that plot for Mike.

A rumbling behind his car announced the arrival of the gravediggers and their trenching tool. Good they had it; they would abandon this job if their only tools were picks and shovels. They were grim-faced, these three sanitation-department employees. These men spent most of their time at the city indigent graveyard on Hart's Island. Mike had been out there occasionally, fussing over the grid map in an effort to locate the remains of one unfortunate soul or another. It was a bleak place, with a mocking view of the waters of Long Island Sound, gay with sailboats and sun. The men who worked there looked like moles.

Mike started his car and began leading the procession into the cemetery. He stopped at the office and showed a tight-faced manager his EO. "You got it," was all the manager said. He held out a book for Mike to sign. Then there was a disclaimer form, and certifications for the two bureaucrats. They read their forms carefully and applied their precise bureaucratic signatures.

The little procession got underway again, moving down a wet, abandoned road, almost a path. On both sides opulent monuments loomed like watchers from the pages of some dangerous old romance.

Mike soon stopped his car. The trencher ground its gears and the three sanitmen piled down from the cab. "Let's start digging," Mike said. Then he added in an undertone, "There's three fifths of Chivas in my trunk for you guys, so drawing this gig isn't a total wipeout."

There was an immediate lift in their mood. One of them smiled, another gave a satisfied grunt. "That's gonna feel good, man," the third and most articulate said. They set about their labor with something close to gusto. From inside the car the two bureaucrats watched grimly. They had done most of their work; they were afraid that they were going to be cheated.

Mike had been in the business too long to do that to city employees. "Listen," he said as he got back into the car, "you folks want your fees in cash or goods? I got scotch in the trunk or three nickels apiece in my wallet. Take your choice."

"Our fees always come in cash," the coroness said. "We aren't allowed to take goods." Mike counted her out three fives.

The health inspector took liquor.

Outside the trenching tool started up with a roar and began digging away.

So everybody was happy, everybody was willing to work. Most times Mike wouldn't have given these people anything, and nothing would have been expected, but in the wet of a miserable afternoon it was only fair.

He and the two officials sat in the car while the gravediggers did their business, cursing and using their tool like a weapon, spattering mud over the gravestone, a simple but expensive piece of Carrara marble engraved with FRANKLIN APPLE, DECEMBER 11, 1893–JULY 12, 1983. Not even an R.I.P. The trenching tool, a small tractor with a device on it like a huge chain saw, rattled and swayed, its teeth crunching down into the earth. In fifteen minutes a goodly hill of soil had piled up beside it.

At last the men went to work with shovels. Normally on an exhumation this was when you came speeding up in your car, jumped out, and peered down into the grave. Not this time. Mike had learned respect for the Night Church. Best to assume it was always right next to him. The coroness, for example. Or one of the gravediggers. Or the assistant DA who had given him a hard time.

"Yo," one of the men called from inside the grave.

"Let's go, folks, this is what wc came for."

They got out into drifting mist. Mud oozed under Mike's feet, sucking at his overshoes. He huddled deep into his trenchcoat, his old snap-brim faithfully keeping his bald spot safe from the elements.

At the bottom of the grave was a steel coffin cover. At least the funeral home had done a good job, and buried what it had said it would bury. Many a dearly beloved got prayed over in steel and mahogany but went down in pine; it was a popular ripoff.

The wind moaned in the trees, and rain steamed on the car headlights that illuminated the scene. In the depths of the grave the steel gleamed in the flashlight glare. "Pull the damn thing off, boys," Mike said.

They got a rope through the hooks on the sides of the heavy coffin cover and raised it on their winch. Now the coffin itself lay exposed, clean and gunmetal gray, with raindrops beading on its polished surface.

"Go ahead," Mike said. His witnesses stood beneath umbrellas on the far side of the grave, which was the windward side. If there was a ripe corpse in there they were going to want to move upwind with Mike in a hurry.

The coffin was locked, and nobody had the key. Mike thought of it lying in Mr. Apple's living room. One by one the screws holding the locking mechanism were removed. When the last of them came out there was a hermetic hiss. That had been one well-sealed coffin. "It's ripe," the coroness called.

"Come around here. It doesn't smell so bad." The umbrellas bobbed in the mist and soon the two officials were beside Mike. "Okay, open it up."

The gravediggers started to lift the lid. They hesitated, dug their feet in as if it was heavier than it should be, then heaved it back.

The coroness screamed. The Health Department inspector made a sharp sound between his teeth. Mike knew that this moment was going to haunt him for the rest of his life. He had just encountered his worst murder. He was more than a little surprised; he had expected either cinder blocks or Mr. Titus, alias Apple. The spectacle before him was the kind of thing every homicide professional secretly dreads, the one so bad it gets past all your defenses. You know you will be spending nights with it from now on, seeing that frozen scream again and again, hearing the awful ripping sound the fingernails made when they popped out of the coffin lid.

"I'm sorry," Mike said into the silence. Down in the grave one of the diggers covered his face with mud-gloved hands. Another looked up toward Mike, or perhaps past him toward God. Or maybe just to see a little sky. "Hold it, guys, I'm comin' down." Mike descended their ladder, slipping once on a muddy rung.

The grave had the same sweet smell that had come from the fox-holes of the dead in Korea. Foul sweet. "Poor bastard. Coulda at least knocked him out." Mike tried to see the face, but the car lights didn't penetrate that far. He fumbled for his penlight.

"No shit, man," one of the diggers said. "I wish I hadn't seen this." His voice was awed to softness. A lot of people who work with human death do not fulfill the common mythology and become hard. They become very kind. Suffering respects itself.

The victim's fingers had been hooked into the coffin lid so tightly that the whole corpse had at first risen up, then fallen back as the fingernails came loose. Black stains covered the shredded rayon upholstery. Blood from those scratching, clawing fingers.

With just the penlight there was no way to distinguish features.

"Get the big flash from the back of my car," Mike called up to the bureaucrats. In the meantime he played his penlight into the coffin. The mess it revealed told exactly what it was like to die at the bottom of your own grave. It was very, very hard. The eyes, bulging open, had sunk to black holes; the mouth, spread in a last, anguished gasp, was all teeth and bitten, shredded lips. The corpse was so new that all the suffering was still there, in the eloquence and humanity of the frozen scream.

Policemen get good at pretending to be hard, but inside they slowly transform through the years, until the cruelty of human beings begins to seem a monstrous defect in the species, more pitiful than bad. They start seeing criminals and victims alike as cogs in a great wheel of human failure. Need and greed grind them all to pulp, weak and strong, good and bad.

"Cops and clowns are sad men," Harry Goodwin once had said deep into a bottle of Chivas, "and priests are better off dead." Mike recalled his own laughter. But now he didn't feel any of the irony or sadness of the remark. After last night he could feel only one powerful emotion—fear. And this new horror added to it in a particularly ugly way. Mike could imagine himself dying slowly at the bottom of a grave.

The health officer came scrambling down with the flashlight, but Mike had had enough. Let the homicide boys identify the poor sucker, that's what they were paid for.

"I'm gonna call this goddamn mess in," Mike said to the people around him. "Anybody wanna throw up, just do it outside of where people are gonna have to walk. All hell's gonna break loose around here in a few minutes."

Mike didn't know of a ten code for burial alive, so he talked it. "This is Inspector Banion. Location: All Souls Cemetery, Roadway W-3, Gravesite E-144. I have a DOA buried alive. Please respond with a homicide workup."

The radio crackled back acknowledgment. Mike sat staring at the hand holding the microphone. Old hand. Age spotted, especially on the back. Busted thumbnail from that bout trying to repair Mary's hairdryer. The tears he had felt coming passed down his cheeks just about on schedule. He wiped them away fast, trying to replace this big, nameless feeling with something he could understand and cope with, like anger or outrage. Whoever the poor devil was, he did not deserve to die like that.

Sirens rose. Fast work. New York City cops are the best in the world at getting through traffic. Especially with the new hee-haw sirens making counterpoint to the old-fashioned wailers some of the EMS meatwagons still use. Mike could count the cars by their sirens. Six squad cars. A large segment of the precinct was turning out. The Banion legend was still very much alive, at least. And this particular discovery would not do it any damage.

Mike got out of his car and stood in the rain as Max and his lady sergeant trotted up. Their faces were as gray as the afternoon light. "Hello, Inspector. You sure it's not Apple?"

"Looks like a younger man in there."

"Any ID?"

"Wearing a cheap doubleknit suit. I didn't look in the pockets." He paused a moment, too stunned to talk. His heart almost exploded in his chest. "Oh, holy God, I must be gettin' old! I *know* that suit!"

Max started to say something but Mike was running back to the grave, to the place where that poor jerk was buried. He clambered down and grabbed the flashlight from the health inspector, who gave it up gratefully. He looked sick. The gravediggers were huddled at the edge of the hole, shivering. The coroness was off vomiting.

Terry. You poor, innocent man. Terry.

"Max," he shouted in rage and sorrow, "call in a revised bulletin on Terry Quist. Change the goddamn thing from missing person to homicide."

Max turned and disappeared past the edge of the grave. Mike looked down at his friend, looked long and hard. And he vowed vengeance.

Another man might have wanted to be alone at this point, or at least to spend some appreciable time in a bar, but Mike Banion went from being frightened to being downright mad. He was going to *get* the bastards who had done this no matter what it took. And no matter who they had on their side. If he had to face Satan himself to do it, he damn well would.

The Night Church might be monstrous and terrifying, but this cruel murder showed it was also full of the petty viciousness of any criminal organization. Mike could understand that. He could feel contempt for it.

He'd like to find some cop who was a member of the thing and detail him to go down and bag poor Terry's body.

Police vehicles kept arriving. There were a dozen of them here, with men hurrying to the just-searchlit graveside with their equipment, cameras, and crime scene tapes, and all the other paraphernalia that modern detection techniques impose on police officers. Mike returned to his car, tossing away the stale cigar stub as he went. Once inside he lit a fresh one, glorying in the warm, aromatic smoke. A fresh cigar is a nice thing when you're all twisted up inside. It can untwist you like nothing else on this earth.

Max joined him.

Mike had to talk. "They buried Quist alive. Jesus, they *buried him alive!*" Now it all came pouring out. "In all my career I've never seen that. I mean, he was just a small-time jerkoff reporter. Nothin'! What'd they do it for? Fun?"

"Rough, Mike. Real rough. But we're gonna get 'em now. Because of this."

"Don't be too sure, Lieutenant. We got a long hard ways to go yet."

"It seems to me," said Max's assistant, "that we need to physically find this alias. Apple's the key."

"His name is probably Franklin Titus."

"How'd you get there, Mike?"

"Never mind, Max. I been burnin' the midnight oil."

"Well, if we have a name, we ought to be able to find our man easily enough."

"Okay, Sarge, you go do that. Go do it!"

"Relax, Mike, she's as committed as you are."

"Oh, hell, I'm sorry. Just think it out. Obviously Titus is the best thing we could get. But he's the last thing we're *gonna* get. You can put money on that. He's king of the mountain. We won't find him till all the people in front of him have been knocked aside."

Silence followed these remarks. Sitting there in his car, listening to the rain on the roof, Mike realized what he had to do. It was simple enough. He got out, said his goodbyes to his people, passed out the promised scotch, and returned alone to the car.

He was going to stay real cozy with Mary from now on. She was the ticket in the front door. His own lovely wife. Serves you right, marrying for looks.

Damn you, Mary, I'm gonna fry you!

Okay, Mr. Detective, fry her hot but move cool. Move very cool. She's one dangerous lady, Mary Titus Banion.

He drove along the old boulevard, past Farrell's, past the skating rink that had been a disco and before that a ballroom, and way long ago a movie theater. Before that, in the dimness of Mike's boyhood, it had been a grassy field, the kind of place where kids went to smoke and drink, and explore one another's bodies in the summer night.

"Death always sneaks up on us," Father Goodwin said. "Death is the greatest surprise of all."

Mike felt exhausted. The old body was yearning for its supper. Mary would have a meal waiting. First there would be a nice cold martini, the kind of drink that worked. Mary would stand in the doorway to the kitchen, smoking one of her Benson & Hedges cigarettes and talking softly to him. Mary was so extremely sexy. He thought of the places she was curved, and how astonishingly smooth her skin was, the way there was a sound like the whisper of snow when he moved his hands along her thighs. He liked how she smelled at the end of the day, Lanvin powder mixed with a suggestion of sweat. Were women really as innocent as they seemed of the fact that they carried the world? Even the bitches and the wrong ones.

By the time he arrived home the rain had become a deluge. He operated the garage-door opener and parked his car beside Mary's Audi. The woman had style; she looked great in that automobile.

"Mike?"

"Yeah, I'm here."

The door creaked. Footsteps clattered on the paved floor of the garage. She appeared, her dress softly dotted pink, her chestnut hair flowing down to her shoulders. He got out of the car.

He put his big, hot paw into her cool fingers.

She closed her eyes for a moment, as if a blow had passed close.

He realized as he followed her into the house that she wasn't going to ask how he was, or even kiss him. She was afraid of her husband. Behind the sex and the habits of living together, she must feel him an absolute stranger, close only in the way people on a bus are close.

"Jonathan's not here yet. I called him an hour ago."

"Why?"

"You wanted to see him tonight. You wanted to talk about the wedding."

"Hard to believe." He felt heavier, let out a tired sigh. There was a

wedding planned. He had once wanted to give Jonathan some pointers
about how to handle a wife. Funny.

"Forget it. He doesn't need advice from me. Relax me, girl."

She handed Mike his martini. It was exactly right, as usual. Thank
God for alcohol.

"I got another break on the case," he heard himself say. He hardly
even glanced at her, but he made it count.

Inside there was a smell of steak broiling with onions. Despite
everything, he felt for her a passion so beyond his ability to suppress
that it seemed a kind of tragedy.

"I'm glad you came back. I need you." She came to him, nestled
against his chest. Then she kissed his cheek, sought his lips. "Can you
forget about the case for a while, do you think?"

Never, you witch. Beautiful, beautiful witch.

"Is anything going on downstairs, Michael Banion?"

"Find out for yourself."

She brushed her hand against the front of his trousers. "Shall I get
ready for you?"

He kissed her neck. It smelled just as he had thought it would, of
Lanvin powder and sweat. Sweet and sour. She stroked him. "I'd
better go cut off supper. I'll follow you up."

While she was in the kitchen he went up the narrow stairway to
their bedroom and with fumbling, shaking hands took off his clothes.
He arranged them so that his pistol was just under a fold of his jacket,
ready to grab.

He looked at his nakedness in the mirror, his powerful shoulders
and neck, the suggestion of dignity offered by his graying temples, the
bulging swoop of his gut.

Mary opened the door suddenly, light flowing in behind her, tripping softly and soft in her own nakedness, her thatch swimming in
shadow between ghostly thighs, her arms surrounding him and pressing him back toward the bed, her hair tickling his chest.

But when he closed his eyes he saw coffins and bloody clawmarks,
and heard a man howling in his grave. He almost lost it. He opened his
eyes quickly.

Mary worked on him dutifully, he had to give her that. She fondled
and kissed and rubbed. He closed his eyes again, remembering all the
girls he had known who had turned him on. The best was Beth

because she was so sweet and innocent except in the bedroom, where she was wild.

Mary looked down at him, trembling to a fine internal rhythm. Only all was not right: this time Mike was waiting for something, and he found it. That familiar faraway look she got in her eyes at moments of seeming passion was not ecstasy, it was detachment.

She began to act, biting her lips and moaning a little. Her tempo increased. Suddenly, still pounding, she bent down to him and began kissing his face. Her fingernails dug into his shoulders.

A week ago he would have interpreted this as extreme excitement, but this time he understood the truth: she was trying to get him to reach climax as quickly as she could.

No doubt that was always why she wanted the topside position—so she could control the tempo and get it over with as fast as possible.

But, Lord, she knew how to make it feel good. He began seeing her through the haze of higher pleasure; she was as pretty as a picture. "Mike," she gasped, "Mike, oh, Mike!"

He came and she shook and trembled and fell down on him whispering, "Thank you, thank you, you beautiful man," and then became still. Her thanks were sincere too, he knew. He had been quick.

After it was over they lay as usual side by side. Then she sat up and lit a cigarette, drawing her knees up to her chin. There was in her face something scary that he did not want to see, something that looked like suppressed glee.

"Jonathan must be at Patricia's apartment," she said. "I guess he'll stay the night."

Mike did not answer her. She had not failed herself this night. She was a very skillful deceiver—so good that her skill itself gave her away. She had not provided him with so much as a hint, not even a flicker of light on the way to the truth.

When she went down to complete their dinner his mind began drifting back and forth among the elements of the case. Terry Quist. Franklin Titus. Those wicked, insane books in Titus's house.

The anti-man to come . . . and his father, the *monstrum*. And beautiful, sensual Mary.

Somewhere between them was his answer, his whole picture, his truth. Somewhere between the woman and the grave and Hell.

Chapter Twenty ——————+

JONATHAN WOULD HAVE clawed out through the sides of the van if he had been able. "It's a damn cage! They've caged us like a couple of chimps." He prowled the luxurious interior, checking the door, the walls, feeling for some opening, some weakness.

They accelerated, decelerated, turned corners, until he lost all sense of direction.

"Sit down, Jonathan."

"If I could get this door open we might be able to jump when they slow down."

"There'll be a car following. They're very well organized."

He went to her. "We have to try."

"We have to think about what's happening to us, about what might happen when they open the door."

A sudden change in the tire sounds told Jonathan something. "We're crossing the Fifty-Ninth Street bridge, going into Manhattan."

"Jonathan, you and I are vulnerable. We feel like ordinary people, and I doubt if we have the resources to deal with whatever we're facing. We could even be brainwashed."

"They picked the wrong man for brainwashing. I can't *be* brainwashed—I know too much about the brain."

The van slowed, turned another corner.

"We're liable to stop soon, Jonathan. Whether you can be brainwashed or not, I want you to—"

He hated that idea. "I *can't* be!"

"Just listen. I want you to remember one thing at all costs. We may be mutated in a thousand different ways, but we can live ordinary lives if we try. We love each other, and we want as normal and human a life as we can have." She put her arms around him. "If we forget that, they win!"

"What's the game, though? What do they win?"

She sobbed. "Just remember what *we* want."

The van stopped. He found her lips with his own. A cheerful young man opened the doors and with firm, gentle hands drew them apart. "We're home now," he said. "Please come inside."

"The hell I will," Jonathan replied. He broke away, leaping down from the van and managing about ten feet along the sidewalk before he was surrounded by more of them than he could resist. The most pleasant of them, a smiling, pin-neat man in a crisp linen suit, showed Jonathan a vicious little knife.

"There is also the way of pain," he said affably, shouldering Jonathan between two of his friends. "You're best off cooperating."

The house was shockingly familiar. He stood looking up at the aged brownstone edifice, decorated by rows of glaring gargoyles. He had always assumed that it housed university data storage. To his knowledge, he had never been beyond the basement labs.

To the east little golden clouds floated above the skyline. Dawn was coming. The house itself was subtly transformed. The wide bay windows, which had been backed by dark curtains, now stood open.

A bell rang, and sleepy children's voices filtered out.

This was the Titus School, the secret training-ground of the Night Church. Jonathan and Patricia had grown up here.

He was hustled into the foyer where Patricia was being ushered along by one of the most fantastic creatures Jonathan had ever beheld.

Instead of the usual black broadcloth this nun wore a rich maroon silk habit. Her wimple was starched and gleaming, black instead of white. She was beautifully made up with eyeshadow and lipstick. The small foyer was filled with the scent of musky perfume.

She supported Patricia, who dragged along the floor as if fainting. When she saw Jonathan, though, she made a visible effort to pull herself together. She looked at him through haunted, tear-streaked eyes. "Don't you remember her, Jonathan?" she shouted. The nun began hurrying Patricia toward the rear of the foyer. "She's Sister Saint John, the one I put up in my apartment, the one who *raised* me from the time I was thirteen!" Her voice echoed, desolate.

"Patricia!" Strong hands grabbed his arms. He kicked. He had to get to her. "Let me go!"

"I remember now! She was at the Spirit too! She was there with Mary! Oh, God, help me! Help me!"

His ears roared, his blood thundered in his veins. *"Patricia!"*

A great clang. An iron door had closed on her.

He had not counted on them being separated. The sudden, irrevocable fact of it brought a new wave of effort, and he struggled against the men who were holding him, screaming into the silence that had followed the clang of the door. "I love you! *I love you!*"

His own shouts were absorbed by the cavernous hall. "Jonathan," a voice said when he stopped, "we're going to take you up to your room now."

They didn't release their grip even a little as they walked him across the marble floor. He could see that the hall was circular, with fluted columns supporting a small interior dome. Dim light glowed through round windows in the dome. At the rear was a sweeping horseshoe staircase that embraced a tiny, wire-enclosed elevator.

The car was waiting behind its brass grill. Two of the men pushed Jonathan in. The three of them filled the small space.

They rose in smooth silence, passing up in the cage until the floor of the lobby seemed seventy feet below. There was a click and it stopped. The men opened a door on the far side. Beyond was a corridor, softly lit with lamps in wall sconces. The walls were cream; the floor was thickly carpeted in tan.

"You'll remember the senior men's floor," said one of the men as the three of them left the elevator.

"No, I won't," Jonathan muttered. He really didn't want to listen to that sort of muck. They were not going to use disorientation techniques to confuse him. It was going to be a lot harder than that. His mind turned once again to Patricia. "When will I see her again?"

"At your wedding."

"Surely that's been canceled."

"No, it's going ahead just exactly as you planned."

No matter what else might happen, at least he was certain to see her again. "Here's your room, Jonathan. Your uncle will be in shortly." Before he could resist or say another word they had thrust him through a door and closed it behind him.

"No!" He grappled with the knob, hammered the unyielding metal. He kicked the door so viciously it sent a shock all the way up his leg and caused him to fall backward onto the floor, which he hit with a bone-rattling crash. For a moment he lay still. Then he went to the window, but found he couldn't even raise the sash to get his hands on the bars beyond it.

When he looked around for something to use to break the glass, he was frozen with astonishment.

He knew this room.

He knew it perfectly, utterly, completely.

It was *his* room, his own boyhood room. The Hallicrafters was there on the desk, with the model Gemini capsule sitting on it. His bookcase held all his wonderful old friends, *Tom Sawyer, The Once and Future King,* the Complete Shakespeare, the Mary Renault novels, *Life's Picture History of the Earth.*

The bedspread was the one Mother had made, with his name embroidered in red on a background of the Orion constellation. His telescope stood at the foot of the bed under a dust cover, just where he had left it when—

When?

A long time ago. He knelt down, gingerly removed the cover. There it was, his beloved Celestron, the treasure of his youth.

It had been a long time since he had thought of astronomy, of those wonderful autumn nights up in the Connecticut woods with Jerry Cochran, climbing a hillside and searching out Wolf 457 or Saturn or the Crab Nebula. Jerry. His boyhood idol. Tall, cool, a brilliant scientific mind. Jerry's seven years' seniority made him almost godlike to the younger boy. If Jonathan had modeled himself on anybody, it had been Jerry Cochran.

We walked the star path, he and I.

He grew very still as the awesome power of memory began pouring his true past up from his depths. He remembered his old friend with almost sacred vividness, his brown eyes, his great broad smile and the sword-sharpness of his mind.

"Jerry." He touched the Celestron, his fingers caressing its controls. What wonders we found with this thing, you and I. "Earth is just a green bubble in the void, Jonathan. Less than a speck of dust. Out here, lost, falling toward the unknown." You were wise for your years, Jerry, so very wise.

The room was a museum of his own past. There at the bottom of the bookshelf were *The Winter Noisy Book* and *The Fire Engine Book* and all the other books of babyhood, *Mother Goose* and *The Encyclopedia of Things* and *Hiawatha* and *Olly Olly Oxen Free.*

And in the big drawer under the bed—pull it out—yes, there were his models, the wonderful, intricate airplanes constructed of balsa and paper, flown by rubber bands at high summer evening when the breeze was still. His Rascal 18 racer, his P-51 that never flew well because it was too heavily doped, even the remains of Jerry's Cessna 182 that had met fatefully with the rose trellis in—in—

Uncle's front yard?

Who was Uncle, and where was that bungalow full of furniture a little boy mustn't touch?

Never mind that now. He went to the Hallicrafters, turned it on. The heterodyne wail of shortwave met his ears as he twisted the knob back and forth. Yes, here was the BBC and there was Cuba and there Radio Moscow, and down along there were the Africans and the Arabs, and in the middle the rest of the Europeans, Netherlands with its concerts and Germany with its language lessons, and France and Italy and Spain.

Oh, yes, on a thousand deepest nights Jerry and I were at this radio, turning the dial ever so slowly from wonder to wonder.

Let's hear what Khrushchev's got to say about the election.

The Royal Shakespeare is doing Measure for Measure *on the BBC tonight.*

We don't want to miss the Cuban-English–Language News.

We were two adventurers of the mind. And what a wonderful time we had . . . when I was normal. When I was myself.

But there were other times.

"Let me out of here! I can't stand it in here!"

"I see you're beginning to come back to us."

"Who—"

He was a dried-up, incredibly ancient man. Only his bright green eyes had any life. His face was a badland of creases, age-rotted skin stretched across sharp old bones. He wore a beautifully tailored black suit and a silver-gray silk shirt. His head was framed by a white vapor of hair. On his fingers there were complex rings. Jonathan saw skulls and intricate cabbalistic symbols in the gold, and ruby eyes and open jaws. Only his thumbs were without jewelry.

"My dear nephew." He opened his arms. Behind him in the hallway stood a young man easily six foot five, his arms folded, watching from the shadows.

Jonathan did not move toward the little gargoyle with the open arms. He had no uncle.

Patricia's words came back to him: *We may be mutated in a thousand different ways, but we can live ordinary lives if we try.*

Much wisdom in that.

"You act like a cornered rat, Jonathan. I must confess I'm disappointed. I expected more of the Prince."

Crazy. But backed up by a powerful guard. And the windows behind Jonathan were barred.

"Frightened of me. How embarrassing. Am I too ugly for you?" He raised his hands, which arthritis had turned to oak gnarls. There was in this man a density of menace. "You find me ugly, you of all people. You may have a handsome appearance, but inside you are far uglier than I!"

"Get away from me."

"You are the *monstrum.*"

"You need a psychiatrist, you're a paranoid schizophrenic. I can help you. I want to help you."

The sparks of eyes twinkled. "On the contrary, Jonathan, it is *I* who can help *you*. You must prepare, you know. The Ritual Marriage is tonight."

Jonathan backed away from the eerie old man.

"Let me touch you, nephew." The hands, trembling, came out toward him. Jonathan cast around, grabbed the radio, raised it over his head.

"Stop! Don't come any nearer!"

The old man stepped aside and his guard began moving into the room.

Jonathan hurled the Hallicrafters with all his might—and the guard caught it, rocking back on his heels and drawing a gasp of breath. He stood with the enormous radio in his hands, looking at Jonathan. Slowly, he smiled.

"Jerry!"

He put the radio down and locked Jonathan in a strong embrace. "Be careful," the old man said. "Remember, It beat a man to death just a few hours ago."

What a lie. The man had hardly even been knocked unconscious. "I am a human being, so don't call me 'It!' And I barely touched that man, as you well know."

"You crushed his chest and broke his back in three places. You all but tore his head off and popped his skull."

"I—"

"And you are *not* human, you are the *monstrum.*"

"Shut up! Stop calling me that idiotic name!" He thought of the brain scans he had done of himself and Patricia, the incredible results. *Monstrum.* So that was what he was called. And she too. She had the same brain-wave pattern. *Monstrum.*

He turned his gaze to Jerry, just as he had when he had needed help as a boy. Friend and teacher, Jerry had also been his bodyguard. A confused welter of memories flooded him as he looked at his friend.

The old man soon shattered the moment. "Come on, Jerry. Leave him to his memories for now." He indicated an envelope on the desk. "There's a letter that will explain a great deal. I suggest you read it."

They began to leave the room. "Wait!" Jonathan cried, but before he could stop them the door was closed and locked.

Jonathan was furious. This time he lunged at the window, smashing the glass with his hands, uncaring of gashes, and grappled with the bars. He yanked them and yanked them and kicked them and tried to spread them. And was defeated by them.

He picked up the Hallicrafters, which Jerry had placed neatly back on the table, and threw it against the door. It shattered into glittering electronic bits but the door did not move.

What in hell was going to happen next? He realized that this playing on his emotions, dehumanizing him by calling him "It," suggesting that he was brutal beyond his own self-understanding, was all part of an attempt to break him. And a much more skillful attempt than he had expected. But he told himself that he understood what was being done to him, and his understanding would preserve him.

We love each other, and we want as normal and human a life as we can have. Patricia had said that. He repeated it to himself like a prayer.

He longed for her strength. If he could just spend one more minute in her arms he would have the energy to cope with another year of the old man's weird emotional games.

"What have you done with her?" His voice was absorbed by the walls. Frantically, aware of how wild animals must feel when first captured, he tested them. Behind the familiar wallpaper of soaring rockets and moons and Saturns and floating spacemen was plaster. And from the solid *thunk* when he tapped it, the plaster was spread on concrete. The room was more tightly made than any prison.

It was his old room, all right. The apartment he remembered was just a hypnotic suggestion. This was where he had grown up, this prison.

As the realization sunk in, a change began to come over him. The curtains that hid his past were being made to part by the glut of familiar associations.

Nineteen Rayne Street was the Titus School, where he had been a privileged student. The Prince, they had called him. With a cold shudder he remembered his own tragedy: he was a seasonal king, doomed to die in the very act of procreation.

The most excruciating sorrow filled him. If that was true then all their dreams of happiness, of escaping to the world of regular people, were hopeless. He had learned at his mother's knee—there will come a day, a glorious day. . . .

He looked at the letter the old man had referred to. Should he read it, or did it contain some further confusing trick? He picked it up.

On the envelope were three words: "For my son."

It was from Mother!

He opened it. The words leaped at him like fiery beasts, tearing away the last vestiges of the hypnosis which had held him in its thrall.

When the letter said "remember yourself," he did just that.

He remembered his pride in being the *monstrum,* and his love of the demons.

"I will speak to you in the voice of the dry leaves," Belial had said. As Jonathan read of his vision it returned to him: Belial, so hideous that he was beautiful, his unblinking eyes filled with so much intelligence that it was shattering to look into them. Belial was freezing wind on a winter's night, moonlight playing on empty snow, clear space pierced by stars.

Belial was a skull, brown and cracked, bursting with worms.

"Mother! What have you done to me? Mother! Mother!"

He rushed through the rest of the letter, squinting at it as if the words might jump off the page and pierce his eyes. At the end he threw it to the floor, turned away from it. Remembrance blazed in his mind:

He and Patricia belonged to the Night Church, had been born into it and raised by it.

He remembered loving it. Yes, but he had been mad then. He could not believe in something so obviously evil . . . so dangerously crazy.

Technology had lifted the Night Church to immense power. With their bacteria they could certainly destroy the world.

And they are mad, as I was until I began walking the path of ordinary human beings.

No matter how bad he is there is something sacred in every man on earth, something deeply *right* that grants him and all his fellows their lives, and seems to suggest that they procreate, and fill the earth with their kind.

In the old days Jonathan had thought of human beings as having less of a claim to life than even the lowest animals, because of all the species mankind was the most defective.

He did not think that now. In hiding Jonathan among ordinary people Mother had awakened in him his own ordinariness, had made him realize that he was only, finally, and utterly *human*—and that was a very fine thing to be.

Even as these thoughts raced through his mind he felt the *monstrum* within him stirring in its fitful sleep, the oozing, black coils of its evil shifting wakefully in his soul.

It could not wake up on its own, but *they* could wake it up, Mother and Jerry and Uncle Franklin. They could and they would.

He had to get out of here! If he was so brilliant surely he could find some way to escape.

He recalled the flickering strangeness of his own brain-wave patterns as they raced across the oscilloscope.

Like all the beasts, you will do what your nature demands of you.

He had seen his strangeness in the equipment he had himself designed.

He and Jerry had worked side by side in their labs. "You tend to the future," Uncle had said. "You are creating a teaching machine for your son." He put his arm on Jerry's shoulder. "He will take care of the past."

The coldest, most hideous feeling came over Jonathan as memories of exactly what was done in Jerry's lab came back to him. Disease vectors. Delivery systems. Contagion intensities.

A Titus School graduate had joined the U.S. Army in 1975, and delivered over the next five years vast amounts of classified data on biological weapons.

Anthrax 4 median, which killed in twelve hours.

Parrot fever mutant 202, death in four hours.

Bubonic positive 1, death in thirty minutes.

He suddenly had the most poignant impression of his life in Queens —the simple joy of having a hamburger at Farrell's. Down the counter some schoolkids would be giggling over Cokes. A couple of bus drivers would be huddled in a booth. Somebody might play "Lay Lady Lay" on the jukebox.

"Jerry, you can't kill them! You haven't got any right!"

Jonathan had a new mission, and not much life left in which to fulfill it.

"We're wrong! We are *not* the law!"

"You will reacquire the moral precision that has always supported you," Mother had written in her letter. "You will *know* the rightness of our cause." And she had written: "The earth's will is toward evolution. It is your privilege to enact it."

"No! We don't know anything about the will of the planet! We're mistaken, we're doing something terrible!"

Bubonic positive 2 had killed in thirty seconds, but it could not live outside a human host. Transmission only by physical contact.

"Oh, God! Jerry—let me out of here! Jerry, does bubonic 3 work? *Does it work?*"

His memory was now so clear that he could almost see the bacterial colonies in the microscope, swarming and propagating right out of their media.

And he could smell the animal rooms, the sharp scent of fear, the thick odor of sickness. In his mind's eye he saw the rats, exploding with buboes as soon as they were exposed to bubonic positive 3, dying within seconds, and the sheep within minutes, ba-a-a, ba-a-a-a-a, as great welts rose and turned purple beneath their coats, then burst as they knelt and vomited and gasped and fell twitching.

And the rhesus monkeys, brachiating frantically in their cages, screaming, clawing their throats open, buboes raising their arms so that they looked like they were doing the turkey trot as they scurried about, and coughing blood and pus and dying amid their own offal, their eyes fixed on the unearthly figures who tormented them, Jerry and his assistants in their green isolation suits and helmets.

"Oh, no. No!" He ran back and forth across the room, hurling things to the floor, grappling with the mattress, pointlessly searching the desk for a phone.

There was no phone.

They had been about to carry out a human test of bubonic 3—murder somebody, just to test—

My dear God, what have we done? He asked, but he knew perfectly well. Jerry had created from the bacillus *Yersinia pestis* a mutant, hyperactive strain that reproduced itself almost instantaneously. It was respiratory, spread through the air. It could be delivered by simply propagating it from a small plane.

Vector analysis indicated that 21.235 hours would elapse from propagation to complete contagion of a given population. After the first one million individuals the rate of transfer would be very rapid, with a potential of seven hundred and fifty million further infections within another fifty-three hours.

Jonathan wanted to help them, to somehow warn them. But Jonathan was a seasonal king come to the end of his time.

He heard the thundering music that would awaken the *monstrum*, remembered how it felt to change.

"Oh, God, you've got to help me! You've got to get me out of here! Please, somehow, *plea-a-se!*"

The disease would be fatal in 98.237 percent of the cases and so damaging in the remainder that the individuals would succumb to other diseases, especially given the chaotic nature of the social infrastructure in which they would find themselves.

The memories rushed like fiery, hurtling meteors through Jonathan's mind. His nightmares were a pleasure compared to this.

Jerry had read a paper to the assembled Scientific Unit of the Night Church: "The causative organism is a short bacillus which often displays bipolar staining with Giemsa stain. The positive 3 form always displays staining, but the poles reveal flagella under light. The positive 3 is motile."

"Shut up! *Shut up!*"

"The incubation period varies from a matter of seconds in a newborn human infant to three to five minutes in a healthy adult male of substantial volume. Onset is abrupt, associated with deep chills. Temperature rises from 41 C to 42.5 C (106 F to 108 F). Pulse will be rapid and thready, buboes will appear upon elevation of temperature. The femoral or inguinal lymph nodes will be the usual primary sites of involvement. The nodes will initially be tender but firm, sclerosing rapidly and becoming filled with pus. Bursting of the nodes indicates that terminal praeludium has commenced."

"Help! Get me out of here! I've got to tell somebody! I've got to warn them!"

Mike! I've got to get word to Mike.

He began a more organized attempt to free himself. Again and again he ran against the door, using his own body as a battering ram. It hurt when his shoulder impacted the metal but he didn't care. He had overwhelming humanitarian reasons for getting out. The fact that he might break a bone in the process was of little consequence, as long as it did not prevent him from reaching his goal.

The door clicked.

He was running with all his might when it swept open. He staggered out into the hall and hit the wall.

Strong arms enfolded him. "Cool down, Jonathan. It's all right, you're home, you're safe."

"Let me go! You're crazy, Jerry, you and all the others." The arms tightened around him. "Please, listen to me. This is all insane."

Jerry put something against his shoulder, something that stung.

"Jerry, you're a good man. A fine man. Best friend—" It got harder to talk. "Best friend I ever . . . oh, Jerry, it's obscene, it's . . ." He realized that he had just been sedated. The hypodermic Jerry had used was lying on the carpet, glittering in the soft light. Jonathan looked at it, his mind seeming to sink into the reflections. "Not the plague . . . no . . ."

"Sh, take it easy, guy. Get some sleep."

Jonathan's mind tried a final struggle. *I'm letting him drug me, put me to sleep! I mustn't sleep, I haven't got the time!*

Then Jerry picked him up and carried him to his bed.

"Now, just relax, loosen up your muscles, guy. Your uncle says you need a little rest before you learn anything more, and I think he's right. Don't you think so?"

"N-n-mmm . . ."

"Sure he is. Sure."

Resistance just wasn't possible. Deadening, black, hostile waves carried Jonathan away.

To the place where the serpent lived. Laughing, lifeless eyes, so cunning, so sensual, so dangerous . . .

You are the guilty one, Jonathan, you, you, you. . . .

"Please—"

You will hurt her!

"No!"

You will thrust and crush and tear!

"No, No, NO!"

He sat straight up, sweating, his mouth parched, his hands shaking uncontrollably.

The sun was setting beyond the garden wall, casting warm light into his room. Down below he could hear the rhythm of fresh-voiced Titus schoolgirls chanting jump-rope rhymes. This was the hour between dinner and evening study hall, known as the Strolls, when the students had the freedom of the courtyard.

Farther away there were traffic noises, a horn, a shout, and ordinary children laughing together out on Sullivan Street.

The sounds of ordinary people. At that moment Jonathan would have cheerfully traded places with the smallest, most humble human being in the world. The taste he and Patricia had gotten of outside life had been so sweet.

If only they could somehow warn that innocent world of the danger it was in.

Somehow.

He looked down at his own perfect hands. The violence he knew to be in himself literally *was* another creature, coiled beneath his own soft skin. And *It* did not want to escape from the Night Church.

No, indeed. *It* wanted to get married!

If It is the beast, the *monstrum*—then so am I.

I beg to die.

Chapter Twenty-One

PATRICIA LAY IN the dark listening to footsteps approach her door. Others had come and passed. These stopped.

She bit her clenched fist to keep from screaming.

It is looking for me. It knows I am here. Sometime soon It will come for me.

The door was tested, the door rattled. Then the footsteps once again retreated down the hall. Slowly, carefully, Patricia began to breathe again.

When they had been dragging her down to this room she had smelled a thick animal smell coming from behind a door marked LABORATORIES. And she had heard animal-like screaming.

Had that been the thing that wanted her?

Patricia lay between silk sheets, sweating with terror. Her face was cooled by a fragrant breeze. Wind chimes tinkled. She remembered that sound.

Such old friends, those chimes. They are in the courtyard elm. They rang and moaned and rustled all through her girlhood.

She sat up in the bed. Now she remembered. Sister Saint John had brought her down here, had given her a shot. . . .

Forced it on her.

"Jonathan!"

She jumped up and rushed to the door. Then she recoiled. She couldn't go out there! But there was an alternative. One wall of her room overlooked the courtyard. She threw open the French doors.

The yard was full of children, little girls in black jumpers, boys in charcoal blazers and gray pants. There were easily three dozen of them taking their pleasure in the evening light. These were not the noisy children of the Queens streets. These children sat in groups or strolled together. A group of younger girls played jump rope. On the low wall that separated her room from the yard a sister in red habit sat leading a group in plainchant: *"Aeterne rerum conditor noctem diemque qui regis et temporum, das tempora ut alleves fastidium . . . hoc excitatus lucifer solvit polum."*

The chant lit darkened halls in Patricia's mind. *Aeterne rerum conditor!* "Eternal creator of the world, who doth guide the day and night and give the times their times to relieve our weariness . . . through Him awakes the morning star."

The great hymn of the Church, the Song of Lucifer, the Morning Star.

She was no orphan; she hadn't been raised at Our Lady of Victory —if such a place even existed—she had grown up here, at the Titus School, and she was the highest princess of the blood.

Such remembrance was brought by those clear young voices! She had sat on that very wall, singing in the evening with Sister Saint John and Sister Mary and her classmates . . . Jonathan and his friend Jerry Cochran, and Kathleen and Kevin and Susan. . . . "We've brought you to the senior women's wing," Sister had told her as she administered the shot. "Your room is just as you left it."

So true. She realized that she had chosen exactly the same kind of curtains for her apartment in Queens—light green silk. Only in Queens she had settled for rayon.

She wanted the rayon curtains!

The sun passed behind the wall. A bell rang and the children began lining up at the boys' and girls' doors.

Such sweet little children.

Her own lessons, thin Sister Saint Julian rasping on about the evils of humankind, the Inquisition, the Holocaust, Communism. "In man the animal predominates. And in the world man is himself dominant. But not for long. This planet does not belong to animals. It has a far greater destiny."

With a force so great it almost made her cry out, Patricia rejected that belief. She had seen too much of the outside world. There had been bad things, but there had also been much more goodness and decency than she had ever been allowed to know about.

"The anti-man will be the opposite of man in every way. Where man is degraded, the new species will be exalted. He will be selfless where man is greedy. And where man is weak, he will be strong. We believers are the best of a poor lot," Sister Saint Julian had concluded. "Outside these walls there are monsters."

No, Sister. We are the worst of a good lot. As she lay on her bed, memory after memory returned. In all the flood, one single recollection dominated: it was an image, quite terrible, of a wild ritual that had been held during her childhood, where she had witnessed the transformation of one Robert Titus Ungar, gangling, jokey Robbie, into something else. . . .

There had been music and strange dancing and hypnotic words, and poor Robbie, eighteen years old and very self-conscious, had begun to change. Before them all he had actually undergone an alteration of his physical body. At first mucus had come out of his nose and mouth, then out of his eyes too. He had gagged and retched, and then screamed as his skull began to change shape beneath his scalp, blood replaced his sweat, and awful scales came crinkling out from under his skin.

She slammed her fists into her eyes, trying to rid herself of the ugliness she remembered.

If he had lived he would have been the father of the anti-man.

The ritual was to unleash the creature within the human skin . . . for a human body could be nothing more than a disguise, a sort of wrapping paper for something . . . something . . .

She gasped. Then she shrieked wildly and rushed up and down the room. *Monstrum!*

She had to get Jonathan and get out of here. But as she paced, the room whirled. "I'm still so damn dizzy!" The chimes rang and the complex scent of many flowers waxed the air.

A voice said, "Come now, Patricia, you don't belong out of bed."

"Where's Jonathan? I want Jonathan!"

Sister Saint John also had another name. She was Letty Cochran. Her husband George had been Master Accountant for the American Church for years. And their son Jerry—he ran those foul-smelling labs in the basement. "The Cochrans are my best pupils," Uncle Franklin often said.

"Remember," Letty Cochran said. "Patricia, remember who you are."

"I'm me!"

"You are much more than that. You—"

"I know who I want to be. I want to be Jonathan's wife and raise a family, and I want us to live together the rest of our lives."

The way Letty Cochran looked at her, with such a mixture of shock and sadness, filled Patricia with foreboding.

The foreboding focused into a quite specific memory. She was kneeling at an altar rail. She was trying to say the rosary. The beads broke apart in her hands and scattered all over the floor of the sanctuary.

"My rosary!"

Then Sister Saint John was there, in her memory, bending over her exactly as she was now.

She screamed. She turned and clawed her way through the yielding sheets of her bed, she leaped at the door.

And into the arms of yet another sister. Sister Mary. Mary Banion. "Let me go!"

"Oh, you poor darling!"

A man was coming into the room behind her, a man with a mustache and great, bushy eyebrows. He bit his bottom lip up into the mustache. "Now, Patricia, we aren't going to hurt you."

"You're crazy, Doctor Gottlieb! You're one of them."

"Shouldn't we tranquilize her again, Doctor?"

"We can't afford to impede her memory. She's got to recall her part in the ritual."

Gottlieb took her wrist, concentrated a moment. "Pulse is good. And the gynecological exam was very successful, Mary."

"Don't you dare examine me!"

"I did it while you were asleep, dear. I'm not a fool."

"You're evil! All of you! I want *out* of here!"

"Now, wait a minute. What in the world is the matter with you? Don't you remember anything?"

"You're liars, all of you—vicious, evil liars! And the Church is unholy, filthy!"

"You're badly confused, darling."

"I want Jonathan! I want him now!"

"Soon. Very soon."

"You're monstrous, all of you—"

"Patricia, I'm not sure I understand your problem. What's the matter with coming home after all this time in hiding?"

Mary was so clever. So damned clever. Patricia told herself to remember what she had said to Jonathan: *We may be mutated in a thousand different ways, but we can live ordinary lives if we try.*

"You have a great work to perform, Patricia. The greatest of all works. You must remember so you can do it well."

She recalled how Mary had tried to press a cloth soaked in ether onto her face while she lay on the altar of Holy Spirit Church.

As the last effects of the shot they had given her wore off, Patricia became better able to consider her situation. She stopped arguing with her captors. There was no point to it. Instead she tried to seem a little more cooperative. Only by winning their trust would she have any chance at escape.

"What are you thinking, Patricia?"

She couldn't be too compliant, though. That would give her away. She took what she thought might be an expected stance. "You were there when It raped me. You let It rape me!"

It had great, heavy coils and eyes like yellow marbles.

"You were the victim of a terrible mistake. All I can say is that I'm sorry. We're all sorry."

Sorry. That was one way to be.

Again she looked out into the courtyard. At the far side was a ten-foot wall. The only way to scale it would be to jump to a low-lying limb of the elm and vault over. The wall fronted on Sullivan Street. Beyond it would be cars and students and joggers and old ladies and derelicts and kids and all the world. Just being a shopgirl out there would be a privilege compared to the suffocating horror of life in this place.

Patricia had been the highest of them all, but for Jonathan.

You are our hope.

Your child will be a god.

She had been seduced by such praise. She admitted it. If she was clever, she might be able to convince the seducers that she was succumbing to them again. Then they might give her the few unattended minutes she needed. "Our belief is that mankind is a failure, isn't it, Mary?"

"Look at the conditions you encountered on the outside."

Mary touched her wrist. Patricia let a soft and devoted look come into her eyes. But she thought only of escape. Nothing would ever make her believe the Church's propaganda again.

She recalled the rituals, hundreds of them: annuals and seasonals and monthlies. Rituals for the rising and setting of all the major stars, rituals for the rhythms of the body, the phases of the moon, rituals to mark the earth's important passages, and prayers that praised her, the planet of pearly green beauty, whose needs the Night Church served. Then there were the Sacrificials, the bloody rites in honor of the saints of the Church.

Saint Gilles de Rais, accused of torturing and murdering children. Actually the teacher of Jeanne d'Arc, another of the great saints of the Night Church. Like her, burnt.

Saint Elizabeth Bathory, one of the greatest of the medieval genetic experimenters. Walled up in her own bedroom for what the ordinary population called mass murder.

Saint Appolonius of Tyana, killed by the Christians for writing of sorcery.

Saint Iamblichus, crucified by the pagans.

On and on went the list of the honored dead. Magicians, they were called, or alchemists or sorcerers or wizards. All the while, though, their hidden Church was the true guardian of the future, carrying the Treasure of Solomon forth to the millennium.

To the end of time.

"You must be ready to do your duty."

"Yes," was all she said. But she thought, My duty! My duty is to be destroyed.

It had come upon her stinking worse than any animal; its eyes glistening and inhuman, yet piercing with intelligence. It had mounted her with the weight of an anvil.

Patricia's mind twisted and turned between thoughts of capture and freedom. Inwardly she felt like a kitten so desperate with pain that it begins to try to bite itself to death. But she forced herself to sit on the bedside and talk with Mary, and pretend to be a good little princess again.

She belonged only to Jonathan—the Jonathan of the ordinary world. The dark *thing* within was not really a part of him. It belonged to *them.*

"The preparations for the marriage have already begun. You should see your wedding dress! This is going to be the most wonderful ritual in all our history." Mary smiled, touched Patricia on the cheek, on the hand. "Of course, it is the culmination of the Church. It ought to be grand."

"I'm sorry I've been so upset. I have a confession to make. After what happened in June—I'm scared to try again."

Mary hugged her. "My poor darling, I don't blame you, not for an instant. But remember that under normal conditions It can be gentle. And these will be normal conditions. No surprises for either of you. Oh, it'll be a grand occasion, you'll see!"

She returned Mary's embrace. "You're very reassuring."

Mary smiled, pleased by what she assumed to be a compliment. "I'm a faithful member of the Church. And your friend, my dear."

I would like to knock you aside, run through those doors, across that terrace, grab that limb, and swing right over onto Sullivan Street.

I want to be *free!*

But she also wanted Jonathan. Somehow she would have to get to the senior men's wing, find him, and free him so they could both escape together. Woe tugged at her heart when she thought just how hard that would be.

They sat side by side in the deepening dark. Just when Patricia was deciding that Mary was never going to leave, she kissed her on the cheek and stood up to go. "I'm glad you're getting yourself together so well. We need cooperation from both of you if this thing is going to work."

In the distance a gong sounded. Mary moved toward the door. "Dinner. But I think it best that you don't attend Commons just yet. I'll bring you a plate myself."

Patricia looked to the French doors, her heart already beginning to pound with the thought of escape. "Thank you, Mary. I'm really hungry."

She almost burst into tears when Sister Saint John came back the instant Mary left. She was all bright and admiring. "You *are* coming along well," she cooed. Patricia could have choked her.

"I feel much better."

"You must be so excited," she breathed.

That hardly seemed the right word. "Why?"

"I mean, with the wedding in a few hours—"

The words, so unexpected and so shocking, made Patricia literally stagger. Sister caught her before she could fall, and cradled her gently.

A few hours!

Her mind raced along. "But what about Jonathan? Won't I see him again—beforehand?"

Sister laughed. "Not before the wedding."

But she would see him then, before he sank into *monstrum*.

They would have to make their escape from the church before the ritual.

Oh, God, protect us and preserve us!

She looked up past the doors into the dark sky. There was a little patch of heaven there, the moon riding in twisted clouds, the moon so free, the moon so far away.

Chapter Twenty-Two ————

HOLY SPIRIT RECTORY was hidden in a forest of dark trees, only its tall, silent gables rising above them into the moonlight. A weed-choked path led to the front door. Mike had no intention of knocking. After the disappearance of Patricia and Jonathan and his suspicions about Mary, he trusted no friend, not even old Harry Goodwin.

He had ceased to trust his own men weeks ago. He had ordered a stakeout of Holy Spirit after the rape—which had been quietly canceled by Max while he was at Lourdes. No results, Max said.

Scratch Max and the whole Sex Crimes Unit for good measure, and God knew how many other cops. There must be something damned appealing about the Night Church to bend decent people the way it did.

He intended to carry out the rest of the investigation alone. At least he didn't have to worry about loyalties. He was on the side of the little guy, the schmuck who got kicked, Mr. Nobody. Outfits like the Night Church were just like organized crime, maybe worse. The Enemy.

He wasn't here for evidence. There was plenty of that in Titus's house. As the days had passed, each person Mike loved had been implicated.

Harry was a fine old friend. More than that, he was Mike's confessor, his priest. But the rape had happened in Harry's church.

Mike had shared his truth, his sins and deepest sorrows with this man. He hated to test him now.

What a luxury it would be to sit across Harry's kitchen table and talk this thing out with someone he could trust. Surely Harry would check out. He was among the very best men Mike had ever known.

Mike looked up to the second floor. Harry's bedroom window was dark. It was ten fifteen and Harry Goodwin was, as always at this hour, asleep. Those six A.M. Masses did it to him.

Rather than try to pick the difficult deadbolt lock, Mike went around the side of the house, looking for a window to enter. It wasn't hard. Harry was hardly buttoned up. All Mike had to do was apply a little force with his fingers and the sash of the office window went up with a dry rasp.

Mike observed thirty seconds of silence, then began the painful and difficult process of hauling himself in. He hadn't climbed into a window in fifteen years or more.

He put his hands on the sill and struggled. His legs windmilled, caught against the side of the house. Then he got a knee over the edge and heaved. The central bulk of his body swung inward, and he landed on Harry's desk with a subdued thud. He had to lie there a moment letting his heart calm down.

The house was silent. By the faint light from the window Mike could see that the door to the hall was standing open. He went over to it. The only sound came from outside, where a restless breeze snatched at the eaves and rattled the windows. Upstairs Harry would be sleeping—if he slept at all. He looked awful these days, nervous and thin and ill.

Conscience-stricken was how he looked.

Mike returned to the office. The Parish Council sometimes met here, the men sitting on the black, vine-carved chairs, some of them smoking the stale cigarettes Harry always kept in a box on the coffee table. Harry would preside from behind this desk, his glasses gleaming, his eyes as grateful as a dog's. You pitied him, and it made you squirm.

Mike pulled the blinds down and closed them, then closed the door to the hall. He risked a light. If there was any evidence of the Night Church here, it would be somewhere in these records. Mike sat behind the desk and began going through the file drawer. The sections were marked CCD, H. Name, PC, Confraternity, Altar Society, Oil, Insurance, Mscl. Bills, on and on, all the details of parish management. There was nothing suspicious, nothing even a little out of the ordinary. Mike opened first one file and then the next, scanning their contents, lists of names, ideas for sermons, parish bulletin notices, diocesan directives, bills and more bills.

Through all of this desperation one could glimpse the determination of Harry Goodwin. Despite the desertion of his people, he was keeping his parish going, robbing from one account to fill another, practicing every imaginable economy, even to cleaning his vestments himself in the basement, and from the look of some of these bills, not paying for the cleaning fluid. Keeping it going in case his people returned. Or *when* they did. Probably it never crossed Harry's mind that they might not.

He was not getting support from the Night Church, at least not on the surface. Mike scanned the shelf beside the desk until he found the buff-green journal where he knew the parish finances were recorded. It was a simple double-entry journal. No fancy bookkeeping for Harry. He could no longer rely on voluntary help from Catholic bookkeepers in the parish. The entries were in Harry's own spidery hand . . . in pencil overwritten with ink.

Mike looked at the endless, meticulous entries for collections, the amounts dwindling steadily as summer settled in and people's air-conditioning bills took more and more of their money. Last Sunday Harry had taken in $171.29. Paging back through the journal Mike could find no entry so low for a Sunday. It was a parish record, forty dollars below the next lowest figure. But then, just a couple of days ago, there was a stunning contribution, fifteen hundred dollars from the Hamil Foundation, especially earmarked for painting and cleaning the interior.

What the hell? That was the philanthropic arm of the Hamil Bank. Did Laurent Hamil have a program supporting indigent parishes? He was certainly a big-time Catholic. His foundation might well be called on in emergencies. Not too suspicious. But Patricia worked there. Was there a connection between Hamil and the Night Church?

Mike looked at the entry. The hand was a little more spidery, and there was no penciled trial entry. Harry had known the exact amount of this particular contribution.

He closed the ledger. Now it was time to investigate the older parish records, which were in the basement. It was critical to look through the past couple of years. Patterns might emerge. This entry suggested that the Night Church was helping the parish, but it did not tell what Mike most wanted to know, whether Harry was a dupe or a willing partner.

Mike went down the hall past the dining room with its ornate table and wainscotted walls, and opened the door in the pantry leading to the basement. He didn't intend to poke into any dark holes, and looking down those wooden steps made him more than a little nervous. When he saw how the dark down there swallowed his penlight's beam he wished he could dare to get help. But he couldn't. Nor could he just abandon this part of the investigation—it was too important. When you were seeking evidence of payoff or kickback the rule was to look to the time before your suspect perceived the danger of his ways . . . then it was usually all laid out neat as a pin. People kept careful records of their sunny days.

Mike had been here more than once before, both as a boy and as a man. There was a wine cellar from long ago, and Harry still had a few bottles of Sandeman's '37 vintage port in it. Harry had brought one up once or twice for some Holy Name celebration or other. How Harry had resisted selling that port. Mike understood why. He needed those evenings with port and cigars and good company to remind him of the importance his church had once enjoyed among men of power, and to give him leave to dream.

Mike descended the stairs quickly, his penlight beam bobbing on the steps. He crossed the floor . . . and was interested to note that there was a great deal of dust. Good. Nobody was worrying about the old records as yet. Maybe Mike was finally a step ahead.

His light danced as he swung it around, revealing steam pipes, rusty electrical conduit, dark old beams, cobwebs, and shadows behind shadows.

The journals were in a bookcase that sagged against the far wall. As Mike moved toward it he noticed a great crack beside the case. Dank, earthen air drifted out. Deep sounds seemed to come from it, of machinery throbbing. Probably led to some old drainage pipe that communicated to the subway out on Queens Boulevard. Mike peered into the hole, flashing his penlight into blackness. As he painted his light along the walls there was a sound of rustling movement. A shadow made Mike jump back. Something the size of a dog seemed to be scurrying toward him. But that was absurd; it was a rat tricked large by the light. Mike shook his head. Harry's rectory was literally crumbling into the sewers. He reached out to grab the last three or four journals and get the hell out of there. His motions were too quick; when he brushed matted fur he jerked away.

Lightning flashed as his head knocked into a cold steam pipe. He sank heavily to the floor, cursing, holding his head, his penlight rolling

crazily away. That light was sanity and protection. Despite his throbbing head he lurched after it, grabbed it, and cradled it like a candle in
his cupped hands. It was still working, thank God.

He had to get himself together. This was the sort of clumsy lack of
professionalism you expected from a wet-pants rookie. He scrambled
to his feet and scanned the bookshelf with his penlight.

The journals went back to the turn of the century, year by year, all
neatly numbered in gold embossing. Mike took down 1963, 1971, and
1975. That ought to be enough, and long enough ago for any records
of connection between the day and night churches to be clearly indicated.

Mike sat down on the bottom step with his penlight and began
reading. He found nothing of interest in 1963. By 1971 every third or
fourth month ended with red ink. The records for 1975 told a more
somber story. Now the red ink was constant.

In April of that year the Hamil Foundation had kicked in twelve
thousand dollars, earmarked for restoration of the portraits of the
apostles in the dome. Mike remembered the scaffolding. Father had
said the apostles were being revised to fit the discoveries of modern
scholars. Afterward they did not look inspired anymore. Now that
Mike thought about it, they looked ugly. In July the foundation had
donated new pews to add seating in the wings.

Additional seating in a dying parish?

Mike took down 1977 and 1978. January of 1977: $9,712 from the
Hamil Foundation to soundproof the windows. July of that year:
$1,270 for three hundred folding chairs.

Soundproofing and folding chairs? It was eerie, to find the records
of the growth of the Night Church this way, so hidden, yet so obvious
if you knew the basic truth that it existed.

Mike replaced the journals. All this foray had done was to confirm
what he had discovered upstairs. The parish received regular contri-
butions from the Night Church. But what about Harry? The answer
to that question wasn't here after all. It might lie somewhere in the
records of the Hamil Foundation, and might even be located—given a
few years of investigation. But the quicker route to the truth lay in a
direct confrontation with Harry Goodwin. "Old friend," Mike whispered into the silence, "don't join the guilty. Be different."

Using his much abused penlight Mike made his way back upstairs.
He paused in the front hall. He hated to do it, but he was going to have

to play one hell of a rough game with Harry. "Hey, Harry," he bellowed, "wake up and get the hell down here! Come on, Harry, get moving!" That would scare him thoroughly, get him good and vulnerable to unexpected questions. He unholstered his pistol.

From the distance there came hurrying feet. Then the hall was flooded with yellow light and the tall figure of Father Harry Goodwin came gangling down the stairs wearing grayed pajamas under a raincoat liner.

"At least you remembered that pistol I gave you," Mike said from his position in the doorway. As he had known it would, his voice caused Harry to throw up his arms, and in so doing to hurl the little twenty-two almost to the ceiling.

"Mike Banion!"

"Good morning, Harry." Mike did not put his own pistol away. Not just yet. "We have to have a discussion."

"Yes, Mike, certainly. By all means!" He was staring at the pistol. "Mike?"

"Let's go into the office, Harry. It's a couple of degrees cooler."

"I don't use the air conditioners. Out of the question."

"I understand." Mike followed the stooped, shaking man.

"Mike, you're pointing your gun at me."

"Yes."

His eyes were awful in the grim light of the office. With absurdly clumsy hands he put on his glasses. "Now," he said, "please, Mike, tell me why."

Best to get right into it. Make him think his interrogator knows more than he really does. "How well are you acquainted with Franklin Titus Apple?"

"Oh!" He blinked furiously. "Hardly at all, Mike. And you should use the past tense. He's dead. I buried him in July." He looked again at the gun. His eyes were practically popping out of his head. "What is this about?"

"It's about you and Apple. Or Titus. The Apple is an alias. You'll be happy to know he isn't dead at all. You buried another man. A very old and dear friend of mine." Mike stared hard at the priest. "I want to know about your financial relationship with Titus."

"I don't understand, Mike." There was hurt in his voice.

"Let me try another approach. How much does Mr. Titus pay you to let his congregation use Holy Spirit at night?"

"What do you mean, Mike?" The tone pleaded.

"The Night Church. *Surely* you know of it?"

He shook his head. His eyes were frightened, his lips slack. Mike put the gun away. When he did so Harry blinked.

"You're innocent, you darned fool! Aren't you?"

"Well—I must be—I suppose—what Night Church?"

"Good God almighty! Harry, we'd better get ourselves some coffee made." The old priest stood up, his eyes still wide, his mouth working. Mike clapped him on the shoulder. "Come on, Harry. I'm afraid I have some bad news for you."

Mike found the old-fashioned circular toggle switch that controlled the kitchen lights and turned them on. "Our second bad-news night," Harry said. "We mustn't make them a habit."

Mike didn't answer. He put the kettle on and got out the jar of Folger's Instant, pulled a couple of chipped mugs off their nails. "Harry, I think you might be one of the few priests ever to learn this—" The kettle whistled. "Excuse me." Mike made them their coffee, took a swallow from his cup. All these delays were intentional. He wanted to observe Harry. Maintaining an impression that he was in suspense was one of the most difficult things for a man to do. But Harry squirmed. He wasn't having any trouble at all, poor guy.

"My word, Mike, this is strong. What are you going to tell me—my church has been declared off-limits to Catholics? That I know, believe me."

"What I've got to tell you is that your parish is being used by a group called the Night Church. Mr. Titus, known to you under the ridiculously inoffensive alias of Mr. Apple, is their leader. They meet in your church in the small hours. They are probably the most vicious group of people you or me or anybody else has ever heard of."

"In my church?"

"There are hundreds of them. They must fill the church when they come, and they do that often. During one of their rituals, Patricia Murray was raped."

"But I often wake up at night. When I check my church it's always empty."

"Oh?"

"These people are using my church?" His voice sounded hollow. "Mike, are they desecrating my altar?"

"What the hell do you think, Harry? They practically tore Patricia in half on your altar!"

Harry reacted to Mike's words as if they were actual blows. Mike knew this was going to destroy the poor old guy in the end, no matter what happened now. The whole sense of Harry Goodwin's life was being extinguished.

"You say that the people attend these rituals? My Catholic people—the ones who don't come to me anymore?"

Why lie to the man? To do so would be to disdain him, and Mike did not treat his friends with anything less than respect. "I suspect that they fill the church."

Harry closed his eyes. His face screwed up into such pain that for a moment Mike thought he was having a coronary.

At last he let out a long, ragged gasp. He stared at Mike through devastated eyes. His hands were shaking so badly that he could hardly get his coffee cup to his lips.

"We're going to get rid of them, Harry."

Harry Goodwin continued to stare.

"Harry?"

There were perhaps words, but Mike couldn't understand them.

"Tonight it's going to be different. They are probably going to come here, and I suspect they will have Patricia with them, and Jonathan too. I haven't been able to get in touch with the kids all day. That tells me the Night Church has them, and it's going to do its business with them. But Mike Banion is going to be waiting for the Night Church. And I am going to break it into little pieces."

In the absolute silence that followed Mike could hear the priest's tears dripping onto the oilcloth tabletop. It was as desolate a sound as he had ever heard, in a life that had witnessed all the kinds of grief there were.

Harry Goodwin bowed his head. In the grim light Mike saw that speeches weren't going to help him. It was too much. The priest was still breathing and thinking and living, but inside him everything important was blowing to dust. The words from the Funeral Mass came to mind:

Man's days are like those of grass;
Like a flower of the field he blooms;
The wind sweeps over him and he is gone,
And his place knows him no more.

Mike prayed then, a wordless, desperate prayer—not for God's love or His protection, but for His vengeance, that it might roar through the Night Church like holy fire.

"I'm going over to the church now, Harry."

"I'm coming too."

"I know."

They walked across the grassy parking lot to the black and silent building.

Chapter Twenty-Three ———————┼——

THOUGH HE HAD entered this old church a thousand times through the seasons of his life, Mike Banion had never approached it as he did now, with the caution of a professional intruder. He was here to investigate, not to pray.

He had no illusions about what he was doing: coming to this place was as dangerous as going to Titus's house had been. A cop would run out of luck if he did this sort of thing often.

From the end of the block the streetlamp cast a dissipated, silvery glow. There was a smell of wet in the air. Perhaps toward dawn it would rain as it had yesterday and break this suffocating heat. The sky was green and dense. New York summers often ended like this, with thick, humid clouds and muttering storms. Wind soughed around the belfry and eaves but here on the ground it was stifling.

Mike reached down and grabbed an unexpected object from the grass—a bit of crumpled paper. It was no blessing of evidence, though, only a Junior Mints box. It had probably been dropped by kids on their way home from the Cinemart on Metro Avenue. Mike held it a moment, unwilling to let go of something so comfortably of the known world.

They mounted the worn granite steps to the church. It seemed a hundred years since he had gone up these same steps as a little boy all in white, on his way in to receive his first Holy Communion. The boy he had been waved and shouted, "Remember, remember me!" And the wind blew, and the rain rained, and the aging cop could not deny that there had once been a poet in him, but the damn thing had died.

He put his hand on the knob of the big oak door. Unlocked, of course. No matter how he was told or who told him, Harry was never going to lock his church. Very, very slowly, Mike turned the large, cold knob. It was well oiled, and obliged Mike by not making a sound. He pulled the door a bare quarter of an inch. There was a single, distinct click, which Mike heard echo through the nave.

"Are they there?"

"Quiet, for God's sake. Just stick close to me, and don't talk."

The priest was one hell of a liability, but he had such a stake in this, he could not be left behind. No matter the consequences, it was his church and he had a right.

If Terry's terrible death had been intended to frighten anybody smart enough to open the grave from further pursuit of Franklin Titus, it was certainly working. Mike admitted his fear. He had come to think of these people as ghouls.

Poor Terry. Whatever had they done to him? The coroner had found evidence of severe infection in the corpse. It had been quarantined pending virological and bacterial studies. One of the morgue guys had said something about plague. Mike thought of the chart he had found in Titus's house. They gave Terry their disease before they put him in the coffin. Now that the chart had been enhanced by the lab, it was perfectly clear that it recorded the progress of an illness so virulent it could kill in minutes.

The church door swung open on absolute darkness. The Spirit seemed empty, but Mike still did not want to go in. The way he saw it, this was as much Mr. Titus's church as Harry's. Maybe more.

The air that came out of the dark interior was dry and had an unexpectedly familiar smell.

"Been doing some painting?"

"No. It hasn't been painted in years."

The smell told a different story. Earlier this evening they must have spruced the place up. How were they planning to hide that from Harry?

Was all as it seemed here?

Harry, old buddy, have you put one over on me? If they feel free to paint, they don't care whether you know about them or not.

Mike felt very isolated, standing here in the black foyer with his old friend beside him.

Your faith matters to me, Harry. You're my damn priest!

He waited for their eyes to get used to the faint glow filtering through the stained-glass windows from the street. It didn't amount to much, but they could see the aisle clearly enough to avoid tripping.

Mike began the long journey to the altar rail. He intended to hide in the narrow, dark space behind the high altar against the likelihood that the Night Church would be here tonight.

Before him he could see the dim outline of the altar where Patricia Murray had been raped—not by some poor screwed-up jerk but by intelligent people in a brutal ritual.

Patricia. Pretty kid. Be a great wife for Jonathan. To see those two at this altar, her in white, him jammed into a blue suit and looking sheepish—the thought was enough to make a man weep.

Wordlessly, because words weren't his way, Mike prayed for the kids. He looked toward the votive candle and was conscious of something so real and true he could hardly begin to understand it. But he loved something about it. The mystery of it, maybe.

He went up to the altar, genuflected toward the looming dark hulk, and made the sign of the cross. He really wasn't much of a Catholic anymore. His faith, he supposed, was like the love of an old divorced man who has long known that the reasons for the split were insubstantial and recalls his partner with wary fondness.

He became cold. The sensation warned him of how dangerous familiar places could be, transformed by dark and fear. Cops got killed as often as not on friendly ground. He could as easily imagine Patricia screaming on this altar as Harry saying Mass here, or altar boys pouring from cruets as blood running.

Progress was interrupted for the moment by an exceptional blast of wind. Tonight's storms were not going to wait for dawn. As large as the old building was, it shook with the force of the gust. He grabbed Father's arm and stood a moment after the noise died down, listening for the extra little sounds that might be made if somebody had used the roar as a mask for getting closer to them.

But there were none of the rustles and shuffles that people made when, for example, they suddenly stopped running.

Harry, however, had made use of the disturbance and the dark. Mike first realized this when he felt a distinct tug at his shoulder holster. He jerked away—and his thirty-eight special ended up in Harry's shaking hands.

"I've got it! Don't move, I've got the gun!"

"Hell, Harry. Give me that thing back. You couldn't shoot me."

"Don't force me, Mike! You stand right there." Harry put a few feet between them by sliding along the altar rail. "Don't come near me.

I'm not at all good with these things. If you startle me it's sure to go off."

Mike was more saddened even than surprised. With the loss of Harry he had only one thing left that was worth risking his neck for. "What about Patricia and Jonathan? What's happening to them?"

"That isn't your business."

The Night Church was just too strong. From the moment he smelled the paint, Mike had suspected something like this was about to happen. Harry marched Mike into the sacristy. "Mike, I'm sorry. There isn't anything else I can do. If you're cooperative they may spare your life. Please, Mike, play along. I've been playing for years." His voice became high and frantic. "They keep my church alive."

"You poor bastard." Even now, there might be some chance. He had always had clout with Harry Goodwin. "We can talk."

"No, we can't. I've already talked too much. Titus knew you were coming here. He even told me the time."

"So you were waiting for me."

"And wishing to God you wouldn't come."

"You're still on the side of the good. I can hear it in your voice. Give me the gun, Harry."

"Mike, please be quiet!"

"I'm your conscience. I can't be quiet."

"Don't try the sentimental approach. I'm finished with that. I don't care how good a friend you are. I've been tangled up in this mess for a long time, and you can't untangle me."

As Harry spoke there was a change in him. When you saw him like this, sharp and mean, you realized what tragedy was all about. "How long?"

"They've been using my church for years. If it weren't for them, the parish would have been abandoned in the seventies." The bitterness in his voice was almost shocking. This was an astonishingly angry man. "What a joke to waste your precious life on a vocation!"

"I want you to give me the pistol. I want to forget I ever saw you pointing it at me. No matter how bitter you are, Harry, you aren't bitter enough to do something so evil to a friend. If you allow the Night Church to capture me—my God, you know, don't you, that they buried Terry Quist alive."

The gun wavered. Harry seemed about to hand it over.

"And that man who died in the fire across the street—Parker was his name—that was no accident. I'm now convinced they burned him alive because he apparently knew too much. And Patricia—remember what they did to her."

Harry groaned, took a step closer. Mike reached out his hand.

Just at that moment the sacristy door clicked and creaked open. A small, elegant old man in a raincoat and hat hurried in. He removed the hat to reveal a crown of wispy white hair.

Titus.

He smiled. "So our last problem has solved itself. Good evening, Mike. I gather you're here to see me give away the bride."

"Give me the gun, Harry! Now!"

With a growl Titus took the gun, trained it expertly at the center of Mike's chest. "Shall I shoot?" he asked in his soft, polite voice. "Or will you shut your poisonous mouth?"

Mike fell silent.

---

15 AUGUST 1983

MOST PRIVATE

To: The Prefect of the Sacred Congregation for the Defense of the Faith

From: The Chancellor for the Inquiry in North America

Your Eminence:

I have prayed day and night over the request made in your last letter.

Is it morally right for me to go into a situation where my own death is a virtual certainty? I wonder. Or is this moral question spurious—a way of justifying my fear? And, Eminence, I can assure you I am afraid.

I keep thinking of Alex Parker and the blowtorch. I know I shouldn't, but I can't help it. The real issue is whether or not I love Christ enough to risk that.

Eminence, I am so afraid. Help me.

Sincerely yours,
Brian Conlon

Document Class: Urgent A, most private, Swiss Guards courier

Destination: Paolo Cardinal Impelliteri, the Hidden Collegium, Prefecturate for the Defense of the Faith, Vatican City

18 AUGUSTUS 1983

FURTIVISSIMUS

Ad: *Cancellarius Inquisitionis in Septentrionalis Americanensis*

Ex: *Prefectus Congregationis Defensioni Fidei*

My dear young man, I only wish that I were not so aged and infirm, so close to the end of my time. I would count it an honor to suffer at your side.

Recall the gospel: "In His anguish He prayed with all the greater intensity, and His sweat became as drops of blood falling to the ground." And remember your consecration into the Holy Office, my boy.

You lay prostrate before the altar in the Chapel of St. Paul the Apostle here in the Hidden Collegium just eighteen years ago. Remember the words: "Oh, glorious St. Paul, sword and shield of the Church, consecrate me to the service of our most holy Catholic and apostolic faith. Intercede for me in time of trouble, that I may not shrink from martyrdom, indeed, that I may give my life gladly, as thou gavest thine, for love of Him."

Let me be frank with you. When you asked me for a warrior-priest—a man who would die for love of Him—the only name I could come up with in all the Holy Office was yours.

You, Brian.

You are the last warrior-priest young and strong enough to carry out this difficult mission. All I have here are myself, laid up with my damn stroke, and a bunch of dry old historians.

Brian, it is not my way to beg, but now I do beg as I think Christ wants me to beg. Please, Brian, drink of the cup Christ holds out to you. My dear boy, pray for courage!

Holy Mother Church needs you now, and Our Lord needs you now. And I trust in you. I wish I could give Our Lord an army of Brians!

But all I can offer Him is my last, precious one. Go in grace to your duty. Man will not show you mercy, my son. But God will. You shall have mercy and love in endless abundance, and all the wonders of heaven besides.

I envy you.
Paolo

Chapter Twenty-Four ————————+——

HARRY STOOD FROZEN, listening to the echoing footsteps as Titus marched Mike off into the dark. There came a creak of hinges, then the sounds dwindled as the two men descended into the crypt.

"Please, Mr. Titus," he said. His voice was so low it didn't even echo in the empty church. He swallowed. "Please, Mr. Titus, don't hurt him."

There was no answer. From the depths of the crypt there came a loud, angry shout. Mike, protesting whatever indignity had greeted him there.

Mike, Mike. What is the sense of friendship? At our age it is a dance of mourning . . . and remembrance. "Mike, do you remember—oh, Lord, there were great days!" Like the day he had married Mike to little Beth Herlihy. Jenny Trask was organist then, young, dedicated to music, capable of anything from Bach to *Tantum ergo*. She could do a wedding march of rousing splendor.

From the crypt there came a rush of argument, then the muffled slam of wood against wood.

Harry put his hands over his ears, screwed his eyes shut. As never before his church was oppressing him, the ghostly images in the dome mocking his faith, the vigil candle burning like an accusatory eye. He ran from the sanctuary, and across the muddy parking lot.

He came into his kitchen—and remembered how Beth would make them both dinner while he and Mike sat around that table drinking beer and talking.

Harry snapped off the light, sank down at the table, and wept for his betrayal.

To keep from doing it aloud he bit his lips. His mouth began to taste sharply of blood.

Yes, and who were all the histrionics for? Our Lord?

The traitor deserves a traitor's death. Iscariot, send yourself to Hell. His mind went to his twenty-two pistol. It must still be lying on the stairway where he had dropped it. If he took that pistol and pointed it at his stomach and fired, he would die in deserved agony. Unconfessed, he would sink for all eternity into Hell.

A worthy end for a coward. He went to the staircase. But there was no pistol. Harry moaned. Even his suicide was going to be denied him.

"Do you want this?"

Standing in the doorway of his office was a small, mousey sort of man. Harry had never seen him before, but that meant nothing. The Night Church was well supplied with people. The man held Harry's pistol in his hand. The barrel was trembling.

"I'm a priest," the man said in a rushed whisper. "My name is Brian Conlon." A haunted expression passed across his face, but he blinked it away. "I am here to appeal to you to return to Our Lord, and help me in His cause against the Night Church." He stepped forward into the hall to show himself more clearly. His pants were torn and dusty, his gold-framed glasses were bent. With his free hand he brushed some dust from his suit. He was wearing a Roman collar. "Father Goodwin, I am a secret agent of His Holiness." Beads of sweat, which had been collecting on his hairless pate, began to roll down his wide forehead, making trenches in the dust. He smiled weakly. "I'm a bit of a mess, I'm afraid. I shouldn't have attempted the window."

Harry was far too amazed by the mere appearance of another priest to care about the state of his attire. "You mean His Holiness knows? Rome *knows* about the Night Church?"

"Rome knows. And Rome has sent me to help you."

"Father—Father—" Harry couldn't go on. Hopes he had given up for dead were soaring as they hadn't in years. He simply stood, wordless, trying to keep himself from breaking down completely.

Father Conlon came and embraced Harry. He was short; Harry found himself looking down at his hairless scalp. Then Father Conlon met his eyes. "Rome knows everything, Harry."

"Even—you know that I'm—" Harry couldn't say it. *A traitor to Our Lord.*

"You're a participating member of the Night Church."

"No—that's stretching a point, isn't it? I never go over there. I just let them use it, you know."

"I know. And they pay you."

"It keeps the parish afloat! Without that money—"

"Yes, I see. Now I know exactly where you stand, Father." He put the gun into his pocket. "We have work to do this night." He glanced at his watch. "The *Rituale* will begin at midnight. That gives us less than an hour. We've got to work fast. Tell me, are they about yet?"

He thought of Titus and Mike in the crypt. "One of them is, and he's holding a friend of mine, a police officer, prisoner in the crypt. I think he's killing the policeman." As he said these last words the utter moral corruption of his own soul was agonizingly apparent to Harry. He was letting Mike die!

"And you're up here, looking for a gun? To help whom?"

Harry could hardly bear to answer. "For me," he managed to mutter.

Conlon smiled wearily. "I see. In your opinion you're beyond absolution."

"I don't want it! Absolution is the last thing I deserve!"

"But you regret your sins—your apostasies, your lies, your sacrilege, your cowardice?"

No man who was free of them could know what it felt like to bear such sins. "I regret them," Harry said. How small, how hollow were those words!

"May Our Lord Jesus Christ absolve you, and by His authority I absolve you from every bond of excommunication and interdict to the extent of my power. I absolve you from your sins in the Name of the Father, and of the Son, and of the Holy Spirit."

For a moment Harry was furious. Then an enormous relief spread through him. He could feel Conlon's words as truly as a tonic in his blood. They filled him, revitalized him, gave him immediate help. And he said, "Amen."

Father Conlon looked up at him. "You're still very much the priest, you. You've just been frightened up to now."

"I can't help it. I'm easily frightened."

"Well, you have another chance to overcome it. Better that than letting a little fear send you to Hell."

"They threatened me with torture!"

"I think we'll both face that, Father. They do torture priests." The haunted expression crossed his face again.

Harry's mind returned to Mike. "We can save my friend. We've got to! They're torturing *him* now!"

"Who, exactly, has captured your friend?"

"A man named Titus. Franklin Titus."

In an instant Father Conlon's face shifted from calm resolution to terrible dread. "Titus! He's *here?*"

"In the crypt."

He smiled ruefully. "Very well, Father Goodwin. I may already have lost my particular battle." He held out Harry's pistol. "Will you be at the wedding?"

"I am being made to officiate."

"Titus and his mordant wit. When the moment is right, I am afraid we have no alternative but to kill the groom. If I am prevented from doing it, you must."

Harry was astonished. A priest, plotting murder?

"I know how awful it must sound to you. But you don't know the alternative. Believe me, this execution will be a great mercy not only for the groom, but for all mankind."

"His Holiness condones this?"

"The Holy Office is empowered to act in defense of the Faith. Believe me, it is a terrible thing when we are forced to such a measure. But we do not shrink from duty."

A sudden movement at the top of the stairs caught Harry's eye. As he turned toward it Father Conlon pressed the pistol into his hand. "Hide it, Harry! It may be our only chance!" Conlon began backing into the study, pulling a pistol of his own from under his suit.

"No you don't, Conlon! Drop it!"

Father Conlon threw his large, black pistol to the floor. At the same instant Harry put his own palm-sized one into his pocket.

A troop of armed men came running down the stairs. "Your priest is lucky, Laurent," Conlon said to the leader.

For a moment Harry didn't understand. Then he did: Father Conlon was gambling that the two of them hadn't been overheard. "Thank God you came when you did," Harry blurted. "He was going to kill me!"

Father Conlon was edging toward the window. "Not so fast," the one called Laurent snarled. An instant later they took Conlon by the arms. He commenced a mild and hopeless struggle. They surrounded him, then picked him up and began to carry him away. His bald head was bobbing between the shoulders of his captors, his feet were rattling against the floor. His glasses were gone. There was a gash under his right eye.

"Come with me, Harry," said a voice from the dark. Harry knew it at once: Titus, back from his business with Mike.

"Yes. I'm coming." The pistol felt enormous in his pocket. Surely Titus would see the bulge.

Titus led him through the dark rectory. "That man will burn to death, Harry." They went across the dusty living room, into the overgrown rectory yard.

Harry followed him as if in thrall. Those three words kept echoing in his mind: *burn to death, burn to death, burn to death.*

He saw the young people stuffing Father Conlon into a car. Even with the windows closed his shouts could be heard clearly. "Sounds like he's been given the bad news," Titus commented mildly. Again and again, in a frantic, breaking voice, Conlon called "Je-e-sus! Je-e-sus!" Then the big Mercedes drove away.

"Conlon knows what a hard death is like, Harry. Do you?"

"Yes, Mr. Titus, I do."

"You agree very quickly, for a man who has just been proselytized by the Inquisition. Tell you what, Harry. You go down into the crypt. See what you can do for your friend." He smiled distantly. "You had best be loyal to us if you don't care for hard deaths." The smile broadened. "Go on. Mike needs a friend right now."

With a toss of his head Titus disappeared into the sacristy. Harry wanted to do anything but continue with this horrible mission. Gingerly, afraid to do it but more afraid of Titus, Harry lifted the storm door that led into the crypt.

Chapter Twenty-Five ───────┼───

THE SAME BLOW that had knocked Mike unconscious had also given him a pounding headache, which woke him up.

He heard music. Church music. *"Aeterne rerum conditor noctem diemque qui . . ."*

It was very beautiful, being sung by a children's choir. But so far away. He could barely hear them.

". . . regis et temporum das tempora . . ."

He wanted to hear more. When he tried to get up he was hit a flaring blow in the center of his forehead. He lashed out with his fists and encountered sides and a top.

What the hell was this? They had put him into a box. The box was lined with satin upholstery.

A coffin.

Just like Terry! He sucked air frantically. He beat on the top, he squirmed, he kicked.

Then he stopped. He started taking controlled breaths, trying to quell the panic. If he was going to get out of here he had to do some very clear thinking.

Before they had put Terry in his coffin they had infected him with a disease. Was Mike also sick? He took a deep breath. Lungs clear. And he didn't feel feverish. The only thing that hurt was his head.

He remembered the expert way Titus had pistol-whipped him, a single stunning blow to the side of the head.

He didn't seem to have anything else wrong with him. Then it occurred to him why they hadn't infected him. They already knew their disease worked from trying it on Terry.

They wanted this to be as slow as possible.

It was already awfully hard to breathe. How long had he been unconscious, innocently breathing up his little bit of air? Not too long or he'd be dead. Not a lot of air to begin with.

Okay, guy, let's give this one hell of a good try. He braced his hands against the head of the coffin. Then he kicked with all his might against the foot. The whole thing quaked, but it didn't even begin to give way.

Goddamn!

He spent half a minute in a losing effort to catch his breath. No matter how deeply he inhaled, it helped less each time. The air in here stank. God, it stank.

He was suffocating in his own bad breath.

"Help!"

Silence.

Thank God he had heard that singing. At least he knew he wasn't actually underground.

"Come on, out there, have a heart!" He took gulp after desperate gulp of air.

This was the end. In a few more minutes Michael Banion was no longer going to exist.

He stopped trying to get out. That was not going to work. And he stopped bothering to call. Nobody was going to help him.

He had other things to think about now. This was death. He tried to remember what he was supposed to do at this point. The main thing was an Act of Contrition.

But he couldn't remember the damn Act of Contrition! It was a long prayer, and he hadn't said it in years.

He panicked again, afraid that not even God was going to help him. The frantic physical torment of air hunger overcame him and he drummed his feet and slapped at the top with his hands.

Then he opened his mouth. He began gagging and gasping. Some-where his mind turned over a page. He couldn't remember the Act of Contrition, but Sister Louise had paddled him into the *Confiteor*. He began praying in a loud voice, hoarse with the bad air. "I confess to Almighty God, to blessed Mary ever Virgin, to blessed Michael the Archangel, to blessed John the Baptist, to Holy Peter and Paul . . . all the saints!" Take a breath, take another, take another. Wow, I'm flyin'! I hurt like hell but I'm flyin'. "Sinned in thought, word, and deed, and what the hell's the rest? Oh, yeah—through my fault, through my fault, through my most grievous fault—oh God hurry up this hurts!"

Come on, damn you, die.

I'm gonna be like, like—

Sunken eyes, lips stretched away from teeth, stinking like hell, and fingernails embedded in the lid.

Poor old Terry.

Poor old *me!*

Everything went, finally, all the discipline and fight of a lifetime as a policeman. Only the scratching, screaming animal remained.

He kicked and kicked and kicked and his blood pounded in his brain and he gasped until his throat was raw with his own expelled gases.

When they left her alone in the bride's room Patricia's heart leaped with hope. She had been guarded every moment back there, and had come out here in a limousine with Mary and Letty and Jerry. Maybe this would be her chance. But when she looked around and saw the barred windows and heard the lock click behind her, she could only feel the tightness of frustration in her throat.

Although as secure as a prison cell, the room was pretty. The floors were sumptuously carpeted with a Persian rug depicting a wedding. Ancient brass floor lamps gave off warm, yellow light. A spray of roses graced the delicate antique table in the center of the floor. There was a dressing table for the bride, completely stocked with makeup and perfume of every scent.

Patricia went to one of the leaded-glass windows, wondering if she could squeeze between the bars. They were newly installed; she could tell that by their shine. And they were bolted directly into the walls, not into the window frame. They were also hopelessly close together.

Despite all her efforts to be calm and to seem cheerful to Mary and the others, they had not let down their guard. This was the longest time she had been alone since the capture. They had been very sweet to her. They had also been very careful.

"You are our Princess," they had told her.

She had smiled and accepted their homage. But inside herself she clung to the thought that she could be so much more than their toy, she could be a real wife and make a real home for Jonathan. She thought bitterly, I *can* be a human being!

She kicked the table—but not hard enough to upset the roses. Then she slumped down at the dressing table. The face staring back from the mirror was so very beautiful, even in its pain, that she was rather startled.

Beautiful mutant.

"Hello, dear. We've got to start dressing you. There's barely half an hour left!"

How incredible that words said so cheerfully, by as lovely a woman as Mary Banion, could hold such dread.

First they had taken Jonathan's belt and shoelaces. Then they had put him into a straitjacket. When he had realized how completely his suicide would ruin their plans he had become almost frantic to do it.

They watched him every second.

An hour ago ten of them carried him down to a waiting van. They brought him out here trussed to its seat. Five guards came with him.

He lay now in his straitjacket against the wall of the sacristy, trying to find some new trick of suicide. He had pleaded with Jerry Cochran and with Uncle Franklin. "Don't you understand what I am? A monster! And I'll breed a race of monsters!"

They agreed. In fact, that was the whole point. "They will be in the image of Satan."

"They'll be horrors! They'll destroy everything beautiful and good in this world!"

Uncle Franklin had at that moment done something that had chilled Jonathan to the depth of his being. Very deliberately he had leaned down and smiled beatifically into Jonathan's face. And he had whispered, "I know."

Jonathan had screamed to the others to listen to him. Uncle was evil! He was himself something out of Hell—he *must* be! Something foul, something supernatural. Please, please listen.

He is trying to give this world over to the demons!

Jonathan began to shout yet again. "Please listen to me! Please, please, please listen!"

But they didn't listen. They went on preparing to mate their goddess with their god.

There came a sound of footsteps on flagstones. Somebody was approaching the coffin. Then there was a desolate sigh just outside. The wood creaked. Somebody had knelt down and leaned against it! "Since Almighty God has called—"

"Harry! Oh, God, it's you! I *knew* you'd come if you could! Listen, I'm dying. I've got to get air."

"Mike, you're alive!"

"Air, Harry. Get me air, air!" Mike felt desperately along the seal. His mind flashed again to the coffin key in Titus's living room. "Is there a key?"

"Key?"

Now, that was confused thinking. Harry wouldn't have any keys to this thing. "Harry! Harry!"

"Oh, Mike!" There was a great clattering.

"Hurry!"

"I can't, it's too strong."

"What—were—"

"I'm hitting it with my shoe!" There was another burst of noise.

"No. No." He was drifting into unconsciousness, falling down a well.

A tiny hissing sound brought him back from the depths.

"Mike! Say something!"

"Upend the damn thing and drop it! That'll break it open!"

There came a creaking, scraping sound and a great deal of labored breathing. Slowly Mike's position changed. Soon he was struggling with the fact that Harry had lifted the thing feet first.

Then he dropped it. There was a tremendous, bone-jarring crash. God love that old priest, was the lid actually loose?

People were coming and going in the bride's room, bridesmaids with their dresses and makeup cases, sisters with ironing boards and needles and thread, making last-minute adjustments. Letty and Mary fussed over their Princess, who smiled as best she could, despite the ashes in her heart.

Her mind in its desperation had fixed on the notion that Jonathan might rescue her. He was so clever, surely he would succeed where she was failing. He would find a way to get both of them out.

"Now, my dear," Letty said with great self-satisfaction, "we have something to show you!" She put a large white box on the table with the flowers and opened it. Inside was the most extraordinary dress Patricia had ever seen.

It was sewn entirely of spider-web lace worked with pearls. Tiny diamonds made the collar and cuffs glitter. An emerald belt, green to match her eyes, lay folded on top. Mary drew the dress from the box and held it up. It was purest white silk, the delicate strands worked into flourishes and sweeps of subtle design.

Then she saw the design. She choked back a scream. On the dress, depicted in lace, were bodies struggling in fires, bones and skulls, and grinning devils.

"Feel how light it is! The whole thing doesn't weigh a pound."

Patricia held out her hand, touched the gossamer fabric. "It's very light."

"The dress is over six hundred years old. It was made at the height of the Middle Ages. It's been in the family all this time, waiting for you. It's been worn only once before, during the *Rituale* at Salisbury Cathedral in 1334."

Out of the madness and desperation of the medieval world they had brought this terrible artifact. It was as if the rotted fingers of man's mad past had reached out and clutched her. They were smiling at her. All the bridesmaids were watching. She strove for a steady voice. "It's an inspiration."

Her mind was totally concentrated on Jonathan. Memories of him, desire to see him again, hope of escape. But she dared not even ask after him for fear her tone would betray her.

They had to get careless for a few seconds. They just *had* to! And if they didn't, then he had to come to her and take her away. Nothing else could be allowed to happen. Because if there was a *Rituale* then he would become the *monstrum*.

That must not be!

Mary gave her an excited little peck on her cheek. "Before you put on your makeup. For good luck."

Patricia looked down at the awful garment in her hands. A lace skull smiled up at her.

This had never been intended as a wedding dress. It was a shroud.

"Jonathan, you might as well accept your situation. You aren't going to get away," Franklin Titus said.

"Maybe not."

"And we won't give you a chance at suicide."

Jonathan did not reply. That was his one hope.

"I really feel terrible about this. If I had known what it would do I never would have tried the hypnosis. You're pitiful now, son. I find it most upsetting to see you this way."

"You're evil. I'll never stop fighting you."

"If you don't cooperate tonight things will turn out far worse than they did in June. Should the insemination fail because of your resistance I will not stop you like I did in June. This time I'll let you kill Patricia."

Jonathan fought against the straitjacket; he spit at Uncle Franklin and cursed him. "I don't want to hurt her! I mustn't be allowed to hurt her!"

"I agree. Which is why you must cooperate."

"Get away from me!"

"The wedding is going to start in ten minutes, son. You might as well reconcile yourself to that fact." He turned and walked away.

"Don't do it to me! Don't, in the name of all humanity!"

His uncle said something to Jerry Cochran. Jerry came over. "You're disturbing the congregation, Jonathan," he said in an embarrassed tone. "If you can't be quiet we'll have to gag you."

Jonathan became silent. Gagged, he would be helpless even to warn her away. He began to realize that this terrible ceremony was probably going to happen just about as Uncle Franklin wanted it to happen.

He hoped, he prayed that he would somehow manage to be gentle with her.

A great, booming note resounded from the choir loft. The ritual had begun.

By pressing his mouth against the crack that Harry had made and sucking furiously, Mike could get a little air. As he drank it in his whole body seemed to come alive with tingling relief.

The next thing he knew there were fingers in his mouth. Harry was trying to reach in and widen the crack. Mike forced himself to turn aside into the foul air of the coffin. Harry strained. Suddenly a loud snap brought a flood of cool, delicious breeze. Mike found the damp concrete smell of the crypt delightful.

Then Harry's arms were around him, lifting him. "Mike, Mike!"

"I made it. I'm alive."

Harry embraced him. "Thank you, O heavenly Father."

Mike saw a long piece of tubing curling down from the broken coffin lid. He took it in his fingers.

It had been leaking a trickle of oxygen into the coffin all along. "What the hell—look at this, Harry."

"What does it mean?"

"They were feeding me just enough air to keep me alive!" He stood up, examined the mechanism of torture. An oxygen tank, its valve set just to bleed. This was perhaps the most hideous torture he had ever heard of. They could have kept him at the edge of death for a long, long time. "No wonder I didn't die. They didn't want me to."

"But they must have. You're dangerous to them."

"Oh, they were going to kill me, all right. But not soon. The point is, I would have lingered in there, slowly suffocating, until they decided to cut off the oxygen."

"Hours?"

"Maybe days."

Harry hugged him again. "Let's get out of here! We can run! Your car's outside, we can go over to the precinct! We'll be safe there."

"Who knows where we'll be safe. What about the kids?"

Harry closed his eyes for a long moment. "I'm due upstairs in a few minutes. I'm supposed to marry them."

"And I have to rescue them. Somehow."

Harry dug in his pocket and came up with what was to Mike a fist-sized chunk of gold. "You gave me this, Mike. Maybe you can put it to better use than me."

Mike took the little pistol. "Thank you, Father." Mike hefted the weapon. Good for head shots. He and Harry walked together across the crypt, to the spiral staircase that led up to the sacristy. From the top of that staircase light shone down. There were excited voices. "I don't want to do this, Mike."

"You go up there. If they miss you we'll both end up getting caught." To reassure Harry he smiled. "And don't blame me if the wedding doesn't come off quite as planned."

"I hope it doesn't, Mike. I hope to God it doesn't."

"It won't."

Chapter Twenty-Six

THE ALTAR RAIL seemed very far away, a dim white line at the end of the long stone aisle. Beyond it was the dark, ugly bulk of the altar. The sacrificial stone.

"Do you see him?" one of the bridesmaids whispered.

Her heart began to flutter. *See him?*

"Look—he's just to the right among that group of acolytes."

She saw that noble head, those delicate features. "Jonathan!" His eyes met hers and there was lightning between the two of them. Through all the pain and horror of the moment their love shone clear.

Then she was running down the aisle. Footsteps pounded behind her. She was halfway to him before the bridesmaids managed to stop her. "Not too fast," one of them said. "We have to wait for the music. This is supposed to be a procession."

Standing there in her delicate shroud, captured again, she cried.

The flower girl in her white taffeta dress slipped around Patricia. The procession was reorganized.

Mary, standing behind the bridesmaids in the ranks of nuns, called up to the choir loft. "Very well, Mrs. Trask, I think we're ready now."

The most beautiful, ethereal music began. Patricia recognized it as Bach's "Sleepers, Awake," from one of the cantatas. Sleepers awake, indeed. They had lost their chance for that. The two of them were doomed to carry out the living nightmare of the ritual, and nothing could intervene.

Her flower girl began moving forward, spreading rose and gardenia petals. Patricia followed, her heart full of the most exquisite anguish. She felt the weight of the procession behind her, the six bridesmaids, the deaconesses in their dark-red silk festive habits, the common sisters in their white ones. Behind them came the children of the Titus

School, the girls in blue dresses, the boys in tuxedos. And the pews were filled with the whole congregation of the Night Church, resplendent in the dim candlelight in their jewelry and fine dresses, their tuxedos and gleaming studs.

"Patricia!"

She heard him cry out, quite clearly. The music got louder. There was a stir around him. He was entirely surrounded by acolytes. She could no longer see him.

"Run!"

Her bridesmaids began pressing her from behind. "I can't, Jonathan!"

He screamed then, an awful, wild, trapped sound that made her scream too. It reminded her of the sound of a rabbit dying in the country night, crushed in the coils of a king snake.

"Please don't do this," she wailed. "Please, all of you, listen to me! This is evil, it's terribly wrong! Don't any of you understand? Don't you realize it? You must!"

The music swept along, so gentle, so intensely sweet.

Then they reached the altar. The music stopped.

Mike had gone up the winding stairs from crypt to sacristy with the utmost care, pausing in the shadows behind the half-closed door. From here he could see most of the sacristy and an edge of the sanctuary beyond. He had watched Harry vest and go out into the sanctuary behind his retinue of altar boys. Titus and his own retinue of six of the quietest, best-behaved acolytes Mike had ever seen remained behind. Even so one or two of the boys amused themselves by swinging their censers at one another. From time to time Titus would snap at them.

Why the hell didn't Titus get moving? As long as he remained where he was, Mike was stuck here.

One of the boys took a quartz wand about ten inches long from a little black case. He handed it to Titus, who began examining it carefully and wiping it with a bit of felt.

Outside the wedding started. Mike could see Father and Patricia clearly, but where was Jonathan? He must be among the crowd of men off to the side. Some marriage, when the groom has to be held by force.

"At the beginning of creation God made them male and female; for this reason a man shall leave his father and mother and cleave unto a wife, and the two shall become as one. They are no longer two but one flesh. Therefore let no man separate what God has joined."

Harry's voice was quick and strained. Titus had noticed it too; he grew as still as an interested snake.

"Now he enriches you and strengthens you by a special sacrament so that you may assume the duties of marriage in mutual and lasting fidelity. And so, in the presence of the Church, I ask you to state your intentions."

A horror that made Mike's skin crawl and his heart beat thick and slow came over him. He remembered the picture of the dying monster he had seen in Titus's library. To create anti-man a human being must become like that poor, destroyed thing.

To twist and contort and bulge with whatever crazy drugs or trances they used, until you became—

Dear God, poor Jonathan! Poor damn kid! No wonder they've got him trussed up like a hog in a slaughterhouse. *He's* their damn monster!

His dream! The poor kid, he *was* guilty all along just like he thought. What a damn sad, terrible thing! And he told me, he *told* his dad he was guilty! He was begging for help and all he got was a pat on the back. I can be goddamn thickheaded!

Tears were blurring his vision. Poor kid was crying out for help and his own dad wouldn't believe him.

Oh, Christ, help him! Her too. Help all three of us!

To the core of his soul Mike wanted to rush out there and stop that wedding. But he couldn't, not while Titus was between him and the altar. Among so many people his only chance, and a slight one at that, lay in achieving absolute surprise.

The old sorcerer waited in the wings. And the wedding went on.

Jonathan had struggled so hard to break free that he was becoming exhausted. They had gagged him after he had tried to call to Patricia. Despite his hopeless situation he strove against the straitjacket, frantically chewed the gag.

"Patricia and Jonathan, have you come here freely and without reservation to give yourselves to each other in marriage?"

Jonathan wanted desperately to tell her that he loved her, that he wouldn't hurt her as long as there was a particle of humanity left in him. But the gag was a skillful one. It went all the way down into his throat. He could barely groan.

"They have," his mother said in a firm, clear voice. Father Goodwin looked as if he wanted to disappear into the floor.

"Will you accept your issue lovingly from God, and bring him up in the law, Patricia?"

"No! Not unless I hear Jonathan say he wants to marry me. And you won't even let him talk!"

"She will," Mary said. Jonathan begged God to stop his heart, to somehow preserve Patricia from seeing what was inside him. How he longed to spare her that!

Twisting, grinding into her, crushing bone and flesh, listening to the piercing ecstasy of her screams.

"Since it is your intention to enter into marriage, join your left hands, and declare your consent before God and His Church."

"Their hands are joined in spirit," Mary said.

From where the deacons had forced him to crouch down among them Jonathan could just see a bit of his mother's face. He looked at it with utter loathing. That was not his mother. He considered Mary Titus Banion dead. The body might be walking and talking as if she were alive, but the human being inside was dead. By loving Satan Mother had committed suicide.

I want to be dead too. I want to be dead!

But he was far from dead. In fact a new life was beginning to stir within him. Even as the wedding proceeded a strange, low hum began under the soaring music of the organ.

The hum got louder, and as it did Jonathan began to feel more and more and more *ANGRY!*

Patricia could hardly bear the bone-jarring sound that had replaced the organ music. It hurt her ears and stirred her deepest senses to loathing. Her bridesmaids took her by the arms. When she felt their strong hands on her she had a wave of panic. Not ten feet from here she had knelt while It strode to her across the sanctuary. She had broken her rosary, and listened to the beads scattering in the dark.

Altar boys began dousing the few candles, leaving only the vigil candles in their cups and the unwinking red of the votive candle.

God, give us light!

Altar bells began jangling, dozens and dozens of them in the dark. The music boomed to a crescendo. The sisters and the schoolchildren had filed into the pews. Patricia was surrounded only by her bridesmaids now, and the deaconesses.

All heads turned to the back of the church. A gaudy and amazing procession, far different from the wedding party, was starting there. Acolytes carried bejeweled invert crosses, blood red. Behind them deacons held aloft banners of richly worked silk depicting magical symbols, pentacles and six-sided stars and rings in rings.

Behind them all came Uncle Franklin, wearing vestments of material too dark to see in the gloom. On his bishop's miter there romped a serpent that called up in Patricia an emotion so strange that it didn't even have a name.

She felt as if swarms of mites were crawling over her body. Her skin became so sensitive that the dress seemed as if it were made of fire. "No! Please, no!" Her bridesmaids were close around her, holding her in strong hands.

The acolytes went left and right along the altar rail until finally Uncle Franklin arrived face to face with Patricia.

"At last," he murmured. His dry old hand came up, touched Patricia's cheek. She bit him. "Ah! Such spirit, you little viper!" He wiped his bloody finger down the front of her dress. "Prepare her, please, sisters."

Jonathan struggled on the floor like an animal. But he was no longer struggling to escape or even to end his own life. He was struggling against the savagery that had been pouring up out of his depths ever since that infernal horn started roaring.

Now something was happening. His guards were moving him. Were they undoing the straitjacket—was there a glimmer of hope?

Yes!

He was more sane than they must realize. Perhaps he would yet have a chance at killing himself.

But then he knew he would not. They had only loosened a few straps to put chains through the loops. He was now standing up just at the gates to the sanctuary, chained tight to the altar rail. He couldn't even bash his forehead against a corner of the rail; the chains were too tight.

Uncle Franklin stepped to the center of the sanctuary. Boys took his miter and staff. He held up the quartz wand in the dim candlelight.

Patricia was dragged to a spot just in front of the altar. How beautiful she was all in white, her face floating in that wonderful blond spray of hair.

"I love you, Jonathan!"

"I love you! I love you!" All that issued from behind the gag was a faint series of grunts. "I want to be gentle with you!"

I want to break you in half with my power! You'll love it too, you bitch!

Her bridesmaids laid her on the floor of the sacristy. She was tied with silken ropes to four rings that had been fixed there.

For me. She is tied down for me.

He rattled his chains, fighting wildly, desperately. "Relax," Uncle Franklin muttered. "You'll have all the strength you need in just a minute."

The madonna purity of Patricia's skin, the way she was biting her bottom lip as she tried to raise her head enough to see him, began to excite him.

No! I must be gentle with her. It's all we have left. To deny himself the pleasure of seeing her helpless he closed his eyes. His body, his very blood, became a prayer.

The serpent within him slithered faster and faster toward the surface of his being.

The nave was filling with an incense that seemed to mix rare perfume with the odor of decaying flesh. Graves must have smelled thus in ancient times.

"Very well, Jonathan. I shall now dance up your demon for you."

I am the genius of death.

Uncle began by striking the tip of the wand on the altar rail. He held it before Jonathan. "Look!" Jonathan shut his eyes.

But the demand was only a trick to get him to do that very thing. Next thing he knew the wand was being pressed against the center of his forehead. Like a tuning fork it resonated with rich vibrations. They penetrated deep into Jonathan's skull, filling him with the most extraordinary agony.

He could not turn his head. And when Uncle Franklin ordered his eyes to open, the lids rose despite Jonathan's frantic efforts to keep them down.

He could not look away from the spinning, gleaming tip of the wand.

Uncle began moving gracefully back and forth. Such was Jonathan's own concentration that it seemed to him as if everything else had simply disappeared, everything except the dancing, turning body of his uncle and the glittering wand.

Jonathan's stomach twisted and rumbled and almost twisted inside out. He began to gag.

"Get ready!" Uncle shouted. "Here he comes!"

Jonathan's guts began to feel warm, then hot. In an instant he felt as if he were boiling alive from the inside. Almost driven mad with the clawing torment, he shrieked and shrieked. He knew that he was going to tear off the straitjacket. But it was not *him* doing it, it was the thing within, taking control of his muscles.

He found himself shaking the straitjacket away as if it were tissue paper, rattling the manacles until his wrists were bloody. The torment of the inner boiling had increased his strength a hundredfold.

Then the manacles parted as easily as if they had been made of wax.

When he tried to tear off his gag it snagged on his teeth. He snatched away the thin cloth.

How beautiful she was!

Clumsily, with the newfound gait of a body that seemed an unfamiliar size and shape, he began to go closer to her.

His own part of the ceremony finished, Harry had come back from the sacristy and crept around behind the high altar with Mike. They were hiding amid the orchids and the irises just to the right of the tabernacle.

When Harry saw the horror out there he tore through the flowers and bolted across the altar. He began struggling with the tabernacle, trying to preserve the Host from the astonishing blasphemy being enacted before it. Acolytes promptly subdued him.

The last gesture of a guilty priest.

Mike watched and waited, hoping for some chance to make a move that would matter. He knew only two things—Patricia had to be saved and poor, pitiful Jonathan had to be given the best care that money could buy. He stood glaring down at Patricia like a great *golem,* bellowing as if in agony. He seemed bloated.

Mike noticed something extraordinary about the poor, pitiful kid, something that made his chest hurt with sorrow. Jonathan was standing over that girl literally sweating blood. Actual, red blood.

More and more of it oozed out, covering his body with a red sheet. Then the most awful thing Mike had ever seen began to happen to the only person he had ever been able to call a son.

His fellow human being, whom he loved, started drying and cracking apart. He undulated like a snake shedding its skin. As he did the bloody skin began to separate from dark, scaly flesh underneath. Suddenly he began pulling huge slabs of himself off. He ripped off his chest, throwing the translucent skin to the floor. Then with a grunt he scraped his back against the altar rail and left a mass of flesh there. Fissures formed in his legs and he drew them off, the suddenly hollow skin of the feet collapsing like punctured balloons. It made a sound like the shrink wrap coming off a record jacket.

Even as he did this his eyes began to bulge out of his head. They fell, two dried shells, to the floor. What appeared from within was bright yellow, as big as the eyes of a vulture. Mike remembered similar eyes staring at him from the sky above Titus's house. He drew the rest of his face away with trembling hands. There emerged a snake's face, glaring with intelligence and insane hatred.

In the dead silence of the church Mike could hear the wet "pop" as It drew off the last bit of Jonathan, the hand and skin of his left arm, and tossed it aside like an empty glove. It flexed the strange, gleaming claw that had been within.

Seeing this hideous miracle, Mike was at once humbled and filled with creeping horror. God was not the only power in the universe.

Jonathan began to scream again, but this time it was an awful, crackling sound somewhere between a reptilian hiss and the yammering of a crow.

Mike couldn't bear it anymore. If he had ever seen human suffering, he was seeing it now. Jonathan's heart and mind were in there enduring the torment of becoming that—something. Mike raised the pistol to put him out of his misery.

But he didn't get a shot. There was a flurry of activity around the *thing.* Two deacons grabbed Father and pushed him up against It. It shrank back. They pushed Father into Its arms again. It twisted away, It screamed, but they persisted. Soon, as if unable to stop Itself, It plunged Its claws into him.

He gasped, he hammered at the bulging, relentless muscles, he kicked the scaly armor that covered the body. The claws sliced his flesh away from his muscles.

Then It threw the agonized, half-flayed priest aside and began moving toward Patricia. Father lay dying on the floor of his own sanctuary.

God, God, why have You let something like this come alive?

Patricia began to cry out, as sharply and desperately as a baby. Mike looked for a good shot but the candlelight and the swiftly moving deacons and acolytes made it impossible.

It knelt down beside Patricia and caressed her with one of Its long nails. Then It lay upon her.

She could do nothing to prevent that shivering, crusty body from assaulting her. "Jonathan," she shouted, "Jonathan, remember yourself! You're not that thing, you're a human being and you love me!"

Somewhere in the depths of what he had become, she could see him remembering. It was just a glimmer in the savagery of him, but it was human and it was good. There was a gurgling sound, and something like sorrow began to battle the hate in the eyes.

"Oh, Jonathan, I know you're still there. I love you. I love you! I'll always love you!"

"I—I-I-ooaaahh!" It glared into her face with Its impossibly huge yellow-green eyes. She could not bear to look any longer. She turned her face away.

It began Its awful croaking again. She felt It beginning to move, to twist eagerly against her, ripping the flimsy material of the dress. "Jonathan, darling, if you can still hear me, don't hurt me! Please, darling!"

It grew rapidly more excited. She tried to remain as calm as she could. She could feel It bouncing heavily on her, making her breath come in ragged gulps. Then It was pounding frantically.

But It wasn't hurting her. It was trying to be gentle!

When she opened her eyes she saw on that hideous face an expression of intense conflict. It wanted to hurt her, but It was resisting the urge as best It could.

"Oh, Jonathan, Jonathan!"

The barrel of a pistol emerged past the edge of the altar above her head.

The thing that had been Jonathan stopped moving on her. It raised Its eyes, facing the gun. "P-lease—shuuuhhttt. P-lease!"

For an instant nobody moved.

Bullets went snap! snap! snap! It fell back onto the steps of the altar, thrashed once, then was still.

Pandemonium. Mary's voice, sharp and collected, rose above the general uproar. "Franklin—was there insemination?"

Patricia saw Franklin Titus smile happily. But who had inseminated her—the *thing* or the little spark of Jonathan that remained inside?

Oh, Jonathan, it was you, I know it was! *And it is your baby in me, I can feel it! Not the thing's! No, not that!*

People were screaming, rushing away from the altar and the smoking snout of the gun. Mary and Franklin moved close together, quite unconcerned about the weapon a few feet from their heads. They held hands, the old man and his faithful helper.

"All right, listen to me! Shut up and listen, all of you!" It was Mike. He came around the altar. Patricia's eyes filled with tears. She had never been so glad to see anybody in her life.

He came through the stillness that had followed his shout, and pointed the gun directly at Patricia's belly. "You cut her loose and bring us a raincoat."

A horrified gasp came from the crowd.

Mike cocked the pistol. His eyes met hers. "Do it. Or she dies."

Silence. Far back in the church there was a single panicky scream. "Cut her loose," Franklin said.

Patricia got up on wobbly legs. Mike helped her into the raincoat. He half-carried her across the sanctuary, through the sacristy, and out into the parking lot. His car was there. He put her in, then got in himself.

She was so grateful and so sad and so frightened that she could hardly think, could hardly talk. She sat as still as stone while he started the car and drove away.

This was escape! She should be glad. But she wept bitter tears.

"Let's just try and remember the Jonathan we knew."

"Oh, Mike, he's dead. *Dead!* And I loved him so."

Mike drove on beneath the yellow ranks of streetlights. They picked up speed on the Grand Central Parkway. They were heading west. "Do you need a doctor?"

"He didn't hurt me. He wanted to but he fought it. You should have seen him, Mike, how he fought himself!"

Mike covered her hand with his own big paw. They reached the outskirts of the city and went into the dark beyond, on and on, toward anywhere as long as it was far away.

Patricia began to allow herself to think of ordinary life again, of places far from the dominion of the Night Church.

There would be one such place, she felt sure, where she could find peace and safety enough to raise the child.

For there would be a child. And it would not be the child of the monster. Surely Jonathan had preserved enough of himself to defeat the plans of the Night Church—she just knew it, could feel it in her singing blood. A little baby, the precious last of Jonathan.

In his name, she would bear this child.

Mary and Franklin remained behind after their stunned congregation had left the church. "We'll have to tell them," Mary said. "They're in despair."

"Let it be a test of their faith. They'll find out soon enough."

It had all gone so very well. Perfectly, in fact. Well, almost. "Banion drew his pistol before the insemination."

"That was a near thing. I must have given him the autosuggestion at the wrong moment. But there was definitely a complete insemination. She's pregnant. And the father was not Jonathan. The father was the *monstrum.*"

"But she believes otherwise."

"Of course. She'll bear the child as Jonathan's baby."

Mary put her arm around the old man. He was stooped, trembling with the weight of his years. The next great ritual of the Church would be his funeral, she suspected, on some moonless night not too far from now. He has come the full distance, and now he is tired.

"I wish them well," he said in his age-soft voice.

"Mike will do an excellent job of protecting her. You can count on that."

He coughed. "I'm exhausted."

She certainly didn't want him to keel over without giving her the last critical piece of information. "Where are they going, Franklin? You'd better tell me."

"I implanted a suggestion of Madison, Wisconsin."

"Name they'll use?"

"Edwards. And her gynecologist will be a young Doctor Jonas. He set himself up in practice last week. A good boy, from the Congregation Saint John Martyr in Milwaukee."

Mary locked the church behind them. The air was cool and clear. The morning star hung low in the east. "Look there, Franklin. Lucifer."

Hand in hand they gazed at the star of the Night Church. Ordinary people called it Venus, but Lucifer was its proper name, and it was no star of love.

As predawn light spread over the quiet neighborhood Mary noticed an astonishing change around the church. "Look, Franklin, there were demons with us."

"How do you know?"

His old eyes must not be able to see the trees. "The leaves—they went to autumn colors last night."

"So they did. Quite a wonder."

"Yes, a wonder." She watched dead leaves race down the sidewalk on an angry little breeze. How sweet was the world in silence.

Softly at first in her heart Mary heard the plainsong of the Night Church, then heard it rising triumphant from dark and hiding, to fill the world.

Aeterne rerum conditor.